PRAISE FO

"A wholly original take on the lands of make-believe from a captivating new voice in the genre. Hayes takes the reader on a journey to the heart of themselves, reminding them of all that was lost and all that can never be forgotten. A book as comforting and as cathartic as your first knocked-out tooth."
Meg Elison, Philip K. Dick Award-winning author of
The Book of the Unnamed Midwife

"This book is messed up in all the right ways. It's as if Pixar's Inside Out mugged Toy Story in a surrealist Raymond Chandler novel. Weird, fun, scary, and a great mystery to boot. Hayes sticks the landing."
Jennifer Brozek, Author of *Never Let Me Sleep* and
The Last Days of Salton Academy

"This is detective noir shot through with technicolor playfulness the likes of which I haven't seen since Who Framed Roger Rabbit. It's pure imagination on multiple axes – with a ton of heart."
Alex Wells, author of *Hunger Makes the Wolf*

"Combining detective noir, Toy Story, and an in-depth look at trauma, Hayes has crafted the most unlikely formula and makes it sing. The Imaginary Corpse is inventive, fun, and touching, in the most unexpected way. The world – real and imaginary – needs more triceratops detectives."
Mike Chen, author of *Here and Now and Then*

"An immensely creative, bittersweet sugar rush of a fantasy-noir novel: Who Framed Roger Rabbit meets Paranoia Agent with a touch of creepy-cute Coraline atmosphere."
Wendy Trimboli, author of *The Resurrectionist of Caligo*

Tyler Hayes

THE IMAGINARY CORPSE

**ANGRY
ROBOT**

ANGRY ROBOT
An imprint of Watkins Media Ltd

Unit 11, Shepperton House
89 Shepperton Road
London N1 3DF
UK

angryrobotbooks.com
twitter.com/angryrobotbooks
Still Reeling

An Angry Robot paperback original, 2019

Cover by Francesca Corsini
Commissioned by Marc Gascoigne
Edited by Lottie Llewlyn-Wells and Gemma Creffield
Set in Adobe Garamond

ISBN 978 0 85766 831 8
Ebook ISBN 978 0 85766 832 5

Printed and bound in the United Kingdom by TJ International.

9 8 7 6 5 4 3 2 1

For Sonya

Look, honey: We made it.

PROLOGUE: WELCOMING

COMMITTEE

Are you okay?

I'm down here. Yeah, the sunflower-yellow stuffed triceratops. I know.

It's okay. I know you're overwhelmed, I was too. We all were.

Do you need anything? Food? Water? To talk about whatever just happened to you? No is fine. No is always fine here.

You've got questions. Of course you've got questions. And I'm happy to answer them. But why don't we start at the start, and I'll tell you why you're talking to a plush dinosaur.

Here are the two things you absolutely need to know. First: In case you didn't know, you're an idea. I'm not sure if you're an imaginary friend or a novel's protagonist or a mascot or what. But if you're here, you're an idea.

Second: You were loved. You were loved enduringly and unequivocally, and that made you capital-R Real. Not an idea; an Idea. A Friend.

But then – whatever just happened to your person, your creator – it happened, and it was horrible, and it affected you. I won't pretend to

1

know what, and I won't ask, but whatever it was, your person couldn't keep you around. For most ideas, that's it, lights out. But not you. You're Real. So… what happens to you?

Well, what happens is that you end up here. The Stillreal. The underside of the Imagination that nobody remembers to clean. It can be a rough place, but it can also be beautiful. Fortunately, you have me to help you find the latter instead of waltzing face-first into the former.

The name's Tippy: ex-imaginary friend and once-and-current detective. It's nice to meet you.

CHAPTER ONE

That case? That one starts with the screaming corn.

Every time I talk about this case, I wish it started differently: some mysterious person walking into my office, or my best friend in the whole world asking for help fleeing to Mexico, or even me trying to help my person learn her ABCs. You know, a real detective story, something that speaks to my soul. Not one where I get hired out of Mr Float's Rootbeerium by the living incarnation of someone's half-baked TV pitch. Of course, if I always got what I wanted, I wouldn't be where I am, so – bigger picture – I guess this is for the best.

The corn in question is growing on the premises of Nightshire Farms, the 'evil' farm down the road from the 'good' Sundrop Farms. The farms are two halves of a children's television series; their person crawled into a bottle and dropped the whole place off in this lovely communal garbage heap of ours before the show got a chance to air. I'm here because Nightshire's proprietor, arch-villain Farmer Nick Nefarious, is worried about the behavior of the crop of singing corn he's stolen from Sundrop's proprietor, his antagonist/sometimes friend Farmer Fran. More specifically, he's worried about the way the 'singing' corn won't stop screaming. He's offered to clear my Rootbeerium tab as payment, but more importantly he's given me a mystery to keep my brain occupied instead of letting it sink into the mud of my memories. (The clear tab is nice though, not going to lie.) So here I am, about to step right into a whole swimming pool of trouble.

Nightshire Farms really tries to drive the whole 'evil' point home, as much as something with the aesthetic of a kid's cartoon can. The buildings are various shades of black and purple, and so lopsided they look like their architects hated the concept of symmetry. Both the farmhouse and the barn have their windows and doors positioned perfectly to look like snarling faces. There's no detail to the horizon, just flat in every direction, and a haze of red dust that makes the sun look like it's dying. The soil is volcanic ash, thick and gray, and all the plants have faces: poison-red berries with wrathful little scowls, street gangs of fat green gourds sneering and looking for a challenge. And between the barn and the house, standing in military-precise rows, is the corn.

Farmer Nick sold the situation short. When he said 'screaming,' I pictured hungry babies wailing, or maybe someone getting surprised in the dark. This is straight-from-the-heart, pants-wetting terror, like the world's biggest predator is one toothy lunge away from devouring the corn and everything it loves. I understand why Farmer Nick was waiting at the Rootbeerium – I don't want to be anywhere near this noise either – but I wish he'd told me that cotton balls in my ears weren't quite going to cut it. I'm tempted to scream just to let out the pressure.

I start my clue-mining on the edges of the cornrows, taking measurements, getting a summary established in my head. The corn's yellow, but more old butter than noonday sun, and the stalks are varying shades of green, none of them healthy. There are sixty-six rows, with six stalks on each row. (If that metaphor seems heavy-handed, congratulations, you now know why this Idea never got past a storyboard.) I do a full circuit for missing or broken stalks, but nothing doing. It's a perfect little phalanx of corn cobs, all of them screaming their darn heads off.

Next, I check the dirt. The ground gets colder the closer to the corn I get. The color shifts, too, turning deep purple instead of choking gray. That could just be a quirk of Nightshire's soil, but my detective stuff says it's a clue.

(The detective stuff is magic. Just trust me; the longer explanation for it doesn't help much.)

I pick up a handful of the gray dirt, let it sift through the cotton stubs I call toes. Other than the temperature, it feels like dirt, moves like dirt, smells like dirt. I pick up some of the purple stuff, and right away it's different – it's thinner and lighter, pouring between my toes in viscous wisps, like I've grabbed on to night-time mist. I have a theory fermenting.

I look at the corn again, and I let my detective stuff speak to me. It says to check their faces, so I take a gander at one up close and personal. It's not pleasant – this close, the screaming's a drill pushed right up against my skull – but that doesn't stop two thoughts from colliding so hard they burst.

I look again at Nick's other crops, and I look back to the corn, and I see exactly what I expect to see. I'm so excited my toes start to vibrate.

"It's the details," I say, to the partner I like to pretend I still have.

The faces aren't like the faces on Farmer Nick's other crops. The others are cartoonish, abstract and simple, just like every other kid-show Idea I've ever come across. The corn, though, has definition. There are veins in the eyeballs, contours and deformities in the teeth, and an all-around stink of compost coming off them.

"This didn't come from Sundrop Farms," I mutter.

See, the one advantage to your creator dropping you in the Stillreal: you can travel to Ideas other than the one you were dropped in. The catch is that when Friends travel to an Idea they aren't originally from, they bring a little of their home with them. If you're just passing through like I am, it's pretty minor and pretty brief; the colors around here might be brighter after I leave, or a few ears of corn might look like they're made of fabric, at least until Nightshire Farms reverts back to its version of 'normal.' But if something from another Idea sticks around too long, things start to go really sideways – like, say, horrifying faces on your ill-gotten crops.

I follow the purple dirt, watching the way it blends into the gray. It was easy to miss at first, but on second glance there's a hint of purple extending into the shadow of the barn. It's more a general smearing of color than a simple trail, but still, my theory is putting on muscle.

Conclusion: The corn was absolutely stolen from Farmer Fran, but something else made it change – and that something appears to have hidden in the barn, recently enough that the crops haven't had a chance to reassert themselves.

The doors to the barn are wide open, although given the kind of place Nightshire is, they're probably always wide open, waiting, beckoning, hungry, et cetera. The diseased sunlight does less than nothing to light up the barn's insides.

The safest place in this Idea right now is anywhere but inside that barn, but inside that barn is where the puzzle is. I swallow a little knot of fear, and walk inside.

The sunlight cuts out the second I step through the open doors. The inside of the barn is in perpetual twilight, just enough light to see the odd spooky detail you're sure is just your mind playing tricks on you. The floor is covered in pungent, past-prime straw. To my left is a wall of hay bales. To my right is a long row of stable stalls, stretching into the endless shadows. Right in front of me is a wall full of farm implements designed to scare the poop out of people. I tear my attention away from the most barb-laden one, and remind myself to breathe.

Clues will help. Clues will always help. The stalls are the place to start. I walk along the row, my head as low to the ground as I can get, checking under every door for evidence of inhabitants. Nothing; my detective stuff isn't even kicking up. There's no sign of anything alive in here except me and a couple of oily-shelled beetles.

And that shuffling noise…

It's coming from behind me, from one of the stalls I already checked. It's just on the edge of normal hearing, like socks on a shag carpet as heard through a thick oak door. As an experiment I turn around, and sure enough, the shuffling has moved with me, sounding out from behind again, except this time it's closer. I turn around once more, and the sound whickers out. My sense of calm clocks out early.

This creature has to be a nightmare. Only nightmares move that fast, that particularly, calibrated to maximize your fear. Nightmares also tend to be the most dangerous Friends; the threat of harm is vital to their sense of purpose, and it's not like they can help backing it up if they're pressed. On the bright side, screaming corn doesn't seem as worrying anymore.

The shuffle comes again, close enough to set my nerves on fire, waiting for a hand or tentacle or claw to come down on my waiting shoulder. The worst thing I could do right now would be to run. The second-worst thing would be to call out to whatever is making the noise.

"Hello?"

If I do the unexpected, I usually catch the bad guys off-guard.

More shuffling. Ordinary senses wouldn't be able to place it, but detective stuff says it's two stalls from the end, behind another nondescript wooden door. I creep toward it, stop one stall shy, and take a long, theatrical look around, like I can't figure out where the sound is coming from. Then I duck as a blur of shadows and drill bits comes whooshing by, gleaming talons raking the air just shy of where my head used to be.

I blink, and the blur is gone. A silk-on-silk hiss echoes through the barn, coming from every stall at once. I hear sharp bits grating against each other, and huge, heavy things skulking around in the darkness above me. They must have gone up into the rafters, which is basically the last place I want them to be. If I'd known this thing could fly, I might have charged Nick extra.

Some nightmares will stop and talk to you as soon as they know you won't get scared. Some nightmares double down when you get courageous, start getting truly violent. And some are animals, knowing nothing except the chase and the pounce and the fear. And this one chose the spookiest barn in the Stillreal to camp out in, so practicality demands I assume it's type three.

I pivot in place, trying to bait the nightmare back out, trusting my detective stuff to keep me on the ball. There's another rustle off to my left, and a growl of admonishment that I'm sure soaked many a bedsheet in its day. I need to get it down near the floor again, where the tighter quarters created by the stalls will limit its movement.

"Are you a bed monster?" I ask the darkness. "Or maybe a window-scratcher?" I slather the mocking tone on thick, which as a bonus helps cover up my shivers. "What kind of half-scary nonsense were you before you came here?"

The barn stays quiet, that aggravating silence you can tell is going to be filled with noise any second. This Friend has definitely been here for a while if they've got the acoustics down like that. There's more movement, but nothing dramatic enough to suggest they're coming down my way. They won't come down without an opening. This thing is good at their job. I shrug, and start trotting off toward the barn doors, looking as casual as I can manage when my head feels like an alarm clock.

"If you're just going to hide in the dark, I guess I'll go tell Farmer Nick there's nothing to be scared of."

That gets a response. Unfortunately, that response is a whirring, buzzing, impossibly fast blackness diving down at me. Well, I can't say this case is boring.

The nightmare tries two dive-bys first, shooting past one way then the other, glowing dinner-plate eyes flashing as they cross my path. A stall door creaks open behind me, and the shadows on the wall grow long and hungry. This nightmare knows their stuff. By which I mean 'Help me.'

Focus. I need to ground this thing, and I need to do it fast. The blur sails past me again, close enough to blow icy wind across the fabric of my back, and my hindlegs tighten up, ready to use my last resort. I'm a detective first, but I'm also a triceratops…

There's a skittering noise behind me. I pretend to take the bait, craning my neck in a desperate attempt to see around my crown. A single nail pings across the floor right behind me, and I have to stifle my chuckle. The distracting surprise. This nightmare's younger than I gave them credit for. A dropped nail, a creaking floorboard – those are tricks you use on kids to get their attention diverted.

Another nail drops somewhere in front of me, a sound that would leave a typical victim spinning in place – so, of course, the nightmare comes at me from the side, a ragged wingspan of buzzing power tools that fills my peripheral vision. I hunker down, let them sail over me, and spring up into the air for a short-range charge. All three of my horns connect with a stumpy, buckle-laden back leg, and the nightmare bowls head over heels and crash-lands in front of me.

"Ow!" it says, like a toddler with a skinned knee.

All my fear, anger, and curiosity pops like a soap bubble. "You alright?" I ask, not bothering to mask my concern.

"No!" they cry, in a tinny, air-duct wail. They curl in on themself, rubbing at their leg where I connected. I'm pretty sure they're actually smaller now. I feel awful.

Now that they're not moving, it's easier to get a bead on what they look like: black, some hints of purple and red, like the night sky just outside a city. They're about six times my size, four limbs, the hunched stance of a dog or a cat, but their head is roughly human shaped. Given the fluid way they move, I think they're always shaped like whatever they think will terrify their target the most. And then there's the machinery, the eyes like welder's goggles, the whirring drills in place of claws, the saw blades spinning along the ridge of their back, all anchored in place by a spaghetti dinner of leather straps and big chrome buckles.

This is a nightmare, which by the logic that made me means it's a bad guy. I can feel in my stuffing that I'm supposed to mock them, insult them, play it cool. But that's not what they need, and that's probably not what I need, either. I swallow my first instincts and go with the second wave.

"Anything I can do?"

The nightmare sniffles, still curled away from me, continually rubbing their leg. "No." They don't sound sure.

"I'm so sorry," I say. "You scared me, and I reacted. Doesn't mean you aren't hurt, but…"

They sniffle again. "I was trying to scare you," they say. "I understand. It just… it really hurt!"

"Yeah. I'm sorry."

They rubs at the affected area for another second. "I'm okay. I'll be okay." They don't sound okay, at all.

The good news is, I have a job to do here, and it might actually make things better. First things first. "What's your name?"

The nightmare tenses up in confusion. "What?"

"Your name. If you're willing to give it to me?"

When they blink, there's a sound like a garage door opening and closing. "I'm... Spindleman."

"Hi, Spindleman." I extend a cloth paw. "I'm Tippy."

Spindleman looks at my paw, trying to decide what to do, then brightens before enveloping it with a hand that's mostly screwdrivers. Shaking it makes me glad I'm kind of hard to hurt.

"Can I ask you for your pronouns?"

"Huh?"

They're very young, then. "When I don't call you by name, do you prefer he, she, ze, it..."

"It," Spindleman says. "Matthew always called me it."

"All right then, it." I smile, and log the name Matthew for later. "I'm really sorry."

Despite itself, Spindleman brightens. I take the opportunity.

"Can I ask you a few questions? No is fine, if you're too upset."

Spindleman sniffles again. "Okay."

"Thank you." I sit down on my haunches, removing what threat I can, and get ready to memorize. "So... judging by appearances, you're a long way from home, aren't you?"

"... yes?"

I nod, trying to act as casual as possible. "Okay. Can you tell me where you came from?"

"The bushes around the house," it says. It sucks in air like a drowning man. "The, the night-time house with the big orange moon. The one that Matthew sleeps in."

Okay, this I can work with. My stuffing is starting to unclench. "What can you tell me about Matthew?"

"Small," Spindleman says, almost awe-struck. "Small, and defenseless, and... vulnerable." There's a glaze of saliva over its words, but it's hard to hold that against it; we're all what our people made us. "Every night, he has to sleep in his huge room all by himself, and the light in there is bright, so much brighter than the sky I live in during the day..."

"So Matthew is your person?" I ask.

"My person?"

So it's a *very* young nightmare, then. "The one who created you," I explain. "The one who made you Real."

Spindleman sniffs, nods. "He was my... person. But he's not anymore." Its head sags on its long industrial accident of a neck. "He didn't need me anymore."

This sounds familiar. I never stop hating it, though. "Are you here because you got separated from Matthew?"

"He stopped caring about me." Spindleman's goggle eyes widen, and in their glass I see a towering silhouette offering a big, thick hand to me. "He said I wasn't scary anymore, and then he kicked me out, and I had to leave the house and come out here and I... I..."

"Shhh. Shhh. It's okay."

I lay a gentle paw on one leg, and Spindleman recoils from me, huge again, saw blades sparking where they connect with the cross-beams overhead. I back up, partly calculated and partly panic. Spindleman doesn't have any facial features, but I can still tell it's upset.

"I'm sorry," I say, keeping my distance. "I should have asked before I touched you. And... I'm sorry you got separated."

Spindleman hesitates, but from my detective stuff's read, that's only because it has no idea what an apology looks like. This is going to be a steep climb.

"Is it okay if I ask you some more questions?" I ask.

Spindleman whimpers. "Yes?"

"Is this the first place you went after you left Matthew's house?"

"Yes. I mean, no. I didn't leave very long ago, but, this isn't the first place."

I sit down on my haunches. "Where was the first place?" I think I know, but that's when I most need to ask questions.

"I went to the big motel. The one in the big sandbox. The... the bird woman, she helped me find my way there."

"Bird woman? Tall, muscular, eyes shine red, white, or blue?"

"Yes!" Spindleman says, excited to be able to answer in the affirmative.

"That's Freedom Frieda. You were staying at the Freedom Motel?"

"Yes!"

I nod. The Freedom Motel is a common first stop for Friends newly booted into the Stillreal. The question is how it wound up out here on Sundrop Farms. My toes are starting to vibrate again. "Why did you decide to leave?"

Spindleman shrinks again, now about my size, its machinery partially retracted into its body. "It wasn't safe there. And everywhere else I went was so, so big, and so open…"

It's afraid. Hopefully a small distraction will help. "Your home Idea's pretty small, then? The house, I mean." I need to be careful of my phrasing.

Spindleman cocks its head. "The sky is big…but the house, and the little garden, and the… car…" It shivers. "Yes. It's pretty small."

"So you left there because Matthew didn't think you were scary, and then the motel was too wide-open for you?"

"No," Spindleman says. "No, everywhere *else* was too open for me. The motel was perfect." Its voice brightens for a second. A very short one. "I left the motel because of the Man."

"What man?"

"The Man in the Coat. He came by the motel, and he looked in all the windows, and… and he was like me, scary like me, and I had to get out of there…"

"He was like you?" I ask. I try not to sound too excited.

"He was… Real, you said? He could travel like me. He was there looking for me because I left the house."

My brain sets off fireworks. "He was at the house, too?"

"Yes!" Spindleman says, excited at my comprehension.

That makes only a limited amount of sense. This man has to be from Spindleman's home Idea if it saw him there, but if he were from Spindleman's home Idea he wouldn't be a stranger. Well, probably – plenty of weird fish in the Imagination…

"So… this man came to your home, and you had to leave. But then he showed up at the Freedom Motel after you started staying there, so you fled… here?"

"Not right away. I had to look around. I had to find somewhere safe."

This thing is lucky it didn't wander off into an Idea it wasn't going to wander back out of. I start to ask a follow-up question, but it's drowned out by a clap of thunder.

"You–" The rain starts, pitter-pattering down onto the ugly gray soil outside. It's so loud, like it's right in my ear. "So, you came here after you–"

I already feel wet. I hear the squealing rubber, and I hear Daddy shout, and then I'm turning over on my head –

I snap back into the barn. Spindleman doesn't look concerned, so the pause can't have been that long. Then again, I'm not sure what a concerned Spindleman would look like anyway.

"Was, uh – was there a particular reason you came here?" I ask.

"You asked that already, didn't you?"

"Maybe? I meant how did you get here?"

The rain is so very loud…

"I – thought? – my way here." It sounds proud. "I like it here. It's got big sky like the motel does, but, but there's this…" It gestures at the shadows overhead. "This dark place, like my home…"

"We need to get you out of here."

"But why?" Spindleman wails.

The rain is constant now, hissing like some big snake – focus on the drill-monster, Tippy.

"I'm sorry you got scared," I say, back in my soothing voice. I'm good at the soothing voice. She always needed me to be. "But, Ideas like these, they're… impressionable. You're bringing parts of your home Idea with you."

"You mean like the house?" it says with hope.

"No," I say. "You're from a – you're a nightmare. So this place is becoming nightmarish because you're in it. Just a little bit right now, but it'll get worse the longer you stay here, and it's not supposed to be like that."

"But… I miss home…" Spindleman says, tapping whole new reserves of sorrow.

"This isn't your home," I say.

Gosh dang it, why is that rain so loud?

"This is someone else's home." I normally have a whole speech for this, but I need to go. Now. "Turning someone else's home into your home isn't nice. You could hurt people."

"Oh, no! No!" There's a whimper under the whirring of drills. "I don't want to actually hurt people."

A nightmare that doesn't want to hurt anybody? How young was its person?

"But…" Spindleman shakes its head, its whole body. "But…"

"Listen." I take a frustrated step forward. "I know that you're new, but–" Spindleman whimpers again, and I catch myself. Easy, Tippy. "We need to take you somewhere you can stay."

"But where? Where do I go?"

"There are places that are – that are where we all live. Places your changes won't hurt anybody."

Spindleman lets out a deflated whine. "I didn't mean to hurt anybody."

But what I say is, "I know." I'm supposed to comfort it, I want to comfort it, but the rain is like a bag of wet hammers. "I'll take you where you won't."

"The motel?" Spindleman says with horror. "But the motel, that man–"

"Not the motel," I snap, and immediately feel terrible. "I live in a place called Playtime Town," I say, trying to soften my words. "It's meant for Friends like us, who aren't at home anymore."

"Friends?"

"It's what the people who live around here all call each other, long story, but – Playtime Town. I can take you there right now, if you'll let me. My buddies can get you set up with somewhere nice to live."

"And I will be safe there?"

"From there we'll find you the safest place you can be, where you can live with Friends like you. Frieda was probably going to send you there as soon as you were ready."

"I wish she'd told me…" Spindleman says. "I… I wouldn't have hurt anybody that way…"

"It's fine." Really, she just knew it wasn't ready, but it had to go and… rain… water… I shake my head again. "Are you ready to go?"

"Right away!" Spindleman says. "Oh, yes, I would love to go and be safe and have a home again. Right away!"

I should be touched, but mostly I'm relieved. "Great," I say. "Let's get you out of here."

I hold out a paw. Spindleman examines it, shaking, and finally takes my paw in its own. I want to give this poor drill-monster a hug, but there'll be plenty of time for that when we get to Playtime Town, I figure.

Remembering that moment feels awful.

CHAPTER TWO

The Stillreal? Gosh, how do I explain the Stillreal…?

Short version: People (actual people, out there in the real world) have ideas. Nightmares. Mascots. Scripts. Conspiracy theories. Those ideas exist in the Imagination. For the most part, they're ephemeral – they come into being, they hang around your head, they surface when they're needed and duck down when they aren't.

But sometimes, an idea is bigger than that. Sometimes you have a recurring nightmare that helps define your personality. Career aspirations you can see in full 4-D in your mind's eye. A novel that speaks to the depths of your heart. An imaginary friend who gets you through the darkest times. Sometimes, you have an idea you love so much, you make it more. You make it Real – a true citizen of the Imagination, dependent on but separate from its person.

But then what happens?

Well, for some of us, our reason to be Real fades away naturally – kids grow up, scripts get abandoned – and we waft off into the After-Real, imaginary friend Heaven (or so we hear). Some people share their Real Friends with others and they're lucky enough to become Big Ideas, cultural touchstones, surfing between minds as everyone concocts variations on Tom Sawyer and Scheherazade and Superman.

But then, there are some Friends whose people experience something that goes too hard against the grain of our existence – something that makes our continued presence too scary, or too painful, or too lacking in internal logic. They need to get rid of us: stop writing that novel that their husband left them over, let go of that career goal that will never happen after the accident… stop expecting an imaginary friend to make sense of a world that doesn't actually make sense. They need to get rid of us, but we're still Real…

For us, there's the Stillreal. The underbelly of the Imagination. The place for Ideas too Real to fade away, too anonymous to go Big, and too messed up to stay where we are. We're a patchwork of places, a population of emotional refugees, all knitted together at random and doing our best to survive without literally life-giving love. In other words, we're a mess.

Welcome.

For real-world people, travel's simple – places are next to other places, and you get from Point A to Point B by physically moving yourself there. In the Stillreal, it's a bit more complicated. Ideas might look like places, but they're still just ideas, separate and distinct; there's no guarantee that time flows the same way at Point A as it does at Point B, or that gravity even works there, or that the Friends there need to eat or sleep or breathe. So, getting from Point A to Point B safely is a matter of finding the symbolic links between the two points and envisioning yourself at Point B. Preferably, you do this by focusing on something unique from the Idea you're traveling to, but you can just sort of envision something and try to jump to it – as long as you don't mind the risk of, say, not going anywhere; or aging a thousand years because you end up somewhere time flows faster; or never coming back at all.

If you're part of the ninety-nine percent of the Stillreal who don't like pioneering with your face, then short, precise jumps are what you need: find something unique in your surroundings you can focus on, and imagine it changing into something similar in an Idea that has more in common with your destination. Then refocus, do the same thing again, but jump a little bit closer to your destination this time... and eventually, you get where you're going. If that sounds complicated, good; you won't be one of the Friends who are never heard from again.

I hold Spindleman's hand, and think us from the barn at Nightshire Farms to a barn I know in Merrysville, a similar design to Nick's but with a smell like someone gutted Christmas and hung it from the rafters. From there we go to a deserted old ranch in Perdition, our local Wild West town, the skeleton of a farmhouse looming at the back. Then we head to a big, candy-apple-red farmhouse in Small-Town America, all fireworks and factories and grandmas, our last stop before we arrive the gingerbread and pastel of Playtime Town, just in time for the gold-chased Playtime Metro trolley to go smirking and joking past us, a five-o'clock shadow of rust on its apple-cheeked face.

Some Friends, like Farmer Fran and Farmer Nick, show up in the Stillreal with a place to call home, but most of us aren't so lucky. Luckily for us homeless Friends, not everything that washes up in the Stillreal is a person – some of them are places. (Well, and some are both, but that's off-topic.) Over the course of imaginary history, different places have attracted different sorts of Friends. Your superheroic and funnybook-dwelling Friends tend to drift toward the four-color style of Avatar City. Your grittier, but still science-fictional Friends prefer Chrometown's cyberpunk aesthetic. There's Santa Erzulie for the urban-fantastical ones, or the Hex Dimension for the ones that like their dungeons full of dragons. And for those of us who trend toward the more youthful persuasion, there's Playtime Town.

Playtime Town is a big city by way of a kindergarten playground, soft edges, simple shapes, bright colors and smiling faces on everything. It's got poor districts and slums, but they're cozy and familial instead of bleak and oppressive. It's got dark alleys, but the shadows are about as threatening as the ones underneath your favorite blanket, and the criminals are just there to learn valuable life lessons they can impart to you. It's a big American city as described by someone who loves the city to its core; its joys are supercharged and its ills are downplayed and everything is all set for you to have an adventure that will never, ever really hurt you.

Or that's how most of it is, anyway. Us imported Friends have messed around with it in our special symphony of ways, shifting the colors here, altering the decorations there, until the building facades come out looking like patchwork quilts.

I thought us in by the History Building downtown, and, thank Sandra, the place is dry. The Idea's creator thought his characters would come here to learn about exciting bits of US history, but us immigrants love it for the view. From here you can see the whole sweep of Playtime Town, the brightly-colored buildings shaped like crayons and balloons, City Hall and its huge jungle-gym sculpture in the center. The outer rim is a different story, with half-finished buildings in a dozen different styles, the King of Cowboys Saloon right next to the crystal spires of Jove Base Gamma right next to the Victorian crags of the Terrible Old House. Those are the orphaned buildings, the places whose foundations stayed behind with their people. The homeless homes.

Spindleman trembles at the sight. I was sort of hoping for a gasp of joy, but any optimism I was feeling washes away when it says, "Oh, oh, it's – it's so *big* here!"

"Come on, I'll take you over to the rental office. We'll get you someplace smaller." Good job, Tippy. Very comforting.

"Oh-oh, thank you!" Spindleman says breathlessly, skulking close to me as we start walking.

"It's my job," I reply. I'm still too shaken to be very empathetic. At least I'm keeping my mouth from shooting off. "Let's get down to business."

We walk down the street; a stuffed dinosaur detective and a towering, cowering black nightmare mingling with the rest of the weirdoes that hung their hats in Playtime Town. I nod to the Worst Cat as he lurks on his usual catnip-hustling corner, wave to Prince Hekau the mummy as he looms past with an armload of groceries. People are happy to see me; the feeling is not as mutual as usual. I'm looking forward to a root beer and some time in my dryer.

"Are you alright, Mr Tippy?" Spindleman asks.

We're passing the Rootbeerium, a building-shaped cookie complete with frosting roof, the usual three stanzas of pipe-organ theme music spooling endlessly out of the frosted-gingerbread batwing doors. I want to go inside, but it can be an overload for newcomers.

"I'm fine," I lie. The fact that Spindleman has time to ask that when it's already scared doesn't exactly make me feel better about myself. "I just… I really don't like the rain."

"Oh." He waits another half-block before he forces out a "Why?"

My thoughts billiard-ball around the inside of my head. "Long, long, *long* story. Let's just get you a home."

"Okay," he says, nice and cowed. Oh, good job, Tippy. Way to not be a jerk.

The Playtime Town Rental Office is a tall, skinny shack, like the kind you might serve hot dogs out of, but with blank forms lining the walls instead of menus. The proprietor, Golem Jones, is in the process of organizing all that paperwork when we walk up. He's almost as tall as Spindleman, and twice as broad, a wedge of brownstone carved into the shape of a linebacker wearing a bomber jacket and a yarmulke.

"Hello, Detective Tippy," Jones says in his big earthquake voice. "And hello, big fella." His H's are razor sharp. "Another new resident, I see."

Golem Jones is happy to see us, and I reward that enthusiasm by being as abrupt as I can possibly manage. "Golem Jones, Spindleman. Spindleman, Golem Jones."

"I'm looking for a home!" Spindleman announces, high-pitched, hopeful, and a little rushed.

Jones nods, and looks down at me, waiting for an answer to the usual question.

"Kid's nightmare," I say. "We found him hiding in Farmer Nick's barn."

"I had to leave the motels because of the Man," Spindleman says.

Dust crumbles off Jones' eyebrows as he raises them. Spindleman takes in a long breath, and I can tell he's about to reiterate the same story I've already heard, so I intervene. It's for Jones' sake, I tell myself.

"I'm guessing he's Playtime-Town-material given his person's age," I say. "But please make sure he's in one of the safer buildings, yeah? As a favor to me?"

Jones shifts from concern to a smile with a noise like tectonic plates grinding. "Sure, little buddy. I'm always happy to help out a stray."

"What's a stray?" Spindleman asks, with genuine confusion.

Jones' grin just gets bigger. This is why we let him run the Rental Office. "You look like you'd prefer the Terrible Old House, I think, but they're full up right now." He looks grim as he says it. That must be where he put the necromancer whose person overdosed. "For the moment, though, I think I've got a spot at Smile House. Yes, yes, that'll work," he says, wagging a knowledgeable finger for emphasis. "Right next door to the Sadness Penguins. Long-time residents, they can get you up to speed no problem."

There's a pointed glance my way; he thinks that should have been my job. If I explained, he'd understand.

"I very much appreciate it!" Spindleman says.

"Can I leave this fella with you then, Jonesy?" I ask. I want to help, but I'm out of help for the day.

"No problem, buddy." Jones waves me off and sets about pulling paperwork off the walls and stacking it onto a clipboard for our soon-to-be-neighbor. "You get back to keeping us safe."

"Thank you so much, Mr Tippy," Spindleman says. "I really appreciate you finding me a safe place to live."

The Friends of young kids are the worst when I'm like this. I force a smile. "Don't mention it, kid. You stay scary out there."

Spindleman nods enthusiastically, and lets out a gleeful squeal as Golem Jones shoves the now-ready clipboard into signing range. With the attention off me, I take the opportunity to duck out of the conversation.

Case closed. Farmer Nick's ill-gotten corn should reset to normal soon, and within a week or two, Spindleman will be just another displaced Friend, learning how to cope with the Stillreal. I've earned a root beer. Maybe even a sundae.

Yes, I know I was a jerk. But stay with me; there's an explanation coming.

CHAPTER THREE

I head back exactly the way I came, already chiding myself for how badly I handled that. I let my damage get on top of me and made Spindleman's transition rougher than it already had to be. I'm not going to feel good about that any time soon – nor should I.

But dealing with things badly doesn't mean I don't deserve self-care after that rain, so it's a good thing the tail end of my case is already depositing me at Mr Float's. I stop at the gingerbread doors of the Rootbeerium and take a deep breath, letting my dreams of soda and ice cream gain momentum before I step inside. My toes are tingling again.

Mr Float's Rootbeerium is a bar as only Playtime Town can give you; big and sprawling and way too bright, with décor like a wedding cake and a menu of nothing but desserts. The titular Mr Float is the mustachioed ice cream-ghost behind the bar, cleaning out a sundae glass and smiling at his mid-day stock of patrons. Prince Hekau has staked out his preferred dark corner to eat his lunchtime baklava. Mrs and Mrs Svezda, the beige-skinned astronaut and the green-skinned alien, are tucking into a shared plate of chocolate-covered apricots. Chip Dixon, our plucky local journalist/two-fisted adventurer/fifth-grader, is sitting alone at the bar, propping up one of the apple-pie-shaped stools while he sips a chocolate milkshake. He tilts his fedora at me in greeting and goes right back to his drink. The one that gets my attention, though, is the hulking, hunched-over figure of Farmer Nick in the other dark corner directly opposite Hekau.

Nick has exactly three character traits – greed, brutality, and sleaze. He embodies all of them in his appearance. He's tall – the kind of tall that's always a little bigger and scarier than you remember – with sickly skin the color of wet newspaper and a beard like a felonious pinecone attached to an angry, hatchet-nosed face. His overalls are over-starched denim, and his straw hat is decorated with rat skulls. His style is cartoony and exaggerated, but that doesn't make him seem any less dangerous when he glares at me over his banana pudding.

"Detective," he twangs. The note of hope in his voice sounds completely out of place.

"Farmer," I reply.

Nick shifts, knobby fingers fidgeting with his spoon. "How'd it, uh…"

"It went fine. If you consider almost getting chewed on fine. Your problem should be taken care of now, at any rate."

Farmer Nick grins. His teeth look like a busted piano. "You sure?"

"Yeah. Turned out a nightmare had holed up in your barn."

"A nightmare?" Nick's nose wrinkles.

"Nothing serious," I say. "Sorry it was messing with your carefully cultivated evil." That jab isn't because I'm anxious; with villains as bad as Nick I don't have to feel bad unleashing the snark.

Nick chuckles, showing off the damaged piano keys of his teeth. "That it, then?"

"Your Idea will take a little while to get back to normal, but it will. Pretty soon your stolen corn should start singing lullabies again."

Nick tilts his straw hat back, scratches at his pate. "Well then I reckon I'll get back to my farmin'," he says, with one more fixer-upper grin. "Since I can get a good night's sleep now an' all."

"I think everyone will be happy with that arrangement," I say.

Nick slides off his chair, standing up to his full terrifying height, and flips a handful of mixed coins from his overalls onto the table.

"Thankee for the puddin'," he calls over to the bar, and starts searching the walls for his way out.

"Thank *you* for the case," I say.

Farmer Nick's only answer is a shrug. His eyes lock onto something over my shoulder, and before I can check what it is, he fades out of view, leaving an empty booth and a half-eaten bowl of pudding.

I shake my head, and walk over to the bar where Chip Dixon is sitting. He's wearing his blue vest and sapphire tie-tack today. That usually means he's feeling chatty, which is perfect. Chip is the only Friend I know of who can access the Realworld news, and you'd be surprised how often a Stillreal detective needs that. Plus, I like talking to Chip.

"Hello, Detective," pipes Mr Float as I walk up. His mustache lifts in the usual expansive grin. "What can I get you?"

"My tab clear?" I ask. I'd banter, but I don't think I have another quip in me.

"Absolutely," Mr Float says.

"Perfect," I say. "Let's fix that." Okay, maybe I lied. "I'll take a root beer float, vanilla bean ice cream, not vanilla. And get another one queued up for when I finish that."

"Right away," he says. He mops the bar for a second. "Let's call it one big favor and one little favor?" The barter system is the norm in the Stillreal; not every Idea has a concept of money, and not every Friend understands it.

"Done."

I turn to Chip, and find him already looking at me, milkshake gripped in one brown, scar-knuckled hand. "Detective," he says, cordial as ever.

"Reporter," I respond. "What's got you scrutinizing me?" Even on a good day, I don't like to beat around the bush unless I'm the one doing it.

Chip pushes his fedora back on his head. "My favorite detective comes through the door at lunch, I assume he's here to talk to me."

Chip's smirking, expectantly waiting for what he's sure my next move is going to be. There's something in his eyes, though; this little flicker of a different mood. I ignore my detective stuff poking me about it, and ask the question I want to ask instead.

"Can you give me the weather report?"

"The weather report?" Chip's disarmed for a second. "I figured you'd be hunting for a new case."

With most people that's an opening to a verbal fencing match, but insulting good people is selfish, not self-care. "I just got back from a case," I say. "The weather there wasn't so great. Sort of rainy…"

Chip winces. "Oh heck, Tippy." His face looks like a funeral procession. "I'm sorry."

"It's cool, I've calmed down, I just – I need some normal right now."

"Alright," Chip says. "We can hit the rest of the news that's fit to print later, yeah?" He gives me a little slice of smile, and I give it right back.

"Yeah, okay," I say.

Mr Float swings by our end of the bar, dropping off a big, beautiful soda fountain glass, a little blob of ice cream bobbing at the top of a fizzy, spicy lake of root beer. I take the glass in paw, toast Chip, and drink a long, muscle-unkinking slug while my good friend and plucky reporter clears his throat and digs into the Realworld news.

"Portland residents are rejoicing today as old Mr Sun finally shows his face," Chip says, already deep in his old-time newsreel narration. "A week of furious rainfall has finally passed, and citizens are out and about, enjoying the sunshine and assessing the damage. Roads remain closed in parts of the county, and flood warnings are still in effect in the mountains, but that isn't stopping our tireless schoolteachers from…"

I let the sound of his voice and the rush of sugar carry me away, and for a few minutes, I don't have to think. Pretty soon, I might stop hearing the rain.

So. That explanation I owe you, right?

Let's just say right off the bat that I should have asked more questions back on the farm. I should have asked more about the Man in the Coat, or the events preceding Matthew abandoning Spindleman, or any of the other things that are oh-so-weird about this whole scenario. But I don't think well when I've been rained on.

See, my person was a little girl named Sandra Moon. When she was two, her Daddy – an ambulatory smile with spiky black hair – came home from a Work Trip in some other country, and he brought a stuffed plush triceratops with him. It had a little stitched-on smile, like the one I flashed at Spindleman to calm him down; little black eyes, like the ones that studied the corn; soft yellow fuzz, perfect for snuggling at night. What it didn't have was a name, so Sandra gave it one: Tippy. And there I was.

I became a detective because Sandra wanted to be a detective, and because she thought Daddy brought me into her life to help her figure out the mystery of why he kept having to leave for so long, and why Mommy got so mad when he wore that special cologne we both loved.

We had adventures. We solved cases. We battled bad guys. The details of my life filled in: how much I loved root beer – Sandra's favorite drink. I was sarcastic and cynical, just like the detectives in Mommy's favorite TV shows. How my horns burned in the presence of the words Sandra wasn't supposed to say. My case file became stuffed to the rafters with success after success, a solve rate that no TV character could even hope for. Because of Sandra's love, because of the energy she invested in the details of my life, I became more than a normal idea; I became Real.

The fourth autumn of Sandra's life was her first year in Portland, and the first autumn Daddy stayed home. It was also the first time she saw rain. It was a bad storm even by a Portland family's standards, one of those deluges that puts confused gee-golly faces on all the weathermen. Sandra was fascinated, so Mommy got her camera, and Daddy took her outside.

Somewhere in the Realworld, there's a video of Sandra and me – the original me – awed as we investigate the mystery of rain. Sandra is ecstatic, shrieking nonsense about this magic thing happening to the sky. I'm just staring, because that's all stuffed animals do.

We got soaked to the bone. Daddy waited until Sandra was exhausted to pick us up and bring us inside to get dried off – my first pass through the dryer. That night, Tippy and his Stuffed Animal Detective Agency took to the streets to unravel the mystery of rain.

We determined it was the fault of Mr Sky, who envied us our lives on the ground, and tried to force us above the clouds so he could have friends. We defeated Mr Sky by offering him some jellybeans. Cloud-people love jellybeans.

All my new cases were set on rainy nights. We stayed up all night in the winters, just to listen for a burst of thunder. Sometimes, from my prized perch on the window, I got to watch Sandra go outside and spin in the front yard, Mommy and her camera capturing the sheer, naked joy on Sandra's face.

But that winter, Daddy went away again – another Work Trip – and we renewed our hunt for the reasons behind Daddy's constant disappearances. We were just starting to make headway, unearthing clues that drew links between his absences, the lack of rain, and the times he suddenly stopped wearing his favorite cologne. Mr Sky was just one link in the Co-Spirity, the mysterious organization that controlled the whole town. Sandra was pretty sure the corner store was involved, from the way her parents talked.

But then Daddy came home just before Christmas, apparently for good, and she abandoned the search. We couldn't risk the Co-Spirity putting our family in danger. I ached to unravel the mystery, because she'd told me I should, but I understood: mysteries are important, but Sandra's happiness came first.

Winter was particularly rainy that year. Sandra was up late every night and out of bed before her alarm every day, trying to enjoy as much storm as she could before school. Usually, Mommy drove her to school, leaving me at home to catch up on cold cases, but then came the magic day when Daddy offered to take her instead – and even said she could bring me along. Finally, I thought, we'd get a chance to question Daddy without the Co-Spirity finding out.

We were three days shy of her eighth birthday. The road was full of puddles, deeper than Sandra had seen before. She asked Daddy why they were so deep. Daddy was just explaining this thing called 'potholes' when he lost control of the car.

The first thing I remember is the spinning; after that comes the squealing and the screaming. I remember Daddy giving us orders, but I don't remember his words. I remember the awful, high-pitched punching sound of glass giving way. I remember Sandra's legs, hurting and not hurting at the same time, and this heavy feeling like she couldn't quite move. I remember the crimson color of Daddy's face, and the weird way he hunched over the steering wheel, and how everything smelled like thawing steak and Daddy's cologne. And then we noticed Daddy wasn't moving…

And then we were falling out of the car, laying splayed out in a puddle, cold and wet and screaming for help. Sandra was hoarse before anyone arrived.

The rain took Daddy. Not the Co-Spirity. Not Mr Sky. Not anyone. There was no reason to it, no malice or intent of any kind. Nothing a detective could do anything about. It was our world, our favorite things, suddenly deciding to betray us.

That moment, there in the rain, was when the link between Sandra and me shattered. When her world had to change, and everything that made us Friends fell away, I got catapulted out of my home Idea and into the Imagination's old rusty wastebasket.

My horns still burn at cuss words. My detective stuff still works. I still love root beer and clues and dryers. Those things were Real before I left. Now, I'm still a detective, because there's nothing else I can be. I still care, because I can't help it, but it's a little bit easier to lean on the snarky side of me these days. The biggest difference for me is the rain. I used to love it, but now it always brings me back to the moment when the best possible part of my life ended.

I'm Tippy the Triceratops. I'm the best detective in the Stillreal. My detective stuff started telling me from the jump that the Spindleman story stank. But when it comes down to it, I just can't think in the rain. And that's why everything that's about to happen is my fault.

CHAPTER FOUR

My office/apartment/hiding place is a unit at the Welcoming Arms, written as Playtime Town's premier hotel and converted to apartments when its person punted it out into the Stillreal. These days it mostly looks like an apartment building, plain and square where displaced Friends haven't distorted it. But a perceptive Friend can see the remains of the hotel around the edges; the regal loops of gold thread in the carpets, the fancy paintings hung here and there in the halls. Surreal, and a constant reminder that we're refugees, but hey, it beats being outside.

Thoughts of the dryer power me up the stairs and through my door. I wade through the mound of letters, all shapes and sizes of envelope and postcard, all asking for my help, and jog down the hall. I close my bedroom door behind me and climb behind my heavy oak desk to fish out quarters for laundry and to make sure there's nothing immediate that I'm forgetting to handle.

Visitors claim my room is hard to navigate, but with my background the too-bright desk lamp in a too-dark room shouldn't be a surprise. I rummage around among the scribbled-on notepads and empty root beer bottles on the desk, picking up change as I go, then check the equally large heap of bottles and Encyclopedia Brown books next to my Murphy bed. To my great relief, there's no blinking answering machine or grieving woman or angry hitman today. As always, I can scrounge up exactly as much change as I need for the dryer.

I grab my towel and my shower cap from underneath the desk, but I'm barely out my bedroom door before my roommate Spiderhand prances out of his room on his middle and index fingers and gives me a frenetic wave hello. For future reference, Spiderhand is the slender brown hand the size of a dog with no arm to match. His person meant to make a puppet – his husband loved puppets – but he had to improvise one night when the husband was crying, and lo and behold, Spiderhand.

"Hey, buddy," I say.

He answers with a complicated twist and swing of his fingers. He's excited to show me something. The lack of sounds throws some Friends, but his language makes perfect sense if you spend enough time around it.

"What's up?"

He beckons me with one finger and dances backward into his room. I follow, ever the good roommate, and watch him give me a huge, presentational flourish as he shows me the new set of teacups sitting on his bed. This set has a cornflower-blue floral pattern, impatiens and clinging ivy, which helps differentiate it from the other whole tea services he has sitting on every available flat surface in his room.

"Huh," I say, because what I really want to say is 'I'm so sorry, Spidey.' Spiderhand's person loved tea parties; he and his husband had them once or twice a month, right up until his husband hit him one too many times. So now I hate the rain, and Spiderhand collects teacups. We're all smiles here in the Stillreal.

Spiderhand darts closer to the cups, waving at them, pointing at them, hopping up and down to convey his excitement. He's so proud of these pieces, he doesn't even mind that there are obvious seams where some have been glued back together. Or that they smell like low tide.

"They're very nice," I say. Being a good detective sometimes means being a good liar.

Spiderhand stands up on the points of his fingers, expectant.

"No, really. I love the, the… color."

Spiderhand nods, still expectant. I sigh, and I try to imagine how I feel after I solve a case.

"Good work, buddy. It had to take a lot of work for you to find this set." That's true, at least. Finding things that stay coherent outside their home Ideas is at best a challenge.

Spiderhand gives me an eager little nod of his fingers, and a frenetic series of gestures that takes me a second to put together.

"You repaired them yourself?" I ask, keeping my voice high and happy. I avoid looking at the seams.

His fingers blaze. He's saying it took him over an hour to repair each cup. At that, my empathy takes over. "Wow, buddy! Good work!"

Spiderhand vibrates in place. That's him beaming with pride.

"I love them," I chuckle. "I really do. And... um, listen... is it cool if I go take a spin?" I shrug a horn in the direction of the apartment door. "Had to work a case today. Feeling kinda beat up." Spiderhand sags, and with great alacrity I add, "We could do tea and sweets after?"

That perks him up a little. He loves to host, and he loves to know he's helped me cheer up after a case. That's my roommate all over.

"Great, buddy. We'll do tea right after this. I promise."

Spiderhand salutes as I duck out the door. I all but sprint downstairs.

The laundry room never looks so white, the dryer never so welcoming, as right after I've finished a case. I fold my towel just so, set it on top of the dryer like a set of royal jewels, throw my exact change into the coin slot, and close the door on thirty minutes of bliss. The heat punches on, and the slow roll of the barrel begins, and the rain finally slips away into nasty memories.

Now that my thoughts aren't slipping on greasy patches of flashback, Spindleman's story has some dangling questions I need to answer. First up: Why did Spindleman come unstuck from its creator? Usually it's the companion Friends who go, the ones who were supposed to *protect* their people, not the nightmares. And while Spindleman did say

Matthew didn't need it anymore, age is usually a graceful exit, a slow fadeout. It takes a shock to put you in the Stillreal.

Its story doesn't add up, and my stomach never sits right when the story doesn't add up. It's possible Farmer Nick is up to something. Maybe he's got some contact who can hook him up with a spare nightmare, make Nick look like the victim, keep us looking elsewhere while his next big scheme comes to fruition…

The dryer stops, and I'm shunted back into the slightly damp present. I can pursue leads in the morning. For now, I owe Spiderhand tea. I wrap myself up in my bathrobe and mosey back upstairs.

Some time after I left, our apartment became occupied by a cloud of dark, tangy smells; the unmistakable musk of Spiderhand's favorite pink peppercorn tea. He loves alliterative tea blends the way I love the smell of laundry. He's got the table all set up, his new cups (freshly washed), a cherry red sugar cellar, and a dragon-shaped pot for the cream. One of my cracked white plates is in the middle of the table, empty in anticipation of the pastries he has baking. The unrepaired crack is how I know it's mine. Detectives aren't supposed to own anything nice.

"Nice setup, buddy," I say. It's the same setup he uses every time; only the patterns and the pastry vary.

Spidey scuffs two fingers together, his 'aw, shucks' gesture, and pours me a cup of tea. The smell is even stronger up close; if it had steeped any longer it would make my eyes water.

"So," I say, prepared for the digital deluge, "how was your day?"

I won't try to translate directly. Suffice to say, he had a very normal day that he found very exciting. Finding these teacups was the highlight of it. When he starts asking about mine, I tell him all about Spindleman, and he gives me one of his friendly little finger-bops for helping the poor nightmare find a home. I don't get into my concerns about how he got where he was in the first place. If Spidey hears too much, he'll try to help me solve the case, and I'm not ready for a new partner yet. Still. Maybe ever.

The tea party lasts through the better part of the evening before the weight of the day catches up to me. I tell Spidey I need to get to bed, wave off the obligatory tsunami of apologies for keeping me up, and head off to get under my covers and try to sleep.

Unfortunately, Spiderhand brews his tea strong, so I'm going to have to lie here awake and think for a while. Fortunately, that means I'm awake to hear someone breaking down the door of Smile House.

CHAPTER FIVE

I look out my window first, just to be sure I'm not mercifully hallucinating. But no, there it is, right up the hill from me: the big cartoon face of Smile House, frowning at the painful gap that's been shattered into its mouth/door. There's only one light on in the whole building. One more winks to life in the wake of the noise, but that's it, and there's still no further response by the time I've run out to the starlit street. What can I say? A community of traumatized imaginary friends isn't exactly tops at heroic responses.

I hustle up to the door. Shards are spread across the floor on the inside of the building – forced entry, not hasty exit. There's a huge boot-print crushed into the wood closest to the hole, so whoever did this isn't all that interested in covering their tracks. Great...

I enter the building in stealth mode, creeping upstairs one careful step at a time. The stairs are a square spiral threaded up the middle of the building, perfectly placed to catch every echo and whisper from the upper floors. All I hear is the usual mish-mash of snoring and late-night TV. I don't see any more boot-prints, or any other signs of breaking and entering, but the whole place is still; a held breath before blind panic.

As I'm climbing slowly up the stairs, questioning why I don't carry a weapon, a small, earnest face leans over the third-floor railing, making me glad I wasn't able to blow their darn head off. It's one of the Sadness

Penguins; the one with black spots on his cheeks and chest. Without seeing his cape, I can't be one hundred percent sure of his name. Or their gender, to be fair; watch yourself, Mr Detective.

"Hey," I whisper.

The penguin waves at me urgently. Talking to non-verbal Friends feels awful most of the time. They're a constant reminder of how young our people tend to be.

"Did someone come through here?" I ask, as I sneak up level with it.

The Sadness Penguin nods, the answer I was least hoping for. I glance at the brooch holding their cape together – a gilded 'H.' Harriet.

"Harriet, did you recognize them?"

She shakes her head.

"Can you tell me where they went?"

Harriet nods, and then silence stretches out. The Sadness Penguins can get kind of literal. I keep my sigh locked up tight.

"Harriet, please tell me where they wen–"

Footsteps, my detective stuff says. Upstairs, too far away for anyone but a detective to hear.

I tense up, my back legs shifting into a charging pose. Harriet blinks at me, more confused than scared. The footsteps sound out again. They don't sound urgent, or menacing, but they do sound massive.

"Can you describe the new Friend?" I whisper.

Harriet throws her flippers straight up over her head, and gestures across the black feathers of her sides and back.

"Big and… black?" I ask.

Another nod.

"Is it Spindleman?" Hopeful annoyance creeps into my voice. "The new guy who came in this evening?"

Harriet shakes her head, and stretches her flippers out again.

"Bigger?"

She nods. The footsteps fade away from us, headed down the hallway.

"If it's not the new guy," I hiss, "I really, really need to know who it is."

She flails in a burst of frustration.

No, she's trying to outline a shape. Flapping first around her feet, then a little thinner around her hips, then making a circular motion around her head like –

The brim of a hat. A coat. The Man in the Coat…

"Did it have any weapons?" I gasp. "A hammer? Maybe a club?"

Harriet is just starting to measure out a distance between two flippers when the footsteps upstairs turn into a full-bore charge and an explosion of splintering wood.

I bolt upstairs, stammering my thanks as I go. I see nothing but opening doors and worrying faces for four floors. I stop, listen for some kind of audio cue in among the fearful waking noises of the residents. I get one in the form of Spindleman screaming bloody murder.

Forget careful; I ascend at warp speed. I hear Friends on every floor, spilling and stumbling out of their doors, some with weapons, all scared. Spindleman's screams are coming from the eighth floor, which means there's plenty of time for people to start calling after me, "Who is it?" and "What's happening?" and all the other questions I hate leaving unanswered.

I leap off the stairs on the eighth-floor landing, barrel down the hall, and round a corner straight into Spindleman's desperate goggles, coming at me as fast as I was coming at it.

"He's here!" Spindleman shouts.

"Where?"

"Behind me!" Spindleman shouts, expanding to fill most of the hallway.

I can't see around Spindleman, and hearing over the cacophony of its power tools is a no-go, but my detective stuff has me covered. I catch the Friends worrying downstairs, some yelling for the police, some rattling various makeshift weapons. I pick up the creaks and groans of old Smile House at night, an achy tone courtesy of the damaged front door. And when the footsteps start again, my detective stuff reads them loud and clear. They sound huge, like a giant with anvils strapped to its feet. There's no urgency to their pace, just a slow, casual menace that will round the corner any second…

Spindleman gasps, shrinks down to my size, and skitters around behind me as the Man in the Coat appears.

I can't make out his face, can't make out many details at all in the dull twilight that seems to travel with him. His coat is long, black, and slick; it's topped with a crinkle-rimmed hat of the same light-sucking hue. Underneath the hat, his head is just a black expanse, two stagnant green pools doubling for eyes. He's got huge hands, with a ring glinting on what I think is the marriage finger. I notice it just after I notice the big black baseball bat dangling from the same hand.

"The Man!" Spindleman shouts.

The Man in the Coat sees me and pauses midstride, his tread still resonating through the boards. He studies me, fingers dancing along the grip of the bat, and breaks off the look with a slow nod. A plume of blue cigarette smoke oozes out of his face-shadows and drifts up to the ceiling, hanging like upside-down fog.

"Drink," he says, in a voice like a hungry bear, and starts advancing again.

My word of the day is "Run."

I slip a horn into Spindleman's hand and drag it along with me, trying to jump-start its legs. It gets the idea fast and starts running along beside me as we take the corner, the footsteps thundering behind us.

"Eat," says the Man in the Coat, his voice not quite directly in my ear despite his physical distance. That's nightmare stuff, meant to make you glance back. So I don't.

"He found me!" Spindleman wails, more metal-studded legs jabbing out of its center mass.

"Drink." The Man hasn't picked up speed, but detective stuff says he's still gaining.

There are Friends crowded at the top of the stairs. I see Focred the Dwarf, Harriet, two of the other Sadness Penguins, and a T-rex I don't recognize.

"Clear the landing!" I shout as we charge toward them.

Focred and the T-rex get it faster than the Penguins; we have to brake to avoid running into them, and that gives the Man in the Coat time to come booming up behind us. There's another scream from Spindleman as its hand is ripped free from my horn.

I spin around, end up scrabbling down the stairs and slamming into the banister on the first landing before I stop. The other Friends have scattered down the halls, leaving me a perfect view of Spindleman squirming at the top of the stairs, pinned down by the Man in the Coat's boot while he holds the baseball bat up over his head. Spindleman is tiny, quivering, watching the Man in the Coat with a lost and begging look in its little glass goggles.

"Fine," says the Man in the Coat, and brings the bat down hard.

Drill bits skip across the floorboards. A screw bounces past me down the stairs. Spindleman reaches a paw out toward me, trying to re-sprout its wings and fly.

"Fine," says the Man in the Coat, and swings again.

Spindleman's wings collapse; a lens pops out of the goggles. I start jogging up the stairs, trying to get enough traction to charge –

"Fine."

"…Tippy?" Spindleman asks, right before the bat comes down for the third time.

There's a crunch like a car backing up over gravel, and a faint suction sound like an unstoppered drain. The Man in the Coat stands back up, his shadow falling across bare floor where there used to be a nightmare.

I come off the stairs like a comet, head down and ready for impact. From over my nose horn, I see the Man in the Coat staring down at the now-bare floor. I rocket forward, eyes closed – and pass through empty air.

I open my eyes. The Man in the Coat is walking away down the hall, completely unperturbed.

"Hey!" I shout, to no reaction. "Hey!"

The Man in the Coat steps around the corner, and his booming footsteps disappear completely. I get about two steps before the world tells me it's time to sit down and stare.

The Man in the Coat is gone, traveled to another Idea. Spindleman is gone in a much worse way. All that's left is a Smile House full of shocked Friends, and a single loose drill bit where our newest neighbor used to be.

Friends can't die – not really, not permanently – but reminding myself of that isn't bringing the mental swelling down. This feels wrong. This *is* wrong.

The other Friends file back my way, tip-toeing and peering around each other. I hear Focred's old plasma-axe sizzling the nearby air molecules, feel the change in the T-rex's stance that tells me she's primed to bite. I hear the Sadness Penguins all huddled together, their footsteps a concerned little drumbeat on the floorboards. I turn toward them, and look into the field of expectant eyes.

"What happened?" burrs Focred.

"Where's the new kid?" growls the T-rex.

I draw myself up to what height I'm capable of. I'm scared. But the Tippy they need right now isn't the scared one.

"Don't worry," I say, holding my voice girder-steady. "Detective Tippy is on the case."

I feel the tension zip out of the room as soon as I speak. There's been a murder, and that's scary, but now here Detective Tippy is to investigate it. To set it right.

I pick up the drill bit from where it's fallen, and turn it over in my paw. It smells like Spindleman. I know because sniffing it makes me want to shudder.

"But what was that?" asks Focred, zir fingers fidgeting against the haft of zir axe.

The honest answer is terrifying. So I smile. "Another monster who thinks the world's their bed."

One of the Sadness Penguins signs a question to me: Will the new Friend be back?

"Probably soon," I say. "Listen, I need to analyze this…" I make a big deal of nonchalantly flipping the drill bit up in the air. "You all go and get tucked in. I'll handle it from here."

The other Friends take their turns nodding and assenting, Focred the most hesitant of all of them, but however much they resist, they all go. Every one of them hesitates before they go through their front door, looking back at me with an unsettled expression. Yeah, me too, folks.

I look again at the place where the fight broke out, leaning hard on my detective stuff. But there are no clues here, no sight, smell. Nothing my heart can pass to my brain while it takes a break. My stuffing is tied up in knots.

Friends can't die. We can be already dead, like Lloyd and Rocky, the vampire couple in the Terrible Old House. We can even be dead for a while, like King Max Courage of Pluto after he fought the Steel Serpents. But we don't stay dead. Even in the Ideas where murder does exist, it happens according to set parameters, and it's never really permanent. Yes, it's violent, but no one is really hurt in the end. Trust me, we've asked the victims.

But this…

Everything about this is wrong. No; it isn't that it's wrong. It's that my detective stuff hasn't seen anything like it before. And while that's true of a lot of things in the Stillreal, this feels different than just another new Idea. This feels new, and at the same time very, very old…

I shake my head, and fail to clear it. Between this and the rain in the same day, my head is a mess. I'm not going to figure anything out just sitting here, and I'm not going to get more awake and aware by burning the midnight oil. I need to take this drill bit back to where I can concentrate on it, and if that doesn't get me a lead, then I need to come back here tomorrow when Spindleman's back. Its testimony should tell me the real shape of this case.

I walk downstairs, head back to my apartment, and try to get some sleep.

I don't succeed.

CHAPTER SIX

Morning hits sooner than I'd like. I peel myself out from under the covers, roll out of bed onto the pile of root beer bottles, and check on the drill bit from last night. It's still on my night-stand, still in existence, and that in itself is a clue. And not a good one.

I take a deep breath, swig some root beer from the flask in my desk, and head out for Smile House looking my bedraggled best.

Police tape is plastered over the House's mouth. I duck under it with my heart in my stomach. The tape is normal, but I can't get over how abnormal the rest of it feels.

The Sadness Penguins, Focred, and the T-rex are clustered on the eighth floor landing; the Penguins huddled close together, the other two standing with their shoulders slumped, all staring at the blank patch of floor where Spindleman died last night. My accelerating pulse finally gets me to breathe.

There's another drill bit on the floor, a little ways down the hall from where – from the site. There's another one resting against the opposite wall; a screw a little ways down the hallway; a small piece of leather strap and a buckle over there…

My head is spinning. I feel Focred and the Sadness Penguins looking at me as I march toward the apartment Golem Jones picked out for Spindleman. My detective stuff is shouting that something is incredibly wrong, but I'm not letting myself make the connections yet.

The doors of Smile House are hung with the names of the Friends who live there. Doomster the friendly bed monster. Regina the T-rex. King Max Courage of Pluto. And a blank door that should say 'Spindleman.'

Why is it blank? Why would the idea reset to…this? Please, no…

I'm a detective, but I'm also a dinosaur; when thinking fails, I tend to back it up with headbutts. I put my head down and get ready to go straight through the door to the juicy clues inside, but I'm stopped by a booming call of "Hey!"

The voice comes from all around me, vibrating floorboards and creaking doors and other wood-and-stone noises, all knit together to form a beleaguered tone.

"Were you really just going to break down my door?" the voice asks, doubt teetering on the edge of rage. Only Smile House can manage that perfect mix of tired, mad, and scared.

(Not every building in the Stillreal is intelligent. Just some of the really old ones.)

"I'm sorry," I say from the brink of panic. "I just – I have this feeling that something is–"

"Wrong?" the House interrupts. "Something is always wrong somewhere," it mutters, punctuated with the angry bang of a door.

"Of course," I say, softening under the pressure of my guilt. "But I mean, my detective stuff says this is something really, *really* big, and–"

"And it's a case. And you're Detective Tippy. Which means you will do absolutely anything to get at the next clue. Including breaking my doors."

That stings, but I have to let it go. There's no point in being offended when Smile House cuts to the core of you. It's in a perfect position to see the best and worst of a whole lot of Friends.

"It's about your new resident," I say. "The nightmare. The drill-monster."

"Spindleman," the House sighs in a chorus of rattling windowpanes. "I figured, given the door you're attacking."

"It died last night," I say.

Smile House goes silent, a loaded, nerve-grating stillness that fills the entire building. I hear footsteps coming down the hall, over a half-dozen sets of them, walking with a dull lack of energy.

"Can you please open the door?" I say.

The windowpanes rattle again. "I can… but you won't like it."

"I get the feeling I'm not going to like anything about today."

Smile House sighs, shaking the doors in their frames. It sounds like it pities me, and I think that hurts most of all.

"Thank you for not breaking down my door," it says.

It opens. I see everything I need to see in about three seconds, but it takes another thirty to finally stop denying it.

The room is furnished with a plain white easy chair, a plain white couch, a TV with big rabbit-ear antennas. There are some dishes stacked up by the sink, and every surface is either white drywall, wood grain, or silver metal. I know this look, because it's the look of every other apartment in Smile House before someone starts living in it. There are no photos. No paintings. Not even any stains on the beige carpet. Nothing unique, not even the tiniest thing. And Spindleman was here overnight…

If an Idea stops being exposed to an outside Friend, it stops warping around their presence. It doesn't take long for it to go back to normal. Like, say, a single night. But there are still those screws and drill bits in the hallway…

That's when I get it. Immediately followed by me wishing I didn't.

Spindleman didn't come back to its new home. It stayed where it died.

I back out of the apartment. Only my detective stuff keeps me from bumping into Focred, standing at the front of the crowd of onlookers clustered by the open door.

"I told you," sighs Smile House.

Focred tries to ask a question, but ze's busy looking terrified. The Sadness Penguins offer me a hug.

The empty room, the shattered bits, the way Smile House is talking. The clues all point to one conclusion: Spindleman is actually, really, truly dead. And I just let the clues reset while I slept off some silly little rain.

"Detective?" asks the House. The note of concern is the last straw.

I walk back toward the stairs without a hug or an answer or a backward glance. I get downstairs as fast as I can without running. It won't do Smile House's residents any favors if they have to watch their best hope for justice and reason cry.

I know I get downstairs because my detective stuff warns me I'm about to blunder into police tape. I stumble backward, arch up into my I-meant-to-do-that pose. The tape's been strung up over the door of Smile House in every conceivable direction, which means that not only are the police here, but they've been here for a while. How long was I upstairs? I shake off the question and walk out onto the sidewalk, almost smack-dab into the police.

Playtime Town has precisely two police officers, Officer Hot and Officer Cold. Hot is the good cop: a potbellied campfire with a permanent grin and giant ping-pong eyes, topped with a police cap. Officer Cold is less nice: a spindly icicle sculpted into a uniformed patrolman, his ticket pad always out and at the ready. Hot is mid-questioning, bouncing between Spiderhand, Golem Jones, Rocky, and Lloyd. He's got the energy to deal with all of them, but only enough for them, which means I get to talk to Officer Cold. It's my lucky freaking day, I guess.

I swallow the tennis ball of fear in my throat, and do some mental stretches in advance of Cold's usual onslaught of derision. I'll probably get a ticket for something, probably be told the Chief is howling for someone's head over this case, probably hear about how detectives like me are scum…

"Detective Tippy," Cold says as he bow-legs up to me. His crystalline face is drawn with stress. "What happened?"

"New nightmare," I stammer. "Um. A new nightmare moved in yesterday, and – it was – killed?"

"You don't sound so sure."

"Because I can't be sure," I snap back. I need to get on my game with my comebacks, or this is going to be a miserable experience. "Another new Friend attacked it with a bat, and it just… vanished." The tennis ball is back.

Officer Cold's brows slide up his icy forehead. "So the Friend with the bat took it somewhere?" The tremor in his voice says he knows my answer.

"No, it *vanished*." I shake my head, shuffling back through last night's clues. "There was a pop."

"Pop?"

"Yeah, like when the wind blows through the space between your ears too fast?" I'm starting to get my rapport back, at least. "The guy beat Spindleman to death right in front of me."

Cold taps at his ticket pad. "How can you be so sure this Spindleman is dead?"

"How does the ice you're made of not melt?"

"That's just how it is."

"Exactly."

Cold gives me a grimace. "So when will it resurrect?"

"That's the problem," I say. There's no point in comforting him. "I don't think it will."

It's impossible to miss the silence that comes in the wake of that statement. I can feel Hot's lineup of suspects and witnesses looking at me in a half-dozen flavors of horror. They heard me. Of course they heard me.

Cold raises a casual eyebrow. "Friends don't just die, Tippy." His snide edge is kind of comforting; a dose of normal in all this weird.

"That's why I'm on the case."

"What case?"

"The one I just opened." I know I should be nicer to Officer Cold, but I'm running short on anything except panic right now, and I need to conserve.

Officer Cold looks down at his pad. Tap, tap, tap. "This man with the bat, how was he dressed?"

"All black. Big long coat, wide-brimmed hat–"

"Could you see his face?"

I squint up at Cold. "Um. Not really?"

"Christ." From what I hear, that's the worst swear word Cold knows. "Were there any other witnesses?"

"The guy kicked in the door of Smile House and then chased Spindleman screaming around the eighth floor, so, yes?" I could just tell him about Focred and the Sadness Penguins, but where's the fun in that?

Officer Cold sighs. "You wait right here," he says, with a stern gesture toward the pavement. "We're bringing you in for questioning."

"Can I get a reason for that, Officer?"

"Because your story is the most pungent line of nonsense you have ever tried to sell me, and when you consider what you've already been dealing—"

"Yeah, yeah." He'd keep going if I let him. "See you soon, Mr Congeniality."

Cold taps on his pad again, disappears under the police tape, and I'm left to watch Officer Hot trying to talk to the giant eye-robot that lives downstairs from me, just in case maybe being a giant eye-robot meant she saw something important.

I don't like Officer Cold. He's callous, hidebound, and nasty. But today he's extra-special. He was brief, he was acidic, and he barely stopped to verbally fence with me at all. He's being too mean, too much like the Cold all us Friends think of when we think of him. It's a performance, the kind of performance you put on when you're worried.

Under normal circumstances, I'd blow Officer Cold off, make him come to my apartment to fish me out. These circumstances are anything but normal, though, so I sit and wait for my arrest like a good little triceratops. I need to know exactly what Cold is worried about, and I need to know if I can help. The little mysteries are just as important as the big ones.

See, I don't always come off looking so bad.

CHAPTER SEVEN

Officers Hot and Cold throw me in the back of their midnight-blue armored car, along with Golem Jones and Rocky. Their presence tells me Hot and Cold are really reaching for suspects. Golem Jones is an almost-literal pillar of the community; at worst, he might have tried to give the murderer a bed for the night. And Rocky is so nonviolent he drinks pig blood from a carton so he doesn't have to look at it. This isn't a lineup, this is blindfolded darts.

I try for conversation, but Cold is on top of it, knocking on the barred window behind the front seat every time I say the word "Hello." Talking is pointless anyway, with how stunned the others are. Rocky is taking it worst of all, long black hair hanging in front of a face that would be tear-stained if he could shed tears. Being a monster is rough to begin with, I can't imagine how he feels about an actual killing. Before I can think of a way to check if he's okay, we make it to the Police Station, where an apologetic Officer Hot frog-marches us out of the van, through the main office, and downstairs to the holding cells.

"Just doin' the job," he insists as he crams Jones and Rocky into the first cell, next to the Snitching Snipe's garbage-and-pine-needle nest. The Snitching Snipe is a squat, filthy puff-ball of a bird with unblinking, red-rimmed dinner plates he calls eyes.

"Just doin' the job," Hot says again, a little lower, as he steers me down the hall to the interrogation room.

Whatever the creator's plan for the interrogation room was, regular use for the interrogation of nightmares has shifted the room pretty significantly: it's a cavernous, mint-green chamber with a steel table in the center, covered in enough straps to restrain any Friend regardless of limb count. The buckles stare at me accusingly as Hot shoves me into a bolted-down chair.

"Straps," Cold says, with a gesture toward the table.

Two of the straps shoot down off the table like hungry cobras, and wrap around me, buckling my forepaws in place. Officer Cold paces in front of the one-way glass for a few seconds, then starts in on his usual opening questions, scratching at his fresh new legal pad. Officer Hot hovers behind him, fidgeting in every direction at once.

"Name for the record?" Cold asks.

"Detective Tippy."

"Occupation?"

"Detective. Tippy."

Cold glowers at me over his notepad. This is the way it goes every time we talk. The detective tweaks the cops' noses, the cops treat the detective like either a suspect or garbage, everyone leaves happy. Sort of. This part, at least, feels normal.

"Why were you at Smile House at the time of the murder?" Cold says the word 'murder' like it's in another language.

"I heard someone break in, and I know Smile House's residents aren't really well-equipped for violence. I figured I'd give them a hand."

Cold watches me, dubious. "I understand you witnessed the incident?"

And here we have the lovely corner Cold's hoping to back me into – he wants proof I was somehow involved. This is some Olympic-quality reaching. "Yes."

"Can you describe what happened?"

The memory flashes back to me, and my stomach does its best to escape via my nostrils. I clear my throat, put on my finest monotone, and get down to the unbiased reporting. Cold scribbles on his notepad while I tell them about Spindleman begging and screaming, about the Man in the Coat making his dramatic entrance, about watching

Spindleman get beaten to death with a baseball bat at the top of the Smile House stairs. I'm impressed with myself. I've never told such a horrible story with so little detail.

Officer Hot gets more restless by the second, shifting from foot to foot, rubbing his hands together. He's angry, but I can't quite tell at whom. Cold acts like he's ignoring Hot's mood, but it's getting on his nerves even more than it's getting on mine.

"What did Spindleman's death look like?" Cold asks.

"Huh?" That tennis ball lodges in my throat again.

"Its death," Cold explains. "What did… the incident look like when it… when it happened." He sounds like he's translating from an ancient scroll.

"Well…" Not today, stomach. "Like I said before. There was a pop. Like a plug coming out of a bathtub drain. And then Spindleman kind of… just… shattered."

Hot's breath hitches. Cold pointedly stares at me and only me.

"Most of it disappeared." I feel like I might stutter. What will he do if I stutter? "But, the, drill bits – it was made of drill bits and nails and things – they went flying everywhere."

Scribble, scribble. Stare, stare. "And is this the point at which you engaged the perpetrator?"

"'Engaged?'" I ask.

"Attacked," Officer Cold says.

"No lies," Hot snaps. Officer Cold gives him a withering glance, but it doesn't calm him down much. "We have witnesses."

"Good-cop-bad-cop?" I say, staring Hot right in the face. "Really?"

Officer Hot's flaming eyebrows tie themselves in knots, but he can't make eye contact. Officer Cold is fidgeting more than usual, too. This routine is uncomfortable for them, too nasty compared to the petty thefts and snowball shootouts that constitute their normal cases. I'm off-put, too, but I'm not trying to drag everyone into my upset. Either this is hitting close to their original pain, or there's something bigger.

"Answer the question, Detective," demands Cold.

For now, I need to play along. "Yeah," I say. "I was worried he was going to attack others. I thought I was driving him off."

"Were you?" Cold asks.

"No," I say. "When he left, it was because he wanted to."

Cold tilts his head back, examining me over the end of his nose. "You sound pretty sure about that."

"I'm a detective," I scoff. "I mean, seriously, I have magic detective powers. Body language isn't exactly a challenge."

Cold shrugs. "So you didn't attack him until he had already murdered Spindleman."

"I thought it was just dead, not... *dead* dead." The sentence gets harder to say the longer it goes on. "Or whatever you want to call it."

"So you believe Spindleman has been permanently destroyed?"

"It's the best hypothesis I have to go on."

"Hypothesis."

My temper is starting to rise now, too. I know it's the cops' job to be mean to the detective, but there's being mean and then there's accusing me of *this*.

"Yeah," I say, as caustic as I can. "Clues point to it being gone forever. Therefore, for now, I assume it's gone forever, and keep looking for clues. Just like you keep fishing for me to betray some secret you think I'm keeping."

Hot's face buckles, his eyes huge, his pupils red. Cold stays statue-still, except for the raised hand he uses to stop Hot from exploding on me.

"Tippy, we know you specialize in helping out new arrivals." He says it in a breezy, unconcerned way. "You know how they act, how they think. You were the first Playtime Town resident to see Spindleman, and the last. You were one of two who knew where Spindleman was staying."

They're not just accusing me. They're really trying to put the screws to me. If they're putting this much effort into something this uncomfortable, they think this is bigger than just one murder – which means either they believe what I told them, or they know something else I don't. If I want to learn what it is, I'm going to need to pay out some fishing line.

"Look, I didn't have anything to do with this, okay?" I let the stress and confusion of the day pile up in my voice. If I'm lucky, they'll read it as surrender. "I was just trying to get Spindleman away from the Man in the Coat, I mean, it already had to leave the motel–"

"Freedom Frieda's place?" asks Hot, ever-eager.

The surprise is genuine. I knew something they didn't know.

"Um…" I say, playing awkward for the cheap seats. "Yeah. Yeah, that's the one."

Cold and Hot trade a fearful look. "You're sure it said Freedom Frieda's place?" Cold asks.

"'Said' is a strong word, but when I described Freedom Frieda, Spindleman thought that sounded familiar."

Cold scribbles furiously at his pad. "How did it know this 'Man in the Coat' was after it?"

"Spindleman saw the Man looking in the windows of the motel. Or that's what it said, anyway."

Hot looks at Cold like someone just spilled the last of the day's coffee on his head. "No way," he says. "You're making stuff up because you think we'll let you go if you say smart stuff."

"Officer Hot," Cold says.

Hot is more upset than Cold. Time to egg him on. "Why would I make up smart stuff? I mean, I'm just saying it to you."

"That's not funny, gumshoe!" Hot bangs a fist on the table.

"Officer Hot." Cold's teeth are grinding.

I almost hate upsetting Hot. Almost. "Fine, you got me. I lied to two trained policemen, endangering my relationship with the only people in Playtime Town who want the same thing I do, so that I can avoid being in a slightly uncomfortable room for more than a few minutes. Clearly, this is proof I am a criminal mastermind, and you can now lock me up for having secret contact with a Friend who thought his way into Smile House and erased another Friend from existence, thanks to my long-running secret plan to murder someone none of us had ever heard of before yesterday. Well done, Officer. Take me away."

"This isn't funny!" Hot's about to jump across the table and eat me. "Lying isn't funny! Lying isn't fair!"

"Officer Hot," Cold says. His legal pad is nowhere to be seen.

"But the motel's not one of the–"

"Officer Hot!" Cold snaps.

There we go. One of them finally showed their hand.

Cold stands. He looks like someone just popped all his birthday balloons. "Thank you for your time, Detective," he says. "Straps," – he waves at my restraints – "give us a two-minute head start and then let him go." He looks at me, not a little bit smug. "You still living at the Welcoming Arms?"

"Within earshot of Smile House, yeah," I say, answering his jab with a grin.

Cold narrows his eyes. "Don't leave town for a while."

"I won't," I say. "I mean, unless I'm after the actual murderer we're both hunting."

Cold sneers, and walks out of the room, beckoning Hot to follow.

I count thirty seconds, sixty, seventy, a hundred... at one hundred and twenty, the straps loosen, and I'm off like a race car. I rush out of the mint-green cavern, take a breath of stale holding-cell air, and look down the empty hallway to the stairs.

Golem Jones is standing outside the open doors of his cell, tension carved deep into his stony face. Rocky is standing behind him, face drawn, unwilling to exit until he's sure this isn't a trap. My detective stuff says he's stifling tears. They need to be comforted, especially Rocky. If only someone here had any idea what would make this situation more comforting.

"Hey, Jonesy," I say as I approach.

Golem peers at me.

"You see the officers come by here?"

"Yeah," he rumbles. "Officer Cold muttered something about freedom and opened the door and they just... thought away..."

"Ugh," I say. "I'm glad they let you out, anyway. I'm so sorry you got sucked into this."

"Yeah, hey, speaking of," says Jones. "You have any idea what that was all about?"

"It's a long story," I say, as I head over to the stairs. If I can't be kind, I can at least act like the situation is normal. "And I think it's getting longer."

"I hate it when you're cryptic," Jones calls after me.

"You love it, really."

Jones' chuckle is as bitter as they come. "You're mostly right, Detective. See you soon."

Both fortunately and unfortunately, he will.

I messed with them during the interrogation because I was supposed to, but I also did it because it's a great way to get temperamental people like Hot and Cold to overplay their hand, especially when they're already uncomfortable.

They got scared when I told them the Man in the Coat showed up at the Freedom Motel. Hot said "That's not one of the" before Cold cut him off. There have been other attacks already. And that might mean other Friends have already died. For good.

I need to go to the Freedom Motel. I need to see if I can figure out anything from Spindleman's remains. I need to investigate Nightshire – or better yet, see if I can investigate Spindleman's home Idea, where this Man in the Coat first appeared. I need to get moving and keep moving, because this situation could be even more dangerous than it looks.

The worst part? A part of me feels good. I'm on a case, and that means I'm doing what I'm supposed to be doing. And maybe this time... maybe this time I can make it make sense.

Real healthy there, me.

CHAPTER EIGHT

Spiderhand is in the middle of piano practice when I get home; something light and fun, probably trying to chase away whatever nasty memories the whole thing with Spindleman churned up. I wait in the living room long enough for him to notice me, give him an if-you-need-anything smile that's about all the friendship I can muster today. That accomplished, I head back into my office, take a look at the drill bit still sitting on my desk blotter, and dig deep like only Detective Tippy can.

Sight: It's definitely one of the bits I saw sprouting from Spindleman. It's clean, no stains or scoring, which suggests it hasn't seen much use. (That tinkling sound is my heart breaking again.)

Touch: It's ice-cold, a cold that eats the warmth around it, but vanishes the second I break contact. It's light for its size, light enough I can't pinpoint the metal it's made of. That's not unusual for the Stillreal, but it's still noteworthy.

Scent: It smells less like metal and more like leather and cloves. Again, not unusual. Imaginary objects smell like what their creators need them to smell like, and need and logic don't pal around as much as they should.

Hearing: If I flick it with my paw, it rings hollow, even though it's clearly solid all the way through. I give it another couple flicks, and the same sound repeats, no magic tricks with angle or timing or anything.

Taste: Not today, thanks.

The drill bit is detailed. It carries a strong smell, and a particular sound. It has traits I can look for in other objects, things that might show up in the same Idea as a big house with a scared little boy inside. If Spindleman's home Idea got thrown into the Stillreal along with it, I can use this to get there.

Going to a completely unknown Idea is a bad plan. Going to a completely unknown Idea that a nightmare came from is a worse plan. Add in everything that's happened in the past two days, and it's in the running for the worst plan I've ever had. (Don't worry, we'll add to that list before long.)

I need to follow this lead, but if I'm doing that, I need to get some help. Fortunately, I know where help lives.

I duck out of the apartment before Spiderhand finishes practicing, and head to the alley where Boss Raccoon and his family-friendly gang commit their petty crimes. None of them are here today – probably drinking off the moral of their story – so it's no problem for me to think from this children's book alley to one with a bit more contrast.

The new alley is an inlet between two megalithic buildings, garbage artfully strewn across the pavement, rendered in stark grays, silky blacks, and jazzy blues. A woman in a watch cap and a leather jacket leans against a bold crimson brick wall, pinned there by another woman in an immaculate gray suit and matching domino mask. They're smiling as their faces close in on each other, but those smiles fade fast when they see a yellow triceratops standing in the alley with them.

The masked woman is the Witness, one of Avatar City's supporting heroes; the one in the cap is part of the Syndicate, the local third-string gang. I'm pretty sure their person never thought they'd be engaged in a clandestine makeout session. I guess there are some advantages to getting thrown out of your person's head.

"Sorry to interrupt," I blurt, and hustle out of the alley double-time. People around here can be quick to violence.

Avatar City is everything you'd expect from a comic book that never was, the kind of artistic perfection that only happens in between a creator's ears. The buildings are towering Art Deco swooshes, the sky is full of immaculate shining stars, and the streets are crowded with people of every color and mode of dress you'd want out of an all-inclusive city. It's only the sour looks on the adults' faces that tell you you're in the Idea of a teenager.

My quarry should be down at the Cape and Cowl, the local superhero bar. It's never a very long walk from anywhere in the city, but my short legs mean I still show up annoyed at having to thread through crowds.

The neon sign above the front doors hasn't changed, a garish yellow outline of a man in a mask and cape, shaped to look like he's crouching on the overhang, speckled with little gray spots where the light isn't working properly anymore. The inside is also unchanged, glossy black decor accented in glass and more neon, a disco-goth hybrid that I always remind myself to visit more often. The clientele are the usual suspects, a cross-section of urban fantasy Friends partying it up on the psychedelic dance floor or drowning their sorrows at the long obsidian bar. I dodge a man with the head of a wolf, duck through a conversation between a Viking ghost and a guy dressed in a Union Jack cape.

My quarry always drinks at the bar, but for all the berth people give her she might as well have a private booth. Being the main Friend of the whole place probably helps with that. She's got her blue uniform on today, a sleeveless unitard with a yellow clenched fist across the chest, elbow-length blue gloves to match, and black boots that are hand-crafted to look scary coming down on your head. She's got fresh blue streaks in her bouncy black curls, and a look of flat annoyance on her chubby brown face. The annoyance is actually good. It means she doesn't already have a job distracting her.

Ladies and gentlemen, Miss Mighty. The premiere superhero of Avatar City, justice and proper use of power made manifest, and the best and worst thing to ever happen to her person. (Until Chad Powers' birthday party, anyway.)

"Hey Tippy," she says, without looking away from her beer.

"Darn sixth sense," I mutter, mostly for her amusement. Having a built-in early warning system was the first thing we bonded over, once we were both sure the other wasn't just a villain hanging around the scene of the crime. (A villain from Playtime Town stole Avatar City's moon. I got called in, Mighty called herself in, the rest is history.)

Miss Mighty sniffs, her version of a laugh, and spins on her stool to look at me. There's a scab on her lip; she must've gotten into it with one of the supervillains very recently. "How are things, Tipster?"

"Please don't call me that."

She frowns, uncomfortable. "Sorry." She's snarky, but she'll respect whatever request you make for yourself, as long as you make it straightforward. I wish all Friends were so good about boundaries.

"S'okay." I hop up on the stool next to her, mostly to dodge a group of lizard-men bustling past. "To answer your question, things are alright. I'm on a case that's just about to get interesting. How about yourself?"

Miss Mighty sets her beer down and gives me a good smirking. "Need a few repairs, but nothing some malt beverage and a healing factor can't handle."

"I was just noticing that." I nod toward the scab. "Dr Atrocity?"

"Not even close." She makes an excited fist. "Some sky-pirates from over Pluto way went in on one of Red Mantis's bank robberies."

"Sky-pirates gave you that? Last time I saw you bruised, it was from a robot the size of my apartment building."

Mighty grins, a half-feral look in her eye. "They had a freaking *cannon*." She says the word 'cannon' with more joy than I could ever manage.

"And how did you get rid of it?" I ask, indulgent.

"Tossed it into the upper atmosphere."

"Just the upper atmosphere? You're slowing down in your old age."

She narrows her eyes, but it's a good scowl. Her party scowl. "So you want my help with a case?"

"You got me," I say, forepaws up in mock surrender.

"Thank God, I was afraid I might have to talk to somebody tonight."

She picks up her bottle. "What's going on? Big Business acting up again?"

"More off the beaten path than that. New nightmare got kicked into the Stillreal, and it brought something with it that's like its big, violent cousin. And that something has started making a mess. I've got a lead on where the newbie's home Idea might have been, want to go give it a looking-over to figure out what its worser half is up to."

"'Big and violent'?" she prompts, annoyed. "You're being cryptic again, Tippy." Miss Mighty gives me a piercing stare, the look that says she knows exactly how to kick my butt without getting out of her chair.

"Sorry. I've got a problem." I clear my throat while I organize my data. "Big guy, black coat, no face, baseball bat. He showed up in Smile House last night, made kind of a mess. I need to make sure this isn't bigger than it looks."

She raises a dubious eyebrow. "Wait, so someone you don't know attacked Smile House and you're heading right into its home Idea?"

"Or at least the home Idea of the Friend it attacked."

She cocks an eyebrow. "And the Friend it attacked is…?"

"Little kid's nightmare. Big, lots of drill bits everywhere, but kind of a marshmallow deep inside. It reminded me of someone, made me want to help it out." I give her the biggest smile my stitched-on mouth can manage.

"Also a mystery got near you."

"Yeah," I say. Might as well serve this request with a side of honesty. "You know me. So, new evil in town, in need of a smack in the jaw. You in?"

Miss Mighty looks at her drink, tosses it from one hand to the other. She's considering, but it's not taking as long as she's letting on.

"The only reason I come to this bar is to find something fun to go do." She stands up, flexes her fists. Her gloves squeak under the force of her grip. "Let's go." She grins, and it's radiant. She's always happier when she's fighting evil.

You'll notice I didn't mention the part where I think Spindleman is permanently dead? The part that suggests this is something we've never seen before? Yeah. Sandra was always bad at asking for help. She was always afraid that, like Daddy, everyone would say no. I picked it up from her.

That's my excuse, anyway.

Out on the street, I spin in place, head craned back as far as my crown will let me, but all I'm seeing is building tops and stars. I sigh, and look over at Miss Mighty. She answers with a waiting stare. That doesn't make it easier to ask.

"The place we're going..." I begin. I sigh again, and point a paw upward. "I need to be able to see the moon."

Miss Mighty smiles that determined, understanding, guilt-hurling smile, and scoops me up and flies away to a chorus of awed gasps. Some of them don't even come from me.

I can never get used to flying. It makes my legs tingle, my eyes water, my whole body go gooey and excited. It also always ends way too fast. I don't even get a chance to shout anything before Miss Mighty sets me down on the gravel-topped roof of one of Avatar City's many skyscrapers.

"Here you go," she says, pointing a gloved finger up at the sky.

Avatar City's moon is distant, with a little black spot on it where the United Nations built a moon base. I think us over to a more familiar moon, Playtime Town's big wedge of green cheese. (According to some of the natives, if your troubles are really bad it'll talk to you.) From that touchstone, it's easier to get us to the orange harvest moon over Nightshire, a slightly closer match to what Spindleman described. Miss Mighty drops into a fighting stance when the awful gray soil appears under our feet.

"Just a layover," I say quickly.

I picture the same style of moon, but high in the sky, even bigger and even more orange. I imagine it shining down on a house, and the smell of cloves and leather filling my nostrils. And then I smell them, along with fresh-cut grass and cold night air. I know by the way I shiver that we've arrived.

The moon fills the sky overhead, blotting out all but a few scattered stars. The silhouettes of pine trees rise up below it, a black barrier along the horizon. Miss Mighty and I stand inside a white picket fence, in a yard just a little bigger than the length of my body. Behind us is a humongous house with one window staring out of the top story, lit by the faint orange glow of a single nightlight. The air is still, like the whole place is holding its breath, waiting for something big and terrifying to rise up and blot out that moon. I think, with a lead weight in my stomach, that must have been Spindleman's job.

"Nightmare, for sure," Miss Mighty says, spinning in a slow, angry circle.

"Dangerous," I say with a wry grin. (I'm terrible at asking for help, but I'm great at faking casualness.)

There's a long pause as she studies the sky. "Yeah," she says through smiling teeth. "Let's see how dangerous."

This is why I love her.

"Sixth sense picking anything up?" I ask.

"You don't feel it?" She swings her arms wide. "Whole place is soaked in fear." She looks at the house. "But…"

She takes a step closer, a hand out toward the door, her eyes shut in concentration. Body language says she's testing a theory. She frowns, looks back at the moon, back to the door, and nods. Her theory's been confirmed.

"Something inside the house?" I ask.

Mighty nods, still studying the door.

"How bad?"

She shakes her head. "Not actively hostile. But… wrong."

"Wrong?"

Another shake of her head. "It's hard to explain. It's… a different dangerous than the rest of this place."

I take stock of my surroundings. Not much room to get a running start, but the house looks fairly large; there should be plenty of room for charging. I gesture for her to open the door.

'Tall' is the word I'd use for the inside of the house. It's nice in a basic way, a hardwood-floored living room with a couch and a coffee table and big glass-front cabinets, all stretching up toward a ceiling that feels like it's on another planet. There's plenty of space between the furnishings too, big seas of wood planks, all the space a little kid could want to run around in. Or there would be, except for the broken dishes.

They're everywhere in here: shattered bits of white ceramic, little patterns scribbled on them, spread across the floor from the door to the Stonehenge-sized couch and on into the depths of the house. Miss Mighty picks up a piece and turns it over in her hand.

"What is it?" I ask.

Mighty makes a noncommittal grunt, and picks up a different bit, studying it just as intently. My detective sense alerts me to a weird shuffling noise in the background, distant but audible. I make a note of it and focus on the dishes. First clues first.

Spindleman didn't mention any broken dishes, and they don't match the rest of the house – they're sharper, weightier, Real in a different way than the rest of the place. These dishes are someone else's Ideas, probably an adult's. Something from outside was – or *is* – in this house.

I hop up on the sofa for a bird's eye view. The shards don't come from the same set of dishes, judging by the markings. I make out six, seven different patterns. There's no order to the way the shards are distributed, not even any matches between bits to suggest an individual dish shattering in that spot. It's like someone came in here with six or seven dinette sets and sprinkled them around like birdseed.

Again, my attention drifts to the background noise of the house. It's some kind of near-constant shuffling, like someone's sweeping in one of the back rooms. And I think it just got louder.

"Mug."

I turn toward Miss Mighty. "What?"

She looks at me, and holds out a finger, crooked around a jagged-edged loop of white porcelain.

"Mug," she says again. "It's the handle from a… coffee mug?"

The remark sets my detective stuff on fire, but I'm not quite getting the significance yet. I hop off the couch, make a circuit of the coffee table. This isn't making any sense. Stuff like this is what I loved Sandra for. When we'd investigate together, she could teach me about the way people act, put some level of reason behind the illogical stuff. I remember most of it, but–

Miss Mighty gasps, a quick exhale that says danger just pinged her sixth sense. I turn to her, and then I do the smart thing and turn to where she's looking. All I see is the door to the hallway and the stairs, but what I hear is a different matter.

Footsteps, coming downstairs, from about where the boy's room should be. It's a heavy tread, a long shadow preceding it as it advances down the stairs at a deliberate pace. I put two and two together and get 'this was a really big mistake.'

The Man in the Coat steps into the living room, swamp-green eyes regarding us from under that wide-brimmed hat. He's taller than I remember, broader about the shoulders and stomach, and in a coat that's less glossy black and more liquid midnight, sucking in the light. He's got a bat in each hand, both red aluminum coursing with white-hot lightning.

"Drink," he announces, in a raspy, echoing facsimile of the voice I heard in Smile House.

"Is that–" Miss Mighty begins, before the Man in the Coat lunges at her.

CHAPTER NINE

Miss Mighty jumps up without hesitation, flying at the Man at subsonic speed. I thank her creator for giving her all those extra senses because that is the only reason she dodges his swing. The bat goes sizzling into the lamp next to him, breaks it in half and sends it shooting off in two different directions. If he's trying to intimidate us, he's on the right track.

He wheels his arm back for another swing, and Miss Mighty proves she's faster than any bully. Her punch plows into the Man in the Coat's chest and he sprawls out on his back, the house shaking as he lands. Miss Mighty drifts away, fists up to block her face, and gives me the raised eyebrows and rushed breath that ask 'is he dead?'

He's not moving, but my detective stuff picks up that he's shifting, changing; he's different now, but I'm not clicking on exactly how. I shake my head. Mighty nods and turns back toward him, and gasps as she realizes he's already halfway to standing.

"Drink," he growls again.

That last swing wasn't fast; *this* one is fast. One bat blurs, a red arc in between the two combatants. There's an awful celery-under-a-tire crunch, and Miss Mighty howls in pain, shooting backward until she rams into the far wall. She falls down, her eyes feral and terrified, and I can already see the bruise above her knee. Not only is this guy fast, he's unbelievably strong; I've seen Mighty hip-check a car and not even walk funny.

The Man in the Coat straightens up, and when I see him framed in the doorway, I see how he's changed. He's smaller, two heads shorter and nowhere near as massive. Miss Mighty sees it too. The confusion gives her a half-second's pause, and then he's standing over her, both bats raised above his head...

She's invulnerable. She's taken death rays to the chest. She likes to tell me that she once sprained an ankle holding up a nuclear power plant. But when I look at those bats, I see Spindleman's drill bits bouncing down the Smile House stairwell, and my morals take over from my common sense.

A headlong charge would be gift-wrapping my skeleton for this guy, but when I come at him angled off to the side, he assumes I'm running away. I turn at the last second, reach him right as he unleashes a swing, and send my front shoulder blasting straight into his leg.

The bats fly out of his hands, one of them shattering a floorboard near the front door. He stumbles, windmills his arms, and the change hits him again. I actually watch him shrink a head and a half. But his eyes are just as sickly green as they ever were, and now they're even angrier, and they're focused on me. He reaches into his coat, and there's a bat in his hand again, good as new. Heroism should probably be reserved for the bulletproof people.

Ceramic shards skitter behind me as I backpedal. An overhead swing gouges a crater into the floor, and another comes right on its heels, shattering the end-table next to me. I run around the sofa; the Man in the Coat explodes the middle section of it with a single swing and steps through the gap, once again right in my way. I back up as he glares at me through the storm of stuffing, reversing around the coffee table, back toward the front of the house, until I feel wainscoting brush against the tip of my tail. The shadows covering his face shift. I think that might be a smile.

"Fine."

If Chip and I ever have time to sit and talk again, I will pay him a dozen big favors if he can describe the noise Miss Mighty makes. It's a roar, but it's also a scream of pain, and it's also something no human-shaped throat could possibly make. Its message is clear, though: she's going to destroy whatever she is shouting at.

The Man in the Coat only gets halfway turned around before she drops out of mid-air and wraps her calves around his neck. He reaches up to pry her loose, and she flips forward, driving him straight through the coffee table. Glass busts off in every direction, showers them both in gleaming little shards.

Miss Mighty flies away as he takes wild swings at the air; she comes back down as soon as he starts to stand, catching him with an elbow drop that drives him to the floor in a heap. He swings at her again, and she karate-chops him in the arm, sending the bat to the floor. She follows up with a haymaker that puts him on his back, even shorter than before. If the look on her face qualifies as a smile, I never want her to be happy again.

She sits down on the Man's chest, grunting when she puts weight on the injured leg. The Man in the Coat grabs for her throat, and recoils as she punches him straight in his shadowy face. Again. He starts shriveling beneath her, now the size of Officer Hot. Again, and he's not even as big as I am. Miss Mighty keeps punching, spit flying out of her mouth as her fist rises and falls. The Man's hat rolls away, and there's no head underneath it anymore, just a wrinkled black coat with nothing inside. Miss Mighty just keeps going, the floor quaking and cracking around her.

"Mighty!" I shout.

The fire in her eyes flicks out in favor of shock. She looks at me, and back down at the pile of clothes, like she doesn't understand what any of this stuff is. The coat responds to the respite by sliding across the floor, headed back toward the stairs.

"No!" Mighty snarls, taking off with a wince of pain.

The clothes slither to the junction of the wall and the floor, slide into a crack too small for me to see, and vanish.

"Damn it!" Miss Mighty shouts, scorching my horns. She smashes her fist through the drywall. "God damn it!"

"Mighty," I say, trying to sound soothing over the volcanic eruption the curse word kindles in my horns. "Mighty, it's gone."

"It hurt me," she snarls, hovering there and seething at the wall. "It hurt me."

I climb through the ruins of the couch, and glance over at the Man in the Coat's hat, still lying on the floor. I scan over every inch of it, every centimeter, looking at the width of the brim, the way it catches the light.

"Aren't we gonna catch him?" Miss Mighty demands.

I flip the hat over, look inside the brim. My mouth goes sandy. "That wasn't him."

"Excuse me?" Her rage hits me like a tidal wave.

I gesture at her with the hat. "The guy who killed Spindleman, his hat was more shiny than this, and the brim was wider. And his didn't have a chin-strap inside." I wiggle the hat, let the elastic piece bounce demonstratively. "This looked like our guy, but it wasn't our guy. He kind of looked like…"

Spindleman. He kind of looked like Spindleman.

"It's like, instead of him changing the Idea…" I say, mostly to myself, "the Idea changed him…"

"He broke my damn leg!" she bellows.

I'm not too proud to admit I flinch. "I'm sorry."

"Are you?" Miss Mighty flies closer, hovers right above me. "Are you, Tippy? Really?"

The nugget of dread I'd been holding down takes root in my stomach. "What do you mea–"

"Fuck you, Detective," she yells. "Did you know he could do this?" She makes a sharp gesture at her leg. "Is this how your nightmare Friend died?"

I look up at her – Miss Mighty, the champion of the bullied, the strongest Friend I've ever met, the one who taught me that 'consent' and 'culture' can be combined into one term – and I say absolutely nothing.

"Did you *know*?" she demands. She points again at her knee, at the ugly bruise blossoming there.

I've got plenty of words in my head. Big ones. Funny ones. Smart ones. But I have no idea what to do when she looks at me with absolute disappointment.

"I—"

She raises her eyebrows, waiting for my answer.

"I was so scared," I say, right before I realize that was not the right thing to say.

Miss Mighty closes her eyes, shakes her head, frustrated. "What the actual fuck?"

"Please stop swearing."

"My leg is broken," Mighty seethes. "It's broken because I followed you to this place, and because you didn't tell me what he could do. You did this to me, Tippy!" She snarls that last part, a sound like a punch can't be too far away.

"The Man in the Coat did this to—"

"He would never have gotten to me if you had – no." She shakes her head. "No. You know what? I'm leaving."

Lightning strikes my spine. "But—"

"Screw you, Detective Tippy. We are talking again when dinosaurs learn how to apologize."

She flies out the front door and out of sight. My detective stuff alerts me when she disappears from the cool night air, thought off to some other place far away from my lies.

I sift through the broken dishes some more. The sofa has already returned to normal, along with the coffee table, but the dishes aren't leaving. The changes the Man in the Coat made to this place are irrevocable.

Maybe the changes I just made are, too.

Miss Mighty was created as her person's way of standing up to bullies. She was her person's strength, her confidence, but also her belief in goodness and justice. Whatever happened at that birthday party – Mighty's never told me the whole story – it got her kicked into the Stillreal, and it made her both proud of how capable she was and sensitive about the one time it wasn't enough. And I was so worried about solving this weird new mystery, and so scared of this weird new nightmare-man, that I didn't risk telling her all about something that could make her feel weak.

Without Sandra, solving a case is the only thing that feels right. When I put together new clues, when I get that rush of discovery? That's when I feel most like maybe she's still around. Unfortunately, that means I tend to care about mysteries before I care about people. Maybe if we'd made it through another birthday or two, I would have grown up more.

Congratulations, Tippy, you think you have yourself figured out...

CHAPTER TEN

I slump into Mr Float's Rootbeerium with my head hung low, belly up to one of the cake-stools, and order two double-scoop floats, heavy on the whipped cream. Mr Float slings a clean towel over his arm and gets to work.

I take a look around, trying to read the room. The Worst Cat is gone, along with the sky-pirates, leaving the back half of the room to Lieutenant Burrows and the Brass Legion, all polished clockwork limbs and mustaches. I give them a more thorough once-over than etiquette normally allows. I try to leave Friends to their privacy, but right now I need to be sure of the temperature of the Stillreal.

The diagnosis is worse than I'd hoped. The Legion is swapping quips and war stories like usual, but it doesn't take my detective stuff to hear the tension in their voices, or to see them taking turns watching the room over their shoulders. The news hasn't hit them hard enough to make them abandon their favorite watering hole, but the idea isn't out of the question yet.

Mr Float swings by, his bar towel now flecked with root beer and cream, and drops off a glass that might qualify as a vase. It's comfort food – a foaming, towering, foot-plus-tall heap of comfort food. I bend the extra-long straw to my lips, take a sip of carbonated brain food, and review the clues.

We have a new loose Friend, some kind of super-nightmare. I know first-hand it can get to Playtime Town and Spindleman's house, and from second-hand accounts I know it can get to the Freedom Motel – any number of places, judging by that 'not one of the' comment Officer Hot started to make.

No, correction. I don't actually know that the Man in the Coat can get to Spindleman's house. The one I saw in Spindleman's house didn't look like the one that killed Spindleman. There's no empirical proof the Man in the Coat Spindleman saw was the same one that killed it – they're similar enough that a casual observer might mistake them for each other, but–

Laughter explodes behind me, jarring me out of my nasty little thoughts. One of the Brass Legionnaires has detached her clockwork leg and is waving it around, making a silly voice that doesn't make sense without context. The others are laughing a little louder than that probably warrants, but detective stuff catches the reason for it: they're relieved at the distraction. The distraction is helpful for me, too. It lets my thoughts ripen on the vine.

The Man in the Coat in Spindleman's house looked more like Spindleman itself. But why would Idea warping work in reverse? And why did it shrink when Miss Mighty hit it? Was that just a defense mechanism, or was it something else?

And then there's the broken plates. That the Idea changed from an outside Friend makes sense, but what do broken plates have to do with a murderous man in a long black coat? Why did the version of the Man in Spindleman's home look like Spindleman, not the other way around? How is he leaving alternate versions of himself anywhere anyway? And how the heck is this thing able to permanently kill Friends?

"I say," says a creaky, dignified voice, ripping me back into the present. "Is that Detective Tippy I see?"

I look over at the stool next to me, now occupied. Lieutenant Burrows is in his off-duty uniform, light brown cottons instead of the usual heavy leathers, but he's got enough medals pinned to the thing for it to qualify as armor.

"That *is* you, isn't it, Detective?" Burrows says. His monocle whirrs as it telescopes toward me, bushy eyebrows beetling with the effort of examining me. "Yes, yes, I'd know that stitching anywhere." His speech is as forced as the tale-telling I heard back at the Legion's table. He's trying to get through the pleasantries to ask a question.

"Because the stitching is how you recognize a yellow triceratops," I reply, as withering as I can manage. I want to be alone with my thoughts.

"You'd be surprised how many oddly colored dinosaurs I've dealt with," Burrows says. "Why, Epsilon Eridani is lousy with the things. Yellow ceratopsians, red brachiosauri... there's a particular crimson tyrannosaurid specimen that seems to be their leader, actually. Smart as a whip and ten times as deadly, that one."

"Is that what you wanted to ask me about?" I'm in no mood for banter. Well, actually, I'm in a perfect mood for banter.

"Well... actually, no." A clockwork finger traces a discomfited circle on the bartop. "It's just that, the lads and I, we've... heard the rumors." He fixes me with his half-robotic gaze. "The nasty bit of business up at Smile House."

"Yes...?" I draw it out extra-long.

"Is it as bad as we've heard?"

Probably worse, knowing the Playtime Town grapevine, but nobody needs to hear that.

"Still figuring that out," I say. "I won't lie, it looks bad, but making assumptions in the Stillreal is a worse idea than in the Realworld, y'know?"

Lieutenant Burrows gives me a sad smile. "Indubitably."

He isn't moving. I stir my drink with my straw for a second, take another sip just in case he's waiting for a hint that I'm done talking, and give him a sidelong look.

"Is there something else you want to ask?"

"Well..." Burrows flexes his clockwork fist. "I was wondering if you needed to talk about it?"

The question is a sucker punch. "Needed or wanted?" I ask, eyes reflexively narrow.

"Either one," Burrows says. "I know that sometimes the advice of the lads helps steer me in the right direction."

He's being kind. Of course he's being kind, kindness is the undercurrent that brings the Playtime Town regulars together. I never know what to do with that, so I frown. It seems like the Sandra-approved reaction. "If you don't mind me bringing down the mood of the room."

Lieutenant Burrows' mutton chop levitates above his smile. "We're the Brass Legion, Detective. Grim adventure is where we're at our best."

I sit up tall, just to make sure everyone in the room knows Playtime Town's greatest detective was not at all about to cry.

"A nightmare died last night. *Died* died, not the deaths you just spend a night in a magic Martian cave to come back from."

Those floating mutton chops crash to his chin.

"It was killed by this other Friend," I continue, "the kind of nightmare that other nightmares might have. Big guy, broad shoulders. Baseball bat…"

I tell him everything, leaving off the names just in case the Brass Legion gossip outside their ranks. There's no need to spread the panic any wider. Burrows' mutton chop finds new lows to sink to as I'm talking, but never once, to his credit, does Lieutenant Burrows take his attention off me.

"I say," he says again, his flesh-and-bone hand tugging at his collar. "Well, then." He clears a throat that has no need for clearing. "That sounds like a stickier wicket than I expected, to be honest."

"Yeah, me too," I scoff. "It's the case of the century, for sure. It'll feel great if I can crack it. And not be cracked by it," I mutter, taking another pull of my float.

Lieutenant Burrows nods an unfocused nod, drums a moment on the table. He glances back toward his crew, and has a flash of memory that results in him waving over Mr Float.

"Put this esteemed detective's drinks today on my tab," he tells the ice-cream ghost. "And another round for the Legion!" he shouts, loud enough to get a mighty cheer from his unit. "In fact," he says, with a quick glance my way, "keep the rounds coming!"

The cheer is loud enough that it covers him leaning in and saying, still concerned but a little softened, "I have faith in your abilities, Detective. But if you need advice – I am always willing to listen."

I nod, say a muddled attempt at "Thanks," and look away before I show any emotion on my face. Being a father to his men is Lieutenant Burrows' whole thing. That he's extending it to me is probably just him coping, but it doesn't change how hard it hits me. Fortunately, looking away from Burrows means I see Chip Dixon come in the front door. He's on that red, puffy edge of tears that kids specialize in, hands stuffed into his slacks pockets like they're drilling for oil.

"Well… okay, a quick question," I say, making myself look back at Burrows. "What do you think I should do next? I've got all this stuff I can look at, and I just… I don't know which ones are more important. Not yet, anyway."

"Well, then I'd say what you need is a tactical assessment," Burrows says. "If you do not have enough raw data to form a plan, you should rely on scouting reports. In layman's terms, talk to people you trust to have information you can use. Let that guide you to your next move." He shoots a meaningful glance toward Chip, and gives me a smile that tells me he knows I want to go check on my friend.

Unfortunately, the other things his suggestion is making me think aren't as pleasant. But before I let those occupy my mind, I take a quick drink, nod, and extend my paw. "Thank you, Lieutenant. And, uh… sorry I was so rude to you when you walked up."

"It's quite alright, Detective," he says, his metal hand giving me a surprisingly gentle shake. "Believe me, when the heat is on aboard the *Argonaut* we're a bit prone to lapses in propriety ourselves." Worry weathers his face again as he steps away from the bar. "Do be careful, though, wot?"

"Wot," I say, with a solemn nod. "You do the same."

He smiles, and gives me a cuff on the shoulder. "There's the Detective Tippy I know. Good day, chap."

"Good day," I say, and look past him at the hangdog expression of Chip.

Tactical assessment. I take another long slurp of ice cream – the things I'm thinking about do not taste good going down – and I hop barstools until I'm chatting distance from Chip.

"You want company in your misery?"

Chip looks up at me. The tears have started to leak out the corners of his eyes. He's an emotional guy, so this isn't necessarily cause for alarm, but right now I can't ignore anything even a little outside my routine. He sniffs, and shakes his head.

"It's not big," he says. "Just, today's news is all really sad."

That hits me right in the feels. "All of it?"

He sniffs, starts to nod, and pauses. I give him a knowing smile.

"So there's some good, then?"

Chip shades his eyes with his fedora, mouth twisting back and forth in consideration. He lifts his hat again, and his eyes aren't quite as puffy. So, progress. "Some good," he says, with the glint of a smile. It gets bigger when Mr Float drops off his order – plain root beer, no ice. A stiff drink for a hard-hitting reporter.

"You want to tell me about it?" I ask.

He pauses, studying the rim of his mug. "Maybe. What's in it for you?"

"The comfort of good news." Now's as good a time as any to be honest with my pals.

"Why do you need comfort?" Chip asks. He's got laughter in his words. He's touched, but playing hurt to get some sympathy out of me.

Unfortunately for him, I'm playing hardball. "I think I need to go talk to Big Business."

Chip thumbs his fedora up to make room for the stare he gives me. "You really want to deal with a bad news Friend like Big Business?"

"Bad news is going around," I say, with a nod Chip's direction. "Maybe bad news Friends are what I need."

"Yeah, but, he's… dangerous…" Chip says, making a solid punching fist.

I sputter. "What, have we never met?"

Chip's grin finally comes out of hiding. "You're fun, Tippy."

"That's what they tell me. Now why don't you roll the newsreel?"

Chip holds up a finger, swigs his root beer, and slams the empty mug down on the counter. "Another one, mack!" he shouts down the bar, and turns to me, rubbing his hands together.

He closes his eyes, tilts back his head, and starts in on the story of a record number of kitten adoptions, and one about a local comic book convention that's donating its proceeds to charity. For a few minutes, there's no death, or broken legs, or angry faces, or car crashes. For a few minutes, I can remember what Realworld feels like. It's not enough to take all the tension out of my stuffing, but it's enough to fuel me up for what I have to do next.

"Thank you, Chip. Thank you so much."

"Hey," he drums his scarred knuckles on the bartop, "what are fighting journalists for?" He hops down from the bar, and gives me a cocky salute as he heads for the door. "I feel a lot better, too, Tippy. Thanks. Good luck with Big Business."

Oh, right. That's why I needed cheering up. I wave to Chip, and then I wait. I want to give him some lead time before I walk out onto the street, and I also want to give Spiderhand time to go to bed. I can't deal with Big Business without a full night's sleep, and sleeping at all tonight is going to be hard enough without having to give Spidey a recap.

Before I leave, I take one last sip of my float. It's gone warm.

CHAPTER ELEVEN

I get started early the next day, mostly because I never actually fell asleep.

There's exactly one billboard in Playtime Town, on the outskirts where the highway curves toward the forever-bucolic foothills. Coming into town, it shows a family of waving teddy bears beneath bright yellow letters saying 'WELCOME HOME!' Leaving town, it shows the same teddy bears, a little sadder around the eyes, waving arms at half-mast, with the slogan 'COME BACK SOON.' I don't know who the creator thought those signs were for, but today I've got bigger mysteries to solve.

I focus on the mother bear's welcoming eyes, and think to a place where billboards dominate a sunset-tinged skyline. It's morning in Playtime Town, but here in the Heart of Business it's always just a little before closing time, when the moon switches shifts with the sun. I know I've arrived when I gag on the smell of car exhaust and toner.

The buildings in the Heart of Business are taller than anything I regularly think to: huge staring skyscrapers, black against a night sky stained yellow by all the signs, shouting messages at the most primal parts of my brain. 'BUY,' 'DIVERSIFY,' 'OVERTIME,' 'PROFIT.' A rainbow of neon, and not a plant in sight. And looming at the center, the Heart of Business itself, the tallest skyscraper of them all.

Its windows are pitch-black. Its base is a riot of girders that shoot out in every direction, burrowing into other buildings like mosquito beaks. Its logo is just a neon Valentine's heart, complete with arrow. (The meaning there comes in waves.)

By one telling of the story, the Heart of Business came together gradually. Every time a business didn't get off the ground, those crushed dreams of prosperity and ruthless corporate dominance wound up here. By another telling, the Heart of Business was a metaphor from someone's Internet manifesto about the evils of corporate culture, a bottom-line parasite with an equally bloodsucking CEO. I've also heard the Heart was part of some young-adult book about capitalism, or a living conspiracy theory dreamed up by bedraggled faces on the unemployment line. Really, all this means is that nobody in the Stillreal actually knows where it came from, which is why no one ever goes there unless they need something from it. Friends are rarely good at history, but they are good at self-preservation.

I walk along the shadowed streets, looking up at the buildings. Most of them are dead, no power to their windows or signs. Here and there I see squares of light, occupied by what probably used to be people, their skin less 'pale' and more 'without color of any kind.' They're all typing away at computers, or filing stacks of folders as tall as them. I see tall, skinny figures in the background, watching over their activities – or rather, I see the same tall, skinny figure, with the same shape to their tall bouffant haircut, repeated from building to building.

I hate this place.

The doors to the Heart are already open when I get there. The doors to the Heart are *always* open, and they always hiss shut as soon as you come through them, right before a spine-scratching sound like some huge invisible lock has clamped tight over the doors. I've never had trouble leaving, but there's a first time for everything terrible.

The doors feed into the bottom of the Heart's main shaft, a canyon of brushed steel and glass, like something you'd expect a particularly fastidious earthquake to produce. The walls are armored with elevators and escalators and wheelchair ramps, scrambling up to a maze of carpeted walkways and majestic oak doors. I hear typing and talking wafting down from above, and the occasional polite applause as yet another of the infinite meetings comes to a close. I can't see the ceiling through all the fluorescent lights, but if I squint, I can see that same tall, skinny person observing the ground floor. I'm not looking forward to dealing with that, but before I do, I have to deal with Front Desk.

A tongue of silver tile, lined with big fake plants in big beige pots, leads from the doors straight to the front desk, a wedge of white marble about the size of a bus. The desk blocks any possible way in, but still provides a perfect view of the goings-on upstairs, just in case new arrivals don't feel small and alienated enough. Seated at the wedge is Front Desk herself, a brown-skinned, broad-framed woman in a smoke-gray suit, her eyes hidden behind glasses that glow like TV screens, her red hair styled in waves that honestly look like flames. She's wearing a headset with six different microphones on it and typing on three or four different keyboards. I guess Big Business has started taking it easier on her.

I stop in front of the big marble slab, far back enough so that Front Desk has a chance of seeing me over the cliff face of her desk, and wait. It takes Front Desk a few seconds to stop typing and swivel toward me. Her expression doesn't change, the same flat, unplugged stare gazing down at me that she'd been aiming at her computer. I'd call it robotic, but I know some pretty animated robots.

"Name?" she asks, in a voice as bored as the rest of her.

"Tippy. I'm a private detect–"

Front Desk turns away and resumes typing. There are way more than ten fingers at work back there.

"I don't see your name in Mr Big's calendar," she says. "Do you have an appointment?"

"Um. No." And there's no way to get one, as far as I know.

Front Desk nods, and raises the one damning finger that tells me to wait. "Mr Big is very busy today, but I'm sure he'll fit you in if he can. Have a seat, please."

Front Desk gestures toward a bank of fake plants, and one of them is replaced with a comfortable-looking leather armchair. I don't sit.

"Ms Desk," I say, in my best and also worst impression of a businessman, "I really do have a matter of great *import* to discuss with Mr Big, and–"

She turns toward me, the exact same motion she made when I first came in. "Name?"

"Detective Tippy."

Again, the waiting finger. "Mr Big is very busy today, but I'm sure he'll fit you in if he can. Have a seat, please."

And the gesture toward the chair, and the return to her typing, all without displaying any actual emotion.

Front Desk is bureaucracy personified; she can keep this song and dance going as long as she wants to. To get past it, I need to get her to think my business is important – or rather, something Big Business would think was important.

First, let's try something that threatens his profits.

"I have it from a reputable source that Friends are dying," I say, enunciating carefully. "It – it could badly hurt Mr Big's bottom line."

The magic words cause nothing more than a pause. "Mr Big is very busy today," she says. "But I'm sure he can fit you–"

"Mr Big's shareholders might be concerned by recent developments."

Front Desk blinks. "Mr Big is very busy today–"

My thoughts are starting to unravel. I like a challenge, but there's a challenge and there's getting in my way. Fine. I go the other direction, make it seem like he has something to gain.

"I have information."

Front Desk stops typing. I swallow the second tongue trying to worm into my throat.

"Information about the goings-on, the – the dying Friends," I stammer. "I think it might be valuable. I think it might maximize his profit margins." That's another term Sandra's dad used to throw around, before the – no, no…

Front Desk cocks her head just a tiny bit. "Name?"

I'm so frustrated I'm shaking. A little verbal sparring match I can abide, but *this*? I need to finish this and knock off for a nice solid freakout. "I – come on – err, overhead."

Nothing.

"Synergy."

Nothing.

"Business opportunity?"

She starts typing again. She doesn't even ask me for my name.

The detective is getting blocked. It's time for the dinosaur to solve the problem.

"I didn't want to do this," I say, as I walk back to the open front doors.

I spin around, and I charge full-force into the desk.

The desk is too thick to shatter, even at a full head of steam, but it does crack, spitting out white shrapnel that pings off the fake plants and the silver tiles. I stumble back from the point of impact, no longer on speaking terms with gravity, but smiling at the me-sized gouge I've created. I like to think it's what Miss Mighty would do.

Front Desk isn't saying anything, isn't moving. There isn't even emotion on her face. I gather what I can of my thoughts, and say, "Call him down here. Now."

Front Desk's body language stays locked up, but her eyes slowly shift. The change gives me the silence needed for what I just did to sink in. I meant to disrupt her pattern, throw a wrench into the snubbing machine, but she looks like I just lit her world on fire. The front half of my brain reminds me she's a minion of the most soulless mobster in the Stillreal, but the back half only has to say 'Miss Mighty' again to get the guilt engines revving…

"Good evening," says a voice like friendly thunder just over my shoulder.

Thank Sandra, a distraction.

Big Business lives up to his name from the second you look at him. 'Tall' doesn't get the picture across; he fills any room he comes into, looming on a level that has nothing to do with his dimensions. His executive haircut is as gray as a mugger's pistol, and his pearly white smile is broader than any human grin. His suit's impeccable and impossible, shifting to whatever color makes him stand out best against his surroundings. He looks down at me with big silver eyes, something black and mechanical hiding behind the pupils, and extends a wedding-ringed hand for a shake.

"Detective Tippy," he says, warm and familiar. "It's good to see you again." He makes it sound like we've been through a war together.

I don't shake; knowing Big Business, he might see it as binding. "Mr Big. How are you?"

"Fine, fine. Though, ah, I need to express concern regarding recent events in the lobby of Heart of Business, Incorporated." His mouth is all diplomacy, but his eyes bear down hard, letting me know retaliation is on his mind.

"Your assistant wasn't assisting," I say, staring right back.

"Heart of Business, Incorporated prides itself on a total customer service experience. We apologize for any inconvenience and–"

Front Desk lets out a whimper. Big Business looks at her, looks at me, and for a second he gives off a wave of anger, like some prehistoric predator whose kill just escaped up a tree. He lets out a quick sigh, and molds himself back into respectability.

"I think this meeting is best conducted in a more intimate setting, don't you? Shall we adjourn to a conference room and continue our interface?"

You could measure my disgust from orbit. But I nod, and Big Business pulls a phone out of that ever-changing suit of his, and says some jargon I don't fully understand. The whole building starts whirring and roaring, like we're standing inside a motorcycle engine. The tiles underneath us fold open like trap doors, and before my inner ear can tell me we're falling, I'm standing in a conference room the size of a train car, white ceiling tiles slamming shut above me. I've landed without incident in a leather armchair as comfortable as my favorite dryer. Big Business is on the other end of a huge oak table, still looming despite a football field's worth of distance between us. There's a blank projector on the wall behind him, a little click-button device in his hand. He smiles, his mouth pleasant but his eyes relishing my confusion.

"Heart of Business, Incorporated is always happy to cooperate with law enforcement. We have an iron-clad policy that all employees are to exercise due diligence in assisting–"

"I get it," I say. I'm in no mood to translate Capitalist into English.

Big Business looks like someone teleported a lemon into his mouth, which is extra-satisfying to see. "What did you want to meet about, Detective?" he says, as he forces himself back into diplomacy mode.

"Information, like always. A Friend was killed over in Playtime Town two nights ago. A nightmare, called itself Spindleman."

Big Business gives me a rock-drill of a smile. "Heart of Business, Incorporated has not yet broken ground on its Playtime Town campus. If you like, we are happy to direct your inquiry to the appropriate law enforcement entit–"

"Not like a normal Friend death. Gone. Totally dismantled. Practically disintegrated."

Big Business curls an eyebrow, but he's not so much 'inquisitive' as 'impressed.' My temper dances down my spine. He already knew, and he was just baiting me into asking first. What a buttface.

"Heart of Business, Incorporated is aware of the situation," he says.

Yep, total buttface.

"But we do not know much more than the action items we have already discussed."

This game never changes: the detective forcing the informant to inform. Let's try the witty jab approach, that might make me feel better. "'Not much more' still means you've got *some* more, Mr Big. You tell me what you know, I'll tell you anything I know that you didn't cover."

Big Business flashes his real smile – the big, terrifying one. It fills the entire bottom of his face, his cheeks folding up into a flying V to accommodate all those professionally polished teeth. I've seen that smile on one other being in my entire memory. It was a T-rex.

"I have kept myself abreast of the situation as it develops," he admits, in careful, over-enunciated syllables. "But you have to understand, I am a very busy man. Heart of Business, Incorporated is a multinational, interstellar business concern, and tending to the needs of our customers and shareholders–"

"I'll tell you what I know, and I'll owe you a favor," I say, swallowing as much regret as I can manage.

Big Business stops, and unveils that horrifying grin again. "The needs of a firm like Heart of Business, Incorporated can be complex. Difficult to understand. We are aggressive innovators, and our employees are big-picture thinkers who display top-notch leadership qualities. Now, for unusual, possibly temporary situations, Heart of Business, Incorporated does see the value in employing contract workers…"

In other words, he wants me to be on the hook for a job to be named later. No mention in there of how moral or kind the job might be, of course. Unless he thinks he has the entire story in his back pocket, Big Business is highballing me.

"Here's the end-user license agreement," I say. Daddy taught me that phrase. "The next time you have a job that requires a detective, I will do it for free. But: the job has to require travel from Playtime Town to here, and wherever the case is, and nowhere else. I will not do anything where either party knows I'm going to get shot at, slashed, punched, kicked, whatever." His smile doesn't waver, so I deliver the punchline. "And under no circumstances will I ever steal anything for you."

Big Business doesn't hesitate for a second. "Heart of Business, Incorporated does not condone illegal activity by its employees or contractors, but we do aggressively pursue the interests of our stockholders, which include stakeholders in the military and government sectors of several–"

"No shooting," I say. "No death rays, freeze beams, boomerangs, nothing. No violence. And no theft, no matter how daring and dashing my escape might be."

Big Business examines me, like he's checking if I'm level with the floor. He pops a smile heavy on the predatory joy, and extends a perfectly manicured hand. "That seems amenable to me," he says, with an extra side of menace.

I tuck my paw into his hand and give it a solid pumping. To say I feel dirty is to practice new levels of understatement. The things I do for clues…

"Spindleman," I say. "Nightmare. Extremely dead. What do we know?"

Big Business adjusts his lapels, and gives me an unpleasant smile. "Allow me to consult with my people." He leans over the table, and stabs a finger into a big red button on a big black phone that I'm pretty sure wasn't there a second ago. "Send in the fact-finders."

The sound starts the second he's let go of the button. It's the sound of a thousand elevator bells dinging, two thousand hinges creaking, the frenzied murmurs of a crowded stock market floor. At the same time, it's the sound of metal screeching against metal, and the sound of huge beating wings. What happens when the sound stops isn't better.

Standing at the head of the table, flanking Big Business, are about a dozen men in suits, all shapes and colors and sizes. I say 'about' because it's hard to look at them long enough to count them. And I say 'men' because that's easier than getting into all the appendages I see when I'm not looking directly at them, tentacles and stingers and beaks and things I'm not sure exist in my vocabulary.

"Gentlemen," Big Business announces to his fact-finders, his voice loud and commanding. "I want everything about the Spindleman murder on my desk by close of business!"

The fact-finders look at each other. Two of them stand apart from the pack, and each grab hold of one of Big Business' wrists. He bows as if he's going to lend a conspiratorial ear to one of them, and the fact-finders respond by hopping onto Big Business' hands and clambering up his arms. They move like they weigh nothing; Big Business doesn't even flinch as they climb up onto his shoulders and whisper in his ears. They must have been keeping busy; they didn't even need to go scouting before they reported.

Even in the handful of Ideas that do have money, not every Friend cares enough about it to make it worth hoarding. But knowledge? Every Friend has a use for information, even if they're just making sure no one else knows about something. Every Friend needs a favor at some point too, and most of us will trade knowledge or favors for more of one or the other. So, if you're the most ruthless capitalist ever to be cast off into the Stillreal, you figure out the business of knowing things real, real fast… and if your person already gave you an army of sleazy, half-human 'fact-finders' to do your dirty work, why fix what isn't broken?

"Meeting adjourned," Big Business says, after either five minutes or the entirety of human history.

The fact-finders hop off his shoulders, filing back into their hard-to-watch ranks. Big Business fixes his tie, brushes non-existent dust off his shoulders, and gives the click-button in his hand an expert little press. A picture appears on the screen behind him, showing a picture-perfect image of a still-alive, still-uncertain Spindleman.

"Spindleman was young. A little boy's nightmare. Something that scratched at the window at night."

"Yeah, he was a textbook bogeyman." And he knows I already know that. This is just a display of dominance, a test to see if I'll get impatient and let him short me on his end of the bargain. Not today, Mr Big.

Big Business nods, and clicks the button again. Now the picture is the silhouette of a man in a long coat and a broad hat. "And its killer: a bogeyman to kill a bogeyman."

I scoff. "Big and dark? That's all you have?" You're not the only one who can fight to be on top, kiddo.

The screen distorts, and for a second, the fact-finders flicker into their mish-mashed, incomprehensible forms. Big Business tugs at his tie as he looks down his nose at me.

"If the rumors are true," he says, with a sidelong glance at one of the fact-finders, "the killer had to be incredibly potent." Click: a graph, too small for me to make out the details. "A truly transcendental thought-construct, someone well-anchored in the popular consciousness. Think in the range of Superman, Falstaff, Lisbeth Sal–"

"Don't name-drop at me," I say, a little playful and a little sharp. "Spindleman died right in front of me, I know how bad the killer has to be. You're throwing me peanuts, I want the three-course dinner you're hiding under the table."

Big Business' eyebrows knit together. He really thought he'd get by with superficial data.

"You help me figure out where I should go next," I say, "and I'll tell you about what I found at Spindleman's house."

If there's something Big Business doesn't have, he has to have it; information doubly so. If I'm right, the house is too new to the Stillreal for his fact-finders to have fully explored it, which means I'm waving buried treasure under his nose.

Big Business' lip twitches, but he wrangles it into a smile. "We here at Heart of Business, Incorporated have always enjoyed our working relationship with the Stuffed Animal Detective Agency." Translation: I'm right.

He clicks the button again, showing me a map that doesn't look like anything I've ever seen. "There have been rumors – simple speculations, the rumblings of an inherently unstable market – that this Man in the Coat has been seen in other Ideas." He already knows what we've been calling the Man; his fact-finders have *really* been busy. "Mostly outliers, new and transient additions – markets not yet penetrated by Heart of Business's target demographics. However, there have been some groundbreaking appearances in population centers, and the Freedom Motel is one such Idea."

The place Spindleman fled to Nightshire from. That was on the list of potential places to investigate, but I wasn't sure. I should make sure I'm sure now, too, actually. "Any of those Ideas something that might interest Officer Hot and Officer Cold?"

Big Business' only reaction is to click the button, switching us to a view of the Freedom Motel, the big L-shaped building with the fake Greek pillars and the red doors. "Officers Hot and Cold were recently sighted in the area, yes. They spoke to Freedom Frieda, did some investigating, and… that was that." His grin curdles. He's making sure I know he knows more.

"'That was that'?" I repeat. "'Some investigating'? Look, if you really don't feel like learning anything today–"

Big Business' lip twitches again. His finger hits the click-button without meaning to, sends us to a slide that just shows an empty room in a house, a moving van driving away at speed. Before I can wonder what the heck that is, he lets out a scoff that could launch a ship and clicks over to a close-up view of some of the motel's red doors.

"Officers Hot and Cold performed a thorough investigation of the entire Freedom Motel," he says, "interviewing Freedom Frieda and all her erstwhile guests." Click: more doors with different numbers. "They inspected all unoccupied and recently occupied rooms, until" – click: a single door, numbered 303 – "they went into Room 303. Where the other rooms received cursory inspection, the officers lingered in 303 for quite some time, as long as they spent in every other room in the Idea combined." He clicks again, switching the projector screen back to pure white. "They concluded their investigation there, and presumably went home."

I give Big Business a long, scathing, pitiless look. "'Presumably'?"

"Don't," he snaps, and catches himself with another tug at his tie. "These are the data points we can offer at this time," he says, back to his conference-speech cadence. "The officers did not exit the room, and my fact-finders were unable to accompany them inside due to, ah, human error."

The berth the fact-finders are giving him widens just a little.

"We have seen no concerning trends or red flags in Playtime Town or other high-visibility markets, and as such we have adopted a holding-pattern policy with regards to Heart of Business's stake in the matter. But if anything were to change, we here at Heart of Business, Incorporated would of course be sure that we were at the forefront of any new developments."

The projector screen retracts into the ceiling, revealing a soulless piece of corporate art hung on the room's back wall. (It looks like an abstract view of a suburban street, but my detective stuff isn't sure of the significance.) Big Business is as terrifying as ever, but my detective stuff picks out the little things going wrong with him, the tiny hitch in one corner of his mouth, the precise little angle of his eyebrow. He's desperately hoping he's impressed me.

"Right," I say, "So, my end of the deal. The Man in the Coat was in Spindleman's house. And a few things got left behind there. In fact," I say, "as of my most recent visit, they're still around. Totally solid. Didn't ever fade, and I watched the Idea normalize, just to be sure."

The dam bursts behind Big Business' eyes, letting the anxiety come pouring out. "What was it?" He leans over the table, barely keeping his cool. "What was left behind?"

I'm supposed to taunt the bad guy. I'm supposed make him squirm. But I'm not sure he's the bad guy today, and I've been enough of a buttface for one case. (I keep telling myself that…) "The floor was covered in broken dishes."

Big Business looks haunted. That's… something to think about, then.

"You're sure?" he says.

"Positive."

He nods, totally unfocused. It takes him a few seconds to act like I'm still there. "Thank you, Detective. I… look forward to interfacing with you again. We'll reach out to you regarding our outstanding transactions."

"Thank you, Big Business," I say. I hop down out of the chair and walk toward the conference room door. "Heart of Business, Incorporated seems to have a very bright future."

I pad out into the hallway, and get out of sight of the doors just as Big Business turns to the fact-finders and waves his hand. I hear the sound of a hundred wings flapping, but at least I don't see it.

Room 303 at the Freedom Motel. Lieutenant Burrows was right. I just needed to get the lay of the land.

But, my detective stuff asks, as the rest of me focuses on the task at hand, why was Big Business so disturbed by the dishes? There are a few possible answers, and I wish I liked any of them. I also wish this was a case where what I like had any bearing whatsoever.

Sorry. The story doesn't get more cheerful from here.

CHAPTER TWELVE

I ride down in the elevator, and walk out past an undamaged front desk with a rigid Front Desk behind it, working hard to ignore me. I shudder through my guilt, walk down the shadow-choked streets until I stop shaking, and find the nearest billboard.

The board gets me a brief layover at the waving teddy bears back in Playtime Town. I wander toward City Hall and ride the sign in front of the New Friend Hotel to the sign for the Wyrd Bluff Hotel, a small-town tourist-trap in another rejected story Idea. Wyrd Bluff Hotel easily becomes Motel Turing, a postmodern husk on one of Chrometown's smoggy superhighways. Then, with a little refocusing, Motel Turing becomes Freedom Motel.

The Freedom Motel was dreamt up by a pair of foster kids: someplace safe they could run away to, with no adults to tell you what to do and plenty of ice-cold soda in the vending machines. From the outside, it's as welcoming as ever, the parking lot with the usual mix of minivans, red wagons, and spaceships, all dusted with a friendly coating of desert sand. No doors are missing or hanging off their hinges; I don't even see any peeling spots in the paint. But I also don't see any Friends out in the noonday sun, and unless things have changed in the last decade, Freedom Frieda is all about her high-noon barbecues. Detective stuff says that isn't the only anomaly. I keep my head on a swivel the whole way to the front office, trying to put my finger on it.

The office is, like the rest of the motel, bigger on the inside, with photos on the walls of every wayward Friend who ever stayed here. (That's me on the second row, twelfth from the left. If you look closely, you can see Spiderhand's pinky finger just inside the frame.) There's no one behind the faded gray concierge desk, but the bell is still there, a big gold knob in the middle of the pristine blotter. I get up on my hind legs, give it a quick ring, and wait. I watch the parking lot for any sign of long black coats, then turn back around at the familiar clicking of talons on the floorboards.

Like the rest of the motel, Freedom Frieda is the same as ever, a towering eagle in a stars-and-stripes apron and a matching bandana, her eyes flicking between the colors of the American flag. But I can see problems written all over her: a too-hasty knot in the bandana, more melancholy blue in her eyes than angry red or calm, default white. At least Frieda is someone I know how to talk to.

"Tippy?" she asks, in a deep, concerned voice.

"Detective Tippy, now," I say with a smile.

"What you doin' here?"

"Following up a lead, of course." I beam at her with every positive thought I have. "I mean, what else would bring me by? Nostalgia?"

The color of her eyes shifts: deep blue. She's afraid. Clearly I need to cut to the chase, then. I ease in with a lie.

"I was working a case with Officer Hot and Officer Cold, outta Playtime Town. You seen them recently?"

"Yes." The blue doesn't shift away. "They, um. They left, though."

I don't need detective stuff to know she's lying; that's the only time Frieda stutters. She has surprising moral purity for a political ad. I give the obvious button a push. "That's weird. They were supposed to meet me here. You know what made them take off like that?"

Frieda hesitates, shakes her head. Eyes, still blue. Truth, still absent.

"Huh." I scratch behind my crown, shrug. "Can you tell me what they wanted, then? That might help me find them."

Frieda cocks an eyebrow, one eye turned from blue to pale red. Suspicion.

Crud.

"Thought you said they were workin' a case *with* you?"

"Uh, well…" I sigh to buy myself time. "Hot and Cold aren't really… *forthcoming* partners. They think it's part of the whole cop-detective relationship." I give her a conspiratorial smile. We're friends ragging on co-workers, just like old times.

"Heh." The red eye has gone back to white, and the blue eye has brightened a little.

I think she bought it.

"We're all broke in our way, I guess."

"Yeah. No kidding." That stings. Why does that sting? "So, what were they looking at?" I ask.

Frieda tenses. "They wanted to do a full sweep of the rooms. Said they were lookin' for some nightmare, thought it might have gone to ground here."

She used the 'it' pronoun. Does she know we're talking about Spindleman or is that just her defaulting? "Well, did it?"

Both eyes flicker red. I've offended her. "Nobody has to hide at the Freedom Motel, Tippy," she says, with more edge than I'd expect. "A nightmare wants to live with me, they get to do it same as anybody else."

"Sorry, I didn't mean to imply – sorry."

"It's alright." She smooths a ruffled patch of feathers on her wing. "I mean, the officers asked basically the same thing."

"What did you tell them?" Read: can I catch you spinning conflicting lies?

Frieda shrugs. "I gave 'em the master key, let 'em check around. Didn't figure they were gonna leave with it."

"They stole your master key?" I don't bother hiding how baffling that is. If you'd asked me before now, I would have been unsure Hot and Cold could actually commit crimes.

Her eyes flash deep, oceanic blue, with a dash of the same unfocused pain I saw on Miss Mighty not long ago. Because that's what I need to see today… "I can make another one, but… I can't run a home the cops can raid on a whim. I need to get that key back." Her voice soars with panic.

"I'll take the case," I say reflexively. "As… soon as I'm sure this other one is solved."

That brings Frieda fully back to the present. "Thank you, Tippy. I…" She shakes her head. "How can I help you?"

"Can you let me into room 303?"

The blue in Frieda's eyes plunges most of the way to black. "303?" Surprise, but more important than surprise, dread.

"Yeah. Hot and Cold said they got a tip about it. I figure that makes it the place to start, right?"

"… Right." Frieda nods, faking casual a little better with each rise and fall. She turns to the little electronic key programmer on the desk, and flips the switch that makes it spit out a familiar white keycard.

"Here," she says, passing it down to where I can reach it.

I feel homesick holding one of these things in my paws again. "I really appreciate it, Frieda."

"Be careful."

I grin. "Am I ever?" By her eye colors, the joke doesn't land. I substitute a nod and a hasty exit. "Bye, Frieda."

Frieda watches after me, rigid and uncomfortable.

I take the long way across the parking lot, going past each of the red doors to listen for any occupants in danger (or who might cause danger) and give myself time to process Frieda's behavior. She was upset about the master key, but it was more than that – the master key felt like one link in a much longer chain of upset, something about the sanctity of the motel, about her role in running it. And she was terrified when I brought up Room 303, worse than I've ever seen her, and I've seen her with drunks. (Her person drank herself into a lower evolutionary state when she had to suspend her campaign. The full story doesn't make it less depressing.)

Frieda's world is in obvious disarray – you're not alone, sister – and it has something to do with Hot and Cold, and a lot to do with Room 303. Or at least something they were involved in. It's a good week for upset, I guess.

I focus on the data in front of me. There's a dune buggy outside room 217, big and black and purple, with tombstones for seats and the words 'Doom Buggy' stenciled across the hood. The faux-horror aesthetic isn't the part I'm staring at, though; it's the placement. The Doom Buggy is parked outside a room with no lights on and a plain red door. The car is clearly from an outside Idea, but the door isn't changed at all, not even a single skull or cobweb? There's a vehicle in front of the next room too, a giant stone beetle I'm pretty sure is staring at me, and there's spaceship made out of daisies parked next to that. Both of them are parked by plain red doors.

Just for good measure, I put my ear to 217, knock, and listen. I don't hear anyone inside, so I take my chances with a "Hello," and look over in the direction of 303 while I wait.

Still nothing. It looks like the Idea has reset recently. Which means Friends – at least three of them, by a count of the things in the parking lot – thought out of here in a big enough hurry that they left behind vehicles they or their people thought were really important. And Frieda was twisted up over looking like she didn't have control over the motel…

I head across the parking lot and slide the card key into the lock before I get to dwelling. When I first enter, the room looks like I remember them all looking: bathroom door to the right when you walk inside, then a big square room with sand-colored carpet. Everything usual about the room stops as soon as I get through the vestibule, though. The room smells like wet pine trees, and underneath that, there's just a hint of smoke. There's an off feeling under my right forepaw, and when I look down at the floor, I blink. The carpet is the same dull, homey beige I'm used to, but directly underneath my feet is something different. In scattered patches around the room, the normal too-thin fibers have been replaced with areas of what look like tan scribbles of crayon, complete with flecks of white paper peeking out where the mess of lines doesn't quite mesh.

The crayon is spread across the rest of the room, too. On the left wall are two beds, side by side, sheets covered in rocket ships, with a nightstand between them that's just a cube of brown crayon wax. On the right-hand wall, there's the usual chest of drawers, but the TV sitting on top of it is half flatscreen and half one-dimensional black scribble. The blades of the ceiling fan have been replaced with long, irregular ovals in a not-quite-matching shade of brown, and one of the bedside lamps is just two lines of black connected to a yellow triangle, a black exclamation point where the pull-switch should be. This room is warped enough that it still hasn't returned to normal. Whatever Friend did this had stayed here for quite some time before they left.

Crayon, though? There isn't a lot of crayon in the Stillreal. Imagination is strong; Friends are full-color even when all you have in the craft box is the basic Crayola set. This Friend is from a person whose formative years revolved around drawing with crayons, or someone who works in a crayon factory… or whose dead kid drew them a picture right before the accident…

No. I'm off in Theory Town. I need to be here. Detective time.

Smell first: The pine-tree scent permeates the whole room, but as I get closer to the center of the room the smells gets more mixed up, the trees losing the nose-war to the smoke. It smells dirty, like someone burned a pile of oily rags. The stink is strongest between the beds, so I head there to have a look.

Sight: The bottom drawer (er, rectangle) of the nightstand is open. I lean up to take a look inside one of the badly drawn drawers and find the usual comic book, weighed down by a crayon-etched brown disc. I get the disc halfway to my nose before I realize it smells like birthday cake and nuts. By the consistency of it, I think it's a pancake. I drop it back in the drawer, and spin in a quick little circle before I swear that nothing else of interest jumps out. I lean down, poke my head under the farthest bed, and wince as burnt cloth and jet fuel sear my eyes.

The smell of smoke is coming from a pile of bone-white ashes heaped under the bed. Sitting next to the ashes, brim up, is a blue policeman's hat.

Officer Hot.

I scurry out from under the bed. I need to get out, but the bathroom door is between me and the outside, and I didn't check in there before I put it between me and the only exit. I back up to the far wall, torn between charging through and finding something to think me back to my apartment, and freeze when I feel something sharp and fragile under my left hindpaw. I step forward, and somehow don't yelp when I hear the light rattle of porcelain against porcelain.

The carpet on the far side of the beds is covered in broken dishes.

I barrel for the door at full prehistoric speed, toss it open and slam it shut and keep on running. I can surf the sign back to the Motel Turing, from there back to Playtime Town. I can report the murder of Officer Hot, and then find an Idea with a giant armored fortress to hide in until this all blows over.

And then I remember Freedom Frieda. I put my head down and beeline across the lot to the front office, praying Frieda's person didn't make the door impenetrable. The obliging wood explodes into splinters as I make contact. Well, that's one thing going right for me today.

Frieda lunges out of the back room, eyes electric blue. She's not asking questions. She doesn't need to.

"We need to go," I say.

Frieda's eyes shuttle through shades of blue. "Where will we go?" she asks, voice cracking.

"Playtime Town. We've got plenty of rooms there." Even some that people haven't died in yet.

"I–" She looks around, eyes strobing out pain.

Behind me, the door to Room 303 shatters. I know what's coming, so I leap up onto the reception desk and grab Frieda by a wing. I turn around, looking for the motel sign, and instead see the inevitable dark, long-coated figure standing stock-still in the parking lot.

This version of the Man in the Coat is, as expected, dolled up like the motel. He's skinny to the last one's broad, an all-elbows beanpole, his coat and hat done up in brown and tan desert camo. He has two bats: short, stumpy things made out of hammered copper. But the eyes are the same poisonous, hateful green, and they're looking right at me.

Big Business sent me to Room 303. Big Business also said Officers Hot and Cold 'presumably' left from Room 303. If I'd been paying attention instead of patting myself on the back for forcing him to talk to me, I might have seen it. I'm not sure if I'd have believed it, though.

Big Business knew the Man in the Coat was here. He wasn't sending me here because it would help me crack the case. He was sending me here hoping it would kill me.

I want to know what I did that was bad enough he would do this, but answering that question will be easier if I still exist. I weigh my bad options against my worse ones. I can't see the motel sign from here, and, based on previous encounters, I'm not going to move anywhere near as fast as he is, especially not while I'm dragging a screaming eagle. Detective stuff knocks on the front door of my brain, and I glance up at the photos on the wall. Me, raising a soda with Frieda and Spiderhand; Rocky and Lloyd, hand in hand, stroking their chins in comic villainy; a sepia-toned one of Golem Jones near the bottom, rocky hands clutched around a glass of wine and a pita, fisherman's vest and yarmulke looking the same as ever… oh, hey. Thanks, detective stuff.

"Hold on, Frieda," I say.

The Man in the Coat must have heard me, because he takes off at a speed that makes the last one look like a turtle. I slam the door, forgetting just long enough about the hole I've already punched in it. Bits of wood and drywall pepper me as he widens the opening with his bats, and Frieda's screams hit an entirely new octave as I think us out of there and over to Golem Jones' shack, now with complimentary shocked expression. Jones stands frozen, in the middle of collecting paperwork from a flying (and very surprised) cloud of marbles.

"Jonesy," I say, bright and breathless. "You remember Freedom Frieda?"

Jones gawps at us. Frieda's expression isn't much different, her eyes turning full revolutions in their sockets as she takes everything in.

Frieda draws in a long, deep breath, and starts sobbing.

I step closer to her, let her rest a wing on me. The crying doesn't stop, but she's less tense, anyway.

The marbles say something to Jones in a Semitic language I don't understand. Jones gives them a workmanlike smile and shoves a new clipboard their way. They give me and Frieda an entitled glower before they float over to a nearby bench to deal with the fresh bureaucracy.

"Who's that?" I ask, still letting Frieda rest her weight on me.

"The Kingdom of Living Marbles," Jones rumbles. "Going to be rough adapting to the Stillreal."

"Is it smooth for any of us?" I ask.

Frieda's sobs start to wane, bringing me back to the unpleasant and not-unrelated business at hand.

"She's going to need a room," I say.

"She has a room," Jones says, a stone eyebrow cocked her way. "A couple dozen of them, in fact – what in the true name of God is Freedom Frieda doing in Playtime Town?"

I open my mouth, but go quiet when Frieda gives me a gentle warning squeeze.

"There was a man," she says, her eyes sickly blue with fear.

"A man?" Jones asks.

"A man," she quavers, "all in brown." She looks down at her wings, and her eyes shift to sunrise pink. "He chased off all my guests. I was hidin', but Tippy–"

"Tippy saved you," Golem Jones says. A little *de rigeur* in tone, if you ask me.

"He did," says Frieda. "I'm... grateful."

"Why couldn't you just leave?" Jones asks.

Frieda looks at him like he proposed growing two extra heads. "I run the Freedom Motel," she says. "They count on me... all those poor Friends, walkin' right into that man's trap?" Against expectations, her eyes shift to red. "I had to be sure no more were comin'. I had to be sure word got out. I couldn't just... I couldn't leave them..."

I sort of wondered why Frieda was hanging out in the back room instead of the front desk.

"Yeah," Golem Jones says. "Yeah... I understand that." He gives her a long, uncertain look, and turns away to the wall of keys, mumbling to himself.

It's about now that my emotions catch up to me. Guilt about Frieda, mostly, but also a nice swirl of confused fury at Big Business' attempted hit. I have a tidal wave of questions for Frieda, but I keep coming back to the obvious one: how long were you trapped in that office? When I consider asking it, I know I can't ask her anything at all. Not today.

"Jones will get you set up," I say to her.

"Set up?" Frieda asks, shocked back into white.

"He'll get you a place to stay." I mean, I know we have at least one vacancy…

Frieda blinks. "I… stay?"

"An apartment." The word I don't dare say is 'home.' "He's going to need to ask you some questions. Have you fill out some paperwork." I swallow. "He can pick a place that'll be good for a short-term stay."

Frieda smiles, but it's thin and fake, like someone doing a bad impression.

"You don't need to pretend in front of us," I say.

Frieda stops, baffled. She sniffs, and gives me a wan smile. "I always did like you, Tippy."

I hesitate, questions lining up to spill out of my mouth. I dismiss them with a shake of my head. "I've always liked you too, Frieda. Please, let Jonesy take care of you."

"My name is not Jonesy," Golem Jones says, back still turned to us.

I give Frieda a sarcastic wag of the brows – this guy, right? – tip an imaginary hat to her, and turn to leave, only to freeze at a sound that I've heard way too recently to be hearing it again: the long, high whine of a Playtime Town police siren.

I'm tired. I've had my life threatened twice today, and someone I've worked with for a long time is dead, and basically my entire world-view has been thrown into question. So you'll forgive me when I tell you that I stand there as confused and slack-jawed as Jones, Frieda, and the Kingdom of Living Marbles, wondering with mounting horror what could have Officer Cold out and running the siren like this.

The familiar armored van comes careening up the street, sending a pair of monitor lizards fleeing into an alley as it swerves up onto the curb and bears down on me, taking out a street sign before it screeches to a halt ten feet away. Officer Cold lunges out the driver's side door, his freeze ray already unholstered and glowing blue. He looks at me, his expression either triumphant or hungry. That, unfortunately, is when it clicks.

"Officer?" I say.

"You're under arrest."

CHAPTER THIRTEEN

Officer Cold cuffs my forelegs with a set of golden handcuffs. They leave my hindlegs free, but a tingle of magic saps my strength to the approximate level of a wet noodle.

"Why am I under arrest?" I ask.

Officer Cold circles behind me. "Conspiracy. Fraud. Assault. Obstruction of justice. And murder." He gives me a get-moving prod with the freeze ray. It's even colder than I expected.

"I didn't murder–"

"Save it for the judge," Cold says, and gives my tail a prod that carries a distinct note of 'last warning.'

Cold's parking job has attracted basically all of Playtime Town. I see Rocky, Spiderhand, and the Sadness Penguins, but the face that stands out to me is Golem Jones. He doesn't look curious, or angry; he looks overwhelmed and, even more painfully, disappointed.

Cold opens the back of the van, gestures for me to hop in. I oblige, head held high, hoping confidence will make everyone think I'm innocent. As Cold closes the door I see Spiderhand, waving frantically at me before I disappear from sight. His earnestness hurts worse than the look on Jones.

"What makes you think I did it?" I ask through the barred window.

Cold just starts the van and pulls out onto Virtue Street, headed downtown.

"Evidence fall in your lap?" I ask. "Elemental's intuition?"

There's a glance my way, but that's it. I don't pursue the matter any further; my day's bad enough as it is.

We stop at the Police Station in record time. Cold hops out, throws the doors open, and beckons me with the gun to get out of the van. I do as instructed, and we get through the front door, past the front desk, and most of the way to the stairs before I pause. I don't hear any footsteps but mine.

I take a calculated risk, and turn around. Officer Cold is stopped in front of the two desks, staring at one of them so intently it looks like he's memorizing it. His mouth is pulled down in his usual disapproving frown, but his eyes are two black pits, like he's been washing his face with permanent marker. He's not stuck in his original pain, he's somewhere beyond that. He's half of a pair that will never be a pair again. My heart's broken, and the way this case is going I'm not reaching for the duct tape yet.

"I'll miss him, too," I say.

Cold looks at me, and I immediately know I've made a mistake. The loathing in his eyes could peel paint.

"Downstairs. Now."

Cold points the ray at me as he advances, forcing me to hustle downstairs or be run over. Even going double-time, he runs into me at the bottom. He growls as he shoves me into an empty cell.

"Why do you think *I* killed him?" I ask.

Cold pauses, the key still half-turned in the lock. He shakes his head, locks the door, and starts back toward the stairs.

"Seriously, why me?"

He looks back at me, considering whether just shooting me would be easier than having this conversation. "You know the Freedom Motel."

"Everyone knows the Freedom Motel," I say.

"But not everyone was an eyewitness when Spindleman died," he spits back. "You're the only one who's been to both places where we've had a… a death."

I've got him arguing, at least. This is a place where I can seize the high ground. (Sometimes.) "Big Business travels all over the place," I say. "And Dr Atrocity, she can do almost anything you can think of if she's got a lab–"

"Oh, I know Big Business is involved, too," Cold insists, his lip curling.

"And what, because I went to meet with him, I'm involved? Officer, when have you ever even known me to be violent?"

"If you think it'll get you to a clue?" he says. "Very."

"I'm not violent!" I protest. Tires screech in the back of my mind. I shake, trying to force them back out. "Not really… not like the Man in the Coat…" Not now, please, not now.

"The Man in the Coat," Cold says. He steps closer, swinging the freeze ray with a casual ease I am not at all comfortable with. "You know, funny thing about that." He gets right up next to the bars, glares through them with those haunted eyes. "The only time other Friends have seen this man of yours? You were there, too."

"What? But you–"

"I wasn't there," Officer Cold blurts, with the special intensity of pure, uncut denial. "I was in a different room, I was looking at a–"

The last word vanishes in a tightly drawn breath. Cold rakes an arm across his eyes, and quickly re-draws his bead on me with the freeze ray. "I felt him die, you monster. I. Felt. Him. Die."

My stomach is a dried-up riverbed. "I'm so sorry, Col – Officer. I'm so sorry."

"Are you?"

"I didn't have anything to do with it," I insist.

His eyes open flying-saucer wide. "Prove it."

I go to fire off a comeback, and come up empty. He's right. The only Friend who can prove I'm not connected to the Man in the Coat is Big Business – and judging by today, I doubt he's interested in saving me.

Cold sniffs in satisfaction, holsters his freeze ray, and walks off toward the stairs again.

"Don't bother trying to think out of here," he calls over his shoulder. "No one in those handcuffs can escape."

"I kind of sort of figured," I reply. "You're mean, but you aren't careless."

Cold's teeth grind. He stalks up the stairs, leaving me alone with the shadows. I limp to the back of the cell, and I sit, letting my thoughts drift while I consider options for escape.

There's no telling how long I'm going to be in here. Suspects in Playtime Town are held until Judge Stoneface is ready to try them, and that can take anywhere from a few hours to whenever the officers remember to tell him. Cold might drag it out in spite, or just because he's busy being the only cop left in town. My life isn't over, but it sure as heck is on pause. Which is great timing, what with an actual killer on the loose.

I'm just considering what kind of daring breakout I could pull off with a single loose rock and a crushing sense of dread when I hear a scuffling movement from the cell on my left. I recognize the Snitching Snipe's odor before I recognize his shape: dirt, bird droppings, and layers of cigar smoke, like some kind of olfactory lasagna. He lumbers up to the bars between our cells, gawking at me with those unblinking bloodshot eyes.

"You didn't kill Hot," he warbles, cocking his head to one side.

I am not in the mood to have this conversation. "Officer Cold thinks I did, and in the end that's all that matters."

The Snipe cocks his head one way, then the other, and shakes out his filthy feathers. "Why's he think you killed Hot?"

"Does it really matter?"

The Snipe widens his eyes again, gazing at me with unceasing intensity. "You didn't kill Hot."

"I'm glad at least someone believes me."

"Not belief. Truth."

My detective stuff kicks in. The Snipe is speaking with the weight of the absolutely certain. Suddenly, this conversation fits my mood.

"How do you know that?" I ask, struggling to my feet, trying to decipher the language of his face.

The Snipe shrugs. "Ear to the ground," he says.

"What?"

"Ear to the ground," he repeats, without a lick of annoyance. "It hears things."

"Things."

"About crime," the Snitching Snipe says. Finally, mercifully, he blinks.

My thoughts rotate a couple times around my brain stem. I'm processing what he's implying, but I'm not sure I want to be. "You have a literal ear to the ground that tells you about crime?"

"Not literal," he says. "Just… an ear to the ground."

"Is this like my detective stuff?"

The Snipe just stares.

"My… detective stuff?" I say. I'm mystified. He hasn't heard about Detective Tippy's detective stuff? "My extra sense? My gift from my person?"

"Yes," the Snipe says.

"So you have heard of it?"

"No. Yes," he says.

"And what's on second?" I say, as sarcastic as I can.

"What?"

I'm about to steer us away from my regrettable wit addiction, but my next thought hides at the sound of footsteps on the stairs.

Officer Cold's freeze ray is still holstered, but the look on his face says that isn't because he's relaxed. He looks like someone's been feeding him a steady diet of salt. He walks past the Snipe's cell without a glance the bird's way, and stops in front of mine.

"Are you ready to talk?" he asks. His face is still dark, but it's a colder darkness, closer to the disgust he used to show me during interrogations.

"You mean confess? Because I'll confess, sure." I clear my throat. "I don't always tip twenty percent at Mr Float's."

Officer Cold's lip curls. "A good officer is dead, Tippy."

"And a good nightmare, too. And it's awful." I work overtime to soften my voice. "But I didn't do it."

"The Man in the Coat killed Hot," squawks the Snipe.

Officer Cold gives the Snipe the same contemptuous look he gave me when I said I missed his partner. He resets his face to the usual Cold annoyance, waves a dismissive hand at the Snipe. The Snipe goes back to pecking at a spot under his wing like nothing has changed.

"I don't think you killed Hot," he says. He gives me a leer like he's just caught me in his trap. "I think you had him killed."

What is with this week? "Why the heck would I want to do that?" I blurt. "He was a jerk, sure, but–"

"Exactly," Cold snickers. "That's exactly why."

I puff up my chest. "Okay, Sherlock Snowman. You want to show me some proof?"

"Why else would you have been at both murder scenes?"

"Because I'm a detective?"

Cold stands up tall and triumphant "And who hired you?"

"I don't need to be paid to help people."

"Not historically, no," he says, twisting the knife. "But historically, no one's been able to permanently kill a Friend, either."

For a second, I watch him, really watch. The set of his shoulders is from someone who is dead certain he's won, but his teeth are still gnashing together, and at the very back of his eyes, where no one can hide what they really feel, there's doubt.

"Okay, Cold," I say, sitting down and trying to act casual. "I'll play. For old times' sake." Yeah, slather on that guilt. "Why don't you tell me exactly how I committed this crime?"

Cold starts pacing back and forth in front of my cell as he explains. "You got the nightmare done-in first. Knowing you, you probably thought he was a risk to Playtime Town. Something off about him; you found out when you investigated."

"Spindleman was an it," I say, "not a he. And what, after I arranged its murder, I creatively made sure I was there to witness the killing and try desperately to help my own victim?"

"You had to confirm the kill." He jabs a finger in my direction. "Being a witness did that, and trying to save it established your alibi."

I glance over at the Snipe, give him a look of are-you-seeing-this-too? The Snipe is too busy staring at Cold to share it with me.

"Then Officer Hot and I started looking into it," Cold continues. "So you got your buddy in the big hat to take us out too, before we could figure out you were involved. But you didn't count on Hot going in alone."

His delivery keeps going more and more off; he's powering through his sentences, gasping for air when he should be breathing. It's the delivery of someone who needs to get his thoughts out before his brain has time to really reflect on them. I try to make him pause.

"And Big Business figures into this master plan… how?"

Cold steps on his verbal gas pedal. "Big Business is the most connected Friend in the Stillreal. He's how you arranged all this. You were probably thinking over to see him when I nabbed you, right?"

"No," says the Snipe.

Officer Cold misses one beat, but only one. I try to work the opening the Snipe has left me.

"There were other murders before you dragged me in," I say. "I didn't know about them. You were mad when Hot told me."

"Wouldn't be the first crook who played ignorant under interrogation," Cold responds, like it's obvious.

I give Cold a long, careful study. He studies me back, looking down his nose, his arms crossed in victory. I take a deep breath, and I pick at the loose thread.

"So… I hired a nightmare to kill another nightmare, and I used Big Business to find me the one nightmare who could make it permanent?" I try not to get too sardonic. I mostly succeed.

"Not a nightmare," the Snipe gobbles, to no reaction from Officer Cold.

"Precisely," says Officer Cold, but there's a wild look in his eyes that says he already knows what's coming.

"And I hired the same hitman to rub out you and Officer Hot – knowing that the hitman was capable of making this permanent somehow, that you would be gone forever, not just on the shelf for a little while – but with this somehow being that important to me, I executed a plan that not only required you two to go to a very specific place that I couldn't be sure anyone would think to check, but that also put Freedom Frieda, one of my oldest friends, in danger?"

Cold's lip twitches in time with his eyebrows.

"Then, when I was done with that chess game, I decided to think straight back to my co-conspirator's very public, very easy to find place of business, without making any effort to shake a tail."

Officer Cold's lower lip is doing its best to swallow the rest of his face, and his eyes are about ready to climb down and punch me.

"We both want to catch this guy, Cold. We both hate what happened to Officer Hot."

"You knew we were going to check the Freedom Motel," he spits, making up for incoherence with velocity.

"How did I know that?"

"Because you knew that was–" He stops, claps his hand over his mouth. "You knew. You knew that would be where we'd go to follow up on the Spindleman murder."

There's my opening. "You think that because you know Spindleman wasn't the first victim. But I didn't."

Officer Cold takes a step back, and breaks eye contact with me. "You knew," he insists, with the ragged rage of someone who has just discovered how wrong they are.

"I didn't know," I say, face pressed up to the bars.

He turns and stalks back toward the stairs. "Yell when you're ready to stop lying, you damn liar!"

I slump back from the bars, shaking my head to clear the curse-burn in my horns. I guess 'Christ' isn't the only swear word he knows. Upstairs, I hear something big slam into something bigger, then the shuffle of papers falling to the floor. I do not envy whoever has to clean up that mess.

I take a few seconds for my heart to start working properly, then I turn to the Snipe, and ask the most obvious question.

"What do you mean, 'not a nightmare'?"

The Snipe looks me in the eye. Then looks me in the eye some more. Then, for variety, he looks me in the eye.

"The Man in the Coat," he finally says. "Not a nightmare."

"He's not?"

"A friend."

"We're all Friends."

"A real friend," the Snitch insists, some of the first emoting he's ever bothered to do.

"What?"

"Friend," he says. "Companion. Not tormentor."

Well that's the next step after unsettling. "What exactly do you mean?"

The Snitch shrugs. "Just repeating what I hear."

"From the ground?"

He gives me another silent stare that takes me just to the edge of my patience.

The word 'creators' fundamentally doesn't make sense. Ideas don't belong to more than one person. Even collaborators who both love an Idea Real are going to have their own spins on the Friend that results. It's possible the Snipe is wrong, or is being misleading by accident. But then again, I've seen three different versions of the Man in the Coat already; multiple creators would fit with that. It doesn't explain why two of them seem to have warped to fit the Idea they're living in, and it doesn't explain all the broken dishes, but it's a start.

The Snitching Snipe has gone back to picking at whatever's bothering him under his wing. I guess it's up to me to carry this conversation.

"How do you know he's a 'real Friend'? Who said that?"

"Big Business," the Snipe says.

And thus did the Snipe get my undivided attention. "You've talked to Big Business?"

"Heard," he chirps. "Not talked. Only last few months, though. Mostly can't hear him."

A whole maze of possibilities opens up in my mind. "Why can't you hear him?"

"Only hear people when they talk about crime," the Snipe replies.

He hears about crimes in other Ideas? Why am I not strip-mining this bird for data already? I have to reconsider my entire approach to… everything. For now, though, I have questions to ask. "What crime was Big Business doing?"

"Lying to police."

"Hot and Cold already talked to Big Business about the murders?"

"Three months, three weeks, two days, eight hours, fifty-five minutes ago."

And drop goes the jaw. "Three *months*?"

"Three weeks, two days, eight–"

"Right," I say, before he can get going. "But, the big story. This has been going on for three months?"

The Snipe blinks. "Four."

"Four?!"

"Four months, one week–"

"Snipe, that is not useful data right now." I try to hide my frustration. "But thank you for providing it," I add hastily. "Do you know who the first victim was?"

The Snipe shakes his head. "No name. Person didn't have a chance to give them one."

That is one of the worst sentences I have ever heard. "Where?" I ask, barely a whisper.

"New place. Doesn't have a name."

That's another one.

"Where else?" I ask, wondering if Worst Sentence Number Three is coming.

The Snitching Snipe shakes his head, flaps his wings a little. "Mostly new Ideas. New Friends. The Freedom Motel. A few less populated places." His eyes scan me up and down. "Until now."

I sit there with my jaw frozen in place. This is the kind of case you talk about at the Rootbeerium afterwards. Really, this is the kind of case where you hope that you even *get* to the Rootbeerium afterwards. While I let it swirl around in my head, I twig back to something he said before Officer Cold buttonholed me. "You said I didn't kill Hot."

"You didn't."

"Then who did?"

"The Man in the Coat."

This is infuriating. I try to picture something calming, like being out of this cell. "Right, but, can you – can you sense peoples' motives or something?"

He nods, pecks at a wing. I didn't want to ask this next question, but…

"What's the Man in the Coat's motive?"

"Anger," the Snipe says. "The Man in the Coat is angry."

"Angry about?"

"The Stillreal." He says it with finality.

I swallow the ostrich-egg-sized lump in my throat, and ask the obvious question. "What about the Stillreal makes him angry?"

For the second time today, the Snipe blinks. "It exists."

I'm steeling myself for the next question, but again, I'm interrupted by footsteps coming down the stairs.

"You ready to talk?" Officer Cold asks. He's shakier than he was last time, teeth set tighter, more fear on his face.

"I'm always ready to talk to you, my friend," I purr.

Officer Cold winces, grips the bars of my cell. "I know you had something to do with this."

I sit back down in the same place I sat when he came down the first time. "You're right," I say.

Cold's eyes flutter. He's surprised to hear me say it so plainly.

"I'm trying to keep it from happening again."

Officer Cold takes a death-grip on the bars. "It can't happen again with you in here."

"It can and in all likelihood it's going to." I limp closer to the bars, hoping the lights in the hallway will let him see the sincerity on my face. "Officer Cold, your partner died at the hands of someone's Friend. Someone's incredibly powerful, totally unique, ludicrously dangerous Friend. And that Friend is going to keep doing what they are doing until we stop them."

Officer Cold growls. "There is no 'we,' here, Tippy. Playtime Town PD doesn't ally itself with malcontents like you."

"Does it ally itself with malcontents like the Snitching Snipe?"

For one spare second, Officer Cold's eyes flick over to the cell next to mine. He looks back at me, but too fast. We're on the home stretch.

"You got those Friends killed," Officer Cold says.

"He didn't," says the Snipe.

Officer Cold doesn't look at him again, but his glare my way does get sharper. I answer him with a shrug.

"The Snitching Snipe always speaks the truth," I say. "If selectively. If you want to know more, you can–"

Officer Cold pulls the freeze ray out of its holster so fast he can barely control its trajectory. The barrel bangs against the bars of my cell and he stumbles backwards, shaking his jarred hand.

"You did it!" he says, shaking the glowing gun at me. "You did it and I am going to prove you did it."

"He didn't do it," the Snipe squawks.

Officer Cold turns the ray on him, and the Snipe jets backward into the shadows, invisible except for his bloodshot eyes.

"You did it," Cold says to me. "I'm going to get you in front of Judge Stoneface, and we are going to put you in prison, and this is going to stop."

"The Man in the Coat did it," I say.

"You hired the Man in the Coat."

"With what?" I ask. "A favor from the Stillreal's new ultimate pariah?"

He rattles the freeze ray again. "Don't test me, Tippy."

"Why, because you'll fail?"

And then he tries to shoot me.

The freeze ray whines, fires an electric blue beam into my cell. I flatten out just in time, and the beam hits the back wall, leaving behind a hockey-ready shell of ice. Officer Cold drops the ray and steps back, goggling at the winter wonderland he's just created. For a second there's a glint of regret in his big blue eyes, but it's quickly replaced by the same brittle rage he's been throwing down all day.

"Go talk to the Sadness Penguins," I say. "Go talk to Farmer Nick Nefarious. I intervened because Spindleman was in danger. I–"

Cold scoops up the freeze ray, opens the door to my cell, and marches right for me. I won't lie, I just about charge him right there, but something in his eye keeps me standing still. At least I'll die thinking the best of people?

Officer Cold grabs my forelegs, yanks the cuffs free, and points to the stairs, all without looking up from the floor.

"Um," I say. I edge closer to the door. "Um."

"Just go, damn it!" He shouts it into my face, then realizes that this requires looking at me and retreats to the wall, face once more aimed at the ground.

The idea that pops into my head is absolutely ridiculous. Fortunately, I'm no stranger to that, so I ask, "Do you need a hug?"

First he looks like he's going to shoot at me again. Then he looks like he's going to throw me back in the cell. And then he hugs me.

It's not a great hug, all things considered. Not only is he literally at the freezing point, it's pretty obvious Cold has no idea what physical affection looks like or how it works. But I grit my teeth through the plummeting temperature and the apparently endless elbows, and I give him the hug he needs.

"No one is going to miss him like you do," I whisper, right before we detach.

His expression is as flat as ever, but there's a smile in his eyes, at least.

This isn't what I'm supposed to do. I'm supposed to be a rough and tough detective. But it feels... right? Like everything else in my heart right now, I file it away for later. There will be time enough in the dryer. If I survive.

Before I leave, I turn back to the Snitching Snipe's cell. "Hey, Snipe?"

Bloodshot eyes open in the darkness. I nod to make sure we see each other.

"Can you help Officer Cold out? He's going to need help running down criminals. You could make a real difference."

The Snipe looks at me, looks at Cold. "Much as I can."

Officer Cold gazes into the cell. "Getting info out of the Snitching Snipe was Officer Hot's job."

"And now it's yours," I say.

Cold looks at me, and for a second he's ready to lock me up again. My sympathy only goes so far when it comes to cops, but I feel like extending myself right now is a good idea.

"He'd be proud of you for handling it." I pay him the courtesy of looking away, and turn again to the eyes in the dark. "And hey, Snipe? Thank you. You might have saved a lot of people."

"That's my job," the bird declares from the darkness.

I think to myself that I'll never disregard a background character ever again. And then I think to myself that if I had thought that a couple days ago, Spindleman might still be alive.

I walk upstairs, out the door, and into the moonlight, trying to stay ahead of my feels.

Even at night, Playtime Town is bright. The moon is never new here, and the city is always lit up with lollipop-shaped street lamps, cozy windows where pies cool and kittens snooze, signs advertising candy shops and ball pits and naptime parlors. Normally, the bright is welcoming, but right now it feels gaudy. All the illumination just means it's easier to see the worry on everyone's faces as I pass them by on the street. It's gotten worse since I got arrested. Or maybe since the Friend who helped most of us find a home got driven here by unspeakable evil. I head back toward my apartment, pause at the intersection of Grin Street and Harmony Avenue, and look up at the moon as I consider my options.

I could chug root beer until an idea comes to me. I could listen to Spiderhand play piano. I could spin in the dryer six or seven times. Ultimately, though, none of that will help me feel right again, or fix the looks on the passersby. What will help is solving this case. I need to know who caused the crayon warping in the motel room, and why the Man in the Coat leaves behind the broken dishes, and why Big Business thought sending me into an ambush was a good idea.

With the day I've had so far, getting angry at Big Business seems like a reasonable next step. So away I go, against my better judgment.

CHAPTER FOURTEEN

I surf the moon over to Chrometown, then ride that moon to its buddy in the Heart of Business. It's still almost closing time here, which means everyone in the office buildings is in a frenzy to finish their work before the end of day that never comes. (Have I mentioned that I hate this place?)

I have trouble staying angry – I'm more of a 'justice' Friend than a 'vengeance' one – but focusing on the part where I almost actually died keeps the militant spring in my step as I march into Big Business' tower and straight up to Front Desk. She looks at me with a blank, dazed expression.

"Name?" she asks, but you can tell her heart's not in it.

"The guy Big Business tried to have killed."

Whatever emotion she was mustering slacks right off her face.

"Detective Tippy," I say. "I need to talk to Big Business about a matter of great import–"

"Mr Big is very busy today," she insists.

"Great. Import."

She turns to her computer, starts blazing away at her keyboard. "I'm sure he'll fit you in if he can. Let me see when his next appointment is."

"Tell him Detective Tippy is here. He's going to want to see me."

"Mr Big is very busy." She's avoiding eye contact almost as much as Officer Cold.

"It's about the Man in the Coat."

Front Desk's eyes widen in time with her mouth, but she keeps her neck rigid, still avoiding looking at me. What's she hiding?

"I'll see if I can reach him," she says. She presses a few buttons on a phone I can't see, and waits through seven rings for someone to pick up. Detective stuff catches that the voice on the other end isn't Big Business. He's a warm, confident tiger purr; this person sounds like iced-over ashes.

"Detective Tippy is here to see Mr Big," Front Desk says. "He says it's about the thing."

'The thing.' The idea that they have a code word for the Man in the Coat doesn't fill me with happy thoughts.

The person on the other end responds, half-doubting, half-interrogating. The voice is raspy, so quiet that no sense I have can pick up their exact words.

"Yes, the thing." Front Desk sounds annoyed and defensive. "Yes, Detective Tippy." She's being yelled at, and she's not sure the yeller is allowed to do that.

"What?" She stands up out of her chair. I wasn't sure Front Desk was physically capable of that.

"No. No, he can't–" She's shaking her head furiously. "He can't – can't *do* that. He can't – he can't–"

The phone clicks over to dead air. Front Desk looks at me, and it's not quite the blank look I got when I derailed our last conversation. That was shock. This is despair.

"That was… one of the fact-finders," she says. Her voice is stilted and stony, gliding up and down in pitch. She's off-script in a big way. "It… hung up on me."

I'm guessing I know the answer, but, "Is Big Business up there?"

She leans on the desk for support, keeping her eyes on her computer like it might tell her what to think next.

"Is Big Business up there?" I repeat.

Front Desk struggles to find words. "The fact-finder said… Big Business is… on vacation?"

On vacation. Right after I find out he knew about the murders. Right. Not suspicious at all. Not infuriating. Or cowardly.

Front Desk sits back down, and stares at her monitor like it's suddenly written in another language. I step out to a non-threatening distance from her, and clear my throat.

"Front Desk?"

She turns to me without a shift in expression.

"Do you keep Mr Big's appointment book for him?"

Her mouth opens an inch or so, but otherwise, no response.

"Appointment book?" I ask. "Or like… a calendar on the computer? The Internet?" I shake my head, clearing out the desire to charge as a memory of an airbag balloons in my head. "Do you have a list of where he goes and when?"

She turns back to her monitor, and looks even more devastated.

"Look," I snap, "I want to help find your boss, and–"

Front Desk flinches, and I stop. What am I doing? Her boss is on vacation. Her world has been turned upside-down almost as badly as Officer Cold's. I take a deep breath, and a new approach.

"How are you doing?"

Front Desk refocuses on me, like she was just looking at a bright light. "What?"

"You're upset, right? This is weird?"

Front Desk blinks. "Mr Big has never gone on… vacation? Mr Big doesn't… take vacations?"

"I wouldn't figure," I say. "Are you going to be okay?"

Her lips pucker. "What?"

"Are you going to be okay?"

"I… don't… this isn't… you aren't… you…" She swallows. "Mr Big doesn't let me keep his calendar. Mr Big… doesn't… let me do much…"

Front Desk's face breaks into the most lost expression I've seen outside the Freedom Motel, and then I realize that from her perspective, the Friend trying to help her right now is the buttface who put a crack in her desk last time. I do the best thing I can think to do, and try to fix this problem.

"Does he give you the power to let people into his office?" I ask. "Because if he does, I might be able to find him."

Front Desk tries to smile, her lips looking like they're doing gymnastics. At least she doesn't look so lost anymore. She presses a couple of buttons on the keyboard, and a little trap door swings open next to me.

"Thank you, Front Desk," I say.

"Find Mr Big," she says. "That's your primary action item."

She's not pausing anymore. I'm marking that a win, if only because I need one.

Big Business' office is all the proof I need that Big Business started as a nightmare. The angles are the giveaway: the whole room's perspective is shifted so the oak desk in front of the floor-to-ceiling window is the central focus, standing bigger and better-lit and more expensive than anything else in the room. The only furniture besides the desk is two chairs, a big, fancy leather one behind the desk, and a bland gray one parked in front of it. The window looks out over the Heart of Business, every street, every building, reminding you that this one is by far the tallest. The other two walls are lined with books, names on their spines like 'POWER' and 'DOMINATION' and 'SUBMIT.' (You know, in case the rest of the room didn't put you in your place.)

I can think of two reasons Big Business would be 'on vacation.' The first is that Big Business is in league with the Man in the Coat, and now that one of his intended victims has survived, he's gone to ground. The other is that the Man in the Coat came after him, and he's either running or he's… the other thing. I'm not sure which thought makes me shudder more, but I'm hoping his office can help me narrow it down.

I start at the desk. From the leather chair it seems even bigger; looking across at the gray chair is like staring down to the bottom of the ocean. What the heck kind of person made this place Real? Unfortunately, that question has to sit unanswered. My job is to look for clues.

There's no smell in here, no taste, no sound; sterile like the rest of the Heart. That leaves sight. There are a bunch of executive office toys clustered on the desk, all polished steel and matte black, totally decadent in their uselessness. The computer is the centerpiece, a sleek black thing that looks like a highly functional spaceship. I hunt for a power switch, but there's nothing. I'm guessing it's some magic gesture only Big Business knows.

I fiddle with the desk toys, turning them over, shaking them, but there are no secret compartments or hidden switches. I rifle the drawers, of which there are about twenty, and do the quickest skim I can manage of the reams of paper stuffed away inside. Contracts, meeting agendas, memos about pencil and coffee usage, expense reports stapled to carbon copies of checks and receipts, all filed in a system that's orderly but opaque, only making sense in that it clearly makes sense to someone else.

Alright, then. I focus on the agendas, starting with the most recent one. It's just two items, written on Big Business' overdone gold-leaf stationery, 'Opening Remarks' and 'Presentation by Fact-Finders on the Current State of the Stillreal.' The previous agenda is the same thing. Third agenda, fourth agenda, fifth, all the same. This is starting to look as fruitless as the hidden compartments idea, until I get to the seventh agenda back. 'Opening Remarks' is the same, and the first 'presentation' is the same, too – but then there's a 'Lunch Break' of thirty-five minutes, and a second presentation just called 'Second Presentation,' directly after.

I shuffle through the rest of the stack, but I have to go back three more months before I see another 'Lunch Break' on any agenda. I've never seen Big Business or the fact-finders eat, and the majority of the agendas corroborate that idea. But there's one near the top of the stack, and one three months ago. What did the Snitching Snipe say? Three months, three weeks, two days, eight hours…

I check the date on the most recent meeting with the lunch break, and compare with the expense reports. I shuffle through receipts for plane tickets, rental cars, hotel rooms. There are a huge number of 'medical expense' receipts even in just the past couple days, leaving a mental picture I'd rather not color in. The receipt for 'funeral expenses' makes me do it anyway.

There's one receipt from the day of the recent lunch break, and one from two days before that. The one from the day of is a receipt from Heart of Business Catering, ordering three six-packs of beer, two pepperoni pizzas, and one crawfish jambalaya. The one from two days before that has a receipt from the Alibi Lounge, logging the cost of twelve beers and three mixed cocktails. Just in case I felt like pretending this clue pointed somewhere else, the address of the Alibi is listed below its logo (a man in a striped shirt and a domino mask, smirking as he sneaks through a doorway stamped with a martini glass): 666 Opportunity Street, Avatar City, California.

My sigh sends me sliding down out of my chair. The Alibi is Avatar City's premier watering hole for superpowered criminals of all shapes, sizes, and preferred victims. It's one of the most dangerous places I could be going that isn't actively trying to kill me, and honestly I'm not so sure it won't be by the time I'm done. But it's also the only clue I have that might point me to Friends who know what Big Business is up to, and the only lead I have to make sure he isn't in danger.

I usually welcome weird trails of clues, strange behaviors, odd cases that take me to far-flung corners of the Stillreal. I usually love adventure. But I'm not usually dealing with my friends being murdered.

I take a deep breath, spin the chair around to face the window, and get comfy while I look for a touchstone to think out of here.

It's supervillain time.

CHAPTER FIFTEEN

The only things more plentiful in the Heart of Business than office buildings are billboards. It takes me less than a second to find an ad for Smiling Heart Cola: a picture of Big Business grinning as he holds up a bottle of soda. It takes only slightly longer to think my way from that to a billboard for Champion Cola – a more angular, dynamic logo, with Superbolt's glowing blue mug holding the bottle instead of Big Business – and I'm standing on a gravel roof, looking down at streets teeming with suit-wearing businessmen and hoodie-shrouded students. Avatar City, I have returned.

I find a fire escape, waddle down to street level, and make my way through the crowd to a less-busy corner where I can get my bearings. From there it's relatively easy to turn myself south, spot the dirtier streets in the distance, and start walking. This is where things get complicated.

Downtown Avatar City is divided into two parts. You've got your shiny, well-lit North End: the Cape and Cowl, Ronell High, Avatar U; plenty of civilians to get in trouble and plenty of wide intersections for super-beings to fight in. And then you've got the South End.

It's easy to tell when you've gone into the South End. You just look for the line where the color palette switches from four-color to different shades of rust. The buildings aren't as tall as they are in the North End, but they loom ten times as big, poised like they're about to fall on you. The buildings are knitted together with alleys that are just horizontal bottomless pits, full of dumpsters and leering people flicking switchblades. The few businesses that aren't boarded up are either sleazy-looking clubs or corner stores that are just there to be robbed. In a way, I'm more at home here than I am in Playtime Town, but no one decent ever feels welcome in the South End for very long. Fortunately, 'decent' isn't the order of the day.

I smell my destination before I see it: old beer, fresh blood and hot metal. The Alibi Lounge. The sign is done up in green neon, the same masked and smirking man I saw on Big Business' receipt. The entrance is a single black door with a bouncer in front of it, a pile of muscles shoved into a coat. She looks at me with eyes just begging for a good fight, quickly decides I'm not going to give it to her, and goes back to glowering at the world like it owes her money. I keep my quip to myself, and head inside.

The interior of the Alibi Lounge is both more over-the-top than the South End at large, and more obviously dangerous. The right half of the room is all bar, a big slab of blonde wood with a big slab of blonde man behind it, keeping the assorted costumed scum from having free rein over the wall of multicolored bottles. The left half is tables and insufficient lighting, yet more costumed people hunched over glasses of this and that. When I say costumed, I mean it in the broadest possible sense. The Friends in this bar are dressed up in all colors of the rainbow, every theme you can put together with tights and a few flourishes. There's a guy who looks like a metal bird of prey, a woman with dyed orange hair and flamethrowers strapped to her wrists, a being that looks like a human-shaped tornado. All of them look at me when I come in, eyes and cameras and other weirder things tracking me through the room. Some are disgusted ("That's so obviously not a villain!"). Some are confused ("Is that a triceratops?"). Some look a little squirrelly ("I think that's Detective Tippy!"). The squirrelly ones are where I set my compass.

There are four Friends at my chosen table. The scrawny guy in the armored backpack and royal blue tights is Azure Armadillo, what I've been told you call a 'D-list' villain, a background character left to rot when his person's art project got an F. The big woman made of spare truck parts is Scrapyard, a bruiser known for cursing a lot and refusing to work with racists. The lean, web-fingered man with the black-and-white mottled skin is K'kota the Man-Gecko. He was a space-pirate originally, but in the Stillreal you take what you can get. The fourth is the one that worries me. She's short and curvy, with eyes the color of a harvest moon and skin the color of brick. She doesn't so much turn to look at me as already have her eyes aimed my way, like she foresaw me coming in. If that's Dame Rouge, and I think it is, she's probably the most dangerous thing in this entire bar.

The second I commit to heading their way, Azure Armadillo stands and backs up a step. Scrapyard grabs his shoulder and pushes him back down. Armadillo is panicked, and getting more so as I get closer to them. Pay dirt.

"Well hello," I say, taking all of them in with the sweep of a paw. "Assorted henchmen. Just what I always wanted." I don't feel guilty saying it, and that's a relief – bad guys are the one place I never need to hold back on the snark.

Scrapyard looks at me like I spilled something on her shoe. Azure Armadillo is still judging the distance to the back door. The other two are impossible to read. The smells at their table are overpowering: vodka, grave dirt and motor oil, which is part of why I have a lot of trouble telling exactly which of the Friends watching me has moved to stand at a table positioned directly behind me.

Dame Rouge clucks her tongue and says, in a bored French accent, "I'm already sick of this conversation."

Skip the banter, straight to derision. That's the move of a bad guy who knows enough they don't want to risk talking to you. I load both barrels of my banter cannon. "I'm going to guess by your friend's need for a sedative that you've been shaken down for information recently?"

Dame Rouge leans back, regarding me like she can't decide what wine to pair with me. "And who exactly is it showing this concern?"

I smile. It's mostly genuine. "I'm looking for the person who did the shaking."

Scrapyard leans against the table, her joints grinding in a way that just can't feel pleasant. "She means, who's askin'?"

I'm a stuffed yellow triceratops; even if my reputation didn't precede me, there'd be no point in lying to them. Besides, if you want results in Avatar City, you play the hero. "Detective Tippy."

That quiets things down a little. There are no dropped bottles, but conversations near us wink out, and the Friends at the bar take up full-time rubbernecking. The one watching me is on the move again, but they're far enough away that I'm not feeling a need to move just yet.

"The stuffed animal detective?" Dame Rouge snorts. "What brings you to the South End?"

"Friends are dying," I say. "And I think you can point me to the guy who knows why."

Azure Armadillo fires uncertain looks at Scrapyard and K'kota. He's ready to say something, but he's hoping someone else will go first.

"People die," says Dame Rouge, which gets a sour look from K'kota.

"Not like this they don't," I say, looking Azure Armadillo's way.

Armadillo has gone to Defcon One; every tell I could ask for is playing out in his body language. I keep my eyes on him as I pluck at the group's nerves.

"The Friend who came in asking questions, he would've been tall. Big hair. Nice suit. Might have been accompanied by either a flock of lawyers or something words can't describe, depending on whether you were looking directly at them?"

That Friend behind me is coming my way – not very fast, but too direct for me to call it coincidence. If they don't know about my detective stuff, this plan is perfect. If they do know, well, death in the Stillreal is usually temporary...

"We don't know who you're talkin' about," Scrapyard says.

"Which means you know exactly who I'm talking about," I shoot back, making my grin extra-broad and double-triumphant. "I just described Big Business. You may know him as one of the most recognizable Friends in the entire Stillreal?"

Scrapyard's eyes narrow, but under the table her foot won't stop tapping. "Dunno. I'm really good at not recognizin' things."

"You really good at covering up murders, too?"

Azure Armadillo puts his head in his hands. "Look, man, we just want to drink in peace."

"So it hasn't been very peaceful lately?" I needle.

Armadillo stammers, reddens. "It's never peaceful in Avatar City," he says, but he knows I'm locked in on him.

"From what I hear," I say, "you're a lot of the reason for that."

K'kota lets out a low hiss. Detective stuff says he's too rigid, too crunched up for simple anger; this is fear turning sour on him.

The Friend behind me is close enough I'm starting to smell them: saltwater, kelp, cheap cigars, and either blood or a diet rich in meat. They're within pouncing distance, and they aren't moving. I clear my throat unsuccessfully, and continue my conversation.

"What's the matter?" I ask K'kota. "Offended at the implication you're a killer?"

K'kota stands up, teeth clenched, webbed hands slammed down on the table. This is perfect. If I get K'kota to look like he's cracking, Armadillo might think the whole house is coming down and spill the beans.

"Listen," I say. "I get that you want to be left alone, but–"

And then the Friend behind me taps me on the shoulder.

I'm an herbivore. I've got a mean charge on me, but I'm not a fighter. On my best day, I can make you think killing me would be too much work. I'm even less of a fighter when I turn around and see the Friend I've been smelling. He looks like a half-man half-shark, and most of him comes from the half that I'd least prefer to encounter. He's enormous, easily five times my size. His skin is slate gray, and his face is about three-quarters teeth. He has a snout so pointed you could use it to open cans and eyes that aren't so much black as 'the absence of hope.' He looks down at me, and says in a voice like a trash compactor, "Detective, huh?" His tone isn't what I'd call curious.

"Yep," I say. "Came over from Playtime Town."

Chairs shriek against the floor as other villains put extra distance between themselves and this mess.

"This is a henchman bar," the shark-man says.

I think I know where this road leads. "And thus the perfect place for me to find henchmen."

"'Thus'?" He says the word with obvious disgust. "That how they talk in Playtime Town?"

"It's how I talk in Playtime Town, so, in a sense, yes?" Unleashing the snark helps me feel a little less terrified. A little.

The shark-man grins. I didn't think it was possible with that face. "We don't like detectives in our bar."

"I'll be happy to leave as soon as I've got my business taken care of."

"You'll only be happy if you leave now."

"I promise, as soon as I finish talking to these Friends, I will go."

I knew he was big, but now I find out he's fast. Webbed hands grab me and pull me up to eye height – or rather, teeth height. The smell of blood is worse this close, and I'm picking up the rest of his diet: wood, metal, cotton stuffing (please, please have my detective stuff be wrong about that last one…).

"Go now," the shark-man says, through his many, many teeth. "Or go when I wash you down with a beer. Your choice." Judging by the tension in the room, this guy is not exaggerating.

Right. Time to make my big play.

"Why are you being so mean?" I ask, as much like a child as I can muster.

His breath hitches, but his voice comes out even angrier. "Not mean," he says. "Hungry."

"Are you 'hungry' with every Friend who comes in here?"

"Only heroes who think they can interrupt our drinking." I can actually hear his teeth grinding together.

"It'll be hard to relax if you eat me."

He lets out an amused grunt. "What, you think I can't digest a set of horns?"

"No, I think it's hard to relax when you've been removed from reality."

His grip tightens. Either I struck a nerve or he's considering his choice of dipping sauces.

"The entire Stillreal is depending on me to get this question answered," I say.

You can tell he doesn't hesitate very often; his face doesn't slack so much as get stuck halfway between a glower and a sneer. "You're lying," he snarls. "You're scared."

"Friends are dead," I say, trying not to look directly at his tongue. "At least three of them. And I don't mean dead like Captain Apogee was dead. I mean gone. Erased from the Stillreal. And these four," I nudge my head to indicate the heaps of flop sweat behind me, "might be the only Friends who can help me get to the bottom of it. You let me go, I'll even bring back a steak for you. Or a salmon. A whole tuna. Just…" The kid in me comes out again. "Just please let me help my friends."

At first, the shark-man keeps me dangling there in front of his wide-open jaws, but after what can't be more than fifty lifetimes, he lets out a blood-scented scoff, and drops me. I have never been so grateful to hit a beer-soaked wooden floor.

"Answer his question," the shark-man says, pointing a gray finger at the four henchmen. The finger spins to point at me. "And then get out."

He stomps away, headed back toward the bar. Halfway there, he's already bellowing out his drink order.

Let them get a head of steam going on their bad guy routine, and then drop the truth right between their eyes. That's how this triceratops deals with predators. And if I do it in front of people, they wind up either impressed or scared of me. Either way, looser tongues.

I get up to my feet, shake off some of the ick from the floor, and look at Azure Armadillo and crew.

"Well?"

Armadillo shakes his head. That look? That's surrender. "Look, only if you promise us that this whole mess never comes back here. The Alibi is the only home a lot of us have."

"I promise I'll do everything I can to make sure you can still get a flight of beer with your criminal conspiracies." I try to make my smile genuine, but with a glint of cleverness. Villains respect a little smarm.

Scrapyard growls. Her eyes drift over to Azure Armadillo, and pretty soon, everyone else's eyes do, too. Armadillo sighs, heavy with regret.

"We're robbers, man. Guns for hire. Working stiffs." He says it with a mix of relief and misery. "But this… if the Doc is making this kind of play, we want to stay clear of it."

"Speak for yourself," Dame Rouge purrs, but underneath I can tell it's all bluster.

The words "the Doc" drop the bottom out of my adrenalin rush. "The Doc?" I say. "As in Doctor–"

"Don't sssay her name," K'kota hisses.

I sweep a look across all of them. "Starts with an 'A' and ends with 'trocity'?"

K'kota flinches. That's a yes.

I find my spine and get a good, solid grip on it. "Exactly what kind of play do you think the Doc is making?"

Scrapyard sighs. It sounds like a steam valve being opened. "Big Business was asking after her because he–"

Armadillo breaks in. "Big Business knew we'd done a job for the Doc recently. He figured that meant we knew where her last lair was, figured we could put him on the right track." He remembers to breathe, and adds, "Don't tell the Doc we told either of you."

"Seriously, don't," Dame Rouge says, with the first edge of fear I've heard from her all night.

"I'll forget if you tell me what kind of job she hired you for."

They all get a little quiet. K'kota, in particular, looks incredibly uncomfortable.

"Robbery," the Man-Gecko says. "What elsssse?"

"What did she have you stealing?"

"Just stuff," says Scrapyard.

"'Stuff'?" I say. "Look, I think we're a little past pretending any of us are clueless–"

"No, no," Azure Armadillo cuts in. "She means it. The Doc sent us out into the Stillreal, said we were just supposed to bring back anything that looked important."

"What did she mean by 'important'?" I'm already connecting the dots in my head.

Scrapyard shrugs. It sounds like an old door opening. "We grabbed a vase from this one house. A brochure from the Freedom Motel. Some wiring. A wrench. Just… *stuff*. Anything that would come with us when we left."

"Don't forget the photographs," Armadillo says.

"Damn it, Dillo!" Scrapyard snaps.

I duck my head so they can't see the pain the curse causes me.

"What?" Armadillo snaps back. "What, you think we should hide it?"

"We could get in serious trouble here," Scrapyard says.

"And exactly which one of us can actually experience pain?" Armadillo turns to me, ignoring her glower. "Doc made us take photographs of everywhere we went, with this special camera she gave us. Said it was… reinforced? It traveled anywhere you thought with it."

That doesn't actually seem out of the realm of possibility for Dr Atrocity. More dots start connecting. "But what is it you think she wants it for?"

Armadillo's face buckles. "I – I don't…"

Dame Rouge sighs, the deep and resonant sigh of annoyance with someone you care about who never stops doing the annoying thing. "The deaths," she says. "Armadillo doesn't want to say it, but the murders."

Scrapyard mugs in disgust.

"We assume Big Business wants to see her because he thinks she's connected," Dame Rouge says.

That's what I thought. That's also what I didn't want to think. "And where and when does Big Business come into this story, exactly?" Sandra taught me to always make them tell you what you already know.

"We ran into him at the motel," says Armadillo.

Or what you don't know.

"He was visiting Freedom Frieda." Armadillo unfocuses, dropping into a memory. "When he saw us, he just kinda… stared…" A terrifying memory, by the twitching of his lips.

"He's always been rude," Dame Rouge interjects.

I'm not so much connecting dots as I am scribbling all over the page. I shake my head and think overconfident thoughts. I just have to get to the end of the conversation, then I can go have a freakout somewhere safe.

"And where did you tell him to go? What's this location I'm going to pretend I never heard about?"

Scrapyard chuckles, but there's no joy in it. "She's outside city limits. Old observatory. Cabbies'll know where it is."

"Flying is faster," says Dame Rouge, "but something tells me you aren't exactly, what's the word? Capable."

"I tried it once. Didn't take." I make a point of turning to Scrapyard and Armadillo. "Thanks for the information. I'll pay you in not knowing who you are."

"Whatever," Scrapyard says. But Armadillo looks grateful.

I walk out of the Alibi, feeling the shark man's eyes on my back until the door closes.

I'll need to walk back uptown to hail a cab, but that gives me time to try to put everything together – even if I don't want to.

Dr Atrocity. That was the one name I really, really didn't want to hear.

CHAPTER SIXTEEN

I hail the first cab I see on the shiny side of town, and take a ride with a gregarious, mustachioed driver out into the mostly empty outskirts of Avatar City. While I'm listening to his life story, I sort through what I know, mix in that disturbing conversation from the Alibi, and hope that wherever I'm going I won't find any clues.

I know that the Man in the Coat can travel freely like any other Stillreal Friend. I know that he leaves duplicates that I can't explain yet. I know that he has multiple creators, not just one. And now I know that not only is Big Business interested in him, but Dr Atrocity is also involved.

Dr Atrocity. Why is it always the most interesting and least appetizing Friends I have to deal with?

Avatar City houses the supervillains, not just the superheroes. The heroes get downtown, but the villains gravitate to the South End. As a result, the South End is a series of block-wide city-states, paying the grunts in the Alibi to wage little turf wars over who gets to build which doomsday device in which abandoned warehouse. But there's not a single Friend anywhere in Avatar City who pretends this is anything but Dr Atrocity's turf.

Atrocity's the number one villain, the greatest in the land, the character who exists to be Miss Mighty's dark opposite, target, and nemesis. Every time Miss Mighty takes her down, she sets up somewhere else.

She'll work with other villains as henchmen or partners of convenience, but none of them intimidate or inspire like the bad doctor. She's evil for evil's sake, make no bones about it. But my biggest concern about her right now is her creations.

Not a lot of Friends can create anything lasting. The Stillreal is too fragmented for things to last unless they were already Real when they showed up. But Dr Atrocity's whole shtick is that she makes Real things; Real things that really hurt people. She's created giant monsters and armies of robots and zombie Popes and every other weird thing you can think of. A few of them have even wound up in other parts of the Stillreal; one of the Popes pours at the Rootbeerium when Mr Float needs a vacation. So if anyone in the Stillreal could create something like the thing – the things – that killed Spindleman and Officer Hot, Dr Atrocity is at the top of a list that consists of her and some question marks. Even the dishes and the clones make some kind of sense if I assume there's a villainous genius behind them that I'm not quite grasping. And if that nebulous part of the puzzle makes me want to dismiss her involvement, there's what the henchmen said.

She wanted important objects and photographs, and that suggests travel. A visual of an Idea is an express ticket right into it. If something important will survive going outside its Idea, perfect, but if not, grab a photograph, and count on Dr Atrocity somehow making it permanent. It's a perfect set-up for a band of dark-coated monsters to slip in and start laying waste with their anti-matter baseball bats, or whatever nonsense Dr Atrocity armed them with.

Azure Armadillo says they did the job a couple months ago. I doubt Armadillo has the Snitching Snipe's sense of timing, but 'a couple months' since they pulled this job for the Doc is tipping past coincidence and into near-certainty.

At least if Dr Atrocity can kill me permanently, I'll die knowing the truth?

To the denizens of Avatar City, I'm sure the Avatar City Observatory makes sense. To outsiders like me, the place is so obviously a villain's lair my detective stuff winds up second-guessing itself. 'Observatory' is technically accurate: it's a silver dome atop a mesa, a telescope peeking out of a gap in the roof. But the dome is ominously backlit no matter which direction you're looking from, and when you look at it from below, it looks like a skull. Avatar City's creator was a teenager; I shouldn't expect too much in the way of subtlety.

I wiggle through a tear in the chain-link gate at the base of the mesa (taking care I don't tear my fabric) and trek up to the summit. The journey is just long enough for me to fully consider what a terrible idea this is, but my other option right now is 'sit around at home and wait to die.' I hate this almost as much as I love it.

About halfway up the mesa, I see the first of the speaker boxes. It's about the size of my head, with a wire-mesh speaker on the front firing off a constant stream of what sounds like sports scores:

"Oakland beats San Francisco, 77-70. St. Louis beats Cleveland, 84-40…" I listen until I'm sure the content is exactly what it sounds like, and keep on walking, one ear open for any kind of change. Around the next bend I run into another speaker box, this one reciting definitions from the dictionary. And around the next bend, an identical box is reading what has to be a book, something about a man in a sheep costume. Next bend it's a recipe for chicken fingers, and the bend after that it's a list of types of hats. No matter how far up I go, there's always someone talking.

It clicks when I run into the seventh speaker box, droning on about how to use a juicer; the noise makes it harder for people to hear what's going on inside the observatory, and the subject matter is boring enough that anyone listening in will dismiss it as unimportant chatter. These are anti-fact-finder devices. Dr Atrocity really is a genius.

Irony being what it is, I think that right as I circle around to the grinning skull of the observatory's front, and find the door has been torn off its hinges. I consider the possibility there are traps in the doorway about the same time as I run through it. I hear a scream down the hall, and any doubt I have shatters in favor of the urge to save somebody.

The main room of the observatory is cavernous, full of high-tech gizmos I can't quite identify. My focus, though, is on the figures standing by the giant laser gun at the far end of the room – or, more accurately, the figures wrestling by it. The laser is a twenty-foot-tall, football-shaped hunk of plastic and metal, wires trailing from it into the board of switches and buttons at its base. Said board is currently the battleground for a fight between Dr Atrocity herself, and two men in business suits who turn into loose conglomerates of claws and eyes every third blink or so.

Atrocity's blood-red medical scrubs are torn at the knees and collar; her raven-black hair falls in sweaty, sloppy waves over the half-metal ski-jump of her face. Her cybernetic eye is flashing red, and her still-human eye, midnight purple, is huge and rolling as she fends off the too-many limbs of the fact-finders. Big Business stands a few feet away, wringing his hands and watching this little display.

"Tell me!" Big Business shouts at the doctor, anger garbling his words.

"I didn't do it!" Dr Atrocity shouts back, in her posh, upturned-nose accent.

"Lying," Big Business hisses, and gestures to the fact-finders, who redouble their efforts to grapple her. "We'll see how well you lie after a laser blast or two, hm? Shall we?"

"I'm – not – lying!" she responds. "I have no reason to lie! I can help you!" The desperation in her voice gives me chills. "I've been studying it, I can help, just–" She pulls an arm free, only to have the fact-finder grab onto her leg. "Just let me go!"

Dr Atrocity is begging. Villains don't beg. Big Business isn't doing so hot either, face coated in sweat, jacket flapping open, tie half-undone. But the big worry is his eyes. He's past angry and into absolute fury, an atomic-hot stare that says he's running on nothing but blind rage.

I have to do something. So I opt for something foolish. "Mr Big?"

Big Business wheels around. His teeth set when he sees me. "You shouldn't be here."

Okay. I've got him focused on me. "What are you doing?"

"Saving us," he gargles, and turns back toward the battle.

"How is killing somebody saving us?"

His shoulders hunch up to his ears. "Friends are dying," he growls. "And this," – he jabs a quaking finger at Dr Atrocity – "this is the woman with the insider knowledge we need." Business-speak to the end.

Dr Atrocity gets her cybernetic arm free, clubs the offending fact-finder away. There's a crackle of electricity as she buries the metal hand in the other one's mass, but before it recoils from whatever nasty bit of science she just did, the other one jumps up and wraps some rubbery, spiny appendage around her throat.

"Tell me what you did," Big Business snarls at her. "Tell me why! Tell me!"

"I didn't do it!" Dr Atrocity bellows. She hooks a finger around the strangling tentacle. "I didn't do it!"

"I get the feeling she didn't do it," I say.

Big Business ignores me. "You lie to the heroes. Now you lie to me." He takes a deep breath that doesn't sound even slightly calm. "Maybe you need some motivation."

Dr Atrocity looks at me, and I see terror in her still-natural eye. "I – I – please – I–"

Front Desk freezes up when people stop their business speak. Dr Atrocity freezes up when she has to ask for help.

"Mr Big," I say. "Would Heart of Business, Incorporated really approve of you undertaking such a drastic–"

"You owe me!"

I shut up because I don't understand what he means. I don't stay shut up because I suddenly do.

"Are you calling in your marker to make me *let you kill somebody*?"

"No one's dying," Big Business says. He won't look at me.

"If anyone appreciates how stressed you are about this, it's me, Mr Big, but–"

I'm cut off by Big Business' half-strangled laughter. He turns toward me again, tugging at the limp knot of his tie. "No you don't," he says. "You don't know the burden of leadership. You aren't someone people look to when they want to see innovative solutions. You aren't known for–"

"I'm known for helping people," I say. "Which is what I'm trying to do. Also, we agreed my favor to you would not involve any crimes."

Big Business stares, lips slack as he realizes I've caught him. He digs a hand deep into his bouffant haircut and wheels around, hair collapsing into a haystack of blonde strands and gel.

"I will kill you," Big Business says to the bad doctor, spittle flying out of his mouth. "I will. Tell me what you did!"

"What?" I shout. "Trying to get me killed isn't enough evil for one day?"

Big Business goes rigid, and I go in for the finale.

"I know you sent me there to die," I say. "I just want to know why."

That gets the wince I was expecting. "You – you–" He's vibrating. I can't tell if he's about to sob or explode. "You don't–"

"I don't what?" I say. "I don't understand how hard it is? Because your fact-finders might be telling you awful things, but buddy, I've lived them."

Big Business hiccups, and sits down hard, staring at Dr Atrocity like she just told him Santa isn't real. The fact-finders pause, uncertain in the face of their master's body language.

"Call them off," I say.

Big Business' fingers rummage through his hair again. "I–"

"Call. Them. Off," I repeat. "And then apologize."

Big Business tugs at his hair, his tie. He rubs a hand across his wrist like his shirt is cutting off his circulation. He lets out a choked noise that wouldn't be out of place on a baby, and slashes his hand through the air in a hurried, dismissive wave. The fact-finders let go of Dr Atrocity, morph back into nondescript men in nondescript suits, and disappear in a flutter of wet, unseen wings.

Dr Atrocity stumbles forward now that the weight is off her limbs, and gives me a forlorn, broken look, like her insides are being tied in knots. She doesn't say anything, but my detective stuff can fill in the blanks. She wants to thank me, and she has no idea how that works. On the list of people I thought I'd feel sorry for, she was near the bottom, but here we are.

"It's alright," I say. That has enough meanings to give her plausible deniability.

"I…" Her voice drops below zero. "I suppose it is."

Emotionless, mechanical, frightening. This is the Dr Atrocity that Miss Mighty keeps telling me about. I think I'm helping?

Dr Atrocity presses at her wrist, and watches intently as a little hatch opens up in the back of her hand. Her cybernetic eye reflects the red LED readouts blinking up at her. Whatever she sees, she seems to find satisfactory. She closes the hatch, and turns to me like she's not sure what I'm doing there.

"Are you alright?" I ask.

"Of course," she scoffs, and walks toward us.

"Okay…" I say. Someone like this bearing down on me has a tendency to steal my words. "Well, I mean, do you–"

She stalks past me, and stalks right up to Big Business, hands hidden in the pockets of her lab coat.

"I–" Big Business gags. If Dr Atrocity is twisted up by being thankful, I can't imagine how he feels about being apologetic.

"Please," the Doc sneers. "Let us not feign empathy. You believed you had something to gain from having your minions accost me, so you took a risk. It is a calculus I have done many times over the years."

And how's that working out for you? I think, in the part of me with no self-preservation.

Big Business chokes again. "I–"

"I am a supervillain," Dr Atrocity continues, without the barest acknowledgment he just said words. "Violence and home invasion are facts of life. You have done nothing I have not endured, even thrived from. You have done no damage to me."

Big Business looks up at her. She takes the opportunity to grab him by the throat with her robot arm. I'm going to hear the noise Big Business makes in the dead of night for a while.

"You have done nothing to me," she seethes into his face. "You are an insect. A paramecium. A slime mold who has managed to steal someone's cheap suit."

Big Business gags out a question mark, and Dr Atrocity gives him a casual toss that puts him three feet away on his back. You'd be paralyzed, too.

"You will be gone before I change into fresh scrubs," the Doc says. "You will never return. We are not enemies, but you are not welcome in my lair." She says it in the tone of a lecturer. She really is that calm.

Dr Atrocity pivots, gives me a sidelong glance with a whole condo's worth of meaning crammed into it, and marches off into the shadowy depths of the conservatory. As soon as she's gone, a thin whine escapes Big Business' lips.

"You knew about the house," he murmurs, staring at his feet.

"Uh," I say. If that's his explanation for all this, I'm going to return it for a new one.

"You knew about the house," he warbles. "You knew about the house the monster came from."

He can't be serious. "You're homicidal because I went somewhere you hadn't?"

"*You threatened my bottom line!*" His wail pairs perfectly with his red-eyed, tear-streaked face.

We lock eyes for a second, and that's all my detective stuff needs to confirm my suspicion. "You really can't handle not knowing things?" I ask.

Big Business breaks off eye contact, and either adjusts his tie or tries to choke himself out. I take this awkward moment to look over at Dr Atrocity, but she's just some rustling noises off in the shadows.

"Are you alright?" I call after her.

Wherever she is, she makes a disgusted noise. I turn back to Big Business; one villain at a time. He's kneeling on the stainless-steel floor, fidgeting with his one intact cufflink and subtly looking around for the other one.

"I–" He swallows. It sounds extra-dry. "The Heart of Business, Incorporated is a stable company with a long track record of success. We've posted healthy numbers each quarter for the past ten years run–" Whatever confidence he was giving himself gets lost in a chaotic snort. This is the messiest I have ever seen him by a stratospheric margin.

"Is this about how you got to the Stillreal?" I ask.

Big Business' teeth grind together as he responds. "Nobody threatens Big Business' bottom line. I am profit, merciless and unassailable."

I'm only half-sure I know what that word means, but I definitely know what his body language means.

"I am where the buck stops. I am the Man." He's reciting at race-car speeds, barely even enunciating his words. "I am the machine that does not run down. I am blank and pitiless as the sun." He's touching every nook and cranny of his beat-up suit, buttoning this and unbuttoning that, grooming without actually making anything better.

"You couldn't handle me knowing something you didn't," I say. "You couldn't handle *anyone* knowing something you didn't."

"If you need to know things, you come to Big Business. Because Big Business knows things. And Big Business knows… Big Business knows no one in the Stillreal… no one in the Stillreal can die. We can't die, and I know things. I know things – I know – I know I know I know–"

This isn't an act. Detective stuff would sniff that out fast. This case has broken Big Business as badly as I worry it's going to break me. Of course, I didn't handle it by torturing somebody…

"I'm sorry for what I did," I say. Even if I feel like he doesn't deserve an apology, it'll make *me* feel better. "You already felt–" powerless "– like things weren't working like they're supposed to, and then I – I told you something you didn't know, and I thought I was just trading on my strengths, but… I accidentally made it worse? I just – I thought I was just matching wits with the bad guy…" I trail off as that thought cannonballs into my brain. Wasn't that what I was doing?

Big Business takes a deep, rasping breath. "I *am* the bad guy!" he bellows, head snapping up. "But, with everything… Officer Hot… the nightmare…"

"Maybe you aren't the baddest guy?" I offer.

He sniffles, and nods. Well, there we go.

"I couldn't feel weak," he says to the floor. "I couldn't feel… like I didn't know things. So, when you came in… knowing like that, when you did that, I–"

"You sent me somewhere you knew might kill me," I say. "So you could feel powerful." How I sound sympathetic on this one, I don't know. But I manage.

For the second time in the past five minutes, I watch a bad guy struggling with regret. "Yes," he says, and lets his head sag again.

I can't let this one go that easily. "How did you know where to send me?"

"Fact-finders," he whimpers. "They told me what happened at the motel."

"You mean four months ago when the Man in the Coat went after his first victim?"

He gasps, then rights himself, studying my eyes. "The Snitching Snipe?"

"A good detective never tells."

And for a second, all the sorrow goes away, and he's wearing that blue-ribbon grin. "I always admired your wit, Detective Tippy." And then it's all frown-lines again. "I had to protect myself…"

"Why did you come after Dr Atrocity?"

Big Business starts to look in her direction, bites his lip, and continues his study of the floor. "The killings. They don't make sense, not by any rule of the Stillreal. When I realized Dr Atrocity had proofed herself against my fact-finders, I considered that there is one Friend who can… who can innovate solutions to a lot of logistical limitations."

"Friends come with their own rules," I say.

Big Business winces, fiddles with his cufflink. "Yes, but… Dr Atrocity's rules allow her to invent new rules. If anyone could have created that… thing, it's her."

"And so you threatened to torture me," Dr Atrocity says behind us.

She's changed clothes, swapped her shredded red scrubs for new ones in black, a fresh labcoat and rubber gloves to complete the ensemble. She's looking at us with one calm, starlight-yellow robot eye, and one human eye that is never going to stop hating Big Business. Her voice sounds right again too, and that's not exactly comforting. Dr Atrocity sounds the way a cobra looks right before it bites.

"You're alright," I say. I don't have to manufacture my joy.

"Science," she purrs back. "Now…" She reaches into a pocket and pulls out a thin-but-menacing little remote control. "I told you it was time to go. I will not tell you again."

Big Business turns to me. If it weren't for my detective stuff, I might not hear the 'thank you' he whispers.

"Get the heck out of here," I say. "Front Desk misses you. And don't think me saving your life means you're absolved. That's not up to me."

Big Business blinks, and smirks. I'd smirk back, but my energy is caught up in not letting my skin crawl away and hide. He looks at the floor, at me, and up past me at the wall, and at the speed of thought, he disappears.

In the ensuing silence, I hear Dr Atrocity's footsteps mincing away. I turn toward the noise, and do the second most foolish thing I've done all day.

CHAPTER SEVENTEEN

Atrocity twigs to me following her almost immediately, looking over her shoulder with an eyebrow arched.

"I believe you," I say.

The bad doctor watches me like she's waiting for the results of an experiment.

"I believe you didn't have anything to do with it," I say.

She sniffs and keeps on walking, headed for a hatch in the floor of the observatory. She spins a few bolts and the hatch opens with a theatrical hiss, revealing a set of stairs and a way-too-wide stairwell. Dr Atrocity looks at me, shrugs, and steps down. I barely hesitate before I follow.

We walk down a sterile gray staircase that leads to three or four hundred more sterile gray staircases, spiraling down a dark shaft with something humming and grinding near the bottom of it. We get halfway down before the Doc looks at me again. She scans me over, shrugs, and keeps on walking – I'm guessing if it doesn't fly and bench-press busses, she doesn't see it as a threat.

"I believe you," I call after her. "But I know you know something."

That makes her pause again. By the set of her shoulders, I'm calling her mood 'annoyed surprise.'

"I'm sorry to drop that on you," I say, lying. "I just didn't want to say anything in front of Big Business," I add, truthfully.

The only movement is her fist tightening on the railing. Either she's wrestling with gratitude or she's angry I'm bringing it up.

"I don't suppose you'd tell me what's happening?"

She looks up at me again, and it's not clinical this time – it's uncut anger, and the uncomfortable look she was giving me back at the death ray. She stares long enough to know I saw it, and keeps on walking into the bowels of her base. I follow without risking any more questions.

The machine noises build as we go deeper, intensifying until they shake me to my core. At the bottom, the shaft opens up into darkness. Dr Atrocity fiddles in the pocket of her labcoat, and there's a sound of enormous switches flipping as rank upon rank of fluorescent lights illuminate the room. We're in a rocky-ceilinged cavern, stalactites and stalagmites poking out among an army of generators and servers and compressors and every other kind of random machine you can think of. The noise is actually quieter down here; I'm guessing the worst of it is embedded in the shaft walls, probably to show off to any invading superheroes. Dr Atrocity looks at me with a detached, withering flavor of pride, and marches deeper into the cavern, moving like she knows I'm going to follow.

"I assume," she calls, "given your perfunctory conversation with Big Business, that you are at least somewhat cognizant of the situation?"

"You want to say that in plain language?" I ask. "Wait, no you don't. So, yes. I know the Man in the Coat has been murdering Friends for four months now."

Dr Atrocity chuckles. It's not a comforting sound; it's the sound you'd expect to hear right after the door locks and the room starts filling with water. "The Snitching Snipe's assessment of the start date is inaccurate."

Friends give information in a wide variety of ways, but ironically, the villainous baiting-and-revealing method is probably my least favorite. I'm about to get sardonic with her before she takes a sharp right down a side passage. The walls of it are lined with reel-to-reel machines, their tapes spinning in a never-ending loom of black.

"The Snipe is one of the best-informed creatures in the Stillreal," Dr Atrocity announces. "Until recently, only Big Business exceeded his capacity for data acquisition. But the Snipe also has a significant limitation on his powers."

"He only senses Friends who are committing crimes?" I offer, hoping to cut this short.

No such luck. "He only senses Friends who are committing crimes in the Stillreal."

"What are you getting at?"

Dr Atrocity stops at the end of the passageway, leans over a console set up against the dead-end wall. She presses a button, and a screen as big as her slides up into view. That screen unfolds, up, down, left, right, and I'm looking at five screens that size. Those screens unfold again and now there are nine of them, a grid the size of a billboard, spewing out data and images faster than I can comprehend them. I see Playtime Town, the Freedom Motel, Spindleman's house, the Alibi Lounge. Awe washes over me, right ahead of the sense I'm about to receive an even more horrible revelation.

"You've been spying on the entire Stillreal?"

Dr Atrocity looks over her shoulder with a brutal smirk. "Only recently." The amusement fades, and I'm seeing that horrified confusion again. "I suspect it may be why Big Business thought I was responsible. That, and he hates the idea anyone could confound him so casually without some sinister motive." The wicked joy returns to her voice.

I try to steer her back on course. "Why are you showing me this?"

"So you can see the data I've been gathering."

I look at the screen – yeah, still incoherent. "And exactly what have you been gathering data on?"

I don't need to see her face to know how satisfied she feels at that question. "Porcelain shards."

She presses a button, and the monitors shift, showing me floors, fields, streets, and parking lots, all dusted with the unmistakable white splinters. Spindleman's house is up there, and the Freedom Motel, but the others are new to me – some aren't even Ideas I've been to before.

"The oneiric infection manifests as broken dishware," Dr Atrocity says.

"What do you mean, infection?" I think I already know, but I'm hoping she'll contradict me.

"This being, or beings – this ersatz Friend in the coat – infects every Idea it invades, a contagion which manifests as broken dishes." So much for that hope. She presses another button, and the camera footage is replaced with a series of graphs and pie charts – all animated, of course. "The oneiric signature of the Idea remains the same, but a second signature is layered on top of it, smaller, less potent, but irrevocable."

"Can you explain that in triceratops-speak?"

If her grin gets any broader, I'll be able to see it from behind her. "This Friend does not warp an Idea the way other visitors do. It folds itself into the fabric of the Idea, as though it had always lived there. The dishes are a symptom, but the core intrusion manifests as the Man in the Coat, itself tinted to match the Idea in question. This parasitic thought-form then works to erase the native Friends, like a virus hijacking cellular reproduction of the host organism."

I feel very, very small. "Except the host organism is the Stillreal."

Dr Atrocity's back stiffens. "Not exactly."

She moves a slider, and each of the screens sprouts a picture-in-picture image, nine graphs, each unique.

"What you are seeing are the oneiric signatures of nine of the thirteen Ideas I can confirm are infected, adjusted to eliminate the noise caused by the infection."

Her word choice is making me itch. "Uh huh?"

She moves another slider, twists a dial. One graph is reproduced across all nine screens. Most of the bars lower compared to their previous readouts, but a few spike sky-high. "This is the signature of the Freedom Motel. Note the large difference between it and the others."

"It's noted, but not understood."

"The other Ideas I showed you are all still new, and thus highly malleable. Their signatures are in flux and still capable of permanent alteration."

"I assume you're going to monologue at me about what that means?"

Dr Atrocity, the scourge of Avatar City, turns and looks at me with confused, saddened eyes. "Every one of those Ideas showed up in the Stillreal with the infection already there. Their creators were forced to sever the link very recently – and after the infection began."

The gravity in my head reverses. My thoughts disconnect, making room for the new one that just hit me. Something traumatic happened to the creators of these Ideas – Spindleman's person among them – and whatever it was, it sent the Man in the Coat and his busted-up crockery into the Stillreal with the rest of us rejects. That only leads to one conclusion.

"The Man in the Coat is somehow the thing that traumatized them."

Dr Atrocity nods slowly. My detective stuff can taste the tears on her cheeks. I'm not sure what's more terrifying: that this is bad enough it's got Dr Atrocity crying, or that Dr Atrocity is capable of crying. What the heck have I walked into?

"Where did it start?" I ask, trying to focus on the task at hand.

"My data is insufficient to determine that. I know the house where you and Miss Flighty fought the infection is a recent addition to the Stillreal, but it's not as though Ideas come here with a time-stamp."

Miss Flighty. Even when the world is at stake, the villain still has to mock her hero. "You keep saying the infection. Even the Man in the Coat is an infection?"

"Again, my data is not concrete, but they appear to be symptoms. Expressions of the infection. I cannot determine which of the Men in the Coats, if any, is the original."

I have a feeling I can. The one in Spindleman's house and the one in the motel, they were slower than the one at Smile House – and less deadly, if the fight with Miss Mighty is anything to go on. Plus, they don't seem to be able to think around the way the one in Smile House did.

But how can he do this? Any of this? There aren't very many rules in the Stillreal, but this guy is making a point of breaking every single one of them. And the Snipe said he was a Friend, which means he shouldn't be breaking so many rules. Maybe the Man in the Coat is the Friend of whoever–

"Is there anything further?" Dr Atrocity asks.

My idea train derails. The bad doctor is once again regarding me over her shoulder, a look of distant, fragile annoyance. Her finger is poised above a big red button that she seems reluctant to press. It probably isn't going to throw me a surprise party.

"Yes," I say, dodging the hint as it passes me by.

Her human eye shrinks to a furious pinpoint. "What do you want?"

"Do you… know what kind of dishes they are?"

Her eyebrows knit, but her anger recedes. "Yes," she says, with easy relish.

I let her vagueness hang between us, don't bother to put a shield over my frustration. With the day she's had, she deserves a chance to feel superior. "Will you tell me?"

She smirks, and twists a dial on the great control panel. The images on the monitors disappear, replaced with a composite shot of the floor of Spindleman's house. She twists the dial again, and the floor drops out of the picture, leaving the shards hanging in an endless black. Dr Atrocity has turned away from me, but I can feel that the grin has returned.

Numbers and letters scroll across the left side of the image. An animation swings into full motion, matching up the edges of the pieces two at a time and aligning them along the breaks. Piece after piece clicks into place, assembling plates, handles, lids, until I'm looking at three complete, floral-printed, four-person–

"Tea services," Dr Atrocity announces.

Tea services. Serving platters, saucers, sugar cellars, the works.

"I gather from your paralysis that you have some inkling as to what this may mean," Dr Atrocity says.

Somewhere in the depths of my mind, I have a comeback, but it's going to have a heck of a time getting out from under all the shock. Teacups…

"Is there anything else?" she asks.

The Doc is facing me now, arms crossed. Her fingers are a little too tight against her arms, her shoulders a little too hunched, for me to buy that she's just annoyed. I look at her, the way her feet are planted, the twitch in her knee; she's pouring all her energy into not visibly shaking.

"No," I say.

"Good." She turns back to the bank of screens. "You will be able to leave the same way you came in."

"You're a wonderful host," I say as I take my leave.

"Detective Tippy." The chill in her voice could kill the dinosaurs all over again.

I turn, reluctantly, and look at her. She doesn't pay me the same courtesy.

"I do not provide my data to just anyone," she says. "I am not what you might call a sharing person."

I have no idea how to respond to that. So I don't.

"Today, I have freely shared data that not even torture by one of the worst monsters in the Stillreal could make me divulge."

I think I know where she's going. I have the good sense not to joke about it.

"I have done you a favor," she says. "Which means I do not owe you anything. Which means we need never talk again unless there is a very specific reason to do so." She looks up at the bank of monitors, every fiber of her body rigid. "Do I make myself clear?"

"Crystal."

"Good." She presses a button on the console, and the screens fold up and retract. "Please show yourself out with all due haste."

I spin on one hindleg, and high-tail it out to the stairs.

I'm barely thinking about Dr Atrocity's mood. I'm certainly not thinking about the sobbing noises that issue from the hallway the second I lose sight of her. I'm too busy feeling ignorant.

Teacups. How did I not realize the teacups were important?

CHAPTER EIGHTEEN

Spiderhand's asleep when I get home. I'm tempted to wake him, but getting this close to the gravity well of my bed makes me think maybe a nap would be best. I'm at least not actively seeking someone in danger anymore, right?

When I wake up, Spiderhand is again practicing piano. He jumps down from the piano bench when he sees me come into the room, giving me a high-octane flail as he asks where I've been and if I've heard about the new neighbor and why I got arrested. If he had a wrist attached to him, he'd have broken it ten times over.

"I got arrested because Officer Cold's brain was pulling double-duty," I say. My mood curdles when I think about the next step I need to take. "Spidey… listen… do you have a minute to talk about something that might creep you out?"

There's maybe a second of hesitation before he presses his fingers together and nods. Coming from him, that second is an entire haunted house full of worry. Brave little hand.

"Okay. Great." I keep my voice high and pleased, my kid's-show-host voice. "Can you show me your tea set? The new one we used a couple days ago?"

He hand-nods again, and skitters past me to the wicker picnic basket by the dining room table. He flicks the basket open with his index finger and roots around, unearthing the pot, cups and saucers, all cross-hatched with cracks where he had to glue them back together. They're decorated with a lovely cornflower-blue floral pattern, climbing vines and blossoming morning glories.

I let out a self-critical sigh, and chase it with a smile before Spiderhand's worried look gets any more heartbreaking. I'm the only one who needs to feel bad here. I might have been able to save Officer Hot if I'd made the connection earlier… but right now, I need to focus on saving the ones who are still left.

"Did you glue these back together yourself?" I ask.

He nods. The self-criticism ebbs a little in favor of fear.

"Where did you get them?"

Spiderhand launches into another bout of sign language. It takes me a few seconds to parse it all, but in the end I get it. He picked them up at 'the sandbar at the end of the world.'

Normally, hearing the name of an Idea gets me rifling through memories of the place, trivia, local dives, geopolitics, the soup of potential clues I keep simmering at the bottom of my detective stuff. That doesn't happen for the sandbar at the end of the world. It's because I've never heard of it.

"You went to a completely new Idea?" I ask. "No, no, it's okay," I stammer, when his fingers start to sag. "I'm not mad. I'm not mad."

Spiderhand pulls out of his droop, and gesticulates at me that he thought I knew about it already. According to him, I know about everything. Roommates who hero-worship you are both the best and the worst.

"No," I say. "But this is good, it really is. Can you tell me how to get there?"

His answer is twice as energetic as the last one, and gives me even more pause. He says no, he can't explain how to get there, but if I want, he can show me.

I sometimes lose track of the fact Spiderhand was already living at the Freedom Motel when I got there. His mannerisms (and let's be honest, his lack of a face) make it easy to forget he's one of the most veteran Friends in the Stillreal. But even with that in mind, I feel squirrelly letting him guide our thought process to this fancy new Idea of his; it's like leashing your pet hamster and expecting it to pull a plough.

The ride is smooth, but diverted. He starts by thinking us from Playtime Town to the Heart of Business, where he uses the glow of the neon lights to think us over to Santa Erzulie, dropping outside a towering, neon-fringed hotel with a fountain in the shape of an angry samurai. The fountain then connects us to a more standard cherub-topped one in the middle of the Carnivorous Hedge, which connects us to a bubbling spring on Plunder Island. From there, it's off to our final destination, a volcano-black sandbar in the middle of an endless ocean.

There are no other landmasses in sight. I'm not sure if there's a horizon, or if the water just arcs up and becomes the sky. The only things around are a three-hundred-foot-long sandbar, two Friends looking around for any sign of something else, and, oh yeah, bits of broken tea services buried in the sand, which leaves me with a pretty good working theory as to how this Idea got into the Stillreal in the first place.

I give the broken shards a closer look. It's the same pattern Spiderhand was using at home, mixed in with the goldenrod spiral patterns I saw at the Freedom Motel. There's a patch of bare black sand just big enough to contain enough shards for, say, a four-person tea service. That confirms Spidey's story, but the really interesting thing is the silence.

"Spidey," I say. "Do you notice what is *not* happening to us right now?"

He gives the finger-twitch that means 'no.'

"Right now, we are not getting attacked."

Spiderhand lacks context, so his confused look is a bit different than mine. I spin in a slow, careful circle, scanning the water for any disturbance, any ripple, any anything. But there's nothing – which means there's no man wearing a dark coat here. Which in turn means the pattern is broken. Unless...

I look down at the sand, and bingo: right next to the bald patch, I see shards in about three other patterns winking at me from under the water line. When I lean in close I can see more of them, twinkling white under the waves. The infection doesn't stop here, and neither does the Idea.

"Did you ever go in the water?"

Spiderhand gestures no. I think for another second, mostly about how I don't want to do this next thing.

"Is it okay if I do something potentially foolish?" I ask.

Spiderhand nods with a troubling enthusiasm. Before I can think better of it, I dip one paw in the water.

It's pleasant to the touch, just between warm and cold. The second I touch it, the water shifts colors from opaque green to clear tropical blue, the change spreading out in a perfect circle from the place where my paw touches down. I see reefs down below, black like the sandbar. I see fish in all the colors of the rainbow. And below both of those, I see towers that look like apartment buildings, the rooftops lined in blue light. I pull my paw out; the glow on my fabric fades, and the water shifts back to the usual marine blue. I'm looking at my own reflection, wondering how many more beautiful things the Stillreal has to show me, and how many of them are going to try to kill me.

I touch the water again, and study the buildings. The lights at the edges are in motion, like a marquee at an old-time theater, and I see shadows moving in between the buildings. Probably fish. Hopefully fish.

I look at Spidey. He's quivering in a mix of fear and curiosity. I know which one I feel like indulging.

"Let's see if we can get down there."

He explodes into excited affirmations. That's my roommate.

I don't see any obvious way to get down there, so I'm probably expected to swim, which means it's time for the far riskier experiment. I keep my eyes closed while I put my head into the water. When I open them, my vision is snorkel-perfect, even without my detective stuff weighing in. I open my mouth, and risk taking a breath. It feels wet, a little cold, but still: inhale, exhale. That's sort of what I expected. This felt like a friendly sort of place.

"We're good," I say, lifting my dripping head above water. I shake off the horrible pitter-patter of water droplets hitting the surface, and dive back in, beckoning for Spiderhand to follow. Predictably, he does a cannonball.

The light encases us in two inviting bubbles as we swim, illuminating all the way down to the tops of the buildings. Below that, it gets so murky my detective stuff can't quite tell what's going on, nothing but shadows swimming around other shadows; but I can see the trail of broken teacups descending the edge of the sandbar, and that's all the guidance I need. At least, until my light bubble gets partway down the buildings, at which point my perspective calls itself into question.

From up above, I guessed the buildings were the size of apartment buildings, and that the shadows at the bottom were about person-sized. It turns out the buildings are actually towering smoked-glass obelisks full of copper circuits, each one the size of a skyscraper; it's the shadows that are the size of apartment buildings.

I try speaking. "What do you know about this place?"

Spiderhand gestures that he doesn't know much at all. He found out about it from Freedom Frieda, and he decided to go exploring, and lo and behold, teacups.

Freedom Frieda again. I need to have words with that eagle.

I look around for the teacup shards, and find them stuck to the side of one obelisk, a poor man's mosaic running the length of the structure. I gesture for Spidey to follow, and swim slow and easy toward the black-coffee murk at the ocean bottom. Electricity flares up and down the circuits inside the glass as we swim past it. It looks like a model of brain activity Sandra once saw in school. Halfway down, I come across a tarnished brass plaque that reads 'Sasha – First Grade.' I've got half a jigsaw puzzle's worth of ideas tumbling around my head. I give them a shake, and keep on swimming.

A few strokes down, I pick up voices from below, and something else layered underneath them, deep beeps and squeals, like sonar trying to mimic speech. At first I don't recognize the noise, but my detective stuff has me covered: it's whale song. I take a few more strokes straight down, and backstroke upward as one of those building-scale shadows rises up from the dark and meets with the edge of my light bubble.

It's a whale, with a warty, fog-gray hide covered in barnacles, wires, and little silver antennas. I don't have time for confusion before I see the speakers and dials of an old transistor radio sticking neatly out of its side. The whale song sounds from the radio, and with it a voice, much clearer up close.

"On my eighth birthday, my mom made me a peanut butter-bacon cake," says the satisfied voice of a child.

Spiderhand taps me on the shoulder, and points at another whale passing by on the other side of the 'First Grade' obelisk. This one is cobalt blue instead of gray, but the radio looks almost identical. The same voice says "I played my first ever game of field hockey today," and describes the game in excited tones as the whale swims on by.

There are more whales, I realise, a whole pod of them, swimming back and forth around the bottoms of the smoked-glass monoliths. Five minutes of watching and they never come up for air, but it looks like their blowholes serve a different purpose: one swims up to the base of First Grade, stops on a dime, and turns on its side to angle its blowhole toward the glass. There's a dangerous hum, and the electricity inside the glass arcs out into the blowhole. The jolt of lightning ends after a couple of seconds, and the whale swims off, its radio chattering away in a stern, annoyed tone, a note deeper than the other two. "I used to only eat corn dogs, but now I only eat green beans…"

Real-world whales breathe air. But this Idea's whales breathe memories. Sometimes I need to stop and remind myself that I do love my job.

Our moment of awe over, I keep following the teacups toward the bottom. Spiderhand follows, swinging around to take in every sight he can.

"Mom can't be home for Christmas this year," says another whale's radio. "I think it's Dad's fault. I'm trying not to get too mad at him…"

"I forgot my homework, I don't know what I'm going to do–"

"Stocks are down–"

That last voice is different, more adult and feminine, soft and sultry, mixed in with the kids' thoughts. It's probably a future memory, something dreamt but not actually realized later on in life. Kid creators do their best to fill in all the details, but there's only so much experience to draw from.

"I've been thinking about it for a while," another memory says, the voice of a teenager getting hit with testosterone, "and I'm pretty sure I'm a girl—"

It takes us a while to hit the seabed, long enough to see another three memory-breaths taken in by the oblivious whales. The sand at the bottom is silver and gold, and the seaweed is a beautiful-if-disturbing blood red. I'm less bothered by that than I am by the sheer amount of broken porcelain mixed in with the sand.

"Well, this is pleasant," I mutter to myself. "Spidey? Stick close."

Spiderhand answers in the fearful affirmative.

The shards radiate out from the bottom of the 'First Grade' obelisk, teapot spouts and cup rims. I try to exude calm as we swim toward the next closest one, hoping Spiderhand never notices how fake it is.

"Last night I got to try a video game at Steve's house." Sasha's voice is younger again closer to the obelisk marked 'Second Grade.' "I think I like them."

The shards vanish after I pass the 'Second Grade' obelisk. I swim us back toward 'First Grade,' watching for something resembling a trail.

"Now that they're divorced, Mom says she'll pay for my transition," says the deeper version of the voice.

The shards continue for a bit longer on the other side, but disappear not too far past that.

"I don't want to have another tea party," says the child version of Sasha's voice, from somewhere to our left. "I don't want to have another tea party."

I look at Spiderhand. "Teacups," I whisper.

He signals the same thing. We both spin back around, trying to track which whale just said that.

"He's setting up the table," says little-girl Sasha, now a little bit farther away. "He sets it up every day, and then when I say no, he tears it all down. I don't understand." Her voice is quaking, right on the edge of either sobbing or screaming.

I tread water and try to pinpoint the direction.

"I want to go home," says Sasha.

There. The black whale, swimming between the nearest row of black-glass pylons.

"Why aren't Mom and Dad looking for me?" she says.

The black whale stops at one of the crackling pillars, slowing to inhale its contents. I guide Spiderhand behind a nearby chunk of reef, the better to listen in without being seen.

This close, the whale's hide looks wrong. There's something angry about the contours of it, something twisted in its button-eye face.

"I hate tea," Sasha's memory says. "He won't stop feeding me tea." The tone is past scared and straight into terrified.

The whale swims past us, deeper into the field of black glass, and I get a closer look. The skin around the radio's dials is inflamed and infected, little ridges raised up where the wires are rubbing it raw, and its face looks wrong because it's miserably sad. Both are probably thanks to the white splinters embedded in patches across its side.

"Every time I say no, he looks over at that bat," the memory says.

Bat. Tea.

"He says he doesn't want to hurt me."

I look forward to the day when this whale's radio shuts up.

Spiderhand taps on my shoulder, points in the direction the whale is swimming. The beast has slowed down, coming abreast of a different glass monolith. I swim out into the open water and get a couple of determined breaststrokes in before my detective stuff screams at me.

There's a quick sizzle, like a frayed wire being thrown into a bathtub, and Spiderhand is encased in – I'd call it a net, but nets aren't made of light – a lattice of the same blue light outlining the edges of the obelisks. Judging by how Spidey is flailing, it's solid. I realize I should watch out for myself right before the sizzle comes again, and my vision is broken up by a similar light cage.

The black whale recedes into the distance, taking its clues with it. I look around, trying to find whatever attacked us, and twig to three Friends rising up from the seabed. They're octopi, all wearing complicated, strappy headgear that looks like someone once saw a mining helmet and tried to reverse-engineer it from memory. Loops of fabric hang off their arms, serving as straps for screwdrivers, pickaxes, and little brass wands covered in switches and dials. None of them are surrounded in light, and that's when I realize exactly how foolish I've been.

"Intruders," says the one on the right, a rust-colored octopus with a deep, breathy voice. "You were right."

The light isn't for our convenience. It's an alert system.

"We tripped an alarm," I groan, taking the blame in the hope that it helps Spiderhand not to panic.

"Everyone trips the alarm," says the octopus at the center, a deeper crimson color with a clipped, sneering delivery.

"What do we do?" asks the leftmost octopus, cherry red and a high, frantic tone. "How do we handle these?"

"The same way we handled the others," the rightmost one says.

In the distance, the black whale's radio says, "I'm so hungry…"

I have a quip loaded up, but I don't get it out before the rust-colored octopus twists a dial on his brass wand. I shudder, and scream, and black out to the sound of coursing electricity.

CHAPTER NINETEEN

I wake up to bright light, and a dump truck backing over the inside of my skull. I become a little more awake, and realize I'm mistaken: there's a whole fleet of dump trucks, and they're doing donuts. Whatever those octopi hit me with, I'm anxious to never go through it again.

I wake up the rest of the way, and my pain is briefly displaced by claustrophobia. I have walls pressing in on three sides, an opening in front of me that shows about a four-foot-by-one-foot slit of ocean floor, just enough to remind me what I'm missing. I give myself a few seconds to scream internally, and take stock of my surroundings. The walls are the same black stone as the sandbar, threaded with flowing light just like the obelisks, and close enough together that I can't even turn around. The opening in front of me looks like a product of erosion. Through it, my view is of the silver-and-gold seabed, and a huge black rock outcropping sitting between me and the towers of black glass. Detective stuff shows me a sheet of now-familiar blue-white light layered over the opening; the water flows through it, but otherwise it's solid enough to nix any chance of escape. I'm in jail. Again.

"Spidey?" I ask. No response. "Spidey?" I repeat, trying to avoid sounding panicked. You know, for his sake.

I pick up a faint tapping by my left flank, a dull sound that has to have traveled through a few feet of rock. I lean toward it, get my face up next to the wall.

"Spidey? Is that you?"

The tapping comes again, even more frantic. There's no way anyone but Spiderhand could drum their fingers that fast. Well, that's a little slice of relief.

"Can you see any way out?"

There's a second's pause, and a distinctly dismayed little tap. That's a 'no.' Well, if I can't escape, I might as well gather clues…

Smell and taste are off the table, but I can do the other three. Let's start with hearing. The whale song and radio chatter is still out there, but distant, unintelligible even with the edges I usually have on it. I don't hear anything else right now, which might be the most unnerving part of this experience.

Touch: The light barrier doesn't give the slightest bit when I press on it, and the rock is similarly solid. Nothing to write home about here.

Sight: There's a hole in the base of the outcropping across from me, so dark it's hard to pick out from the rock. It's about as wide as the entrance to Farmer Nick's barn, deep enough I can't tell how deep. More importantly, I see what look like rusty metal bars lining the opening from top to bottom; most importantly, I think I see something moving in there. I wiggle up to the barrier of light, press my fortunately pliable face against it, and try to get a closer look. My vision fills with a sudden burst of red, and I back up fast, smashing myself tail-first into the rear wall of my cell.

The crimson octopus has swum up in front of me. It examines me with detachment and a tiny sprinkle of pain, and reaches into its toolbelt, producing what looks like a stethoscope with a tiny television on the end. Earbuds attached to the device go on either side of its head. I hear beeps and boops as the octopus waves the little television my way.

"How did you get here?" the octopus asks, in the blithe, jabbing tone of someone who sees the exchange as an unpleasant thing they have to check off their list.

Yeah, I'm not holding back with this one. "Hi. I'm Tippy." I say it as brightly as I can.

The octopus looks up from the device. "Excuse me?"

"Detective Tippy. Playtime Town. That's my name. What's your name and what pronoun should I use for you?"

I want them to feel guilty they've imprisoned an actual Friend with wants and needs of their own, but instead they just look confused. "Where is Playtime Town?" the octopus drawls.

"I can show you. Or I mean, I will, if you ever let me out of here."

Their eyes screw up, trying to sort out what the words I said actually mean. They're not having an easy time of it.

"You've never heard of Playtime Town," I say. It's not a question. I knew they were fairly new to the Stillreal already.

"There is no such zone," they say.

"What's a zone?"

They look down at the device again.

"I said, 'what's a zone'? What? Do they not have etiquette underwater?"

The octopus huffs, and tweaks a dial on the side of the gizmo. They don't like what they see.

"I'm sorry to be a bother," I say. "I just usually like to know who's imprisoning me in incredibly uncomfortable cages." If they aren't going to play nice, I'm not either.

The octopus lets go of the business end of the doohickey, and jets off in disgust. "You deal with this," they mutter as they leave.

There's another blur of color, and the cherry-red octopus comes into view. They've got pain in their eyes, and the sight chills me. It's not a look that says 'I'm sorry your dog died'; it's a look that says 'I'm sorry we're about to kill your dog.'

"Wh-Where are you from?" they ask, high and soft.

"Nice to meet you?" I say.

The octopus blinks, hesitant.

"I'm Detective Tippy," I say. "What's your name, and what pronoun should I use for you?"

The octopus blinks again. "I'm Breaker. I'm… a she?"

"Pleasure to meet you, Breaker." I force a big smile. "I come from Playtime Town. I'm guessing this is where you tell me there is no such zone?"

"There… isn't," she says, with a less heated version of her companion's confusion.

"What's a zone?" I ask.

Her face gets even more screwed up than the first one's. My question is shaking something fundamental in these octopi. Good.

"If you can't answer that question," I say, "can you at least tell me who you all are?"

She treads water, nervous as all-get out. "We're the p-pit crew."

"Pit crew for what?"

"It's not important anymore," says the deeper voice of the rust-colored octopus, as they come swimming into view.

"And you are?" I ask.

The rusty octopus waves an arm at Breaker, shooing her out of the prime interrogation spot. "I'm Cable. We need to know how you got here from… Playtime Town."

"We swam?"

By the motions of their face, Cable briefly considers violence as their response. "How did you get to the Memory Reefs?"

And here is where I test the waters. (No pun intended.) "I thought my way here from another Idea."

Cable's brow furrows. "Which zone did you come from?" they ask, louder than the last question.

"I didn't come from a zone," I say. "I came from Playtime Town."

"That's not a real zone," Cable says. There's urgency dawning in their words.

That's when I make the connection. They've never been outside their home Idea. They aren't just *new* to the Stillreal, they don't even realize they're in it.

I try to dial back a little on the sarcasm-to-diplomacy mixture. "What zones are there, then?"

Breaker starts to answer, but Cable cuts her off. "We're not discussing that with an intruder," they say. "I need your data, and I need it now. It is vitally important."

"I gave you my data."

"What zone did you come from?" they shout, with an edge of pure panic that wasn't there a half-second before.

I flinch back from the noise. Breaker looks pained on my behalf. Cable also hesitates, but covers it with anger at a disturbing speed.

"I'm sorry," I say. "I don't know what you're talking about."

"You're from outside the sea," Breaker says, in the same tone as someone realizing who the murderer was all along.

"Yeah," I say. "Me and my buddy in the next cell." I don't get the feeling this is us reaching an understanding.

"How did you find your way down here?" Breaker asks, in the awe-touched voice of a little kid.

My heart breaks. I accelerate on past it. "Maybe you didn't hear the part where I introduced myself. I said I was a detect–"

"How," Cable grinds, "did you find. Your way. Down here?"

"You're not really making me inclined to answer your questions."

Cable flails their arms in frustration. "You need to answer the questions so I can–"

"Cable," Breaker says.

Cable turns to her, at a loss for how to respond.

"We d-don't need the data, do we?" Breaker says. "These p-people are in a bad enough place now, we don't n-need to put them through–"

"Data is the only way this ever stops," Cable replies. "What if it doesn't work? How am I supposed to know what to fix next time without data?"

"But you're already going to kill them!"

Wait, what? "Hold on, hold on," I say. "I'm not sure I–"

"It's the only option left," Cable says, with not-quite-iron detachment. "We're going to take your data, and then we're going to put you in the cave."

"Well pardon me if I suddenly have a lot of data I need to give you!" I shoot back.

Breaker squeezes her eyes shut. "I'm so sorry," she says. "Th-this is j-just – it's – I said this was a bad experiment, but when – when it st-started happening–"

"When the Man in the Coat came?" I ask.

She lets out a little squeak, swims back a pace. "How do you kn-know about the Man in the C-C-Coat?"

Honesty. Not snark. Honesty might get us out of here. "He killed a friend of mine."

Breaker's eyes widen. "You have friends in the sea?"

"No. The Man in the Coat is affecting people outside the sea, too. He's got – he's hurting a lot of people."

Breaker gasps. "Oh my. Oh my." She turns to Cable. "I th-thought we trapped it."

"'Trapped'?" I ask.

Breaker starts to say something, but she's held off by the reappearance of the crimson octopus. Their reappearance doesn't stop my brain from entering the spin cycle, though. How did they trap the Man in the Coat? I need to pull at this thread as hard as I can, but to do that, I need space to move. Somewhat literally.

The crimson octopus fans both Breaker and Cable away and comes threateningly close to the barrier. "Listen, outsider. I am sorry your friend died." They say it without meaning it. "But the experiment is going forward one way or another."

Breaker tugs at one of the crimson octopus's arms. "Plug, please."

Plug. Okay, I'm getting the theme.

Plug gives Breaker a baleful look, and regards me with even less sympathy. "We cannot help the dead, and we cannot help your friends. That is not our job."

"Not your job?" I shout back. Breaker seems alright, but with the others I'm not sparing even a drop of outrage.

"W-we keep the memory towers working," Breaker says, halfway to despondent. "We m-make sure the memory whales have g-good reception. We keep the sea… running."

"Kept," Cable says, looking down at the seabed.

"Keep," Plug growls. It stares at me with eyes as hard as chunks of amber. "Sasha trusts us to keep the memories going. That is our job, and we are going to do it."

"How does murder fit into your job description?" I ask.

Cable's arms curl up underneath them. "The Man wants to kill. That's his job. Capturing him has worked, for now, but we need to find a permanent solution."

My brain does a backflip trying to parse the logic. "So you just jumped straight to ritual sacrifice?"

"We help him do his job," Cable says, careful with every word. "We allow him to fulfill his purpose, and in exchange, perhaps he allows us to fulfill ours."

"So what, I don't get a vote in this?"

"We cannot risk him hurting the memory whales again," Cable seethes.

The lighting on the world dims. "He attacked the whales?"

Breaker's face crumples. "He t-t-took down Sasha's first Hannukah," she says, voice trembling with tears. "He almost g-got Papa's memory of the birth, but we stopped him. B-but now—"

"Now we do what we have always done," Plug says. "We fix it."

"But how…?" I need to sit down. After I escape, I need to sit down. "But how can you be sure this is going to work?"

Breaker's eyes widen, but Plug cuts her off. "We have wasted too much time," they say, and grab at another device hanging on their belt.

"There has to be another way—" I say, but there's that jolt of electricity again, and I black right back out.

Again, I wake up aching, but this time I'm awake much faster. Terror makes a great stimulant.

Senses. Get a grip. Sight: I'm not in the little cell anymore. This cave is bigger, just darkness on three sides, and the same soccer-goal-sized opening I saw from my prison in front of me, covered in the same light barrier. Just like last time, the water flows through the barrier; just like last time, I'm guessing I won't be able to swim through it. What gives me pause, though, is the line of rusty iron bars stuck into the sand just on this side of the barrier. They're the exact kind of bars I'd expect in Playtime Town Jail, give or take about a century of immersion in saltwater. They're so pitted some of them are only half there, looking so weak that anything stronger than a stiff breeze could bust out of here. We're in the cave across from our previous holding cells. We're in 'the cave' Cable and Plug were talking about. Which means we're about to be killed.

Focus, Detective. Focus. Touch: I take stock of my body. Everything is there, but moving is hard, like my joints have been stitched to my sides. I peek down at my belly, and find I'm wrapped in a length of LED light-tubing. When I try to turn around, I also find there's large mass attached to my back, something irregular and heavy and very likely hand-sized.

Hearing: "Spidey?"

I get a scared wiggle in return. They've tied me and Spiderhand together. Right. This is great.

Scent: Nothing but seawater. Taste: the same. Hearing: I've got total, pre-explosion silence inside the cave, and the faint movement of three small, pliable bodies approaching from above.

"They're awake," announces Cable, as the three octopi swim into view.

Plug looks detached. Cable looks pained. Breaker just looks shattered.

"I'm sorry," Breaker says. "I'm so sorry, I tried to–"

"We have to," Plug says. They're not sorry.

"You know," I say, "we might be willing to help if you, say, let us out?"

Breaker whimpers, looks at Plug. "Plug, we could let them out–"

"Breaker, you could shut up," they respond. "We have no other options," they say to me.

"With help, you could maybe find some," I say, trying very hard not to wheedle.

"We cannot trust your help," Plug says.

Cable looks down at the sand. They think Plug's right, and it's the worst thing they've ever thought.

I load another quip into the chamber, but drop it when I hear the faint shuffling behind me. Spiderhand goes board-stiff. I'd love to say I'm feeling any braver.

"I'm so sorry," Breaker says. "I'm so sorry."

The shuffling gets louder, closer, and here come the familiar footsteps. Boots, big ones, loud despite the muffling of sand and water. Board-stiff gives way to lava-fluid as Spiderhand's panic spins up. I fight against him just enough to turn around.

This version of the Man in the Coat is a barrel-chested hunk of darkness even bigger than the one from Spindleman's house, his clothes and weapons gone nautical to match his surroundings. Kelp and barnacles stick to his flabby, moss-green coat. His hat is a wide-brimmed rubber thing like the ones fishermen wear, but with more jagged edges. He pauses as he looks down at me with those hateful green eyes, hanging back a step like the others did. Then he nods, steps forward, and out of his sleeve comes his version of the club, a rusty length of metal with a barb on the end. It stings just looking at it.

The Man's eyes flick wider the second before he moves. I roll to the side, but I'm anchored by Spiderhand. The swing barely misses me.

"Backwards!" I shout. "Backwards!"

But Spidey's just stuck back there, vibrating, off the edge of the map of rational behavior. I push against him as hard as I can, but the next swing clips me on my nasal horn. It's a glance, but it still leaves my face swollen and my legs struggling to work. No, please, no–

The Man brings his arm back around. His downward chop misses as I dredge Spiderhand backwards through the sand, but then a lateral swing gets me right across the temple, and my world turns into stars and blotches.

I know he's right in front of me. I know he's going to go for my head again. But my legs aren't responding, and my head won't quite move, and I know, in the pit of my stomach, that I am going to die here.

My world inverts. I get a perfect view of a missed swing as I go careening toward the mouth of the cell. Spiderhand has me up on his back, and he's skittering at a speed only a terrified, determined Spidey can achieve. I lift my head, watching as the mouth of the cave rushes closer. At the last second, my view is blotted out by a kelp-streamered jacket.

"Drink," says the Man in the Coat.

Spiderhand dodges a blow. It sends up a cloud of sand that blocks my view again. Spiderhand hesitates, as blinded as I am, and that gives the Man all the opportunity he needs to close in and give us a massive two-hand chop. The crack when he connects with Spiderhand's knuckles is one of the worst things I've ever heard. I feel the shift as his fingers curl under him, too stung to keep moving.

"Drink."

I get clubbed in the belly. My torso is burning, my limbs tingling like their power cords came unplugged. Another head shot; the water is a black blur, except for a tiny white speck drifting away from me. It's my stuffing. This jerk has ripped open my stitching.

"Fine," the Man in the Coat gurgles.

The Man leans over us, and stumbles backwards as he's drowned in an upward flurry of white-gold sand.

Spiderhand is shoveling handfuls at the Man in the Coat, as fast and furious as his wounded digits can go. The Man keeps lurching backward, shielding his face, trying to extract himself from the blur, but all that does is buy us time and distance. Spidey digs until the Man is totally obscured, then splays out on the ground. A single quaking digit nudges the back of my aching head. I don't need to see him to know what he's trying to say. 'Your turn, roomie.'

We lever ourselves over, putting me on the bottom. My body tells me right away what a terrible idea this is, but the Man in the Coat is already waving the last of the sand away, and honestly, I've had a very, very bad day. I let anger and excitement and being a dinosaur take the wheel, and I charge.

The Man clears the sand out a half-instant before I plow horns-first into his stomach. He halves in size the second I connect, ragdolling against my horns. I barrel forward, aim us at the bars, trailing fluff as I go. In the background, I hear the octopi screaming.

We hit the bars with a meaty thud, and the Man in the Coat lets out a noise like he just swallowed an entire tube of saltines, a second before the bar bursts like a can of tomatoes hitting concrete, spraying rust in every direction. My own bubble of light surrounds me as I rocket out of the cave and into the open water, sloughing the limp form of the

Man off into the sand. I swim, Spiderhand's thumb still tapping at me, the octopi shrieking below. I swim as hard as legs meant for prehistoric Earth can manage, swimming for the trail of cups, for the lighter blue water above me, until something cold and gluey grabs onto one of my back legs. Spiderhand dances a manic two-step on my back as I'm dragged back toward the ocean floor.

"No!" Plug shouts, wrapping another arm around me, another. "You have to, you have to, it is the only way—"

There's a wet, awful crunch, and the arms fall off me. I spin and see Plug tumbling through the water, down to the waiting Man in the Coat. He grabs Plug by a trailing arm, tosses them into the sand. The Man lets out a thunderous grunt before he drives the club barb-first into the octopus. There's an explosion of bubbles, and a hauntingly familiar pop, and the only thing left of Plug is a tattered tool belt.

I have to go. I have to go now. But I'm looking at the tool belt, thinking of the screaming, of all the water around me, water just like you see in puddles on a highway. I shake my head clear, get moving, and get out three strokes before I'm dragged down into another blow to the head.

My world turns red. Up becomes down. Behind me, Spiderhand stiffens, and the light tubes come streaming down around me, broken in half. The attacks must have weakened them enough for Spidey to escape. I feel the water Spidey displaces as he swims up and away at a speed we'd never have mustered together. Yeah, that's fair, I think, before the club drives me into the seabed.

"Drink," growls the Man in the Coat.

I roll to the side, sand billowing around me as I get to my feet. I try not to think about how loose and airy my torso feels.

Sight: the Man in the Coat in front of me, Breaker to my right, a horrified Cable hovering over the remains of Plug's belt. There's nothing around us now but open ground. The other four senses don't matter right now; that gives all I need. Or all I can use, anyway...

I wait for the Man to step in close. As soon as he does, I back up, trying to seem like I don't know where I am, like I'm scrambling for an exit route. The Man reads me like I'd hoped, and goes for a lunging chop. I dodge out of the way, and use his recovery time to back up even more, to force him to keep on pursuing. He does.

"Drink," he says as he advances.

Good. I can work with this. All I have to do is keep him annoyed long enough for Spidey to think his way home. But maybe if I'm lucky, I'll pull off more than that.

Back I go, and forward he comes; back, forward, back, forward. Whenever he seems like he might change tactics, I make a point of stumbling or wincing, giving him just enough opening to keep him taking the bait. It works, and it keeps on working, but eventually he grunts in frustration and starts glancing around, looking for a way to manufacture an opening. I give him one.

I stumble, let out a pained cry. It's not a performance I find particularly difficult. The Man's eyes widen. He closes the distance with that horrifying sprint, and nearly stumbles himself when I roll and come up to the side of him. I charge straight into his fully exposed belly – or that's what I plan to do, before my left hindleg accordions into a stuffing-less heap.

So. I'm not lucky.

The Man grabs me by the neck and leans in. This close, the shadows of the coat don't hide him anymore. His face is round, chubby, pale as a full moon. His eyes are just green human eyes, distorted through a thick pair of glasses. He pulls me in next to his leering mouth, and whispers in the tiniest, squeakiest voice I have ever heard, "We could have had so much fun."

He tosses me to the ground like a piece of rotten fruit, and lets out a gross, wheezy chuckle as he puts a boot on my stomach. The blackout creeps in again. I look up at him, at the club above his head, at the surface of the water shimmering too far away – and at Spiderhand, streaking down toward me on the back of something blue and gold and fast.

Miss Mighty connects like a freight train. She and the Man in the Coat pile-drive into the seabed in a cloud of dust. Spiderhand comes flying out of the cloud, fingers flailing. A punch like a thunderclap sounds from inside the dust, and the Man in the Coat tumbles out head over heels, barely even my height now, his coat flapping loose around him. Miss Mighty strides after him, grabs his club before he can recover, and uppercuts him off his feet. When he lands, he's about as tall as Spiderhand.

The Man scrabbles forward, hands out for Miss Mighty's throat. Mighty lays him out with a spinning kick, and what's left of him disappears into the coat. She grabs it before it can slither off, wads it into a ball, tosses the ball up, and swings for the fences with his own club. The connection is like a Mariners home run, a hollow crack that sends bubbles cascading in all directions.

The coat is gone; the bat, too. In their place is a battered, wide-brimmed hat and a single cracked teacup, drifting gently to the ocean floor.

I try to say something witty, and settle for collapsing.

CHAPTER TWENTY

I wake up on my back, staring at a white ceiling while someone tugs at the sore spot that used to be my legs. I try flailing, and get shushed and petted with a feather-soft hand until I slump back into bed.

I see more beds in either direction, all white with bright yellow polka dots on the sheets and pillows. The floor under the beds is made of cheerful sky-blue tile, reflecting fluorescent lights that feel like an afternoon sunbeam. I hear cloth swishing against cloth, feet marching back and forth around me. I smell cinnamon, alcohol, and fresh lemon.

It's happened. I'm finally on the 'patient' end of Saint Sunbeam Hospital. Well, it could be worse – Spidey could have not come back for me...

"Spiderhand!"

I try to sit up, and again I'm shushed back into the mattress. I waggle my hind legs in a feeble attempt at a struggle, and find they're both blissfully, agonizingly whole.

"Your roommate's fine," says a kind, twangy voice somewhere near my back legs, talking in a soothing stage whisper that I have to admit really does calm the nerves. "Got him in a bed down the way."

It's Nurse Simon Pawsome, the Red Panda RN. That explains the spice mixed in with the antiseptic. "And Miss Mighty?" I say to the ceiling, not relaxing just yet.

"Didn't see any Miss Mighty," he says. "But Spiderhand did say a flying woman dropped you off."

I'll need to get the full story out of Mighty later, after I'm done being grateful we're both around to discuss it. Survival of companions assured, I check in on my body, and regret it. I've been stuffed with fresh ticking and sewn up with fresh thread, and I can feel every centimeter of it, still sore, still stiff, still Real. The groan I let out could be used as a torture tactic.

"I'm gonna need you to be quiet there, Tippy."

"Will I ever run track again, doc?" I ask, in a voice too hoarse to be tough.

Nurse Pawsome makes an amused cluck, and tucks those soft hands underneath me. "Let me sit ya up so we can talk face-to-face, eh Tippy?"

"Detective Tippy," I say.

"Takin' that as a yes," Nurse Pawsome says, and the entire length of my body is dipped into arctic waters of pain as he gently raises me up to a quasi-sitting position.

"Better?" he asks, coming up alongside me. He looks the way he's always looked, a red panda, lithe and rosy red, with an always-sniffing nose and an always-busy tail, sheathed in polka-dotted scrubs to match the sheets.

"So," he says. He gives me a grim smile that looks like it could use about seven naps. "What exactly happened to you there, bucky?"

"Nothing you want to hear about."

"This about the murders, then," he says, in a voice I can't ignore.

I'm used to seeing Nurse Pawsome concerned, even used to seeing him worried – but I'm not used to seeing him dread. If nothing else, that confirms I'm doing the right thing following up on this case. And also that I'm the worst detective in the Stillreal for letting it go unsolved for even a second.

"How many are we at?" I ask without wanting to.

Nurse Pawsome fumbles his words. The look of utter misery says it's not a number I want to hear.

"We're at eight," says Miss Mighty from behind me.

I spin around, my midsection objecting strenuously. Miss Mighty isn't wearing so much as a bandage. Her costume isn't even mussed. When her person built her to save people, she wasn't messing around.

Nurse Pawsome glances between the two of us, friendly face at a loss. "Your Panacea Potion should be ready soon," he sighs, and backs away from my bed. "I'll just check… I'll tell Spiderhand to come see ya when he's ready to be up and about." He hustles off away from us, scrubs swishing just like all the other nurses.

Miss Mighty frowns at Nurse Pawsome, gives a 'not my problem' shrug, and sits down in the chair at my bedside.

"How long until you heal?" she asks, with a look at my torso that tells me it's as bad as it feels.

"Panacea Potion brings back the dead if you use enough of it," I say. "Spidey and I should be up and kicking butt again in no time."

Miss Mighty's lips quirk, amused and wistful. "He's the only reason either of you are alive. You know that, right?"

"I'm a lucky roommate," I say.

"You're both lucky," she says.

We trade a glance, both sure that's the closest to an emotional moment we're going to have in this millennium.

"How did you know to come rescue us?" I ask.

"Spiderhand dragged me out of the Cape and Cowl."

I consider exactly how many shiploads of tea I'll have to buy to feel like I've thanked Spidey enough. "Okay," I say. "So, one: thank you. Two: I thought you weren't talking to me until I apologized? Three: I'd like to apologize."

Miss Mighty sits back in her chair, blinking. What can I say? Today has left me unwilling to beat around the bush.

"It was…" She clears her throat. "It was Spiderhand," she says flatly. "He was really worried, so I figured now wasn't the time to stand on principle." She gives me a frank, loaded stare.

I start to respond, and then I catch myself. First things first. "Is it alright if I apologize?"

Mighty frowns, clears her throat, and gives me half a wave. "Fine."

It comes barreling out of me. "I'm so sorry about what I did. I was so desperate to, to solve the case, and I got clue-drunk and – I told Spidey that it might be dangerous before we went in. I did. I promise."

Miss Mighty exhales slow and heavy. "Yeah. I figured you might." She runs a hand through her dark hair, looking off to the side while she gathers her thoughts. "I yelled at you because I was hurting, but I was mad at you because you didn't trust me. You thought I would say no to danger, and not only is that a total misunderstanding of who I am, that is not a decision you get to take from somebody." Her teeth clench. "Ever."

"I was clue-drunk," I repeat, nodding. "I'm trying to not let it–"

"You're more than a machine for interpreting clues."

My turn to stare. What did she just say?

"You're an incredible detective," she says. "You've helped a lot of Friends, including me, because of it. But you're more than that."

I blink, still trying to make sense of what she said.

Miss Mighty leans back in her chair, staring an exasperated stare at the ceiling. "I don't team up with you because you're the best at finding clues. I team up with you because I know where you go, there are going to be people who need help, and we are going to help them." She scoffs, "And adventure. Not gonna lie, that's a factor, too."

I snort. It's easier than having a genuine reaction. "Yeah, I'm really good at getting us in trouble."

"Someone has to be." She raises her head to look at me again. "I was going to miss kicking ass with you if you dropped dead on me." She gives me a wan smile, shakes her head, and then she's back to her usual look of disdainful steel.

My turn to clear my throat. "Eight, you said?" Maybe I'm not a machine for gathering clues, but I need a subject change.

Her smile fades as she recites her information. "Eight confirmed. He took down that octopus, the one Spiderhand said was called Plug." She sighs, tension knotting up her voice. "And Azure Armadillo says Victor Crane went down trying to follow up the same leads you were. Sources say we've lost touch with some of the guys from the Mousehole Wars, too." Her eyebrows raise, the only fear she's willing to show me. "Everyone's on edge."

She's saying it that way so she doesn't have to admit she's including herself. "How bad?" I ask.

She looks away from me, shakes her head. "We need to do something." I hear the familiar squeeze of her glove making a fist.

"You did a number on the guy underwater," I offer.

She scoffs. "Yeah, but he went down easy." She glances sidelong back at me. "There was no way that was the… the main guy," she finishes, tongue-tied and frustrated.

"No," I say. "There are copies all over the place." I squeeze my eyes shut, shake my head. My brain still isn't running on all cylinders.

"You mean like the one that broke my leg?" she asks flatly.

"Yeah," I wince. "That."

"I'm over it," she says, and she absolutely means it. "Keep talking."

So I do. "The white shards, the broken plates? They show up everywhere he kills people. Seems to leave behind duplicates with them. Like–" what was the word Dr Atrocity used? "–like an infection."

Mighty cocks an eyebrow. "White shards?"

"They're bits of tea services. He's got – the whales down underwater, they said something about a tea party…"

"We're dealing with an evil murdering tea party?"

"You've dealt with weirder," I say. My brain trips over what I said a second ago. "But… wait." Lightbulb. "There were no teacups in Smile House."

"Huh?"

"The Man in Smile House, he was different than the others. Bigger. Faster. And there weren't any teacups there. At least not when he showed up." I triple-check my thought, because I do not want to deal with the look it's going to get me unless I'm sure. "I think that's the original."

"The original what?"

"He's someone's Friend," I say.

"Someone created a Friend who murders other Friends and mutates Ideas permanently?" You could cut a hole in a bank vault with Miss Mighty's tone.

"Someone obsessed with tea parties," I say, thinking back to the memory whales. "Someone who gets frustrated and says 'Fine' when the tea parties don't go well and then..."

I don't need to finish my thought. I can tell by the way Mighty's gloves squeak that she knows what comes next.

"And I think," I say, letting the puzzle pieces fall into place, "and I think it's what's driving all these new Ideas out here into the Stillreal."

Miss Mighty's eyes widen. "What?"

I nod. "Just figured it out before I got jumped out there on the high seas." I'm staying vague for now – she won't like hearing I've been to see Dr Atrocity. Not my finest decision. "Spindleman and the octopi, at minimum, came here with those broken shards already in their home Ideas. I think whoever created the Man in the Coat is who traumatized their people into sending them here."

Her breath catches. "He's a monster."

"The Man's person?"

"Yes!" she says. "He's – what you're describing – that's a serial killer!" Her jaw works. "The clones, like the one in the Memory Reefs and the house–" her hand grazes her leg "–they're what, like, living trauma? People's grief and fear getting up and walking around?"

"It's more complicated than that, for sure," I say, thinking of the one in the Freedom Motel, "but... oh gosh..." Just saying the name of the place gets me thinking. I'm already getting down from the bed as I say, "Frieda. I need to go talk to Frieda."

This time, it's Miss Mighty who shoves me back into bed. She's not as kind about it as Nurse Pawsome; her hand is like a cement block. Attached to a battleship.

"No," she says. "You need to wait for Spiderhand to be good to go, and you need to wait for both of you to drink your Panacea Potion, and you need to calm down and not rip your stitches."

"I'm made of cloth–"

"You're made of my friend. And you are going to take care of my friend or I am going to knock my friend's block off."

"But–" I say. "But–"

"You plan to solve crimes without working back legs?"

"But–"

"If you say 'but' again I am bending this bed into a cage."

I kind of wanted to shut up before that anyway. I slump back into the bed and stare out at the blue, white and yellow, listen to the swishing of scrubs and the murmurs of nurses, while I wait for my potion to be ready. After a few seconds, Miss Mighty clears her throat.

"So our next lead is Frieda?"

I look over at her, let her know the use of 'our' didn't go unnoticed. "Frieda has been involved in this longer than we have and longer than she's let on. I have that on authority from the Snitching Snipe."

"Why haven't you questioned her yet, then?"

My thoughts twitch at the question. "Well... I figured she didn't need to be reminded of what she went through right away. Not while I had other leads."

Miss Mighty looks me up and down, and softens into a smile, one of the few that hasn't come out because she was making fun of me. "You're a good guy, Tippy."

I wince at the compliment. "Detective Tippy."

"Whatever."

Given everything going on today, I let her dismissal of my hard-earned title slide.

CHAPTER TWENTY-ONE

Panacea Potion tastes like toasted marshmallows and honey, and it really does heal everything, but I still feel like I was put back together with the wrong size parts.

Mighty and I meet up with Spiderhand at the checkout desk. There's a full-sprint hug when he sees me up and walking around. Nurse Pawsome separates us (with a smiling lecture about undoing all the doctors' hard work) and leaves us to limp out of Saint Sunbeam, one of us on each of Miss Mighty's arms, while I weather Spidey's storm of questions. Who do I think the Man in the Coat is? Do I think it's Spidey's fault? Is there any way he can help? I don't know, no, and no, I say, going from confused, to touched, to distracted as we walk through Playtime Town.

Miss Mighty said it was getting bad, but somehow seeing it is always worse than hearing it. The Worst Cat and Boss Raccoon are lurking in one of the alleys, but instead of their usual furtive cigarette-smoking and stolen-candy-eating they're both watching the street like they're waiting for test results. Rocky and Lloyd walk past us with their hands white-knuckled into each other, walking double-time. Rocky twitches away from us when we pass close by, and Lloyd looks at me like I'm a life raft in a stormy sea. Golem Jones is being defiant at least, sitting in his hot dog shack with his rocky fists planted on the counter and his eyes glaring out at the world, still doing the business he does. If I look close though, even he's shaking a little. I need to fix this, and to do that I need answers.

However much Spidey wants to help, he's content to head up to the apartment and practice his piano. Judging by the cant to his gestures, he's nervous that he won't be able to play right anymore. I try to send Miss Mighty with him, but she answers me with a shaking head and crossed arms.

"You're dealing with bad guys who can do damage like we haven't ever seen before," she says, with a meaningful glance at Spidey. "You think I'm letting you out of my sight for a second?"

"Weren't you mad at me?"

"You apologized," she replies, in the way you'd say the sky is blue.

I'm too exhausted to argue. "Alright, but I need you to stay out of Frieda's line of sight. This is a house call, not an interrogation."

"You're no fun," she says with a smirk.

Frieda lives downstairs, in one of the swank corner apartments. Jones must really be taking pity on her. Mighty parks herself in the stairwell, watching me with playing-it-cool detachment that almost paves over her eagerness to punch something. Frieda takes her sweet time answering my knock, but soon enough there's a jingle of keys, the chunking sounds of padlocks coming undone, and the door opens to show me my favorite eagle, watching me with wary blue eyes and every muscle tensed.

"Tippy," she says. She doesn't even pretend to be surprised.

"Frieda. You acclimating alright?"

"No," she says with a scoff. "But you already knew that."

I give her my pre-interrogation smile. I'm getting a lot of practice with it these days. "Yeah, I figured. You got a sec?"

"For you, buddy? Sure." She steps back, gestures for me to come inside. "I think the apartment came with some tea. Ya want some?"

"Ceratopsians love tea," I say, already walking in past her. I hear Miss Mighty's glove squeak as the door closes.

The apartment is identical to my apartment. I take a seat on a familiar big white couch in a living room that lacks only the piano and Spidey's bric-a-brac, and watch Frieda waddle around the kitchen poking her beak into the cupboards.

"What d'you wanna ask me?" she calls, as she opens and closes cabinets.

"I wanted to know more about what happened at the motel."

There's an instant's pause, and then she dives into tea preparation. "Go ahead 'n' ask," she says, over the sound of running water.

"I'm asking about everything, Free. Every detail you can stand giving me, every weird little thing you noticed. How did we get from the Freedom Motel I stayed at to the mess I pulled you out of?"

Frieda stares at the wall like it might have the answer written on it somewhere. "First noticed it about... four months ago," she says, shoving herself back into setting up the kettle.

My admiration for the Snitching Snipe continues to grow. "What did you notice?"

She looks at the kettle, hastily drops it onto a burner. "One of my guests... disappeared. I assumed they were leavin' because they wanted to... but then another one disappeared, and that one was a long-term resident, someone I knew wasn't leavin' without me knowin' where. Then Spindleman vanished. Three is a pattern, s'what I've always been taught. So I checked out their rooms..."

Frieda starts the water boiling, leans against the fridge with her wings folded. Detective stuff doesn't miss how heavily she slumps against it.

"And they had been redecorated with broken plates?" I prompt.

Frieda's eyes flicker red before they snap back to solid blue. She rights herself and flaps over to the cabinets, rummaging through them for something to pour the tea into.

"After Spindleman left, that was the first time I saw the Man in the Coat. He never came anywhere near the front office, he seemed to just lurk around the rooms. I started droppin' warnings on peoples' doorsteps, tellin' 'em to get out." She stops midway through grabbing something from a high shelf. "Your visit was the first time it ever came after me..."

She's clearly wondering why. If I had the answer, I'd give it to her. Instead, I squirm in my seat. "Yeah," I say. "That's going around." I feel as terrible as that sounds.

Frieda shakes her head and pulls a pair of cups out of the cabinet, a sippy cup and a silver goblet. (In Playtime Town we scrounge up what we can.) By the time she's got the tea pouring, she's not even shaking anymore, and her eyes have gone from blue to neutral white. I take the sippy cup from her and take a careful, well-secured sip before I move to the next part.

"Frieda?" I say.

She glances up, eyes back to blue. "Yes?"

"That first Friend you said disappeared…"

The worry brightens. "Yes?"

"Are they who caused the changes in room 303?"

Frieda's beak falls open, and her eyes go so blue they're almost black. That's pretty much a yes. She picks up her goblet, sets it back down, picks it back up again. I've hit my mark.

"Should I finish my tea first?" I ask.

One eye blinks red. "Sorry. It's been a… complicated time, lately."

"You have a funny definition of 'complicated.'"

"Nothin' funny about it." She slams her goblet down on the table, and once we've both winced at the sound, she says, "Yes. That's who stayed in room 303."

"I figured. Everything I've learned about the Man in the Coat and his person tell me they'd be into someone whose Friend still works in crayon." I take a careful sip of my tea, giving her time to stew. "So… are you gonna make me ask?"

Frieda looks at me down her beak, waiting for me to go on.

"Are they dead?" I ask, not beating around the bush.

She winces, both eyes blue. "Why?"

"Because I think I can stop this guy, but I need more," – clues – "information. And if one of the Man's first victims is alive, I have to say, I cannot think of a better source of information that doesn't put me," – in the Memory Reefs, way too close to the rain – "in striking distance of a bat."

Frieda holds her head steady, high and judgmental. "I was created to protect people who can't protect themselves."

"I know."

"Not like this you don't. I don't know how badly you need to solve cases, and you don't know how badly I need to help keep my guests safe. And Wrrbrr…" She closes her eyes, folding up like she's going into a moment of silence. "She wasn't the first one, I don't think. I think she's just the first one who got away." Her eyes go back to that almost-black shade. "She had been runnin' for four days when I found her. She was half-starved because she didn't know what she could safely eat…"

I see how this unpleasant story is going to play out, but I'm not going to get in the way.

"When the Man came lookin' for her… I knew she couldn't survive on her own, not like the Playtime Town residents could, and… she reminded me of…" She shakes her head to and fro. "The Man breaks all the rules. For all I knew, if anyone knew where Wrrbrr was, he could find her. I had to keep her hidden. From everyone."

"He's not a god," I say. "He's just a nightmare who thinks he's special."

Freedom Frieda nods, takes in a deep breath, and looks me in the eye. "You really think Wrrbrr can help you?"

I return her look. "I really do."

Frieda draws in another deep breath, smoothes a wrinkle in her stars-and-stripes apron, and gives me a resolute nod before getting off the couch and walking down the hall toward the bedrooms.

"Where are you–"

I hop down from my own seat, start to follow, and hear the door to her bedroom slam. Detective stuff picks up the tiny rumble of dresser drawers opening, the dry rustle of paper. Frieda steps back out into the hallway, a wrinkled white sheet of typewriter paper in her hand. I can see the crayon scrawls on it through the back.

"Fine," she says, angry, but a little bit relieved. "Let's go visit her."

I say nothing. I should go tell Mighty that I'm leaving, but I'm afraid to do anything that might knock Frieda off the track I've finally got her on. I'm a great friend, apparently.

Frieda lays the sheet of paper out on her kitchen counter, pulls me up onto one of the stools. The paper is covered in a drawing so blobby and imprecise it's practically abstract art. I recognize a profile view of some kind of chair, a stick-figure rendering of a table, and a background of brown scribbles that appear to have leaves on them. Not even my detective stuff can get more detail out of that picture.

"Where did this come from?"

"Where ya think?" Frieda says. "Hold on."

We think up and out of the apartment, out of Playtime Town. Frieda's white-on-white apartment disappears, replaced with one decorated in much darker colors. The place is tiny, is my first impression. There's a card table in the corner instead of a proper dining room, a leather easy chair next to it. If I squint, it kind of looks like the chair in the drawing. There's a kitchen as big as a closet at one end of the room, and a hallway off the other end that doesn't look like it leads to much at all. The tree-patterned wallpaper is peeling, water is dripping from a pipe somewhere, and the floor is the kind of dirty that'll never really wash off. Standard rundown apartment, except for the little pixies flitting around inside the light fixture, the runes carved into the buildings outside the stained windows, and the fact that the card table and half the dishes in the sink look like they were made out of chunks of colored wax.

I look out the window. It's nighttime here, and late at night based on the depth of the darkness. The street lamps have the same tiny fairies inside as the one in the apartment, and beyond the rune-etched buildings I can see a tower shaped like a sword sticking up out of the bay. We're in Santa Erzulie, the urban fantasy Idea. And that's when my thoughts finally catch up to the truth. "Oh."

This place is the perfect safehouse, unique enough that the Man in the Coat wouldn't stumble on it accidentally, uninteresting enough that just finding the drawing wouldn't get you here easily. I mean, there are more out-of-the-way Ideas than Santa Erzulie, but they're also less populated, which means fewer people for a refugee to get help from if, say, a homicidal nightmare came busting through the wall. Tactically, this is aces, and the fact I am even thinking about that proves this case is the worst.

"Wrrbrr?" calls Frieda, walking into the little hallway to nowhere. A door opens, and Frieda speaks again, this time with a surge of relief.

"It's alright. They aren't goin' to raise the rent." That's got to be a code phrase. (The. Worst.)

Footsteps come back toward the living room. Frieda's are easy to identify, but the other set barely makes any sound at all, like a cotton ball dragged across a blanket. Frieda steps into the living room, her eyes glowing a plaintive, worried blue. Wrrbrr comes in behind her, and I get the unadulterated fun of trying to process what I'm seeing.

Wrrbrr is alive, that's one thing I can say with authority. Their color shifts up and down the rainbow from second to second, and their shape goes from a sort of rounded, rubbery version of Frieda to a flat, dog-sized raindrop once they stop moving. They have a face, three dents of shadow near the front, and they look at me with a skittish uncertainty that tells me their personality is still mostly composed of innocence. This is a Friend from a very undeveloped mind – probably a baby's. The Snipe said the first victim was too new to have a name, and Wrrbrr is only slightly older than that.

What the heck kind of monster am I dealing with?

"Wrrbrr," Frieda says, "this is Tippy." She gestures in my direction. "He is a good friend of mine, and he wants to ask you some questions."

Wrrbrr looks at me with those marker-dot eyes, and I get dizzy at the fear I see there. It's a face built for smiling that's still figuring out how to show what they feel now, the face of someone who had the joy slapped out of their hands while they were still playing with it. I want to hug them and take them home and offer them some of Spiderhand's cookies.

"Hi," I say, with ashes in my mouth. "I'm Detective Tippy. What's your name and pronoun?"

Frieda clears her throat. "Her name is—"

"I asked them," I say, barely talking my eyes off Wrrbrr.

Frieda's mouth goes quiet, but her eyes glow red.

The blobby little Friend looks at Frieda, at me, face scrunched up as they try to make the hardest decision. When they speak, it's in a breathy little whisper, like air escaping from a party balloon.

"I'm Wrrbrr," they say, a little roll to the 'r's that Frieda didn't quite nail. "And... and..." They scrunch up their face again. "What's a pronoun, please?"

So, so many cookies. "When I call you something besides your name," I say, triple-checking it sounds simple without sounding condescending, "the words I use are pronouns. For some people, it's he, him, and his; for some it's she, her, and hers; I know a few it and its, some ze, zir, zirs."

Wrrbrr again takes a questioning look at Frieda. "Um… I'm… that second one. I'm a she. Like Bonnie."

I'm guessing Bonnie is her person, but I'm not sure she's in a position to explain. "Pleased to meet you, Wrrbrr. How are you doing?"

"Scared!" she admits, with the ghost of a wail.

If I can't pull off cookies, maybe I can try committing violence against everyone who ever hurt her. "What has you scared? Do you want to talk about it?"

"The Man," she wheezes. "The Man who came for her when the other Man, the real Man, came."

The real Man. My rage is cooled courtesy of the chills running up my spine. "Was he a man in a long, dark coat?"

"Yes!" Wrrbrr yelps.

Frieda glowers at me, eyes stop-sign red. I give her just enough glance to let her know the complaint has been noted.

"Listen, Wrrbrr," I say. "I'm a detective. Do you know what a detective is?"

"Yes!" she says. "I – I read about you. Or people like you. You find things that are missing."

She can read, and she can read at an advanced enough level to have read detective fiction. That doesn't jive at all with the age range I'm guessing this half-formed Idea came from, which means either I'm missing my guess, or Frieda's had her stashed in Santa Erzulie longer than I thought.

"So, Wrrbrr, detectives don't just find things. Detectives also stop bad people. People who make things go missing. I'm…" About to scare you more? "I'm trying to stop the Man in the Coat."

Wrrbrr's eyes go wide and hopeful.

"And I'm hoping you can help me."

Scratch the hope, mark up some fear. Wrrbrr's head/body/thing shakes side to side in the universal gesture of half-conscious denial. "I…

I don't know if…" She slides backward, pressing herself flat against the floor. "I don't think I can help…"

"If you can't, that's okay," I say, as quiet and as soft as I can manage while every inch of me is on fire with worry. "But if you can, that's great."

"Um. Ask, please? I want to help."

"Great." I straighten my shoulders, check my tone in my head. "The Man in the Coat. When did he come for Bonnie?"

Wrrbrr squishes herself flat again. "A long time ago."

"Do you remember how long?"

"A little over four months," Frieda says. Her eyes are fading to an annoyed pink.

Three months, three weeks, two days, eight hours… "Okay. That's," – the words I dam up are 'what I hoped to hear' – "Do you remember the place you came from? The place Bonnie put you in?"

"The Space Kingdom," Wrrbrr says. "I'm a space knight." Her pride is the most painful thing I've heard yet today.

"Really?" I say.

"Yes," Wrrbrr says, beaming, the black streak of her mouth suddenly shiny with primary-white teeth. "The youngest space knight!"

"That's very impressive," I say. It probably actually is, but better to act like it either way. "What do space knights do?"

She frowns. "They, um…" She stops for an uneasy breath. "Space knights defend the Space Kingdom, and all three moons, and the peanut butter swamp and the spoon people."

"Against who?"

Confusion creases Wrrbrr's face again. "Against – the fork people," she says. "And the people in the nasty underpants."

"The nasty underpants?" I almost giggle at the raw hate in her voice.

"Yes. The Nasty Party's storm stupors."

Oh. That's a dark twist. "You fight the Nazi – Nasty Party, you say?"

"I used to," she says, again confused, and more than a little pained. "But then… then…"

Her mouth winds up into an actual spiral, and the surface of her body starts to undulate. Detective stuff reads it as nerves.

Freedom Frieda lays one gentle wing on Wrrbrr. "It's okay," she says. "You're okay."

"But I failed…" Wrrbrr says.

I'm not crying.

"There was nothin' you could do," Frieda responds, eyes rocketing deep into blue.

Still not crying.

I wait for Wrrbrr to regain her stability before I continue.

"It sounds like you're very courageous," I say, to a warning look from Frieda.

"Queen said I was the bravest," she boasts. "Because I have the most to fear."

"That makes total sense," I say. "Do you have a sword or any other symbol of office?"

"I have…" If that color is what I think it is, Wrrbrr blushes. "I have Star Power."

"That's very impressive," I say, piling on the amazement. "What does Star Power do?"

Wrrbrr quivers for a second, afraid to meet my eyes. "We can put up stars as shields, or, um, fly around on shooting stars. We can summon the Star Sword or the Star Cannon." The way she says it makes it sound like the best thing ever. "And we can look at the stars, and, um, and we can know the future."

Know the future. There's my opening. "Okay," I say. "Do you think you could use the stars to learn something for me? Or maybe you already know it." I make it sound like that would be the most impressive thing of all.

Wrrbrr grows a tiny bit taller. "What?" she asks. "What?"

Frieda is less looking daggers at me and more throwing entire silverware drawers with her face. I weather the judgment, and ask:

"Do you think you and the stars could help me get to the Space Kingdom?"

Wrrbrr's mouth drops open. "What?" she squeaks.

Frieda goes back from pink to red, her beak clacking in warning.

"No pressure," I say, lying. "No pressure at all, Wrrbrr, but – if you can get me back to the Space Kingdom, I can look there for – missing things. Hidden things."

"Clues?" Wrrbrr snuffles. Her colors have gone paler, her eyes bigger to match her mouth.

I nod. "Clues."

Her face shifts backward on her body, moving as far away from me as possible. "What clues, please?"

"It sounds like – I'm so sorry, but–" if you mess this up, Tippy, you are such a jerk "–it sounds like you were one of the first to be attacked. If you can get me there, I might be able to figure out how to stop this."

Wrrbrr grows a head and neck again, this time so she can shake it. "It's not safe there," she says, voice quivering.

"What kind of not safe?" I ask, and immediately regret it.

I deserve the blazing stink-eye I get from Freedom Frieda. When that terrible question comes out, Wrrbrr pancakes against the ground, huge eyes watching me like I might be about to explode. She shakes side to side again, less like she's saying no and more like she's gelatin that just got knocked off the counter.

"I'm sorry," I say. "I–"

"The Man is there," Wrrbrr whimpers from the floor. "He stayed. He looked for me. He's still looking for me. If I go back, he'll come after me!"

I step toward her, and am blocked by the looming bulk of Freedom Frieda.

"It's alright, Wrrbrr," she says. "You don't have to talk to him about the Space Kingdom."

"I want to help!" Wrrbrr says. Her voice is cracking around the edges. "I really do, please, I really want to help–"

"I know, sweetie," Frieda says, shifting into her knowing mother voice as she turns around. "And you'll be able to help one day."

"I want to go home…" More than the edges are cracking.

Frieda's back arches. "I know, Wrrbrr. I know."

"I'm a space knight," Wrrbrr near-whispers. "A space knight is supposed to be brave, and nifty, and… and…" And then her voice is nothing but cracks.

Frieda picks Wrrbrr up, cradling and shushing her as she walks the whining, whimpering little jelly drop back into the hallway. Or that's what my detective stuff tells me while I'm examining every detail of the floor.

The part of me that's screaming isn't as loud as the part that's thanking the stroke of bad luck. Getting shut down is frustrating, getting stopped just shy of possibly cracking this case hurts at my core, but the thing that makes me feel the worst is how afraid I am. Not for poor Wrrbrr, but for myself.

Frieda comes back down the hall with the mechanical care of a parent trying not to wake a baby. She comes into the living room, eyes blazing like the noonday sun, and crosses her wings as she regards me with disgust.

"What were you thinkin'?" she hisses.

"This case threatens the entire Stillreal," I say. "If there's a lead I can pursue–"

"You don't help the Stillreal if all of us are sufferin' the entire time you're workin'," Frieda spits. "Wrrbrr has gone through enough."

That stings. "We've all gone through a lot–"

"We didn't go through it that *young*," Frieda says.

All the fear, frustration, and pain wells up in me as I consider her very true statement, and the pressure pushes the absolute worst possible response out of me.

"I know you exist to take care of us," I say, "but keeping one Friend hidden away doesn't fix what the Man in the Coat did to your guests."

Frieda rears up, wings unfurled, eyes so bright they turn the entire apartment red. She hesitates, pulls her wings back in, and looks at me with one eye red and one eye sapphire blue.

"I know you're hurtin'," she says. "So I forgive you."

I start to respond, but–

"Now get out."

She's not about to brook another shot from me, no matter how witty it is. So I look out the window, find a trashcan sitting at the mouth of an alley, and admit defeat.

I land back in Playtime Town in Boss Raccoon's alley. There's no sign of him or the Worst Cat, but the piles of strangely cute garbage are disturbed in a way that makes it look like they left in a hurry. I look around the lifeless alley, and I have to wonder if they left, or were killed.

I have to fix this; none of us should have to think like that. The fear comes back to me when I remember what that means, given Frieda won't let Wrrbrr help me.

I have to go back to the Memory Reefs.

CHAPTER TWENTY-TWO

"Tippy, did you forget what a plan looks like?"

I take another sip of the tea Spiderhand has brewed for us. This one tastes like peppermint and rose petals. "If I had, how would I know?"

Miss Mighty takes a deep, centering breath, and sits back down at the table. "I barely pulled you out of there last time, and that was only because Spidey pulled off a half-terrible plan in the first place." She waves an annoyed hand in his direction, and balks when he enthusiastically waves back.

I can't help it, I crack a grin. For a second, anyway. "Look, Mighty, I don't like it either. But a lead is a lead is a lead."

"Because that attitude has done well for us so far," she mutters.

"Yeah," I say. "I know."

That takes her off-guard. "What?"

"You don't like my idea," I say. "That makes sense. This is absolutely a *very bad idea*. We won't be anywhere either of us knows well, we won't–"

Spiderhand stops me with an ornate series of finger motions. If I had a shade besides yellow I would blush.

"Sorry – Spiderhand knows the area alright. Sorry Spidey." I nod at his 'it's okay' finger-dance. "Point is, I know. It's the riskiest risk we could take."

"And you know I am all about that," Miss Mighty says. "But I need to know why we're doing it."

That may be the most subtext I have ever heard from Miss Mighty. I shake out my stitched-up body, and get ready to do what detectives are terrible at: telling secrets. "When you were down there… you saw the whales?"

"It's kind of hard to miss whales."

"Of course." I don't rise to the bait, not even for play. Now is not the time. "The octopi called them memory whales. They stored all their creator's memories. Ones she hadn't had yet, and all the ones she'd had—"

"The night she was attacked…" says Mighty, trailing off. "You think the whales might have her memory of the attacker. The Man's person." She gives me a crooked smile. "This is why we're friends."

"Thanks," I say. "So yeah," I continue, clearing my throat. "We have no idea how much of a mess it is down there, but if we're going to solve this—"

"We are."

Spiderhand agrees, too. I've got something in both my eyes.

"Anyway. It's this, or we start combing through individual teacup pieces looking for a clue."

Miss Mighty grimaces. "I'd rather get punched."

"What else is new?"

Miss Mighty smirks, and bows her head in admission of being one-upped. "I'll take you back to the Memory Reefs," she says. "I wish we had a plan that was more of the good kind of exciting, but if you think this is the best way to get this handled, I trust you." She lets out another sigh, slumps down in her chair. "Jesus, your job sucks, Tippy."

"Lately? Yeah. *Our* job does suck."

Miss Mighty snorts. "After we solve this case, I'm buying you like six dozen of whatever ludicrous excuse for beer you drink in Playtime Town."

I smile, and let this brief calm wash over me. "We drink root beer."

Miss Mighty shakes her head. "Why am I not surprised?"

"Because you're actually one of the smartest Friends I know?"

"If you make me blush, I'm going to invert your face."

"It's nice to know you care. Spidey?"

Our local hand perks up, fingers curled into worry and anticipation. "You good to go?"

He considers for a second, and hand-nods. I look at Miss Mighty, but she's already holding onto his pinky finger and smiling at me like I'm a slowpoke. I love-hate my life.

Spiderhand concentrates on the teacups sitting out on the table, still smelling of mint, roses and so much sugar, and thinks us straight back to the white-gold ocean floor. Detective stuff says the floor has some new irregularities, but before I get moving, I look to Miss Mighty again. She nods and swims a few strides straight up, taking a sentry position while Spiderhand and I get to sifting through the sand.

The nearest irregularity in the floor is a deep tan color, long and lumpy. I'm already pretty sure I know what it is, enough so that I'm shaking when I dig it free. It's a tool belt, like the one Plug left behind, but the color of the one Cable was wearing.

Dang it.

Miss Mighty whistles from above, points once she has my attention. I follow the point, and see Spidey, his hangdog gesture locked in place, holding up a screwdriver just like the one I saw in Breaker's belt. That puts a little extra oomph into my search. I make a gesture that I hope Mighty and Spiderhand read as 'try to find the other one.'

Mighty raises herself up a few more meters, taking a broader survey of the area. Down on the floor, I check outward in a spiral, pawing at every odd patch of color in the sand. I'm looking for leather, buckles, or the other bits I saw dangling off the cherry-colored octopus' belt, but I get to the edge of the cell-caves without finding anything. The weight on my chest doesn't go away, but it does get a little lighter.

I check the caves that served as our jail cells: empty. I swim the length of the outcropping the cells are built into: nothing there, either. I consider a second check of the caves, maybe even a sixth or seventh… but however I'd prefer today goes, in the end, I know I have to check inside their bigger cousin.

I find it difficult to even approach the opening of the big cave. I have to stop every other step to take full stock of my surroundings, make sure no towering monsters in barnacled coats are ready for batting practice. The inside of the cave has gone back to normal, no divots, no silty water, no signs of us nearly dying in the dark. I gulp, and I step a little bit further into the darkness. When nothing in the cave moves, I do the really foolish part of my investigation.

"Hello?"

Still nothing to hear, see, or smell. That's got me more jangled than I expected. I back out of the cave, and start wadding up and throwing away ideas about what to do next. And as if on cue, Spiderhand comes shooting past me, flailing in absolute horror.

Moving fast is kind of Miss Mighty's shtick, but I've never appreciated how fast until now – she shoots out of sight before I've even decided to move. I check that Spidey is sheltered in place behind a stalagmite, and bolt toward the outcropping where Mighty disappeared. I'm not quite halfway there when I hear the crackling sound of electricity coming from around the corner. I rev up into a charge, but Mighty steps in my way as soon as I get going, annoyance smeared across her face, gesturing for me to stop with one hand while the other grips the tool belt of a struggling, shivering octopus.

Breaker's swinging around a cobbled-together wand-club-stun-gun-thing – that's what's emitting the electricity – and spreading her other arms as wide as they'll go. She looks as spooked as Spidey; I'm surprised I don't see ink. She jerks her weapon toward me, and goes into a frantic display of readjustment as she tries to find a way to cover both me and Miss Mighty at the same time.

"Let me go," Breaker whines. "Go away!" Her voice is high and trembling, a voice that only remembers sounding afraid. All of me cringes at once.

"Let her go," I say.

Miss Mighty raises her eyebrows. "She's got a cattle prod."

"And a stranger grappling her isn't going to make her less inclined to use it."

Mighty scowls, but still releases her grip. The octopus backs up, swinging the wand in a wide arc as she puts distance between us and her.

"Go away!" Breaker shrieks again. "Go away!"

I stay as still as I can. "Breaker?"

She keeps backing up until she bumps into the outcropping, spins around to brandish the wand at the rock, and jerks right back around to point it at us, her attention shooting off in every direction as she tries to figure out what's even a threat anymore.

"Breaker, it's me. The guy who escaped from the cave."

"I know!" she fires back. There's anger mixed in with the fear. Progress? "Go away!"

That's not happening. Not today. "I'm sorry, but I really need to–"

"My friends are dead!" screeches Breaker.

I get ice-water flashes of the last time I was down here, me and Spiderhand half-wrestling, half-panicking, my own stuffing drifting past my eyes, and the sound of the club hitting Plug in the head, almost as memorable as the sound of it hitting me. I remember Miss Mighty bringing down the Man, but I don't remember seeing Cable or Breaker as I fled… is it possible to die of guilt?

I don't sit down so much as sag. "I… I'm so sorry. We thought – *I* thought we were going to die, and I just did what I–"

"What?" Breaker says, baffled. "What are you talking about? He killed them!"

Is it possible to die of confusion? "But what are–"

"He came b-back!"

I go numb again as my memory kicks into gear. Cable was still alive when Miss Mighty took the Man in the Coat out. If Cable is dead…

"I've already t-talked to you t-t-too long," Breaker says. "I have to hide. I have to hide."

"But–"

"Go away!" she yells. But she's not moving. I still have a chance.

"Breaker," I say, "that's why we're here. We don't want you to have to hide."

193

She hesitates, attention ricocheting between the three of us. "I don't—"

"We've lost friends, too," I say, as slow and soft as possible. (We also nearly lost ourselves because her buddies thought live sacrifice was the right next step, but I won't point that out.) "Lots of people are dying, and everyone everywhere is hurting."

"Everywhere?"

I nod. "Outside the ocean, too."

"Ou-outside?" She acts like she can't pronounce the word. "Like – like in Sasha's world?"

"No. Other places like this. Other people like you. People who protect people like Sasha." Or used to, anyway. One horror at a time, though. "The Man in the Coat is after all of them. And we're here because we think you can help us stop him."

"H-how?"

"The whales. I need you to help us with the whales."

The ridges over Breaker's eyes wiggle as she processes these bizarre new ideas I'm filling her with. She ends the thoughtful period by curling her arms underneath her and shaking her head. "I can't."

"What do you mean, you can't?" Breathing is suddenly very hard.

"You need to go," she whimpers. "I have to h-hide, before—" Her eyes widen at nothing in particular. "You need to g-go."

What nerves I have left start to unravel. "Breaker, I understand you're upset. But if you help us, we can make sure he doesn't hurt anyone else."

Her arms knot up tighter. "I can't."

I can almost hear, almost *see* the information this little octopus has in her braincase. I can't give up. "Breaker, please." I swim forward, halt when she levels the wand again. "Please. We really need your help."

"I can't," she insists.

"Can't what?" I demand.

"Go. Away."

I have no nerves left, there's just fire. "No," I say, advancing on her again. "Please, you have to understand, we can save the whole Stillreal. Save *everybody*." Breaker points the wand right at me, and I ignore it in favor of more pleading. "This is about all of us. This is about the entire world. We can do it, we can, we just need to go talk to the—"

A hand grips my tail, and I freeze long enough to realize what I'm doing. I've left Breaker almost no personal space. She's backed up against a rock, wand crackling and swinging wild, eyes feral with fright, and I'm so close to her that if I twitch the wrong way, I'll knock into her. I feel Miss Mighty behind me, halfway to berserker rage. Spiderhand is to my right, twisted up in his own ball of nerves. My clarity crashes down into shame.

"I'm so sorry," I say, flailing back from her. "I didn't... I... Friends are dying, and..." I hang my head, and accept my fate. "I'm sorry."

Miss Mighty pats me on the back, just once, and shoves me off to the side. She's not rough about it, but I think that's general restraint rather than concern for me.

"Breaker?" Miss Mighty says. "Is that your name?"

"Yes..." Breaker's still got the wand in a death-grip.

"My name is Miss Mighty," Mighty responds, only slightly softer than her usual verbal battering ram. "Is it alright if I call you Breaker?"

Breaker gives her a gun-shy, measuring look, but squeaks out, "Okay."

"Great. Thank you." Mighty smiles at her, one of the only Mighty smiles that doesn't look like a bear trap. "Sounds like you're having a shitty time lately?"

Yes, my horns burn. Now is not the time to complain.

"Huh?" Breaker says.

"It sounds like some really, really bad stuff happened here." Mighty's voice hitches in understatement.

Breaker uncurls two arms, rubs them together in a worried gesture. "I lost my friends."

"I know. But even before that, it sounds like things here were really bad."

"Yes, but – I–"

"You angry about it?"

Breaker's eyes go big. "I–"

"Sorry," Mighty says. She pulls her hair back from her face. "Of course you're angry."

There's an edge to Miss Mighty's voice, a spikiness beyond the normal that she can't quite conceal. I focus on that rather than how much I want to jump in.

"What I really mean is," Mighty continues, "are you more angry, more hurt or more scared? I know you're feeling all of them," – she lets out the wettest breath on record – "but… what's in control right now?"

"I… I don't…"

"I know exactly how you feel," Miss Mighty says with a thick, smoky tone. "The Man in the Coat hurt your friends, and you know you couldn't do anything about it, but you still feel awful that you didn't."

Spiderhand tenses up into a sympathetic fist. I'm not doing much better.

"Now your friends are gone," Mighty continues. "You feel like your life doesn't make sense anymore. You've started telling yourself you can't do anything about anything, because if that's true, maybe you don't have to blame yourself." Miss Mighty wipes her face so fast I might be the only one who sees it. "That sound about right?"

Breaker's arms squeeze her even tighter. "… Yes."

Color me awed.

Mighty takes a second to adjust her domino mask. "Then can I tell you something? As a reward for me guessing right?" There's the tiniest, shakiest joke in there.

"Y… yes?"

Miss Mighty raises a finger, and points it at me. "When I felt like that, Tippy here was one of the people who made me feel better."

Reality and I go our separate ways. I get my mind screwed back into place in time to hear Miss Mighty explain that "He's a helper. He helps people who have been hurt. People like you."

Breaker doesn't respond. She's still terrified, but her arms are a little looser, and she's giving me a much closer study.

"He has lots of questions," Miss Mighty says. "And he was rude about asking them. But it's because a lot of other people are hurt too, and he thinks you can help them. You can see how that might get someone not thinking so clearly in the moment."

Thanks, Mighty. Glad to know you, too.

Breaker looks at Miss Mighty, looks at me, getting more worried each time she alternates targets. "I – I like to help people…"

Miss Mighty smiles. "Don't we all. If you want to help, though? You're going to have to answer his questions."

Breaker's breath catches again. She looks at me like she thinks I might bite. I smile and float there, looking as innocent as I can manage.

Her arms flop loose in time with her sigh, and she half-whispers, "Okay."

Miss Mighty turns, and with a warning glance at me, moves for me to take her place.

I swim up, clear my throat. I need to start soft. After that display I can't really do anything less.

"Is it alright if I still call you Breaker?" I ask.

"Yes."

"Great. And your pronoun is she, right?"

"Yes."

"Good, good." I glance at Miss Mighty, and get a nod of approval in return. "Okay, so first of all: I'm sorry. You don't have to forgive me, but I shouldn't have pushed so hard and you deserve to hear tha–"

"It's okay," Breaker says. "I f-forgive you. We're all st-st-stressed."

A smile washes over me unhidden. I shrug it off. "So, I know this is going to be unpleasant, so I'll try to make it short. Do you know where the Man in the Coat is now?"

Breaker twitches. "No. After you all left, he, he came back bigger, and meaner. So I took their weapons and I h-hid back here, and I've just been… waiting…"

Her breaths are turning into hiccups, and her eyes can't seem to remember how to focus. I hope questions help her as much as they do me.

"Breaker. Breaker."

With some effort, she gets her eyes locked on me.

"When I was here last, you asked which zone I came from."

"No, I – that was – Cable w-wanted to know that," she says, and she slides back into her warmed-over angst. "Cable believed that y-you c-came from No-Pi's Land. He always said he and I were g-going to… explore them… when… w-when…"

When they were free. I wonder if I can hug her and destroy everything in sight at the same time.

"How are the zones divided up?" I ask, slow and quiet.

"The higher the number, the later the memories." She says it with ritual calm. "The memory towers follow a very clear path of progression as she ages."

"How old is Sasha?"

"Eight right now," Breaker says. Her arms curl. "Or, eight the last time I checked."

"'Checked'?" I ask.

"The – the – the memory towers… there are ways to check which memories are real and which are f-future memories, but, the towers haven't changed in a while. We had been assuming some l-latency in the systems due to the intrusions, but, now…"

I tense bits I didn't know I had. "They stopped around the time the Man in the Coat showed up, didn't they?"

Breaker's eyes are basically made of pain. "…Yes."

I start to ask the next question, but she bowls me over with a truckload of words.

"That was how we figured out he was here. We started having towers stagnate, no new memories, no rewriting of the future ones. We kept running tests, we f-figured it was an error with the tools, b-but we weren't finding anything wrong… we j-just thought it was, was something we hadn't found yet, b-but then the whales started showing up with the bruises, and then… Outlet. Outlet was tr-trying to in-in-initiate a reboot and then he… he…"

I prepare my question again, but my detective stuff nudges me about the tiny, almost subsonic whimper starting to issue from Breaker, and I can only watch in horror and mounting sympathy as the whimper builds into a head-hanging, limp-armed sniffle.

"He…" she says, and sinks into the whimper again.

Miss Mighty and I trade looks, hers uncomfortable and mine lost. I want to fix it, but the last thing I need to do right now is ask her another question. Mighty gestures at me, urging me to do something. I give her a frustrated shrug. She starts to speak, and the sniffles cut off with a gasp.

Spiderhand is floating next to Breaker, his pointer finger extended, waiting without tension or judgment in his manner. Breaker looks... looks... and with a flood of gratitude, wraps one arm around the end of his finger.

How many times is my heart going to break in one conversation?

"It's okay to cry," Miss Mighty says, her voice rough and unsteady.

Breaker sniffles again, louder. And louder. And then she and Spiderhand get tangled up in a heap as she goes into all-out, pedal-to-the-metal sobbing, like I haven't heard since Sandra. This isn't her original pain, but we're not far off.

Miss Mighty floats backwards from the outburst, watching Breaker like she thinks she can wish her better. I wait until Breaker seems to be sputtering out, and look to Miss Mighty for a nod of approval before I continue.

"Breaker?" I ask, my own voice shaking now.

The octopus looks up at me, still entangled with Spiderhand.

"I want to help you – help all of us – figure out this problem. This Man who hurt you and took your friends."

She snorts wetly, and nods.

"Can you take me to a specific time in Sasha's memories?" I ask.

"I..." Her brows knit as she considers. "I... oh." To my surprise, she brightens. "Oh maybe. Wait..." She uncoils from Spiderhand. "Yes! I can!" She's crying again, but this time it's joy. So I've done something right, at least.

"When we were – when everything was working right," she says, still trying to dry out her words, "I proofed the memories. Made sure they weren't losing resolution."

Resolution. I'd say this is weird, but lately I'm dealing with weirder.

Breaker continues, picking up speed along with volume. "So, I had this, this... mental shopping list," she says, tapping between her eyes.

"Wh-where everything was, when it took place, if it was real or f-future stuff, everything I had to know to be sure the memory was good. And I remember… r-right before all the, the," – her eyes widen – "the M-M-Man… stuff. Right before that, one of the future memories got o-overwritten with… s-something about the teacups."

The click of realization sounds inside my skull. "When I was swimming down here the first time, I heard one of the memory whales talking about teacups. Some guy who wouldn't stop giving Sasha tea."

"That's it!" Breaker shouts. "It popped up right before we had the system errors. Cable didn't f-figure it h-had… anything to do with the problem, but…" She loses focus again. "M-m-maybe it… maybe…"

"Do you know where we could find the first memory Sasha has of the tea?"

Breaker's eyes just about cross. "I don't – I can't–" Her voice rises in pitch. "Those m-memories are really f-f-far out in the Reefs, and, and the memory whales may not r-react well to you, and I usually do this with-with-with other people and, and… I…"

Breaker looks between Spiderhand, and me, and Miss Mighty, doubt swirling down into the depths of her pupils.

"You think you can stop him?" she hiccups. "From hurting anyone else?"

"If you can get us to the oldest memory?" I say. "Then I have to believe we can." I mean it exactly like I say it.

Breaker's arms unfurl from beneath her, and she gives me – I think – the octopus equivalent of a determined smile. "Then let's get going."

She goes shooting off toward the memory towers, not even waiting for us to follow. Spiderhand paddles after her, just as enthusiastic. Miss Mighty treads water for a second and shares a long, frayed glance with me before swimming away in kind.

I'm swimming through an Idea that wasn't in the Stillreal until a serial-killing Friend brought it here, and I'm following a trail of clues that's almost gotten me killed three times. I follow after Breaker, trying to find a fitting shape of smile for what I feel.

CHAPTER TWENTY-THREE

The memory towers look different approached from the bottom: colossal towers of metal and glass, blasting electricity into the water overhead. Each base has a piece of packing tape stuck to it, a string of numbers written on it in permanent marker. My detective stuff says the numbers were written using octopus arms, and my eyes verify it by how sad Breaker is when she looks at them.

"Row ninety-seven," Breaker says as she approaches one base. She turns to look at another. "Row ninety-six. This way."

The whale song sounds different too, now that we're not quite so close. They sound more lost than worried, like they're hunting for something that isn't where they left it. It's upsetting Spiderhand; I can see it in the way his fingers tread the water. Miss Mighty is even easier to read: her body language says she's ready to beat someone with a car. Listening to the memories as we swim, Breaker's story holds up. Sasha is around eight years old, maybe nine if there's a birthday I just haven't heard yet. She's a transplant to the local Realworld, her most excited thoughts centered around parks and playgrounds. She likes grape soda, and nature documentaries, and listening to the rap music her mother insists she needs to hear to get 'cultured.' Her mother also seems to be the one who told her about the memory whales.

"I don't like tea anymore," Sasha's voice crackles from above.

All four of us freeze, looking up at the memory whale swaying overhead. Its radio crackles again, and announces, in the same sad, whining voice, "But if I don't drink tea, he gets mad."

Breaker swallows hard, and traces an arm across a label. "Row eighty-nine," she says. "We're on the r-right track."

Hoping to distract her from the totally reasonable horror the whale just instilled, I say, "I have a question."

Breaker glances at me, nods her head, and goes back to counting down the numbers on the obelisks.

"The cell," I say.

Breaker gives me a confused look, but I let the mysterious statement hang until Miss Mighty nudges me, and mutters one word. "Expositioning."

"Sorry," I say, as much to Mighty as to Breaker. "The cell you had the Man in the Coat in. The bars were too broken down to keep him in, and I was able to bust that force field easily, so there's no way he couldn't. How did you trap the Man in the Coat in there?"

Breaker shrugs, not nonchalant but more afraid to contemplate. "We use it – used – w-we used it for k-keeping whales safe if they were s-sick or in-in-injured. When the M-M-Man showed up, he chased Outlet past the c-cell, and the Man, he acted like he was sc-scared. So we…" Breaker shakes her head again. "So we tried to fix the problem," she says, tapering off into a mutter.

Trapped. Scared. The idea we can make this monster feel either of those is making my brain tingle.

"Good thinking," Miss Mighty says into the silence.

"Thanks," says Breaker. She doesn't sound very thankful.

We find our way into an area where the towers' electricity is coursing less intensely than the ones closer to my near-death experience, the taped-on labels more faded and worn. Another shadow passes over us, and Sasha sobs, "I want to go home…" I can't imagine why these memories are in worse repair.

Breaker takes a left turn two rows down. Spiderhand follows, but I'm held back by Miss Mighty.

"Tippy," she whispers. "My sixth sense is going off."

I wish this were shocking. "How bad?"

"Just a little," she says. "Could be the pillars are about to collapse, could be Breaker is planning to feed you to that guy again, but…" Her glove squeaks. "If I'm going to make you warn me when a place is dangerous, I gotta do the same, right?"

At this point, that's all it takes to make me feel warmer inside. "Thanks, Mighty." I nod toward the turn the others took. "Watch Spidey, yeah?"

Her eyes blaze as she nods. My friends are the best Friends.

"H-here we are," Breaker says a few minutes later, as she pauses in front of a tower. "Row eighty-five, log seventeen." She reads the label like it's a headstone.

Most of the towers around here have sporadic lightning at best, little sparks like when you yank a cord out of an outlet, but this one's current is as beefy as any of the ones we swam past on the first visit, a cha-cha of blue arcs every couple seconds. I'm guessing there's more juice in important memories.

"Do we need to get a whale?"

Breaker hesitates, studying the base. "Usually we wait for the whales to feed, take a reading off their radios…" She pulls a screwdriver out of her tool belt, pockets it with an annoyed mutter.

"But?"

"Um… sometimes, the whales get full early. Or, there are zones… spots they don't feed from as much." She pulls out a socket wrench, pockets that, too. "So disorganized…"

"What makes them feed from a spot less?"

"W-we think – thought – think–" She winces, shakes her head. "We think the whales just have different tastes sometimes. And some memories…" She produces and puts back a small pair of pliers. "Some memories just taste bad, we think. Thought. Here!"

She pulls out a little metal tube, pops the lid off, and shakes out a pair of earbuds, the plug more like a house key than anything electrical. The headphones float in the water for a second before Breaker grabs them and starts a slow, inspecting float around the tower's perimeter. I glance back at Miss Mighty. She looks at Spiderhand, and at the rows on rows of memory towers behind us, and gives me a tentative nod. I follow Breaker with trepidation.

I catch up to the octopus halfway around. She's paused in front of a brass panel bolted onto the obelisk's surface, the teeth of the earbud plug hovering in front of a slot next to two little dials. I'm getting to know that fearful look a lot better than I'd like.

"Don't want to listen?" I say.

Breaker looks at the plug, and gives me a shake of her head. "S-some memories really should be allowed to erode."

I should probably take that as a warning. I don't. "Do you mind if I listen, then?"

She looks at the headphones again, and with a heavy sigh, hands them off to me.

Of course fear rushes in on me. Of course I suddenly want to be anywhere but here. But I don't want to dream of black coats and bouncing screws for the rest of my existence either, so I stick the key-plug in the offered slot and close my eyes while Breaker adjusts the dials.

The memory grabs on tighter than I expected.

The first thing I remember is sound: a metallic rumble like baby thunder, somewhere behind me. The second thing is smell: wet leaves, damp earth, cold winter air. The third thing, finally, is sight.

The forest doesn't surprise me – me or the little girl remembering this – and the trail through it doesn't surprise me either. The curves are familiar, along with the patterns of the fallen autumn leaves. What does surprise me is how far away Dad is, engrossed in a little patch of gray off to the side of the trail. Mushrooms. Mushrooms like the ones he keeps trying to cook me for dinner, the ones I won't eat. (He says I might like them when I'm older. He says I'm brave for trying new things with him.) He's got his little pen-knife, and the big white bag he takes the mushrooms home in. He loves to collect mushrooms when we go out hiking. It's his favorite thing, right after me. (Maybe right before me, says something deeper and darker inside me.)

I walk toward him, trying to remember what the mushrooms from this trail are called, the Anita ones or the Philosophy ones or whatever, and then I hear the other sound, the leaves crunching behind me, and feel the warm, soap-reeking hands as they wrap around my mouth and scoop me off the ground.

The forest tilts to the side, blurring as I struggle. I can still see Dad, and I reach out to him, trying to talk around the hand, but the taste is too much, and the fingers are too strong, and Dad is so, so busy with his mushrooms. I don't want the memory whales to remember this. I don't want them to have to remember this.

The man holding me takes a sudden step up, and I'm inside a car, being set down on an uncomfortable seat. The rumble comes again, and my Dad disappears from view behind a closing door. I get out half a scream before the soapy hands cover my mouth again, and I look the man in those dark green eyes for the first time.

"We're going to have fun," he says, smiling with teeth as white as the ones I see on TV. "We're going to have lots of fun, and I won't ever hurt you like those other guys with vans. Just… please…" He adjusts his glasses, "…Don't scream."

I don't like his eyes. His eyes look like he might be lying and not know it. So I don't scream.

He scrambles up to the front of the car – the SUV, I think it's called. I hear the cough of an old engine starting, like the one in Mom's ex-boyfriend's Rambler. The car starts moving, and I can't stop crying, but if I scream he might look at me like that again and–

–I yank the earbuds out. My chest is empty, and it won't fill back up no matter how hard I try to breathe.

I wasn't expecting to see, or smell. I wasn't expecting…

I could feel the Stillreal swallow her up. I could feel her separating from the Memory Reefs, I could feel…

Is that how Sandra felt?

Someone is right next to me. I bristle, scared of them touching me, of the smell of soap. They retreat, and I look up and it's Spiderhand, looking as scared as me, one manicured little finger held out.

"Are you okay?" That's Breaker.

"Or together enough to think out of here?" That's Mighty.

"I think so?" No pun intended.

"'Think out'?" Breaker asks.

Miss Mighty holds up a hand before I try to explain. "That little thing I told you about?" she says to me. "It's big now."

"Little?" Breaker asks, going from worried to panicked. "Big?"

Spidey stands up on his fingertips and points behind us. I look at the same time as Breaker starts screeching.

The Man in the Coat is charging straight at us – not the soaked, seaweed-wrapped one Miss Mighty hit, but the towering, black-coated one, the one with the black bat that shattered Spindleman.

"Tippy?" someone asks me.

He came back bigger, Breaker said. He came back meaner, she said.

It's so wet here… wet like the leaves on the trail… wet like the road…

"Tippy," says a voice somewhere a reality away.

I wonder if his teeth are white…

"Tippy!"

Do I hear rain?

Bull-powerful arms close around me, and the Man in the Coat disappears from view, in favor of glued-together teacups and Spiderhand's table and my apartment. Our apartment.

"Thank you," Miss Mighty says, to someone who is clearly not me.

We're not in the water. We're not with the Man. No coat. No bat. No eyes. I come back to the present when Breaker starts screaming again.

Spiderhand is already on the physical comfort job, hovering close by and trying to look safe. Miss Mighty has taken on comforting sounds, shushing and cooing and keeping her super-strong body far distant, looking both frustrated and dangerous. Neither one is really helping Breaker. Her eyes are rolling and her arms are slapping every which way as she tries to take in something I doubt she was capable of imagining.

"Breaker," I say, stern and fatherly, or as close as a two-foot-at-the-shoulder triceratops can get.

She keeps on screaming. Footsteps of varying sizes are rampaging down the hallway. I'm guessing any second now they'll be joined by sirens, and even if I can't help Breaker, I at least want to keep the pressure off Officer Cold.

"Breaker," I say, a bit louder and a bit softer. (Or maybe just one of those.)

She backpedals into the kitchen, screams higher as her flailing knocks down pots and pans and cookie jars. Why the heck do we have so many cookie jars?

"Breaker, please!" Miss Mighty yells.

I take a wide turn around the kitchen island, get Breaker in my sights. She's hunkered down in a heap of pots, trembling and swatting at the sides of her head in a motion that makes no sense for a couple of seconds, and makes too much sense right after. She's trying to unplug earbuds that aren't there.

The first urgent knocking hits our apartment door; Breaker curls up, punching at her head and muttering nonsense.

"Stop it!" I shout, both at her and at the pounding at my door. It works equally poorly on both of them.

Our front door explodes as Freedom Frieda comes spearing through, eyes blazing red, head swiveling to search for whatever the problem is. Two of the Sadness Penguins come in after her, and Golem Jones after that. The Penguins are holding what look like pried-up floorboards. Frieda sees the motion in the kitchen, spins toward it, and her eyes flicker from nuclear red to confused crimson.

And Miss Mighty shouts, "Everyone *stop*!"

The pile-up of justice in our entryway halts, all stunned and all looking at Miss Mighty. One Friend is still moving: Breaker, who has suckered herself to the top of the refrigerator and is thrashing around up there, still peeling at her head like there's something stuck to it. I shrug off how pointlessly angry I am and inch closer to Breaker's point of ascent.

"Breaker," I say, almost a whisper. "Breaker, it's Tippy. The guy you were helping. I know you think you're stuck in a memory... but if this were one of Sasha's memories, how would I be in it?"

Breaker works with machines. Weird, complicated machines that only make sense to an eight year-old girl who imagines her memories live underwater, but machines nonetheless. If I give her something logical to hold onto, it might get her to calm down.

Her arms drop to her sides, limp, and I can finally breathe. I've still got it. More importantly, I've still got her.

"Breaker..." I shake my head. "Breaker, this is where I live."

She looks around at the upturned pots and pans, the broken shards – oh crud, not the broken shards of cookie jars...

"Breaker," I say, and thank goodness she puts her attention back on me. "Breaker, this apartment is in Playtime Town. Playtime Town is an Idea, like your Memory Reefs. It's part of the Stillreal. It's where... where..." How the heck do I explain the entire world to someone who thought it ended at the surface of the ocean?

"It's where made-up people go when their creators give them up and they're too Real to fade," Miss Mighty says.

Breaker looks over my shoulder. I follow her gaze. Miss Mighty is standing over me, looking like she wants to punch reality on our behalf.

"Creations?" Breaker squeaks. "Wait... you mean..."

"People made us," Mighty says with a nod. "People made us up, all of us, for... different reasons," – she glances the Sadness Penguins' way – "and then, for whatever reasons, they didn't want us anymore."

"Didn't... *want?*" The pain in Breaker's voice stabs straight into my rawest nerve. "Are you s-saying..."

Stop the question, Tippy, stop the question.

"...Sasha didn't want us anymore?"

Horror is the order of the day: me, the Penguins, Mighty, Jones, Frieda, Spiderhand, all of us wincing as we realize where her mind is spiraling to. It's easy enough to guess – at some point, all of us went there.

"No..." I say, and wince again. "That's not what... I..."

"Sasha still wanted you," Miss Mighty says. "That's what he's trying to say."

Six held breaths all come out at once.

"You helped her keep her memories in place," I say, piggy-backing on Mighty's assistance. "Helped her access them. I'm guessing she was a pretty smart cookie, and she counted on you to help her do that."

"But…" Breaker braids her arms together, anxious as she shuffles through her thoughts. "You said–"

"I said something… I maybe shouldn't have said," Miss Mighty says. "Very few of our people don't want us anymore. Usually, they just can't *have* us."

Horror is off the menu. We're now serving pain with a side of empathy.

"Can't… what?" The rest of Breaker's arms twist together.

"We're not here because people grew up, or moved on," I say. "We're here because things… happened. Things that made it so our people just stopped thinking we… that we made sense."

Miss Mighty leans back against the counter, weighed down by gloomy memory. "Some of them realized the world didn't work the way they thought. Some of us, whatever happened made us painful to think about."

One of the Sadness Penguins whimpers.

"And some of us," I add, "I mean… some of us it was that whatever happened was so horrible, our people couldn't be anything like what they used to be, and that included us."

"It happens all the time," Miss Mighty says, throat clenched, eyes red. "We're just the ones who are too Real to disappear. We just… aren't Real enough to protect them."

There's a snap from behind Mighty, and her anger turns to embarrassment. I think she just cracked our countertop.

Breaker coughs, stammers. I try to get her attention again, to explain the Stillreal in a more hopeful tone, but instead I'm thinking back to raindrops, one-two, one-two…

Freedom Frieda steps out of the mob at the door, her eyes switched to a depressed blue. "Breaker?" she asks, in the saddest squawk on record.

Breaker spins toward the voice, and balks at what she sees, the four new beings that make no sense to her, two of them armed almost exactly the way her friends' killer was. I have never seen a Playtime Town arrival go this poorly. Well, not since Spindleman…

"I'm Freedom Frieda," the eagle says with a salute. "My person made me because she was fightin' for better lives for people who had always had worse ones. She trusted me to be a symbol of freedom for everyone in the place she lived, for all those who sought a new home and a new reason to hope. And then… and then she realized she had failed. Not because she was bad at what she did. But because bad people wouldn't let her succeed."

Breaker is a bundle of arms with eyes peeking out of it, but those eyes are fixed straight on Frieda.

"After she gave up…" Frieda looks down at the floor. Her eyes are the deepest blue I've ever seen them. "She did – something – and… I came to the Stillreal."

Breaker uncurls just a tiny bit. She's starting to process, but she's wishing she wasn't.

Golem Jones steps forward. "My person wrote me to be different than the rest of my kind," he says, a voice like an underground cave, deep and secret and hollow. "I was a protector without a rabbi having to control me. I was proof that power didn't need to be leashed to be used for good." Jones' brows sink low. "And then he got sick. And his co-worker, the one who drew me, he – he did something. He did things with me. There is another me, but he is not me. He is greed. Simplified. Goofy. A *schmuck*." Jones shakes his head, sadder than Frieda, but much less raw. "My person couldn't deal with me anymore after that."

I look at Miss Mighty, my head full of the memory of water. She looks at me, her eyes full of rage. We both nod. We can't talk about this now. Thank goodness there are older Friends here who have worked through some of this already.

"It wasn't our fault," Frieda says. "We're Real. That means we're important enough to keep existing. That means we're amazing." She smiles, and she means it – her eyes are finally white. "And that includes you, too."

I drop my head, nod and just mutter, "What they said."

I hear a rush of motion, and a sucking, wet sound that drags me straight out of my oncoming funk. Breaker is down off the fridge, and has all but stapled herself to Freedom Frieda's torso. Frieda has folded her wings around her and closed her eyes, but you can see blue light peeking out from under the lids. I feel Miss Mighty unclench next to me as the Sadness Penguins pile onto the hug. I chuckle as Golem Jones gives me a look of relieved amusement from beneath his fez, and then Spiderhand decides it's time to comfort me, a slow pet across the arch of my back. I go rigid against the touch, and he backs away, palm out, apologizing. I answer him with a smile.

Friends aren't usually good at helping each other with their hurt. I'm lucky to know the exceptions.

The hug ends as fast as it started. Spiderhand, either oblivious or disinterested in the temperature of the room, starts bustling about the kitchen, grabbing pots from that cabinet, tea from this one, cake from the fridge. Forget all us sourpuss Friends, he's hosting a tea party.

A tea party is probably a good idea. Something simple and comforting, something that calms everyone down. It's going to be a very nice time; Spiderhand throws excellent tea parties. So I wait until the others are busy pitching in, and I duck out the door.

CHAPTER TWENTY-FOUR

The Rootbeerium is packed when I come in, but not in the usual happy-hour way we all love. The Friends in here aren't partiers; they're the ones willing to buy soda in exchange for the safety of numbers. Rocky and Lloyd sit in one corner, their hands stacked on top of each other's, Lloyd massaging at Rocky's knuckles as they stare into the distance. The Sadness Penguins that aren't in my apartment surround a table in the center of the room, playing Go Fish and watching the door. Every cake-shaped barstool has someone on it: Boss Raccoon, Lieutenant Burrows, the Kingdom of Living Marbles, and more I don't even recognize, all either tense and silent or tense and way too talkative. When Mr Float sees me, his smile is mostly one of relief. I still feel terrible, but this lets me know I'm making the right choice. I head to the bar, find a makeshift gap between a dragon in an evening gown and an origami sailboat with a penciled-on face, and wait for Mr Float to come my way.

"Detective Tippy," he says, his usual patter a touch more haunted. "How are we doing today?"

"Peachy – just like everyone else in here."

He smiles as he smoothes out his mustaches. "What can I get for you today?"

"Neapolitan with hot fudge and nuts, two extra-large root beer floats, and you pointing in the direction of Chip Dixon."

Mr Float smiles again. There's hope somewhere at the bottom of that look. Far, far at the bottom. "I'll bring the order out to his table," he says, as he gestures to the back corner of the room.

I weave through the crowd, dodging feet and wings and tank-treads, nearly colliding a few times thanks to my freshly mended limbs. Chip is in the farthest, darkest corner, all alone at a big circular table. He's got an empty milkshake glass at one elbow, an empty sundae boat at the other, and a root beer float I could bathe in right in front of him, a twisty blue straw stuck between his lips as he slurps and slurps and slurps. He raises a finger when he sees me, and takes a second to lick whipped cream off the top of the float. Only then does he lean back and look at me like I'm late for an appointment.

"Mr Dixon," I say, trying not very hard to sound casual.

"Tippy," he says. "What's the ruckus? Looking for a drinking companion? Little comfort in the cold night of the soul?" Watching for death itself to come stomping through the door and he still falls into his shtick. The power of imagination, folks.

"Comfort would be grand," I say. "But today it's in short supply." I hop onto a chair.

Chip raises the other eyebrow, waiting for me to ask what we both know I'm going to ask.

"Mr Dixon," I say. "Can you give me all the latest news? Hit the lurid stuff today. Especially anything to do with tea or missing kids."

Chip nods, discomfort jitterbugging in his eyes. He sits back, takes a slug of root beer, and goes to work.

He starts with local political races. That stuff I'm not too interested in today, mostly just scanning for keywords. I'm also not worried about the sports scores or the nonsense about gas prices. But then he gets into the police blotter, and I lean in close. Stolen cars. Muggings. Police brutality. All the stuff you hear about in the darker parts of the Stillreal. I'm shuddering, but it's not like my nerves have been soft and squishy lately anyway.

"Headline," Chip says, clearing his throat, and I already know we've hit the meat of it. "Police Continue Search for Teatime Man."

Pay dirt. Filthy, toxic-waste-laden pay dirt.

"Portland PD continues its diligent search for the monstrous murderer known as the Teatime Man," Chip intones, eyes wide but mouth doing its job. "In a press conference yesterday, Captain Farrah Logue announced that thanks to the hard-working detectives of the Homicide Unit, they are closer than ever to discovering the identity of the dark stranger who has terrorized Portland's families since mid-August. Residents of the Teatime Man's stalking grounds in Hazelwood are relieved, but not relieved enough. One father of two said 'I hope they lock him up and throw away the key,' while a single mother in Montavilla said 'I won't feel safe until I know he's in the ground.'

"The Teatime Man has abducted four known victims, all children under the age of seven. The moniker comes from the one child who escaped the man's clutches; he said the man collected children like him, boys and girls, and that this sick, subhuman snake loved to force the children to have tea parties with him, flying into berserker rages if they refused. One child is confirmed dead; the other two victims are still missing, and everyone presumes the worst." Chip's eyes are welling up with tears. "This reporter hopes that the breakthrough Captain Logue speaks of is enough to drag this monster into the light of day, and that soon the children of Portland can sleep easy once again."

Chip stops, and the silence comes home to roost. Everyone within earshot has stopped talking.

Tea parties and rages. Broken tea-cups. I've almost finished this jigsaw puzzle. I just wish the picture was prettier.

"Thanks, Chip," I say, as I climb down from the chair. "Tell Mr Float every root beer you drink tonight is on me."

"Tippy?" Chip croaks.

I stop and wait.

"Is that where the Man in the Coat came from?"

I nod. "That story you just told me? That story has to be all over the news, right?"

Chip swallows. "Everywhere."

A voice among the onlookers swears. I shake off the burning in my horns. "Then yeah," I say. I turn, and walk away, focused on the horrible thoughts bobbing to the surface of my mind.

"Nail this jerk!" Chip calls after me.

I can't raise my paw enough yet to gesture back that I will.

I leave the Rootbeerium in a daze, meander up the street with my brain in the grave, my detective stuff nodding again and again that yes, it all fits, even though I don't want it to.

Friends are products of imagination. We come from all kinds of places, but we don't think about it because we all ended up in the same place. Or I don't think about it, anyway, and really, that's the problem.

Every adult in the Realworld watches the news. And if the news tells every adult about a monster lurking in the shadows, ready to force their kids into some kind of murderous tea party... and then local kids are attacked, so the kids start hearing about it, too... and they remember what their parents saw on the news... and their parents remember what they saw on the news... and there isn't enough information out there to make this killer human, to make him concrete, understandable, to make him anything except these scary rumors...

Well, then people get scared. People get angry. Kids hide under their covers, and everyone talks about this man in a dark coat, about tea cups and terrified little kids and a long, long black coat...

Then those fears feed into the original Idea, the one the Teatime Man himself created, his vision of himself... and up and up and up it grows, the absolute worst and scariest version of this very real monster. The worst killer the imagination has ever known.

An Idea shared by thousands. Maybe millions. An Idea that can ascend to the heights of imagination, to be something beyond the original minds that birthed it. A Friend like Sherlock Holmes, like Captain America – no, like Moriarty or Doctor Doom. But also a Friend born of rumor, a thousand variations on a theme. So potent it can traumatize creators who weren't even touched by its person, so widespread and nebulous that every attack births its own little monster, different but also connected to the original...

The Man is a world-spanning Friend that can think around freely, but that chiefly cares about the things he hasn't finished harming, the people scarred by the Idea of the Idea… and the stray Ideas, the little pieces of its creator's victims that have managed to survive, just like that one little boy who escaped.

I wonder if the real Teatime Man has a baseball bat. I wonder why a rusted-up cell kept him locked in when he should've been able to smash his way out. I wonder how many kids he's hurt. I wonder how many he's killed.

I need twelve root beers followed by twelve hours in the dryer. I need to have stayed at that tea party and held Breaker and worried about the people who are left behind. I need to have never run up those stairs to save Spindleman.

Except not. None of that is what I need. What I need is to solve this case. And unfortunately, that's going to mean marching up the stairs of the Welcoming Arms and raining all over that comforting little party.

Raining.

This might be the worst day yet.

I head across the street, and get ready to be the bad guy.

I walk back through our busted apartment door and into a tea party slightly less tense than your average firing squad. Spiderhand, Frieda, Breaker, Golem Jones, and Percival the Sadness Penguin are crammed around the dining room table, teacups wrapped up in their appendages, staring at the walls with eyes that could double as mining equipment. No one's crying or screaming, but it's hanging in the air, waiting over everyone's shoulder just in case it's still needed.

"Tippy?" Breaker asks. She's looking across the table at me, a little less scared and a lot more confused.

Spidey darts back to the kitchen for the tea-cakes he somehow never runs out of. The others shift in their seats. My detective stuff says everyone is relieved I'm back.

"Yes?" I say to her, swinging close to the table for a snack.

Breaker's arms tie themselves in a square knot. "You said you were a detective?"

That is such a dinner-party-basic question my first instinct is to laugh. Thankfully, I don't. "Yes. I run the Stuffed Animal Detective Agency. I mean… I *am* the Stuffed Animal Detective Agency… I don't really have–"

"That was what your person wanted you to do?"

The relief makes sense now; I'm guessing she's asked this same loaded question of everyone at the table already.

"Yes," I say. "She… we solved the world together." Somehow, I smile. "I was her proof that your brain can make the world make sense, you know? That there are reasons for things. That bad guys always get caught…"

"Is that why you were in the Memory Reefs?"

"Yeah. It was the most promising lead I had."

"The teacups?" she asks.

Smart cookie. "Yeah."

Breaker holds her teacup up near one eye, studying it. Ideas dance across her face. "What do the teacups have to do with the Man in the Coat?"

"They're… they're like an infection," I say. "Everywhere the Teatime Man goes, anywhere he spends any real time, he leaves behind a version of himself, and a bunch of broken tea services."

"The Teatime Man?" Miss Mighty asks.

"What the humans are calling the person who made him."

Miss Mighty cocks an eyebrow, dubious. Breaker tries some other arm-knots. Golem Jones shifts in his seat, and rumbles, "Chip?"

I nod. "Just got back from talking to him."

More tension leaks out of the room, and I bristle. They thought I had ditched them. I'd be insulted, but these past few days I've probably earned that reaction.

"Spiderhand got those cups you're drinking from on a visit to the Reefs," I say. "When he told me that, I realized these might be older than any of the other ones I knew about. I figured the Friends in your home Idea might have figured out some things I hadn't."

"Was there anything?" She wants so badly for my answer to be yes.

Luckily, I can oblige. "Yeah, thanks to you. You figured out you can trap his duplicates, which means we might be able to trap him. And as a bonus, Mighty here figured out that you can destroy his duplicates—"

Miss Mighty flashes a lioness' smirk.

"— but, when you destroy his duplicates," I continue, "it looks like that alerts the real thing."

Intensity sparks in Breaker's eyes. "We need to stop him. If he can go anywhere, hurt anyone, if he's the first person who's been able to kill things for real like Spiderhand says—"

"The first *Friend*," Golem Jones corrects. "People have had killing figured out for a while." The sadness in his voice is as thick as mortar.

"R-right," Breaker says. "He needs to b-be stopped. Now."

"Sooner than now," Miss Mighty growls.

I shrink back. "I didn't mean to turn this into a war council. This is supposed to be for you to—"

"This is what I need," Breaker says.

Miss Mighty bares her teeth in a smile. Golem Jones frowns. Spiderhand just puts another pile of tea-cakes on the table. I look around, watching the other Friends watch either Breaker or me.

"No one minds?" I say.

Everyone exchanges a tense look, and everyone who has a head shakes it. Spiderhand gestures consent from behind the kitchen island.

"This conversation has been coming for a few days now," Golem Jones says, still heavy.

"Okay," I say, mostly as a placeholder while I re-assemble my thoughts. "Breaker, do you think you could build a – a trap cage? Same basic idea as the one you had the Teatime Man in, but portable until we need to use it?"

Breaker stiffens. "If I have the m-materials."

"We'll get you the materials," I say. My heart is off to the races. Her 'yes' means this is actually happening.

"But, I don't know how fast I can—"

"I'll get you help," I say.

Everyone is giving me side-eye, and that's not unreasonable. Miss Mighty cuts right through it. "What are you planning, Tippy?"

I close my eyes, and make sure this doesn't sound ridiculous before I say it out loud. It absolutely does, but I say it anyway. "We're going to trap the original, and we're going to kill it."

CHAPTER TWENTY-FIVE

Golem Jones' jaw pops open with a sound like a millstone turning. Miss Mighty mugs grim approval. Breaker leans closer with a look of hypnotized horror. Spiderhand just waits, a never-ending fountain of trust.

"Just to save us time," I say, "yes, I'm serious, and yes, this is as terrible a plan as it sounds." Sarcasm helps keep the weight off my brain. "And even if we hammer out all the details and we're positive it's the best it can be, it's going to be dangerous. Like really dangerous."

Miss Mighty all but beams at me.

"But we have to stop this," I say. "We already know this Teatime Man – we already know he can make it to Playtime Town. And based on everything else we've seen, he's going to come for Breaker."

The octopus whimpers. Percival pats her on the arm with a consolatory flipper.

"Sorry, Breaker," I say.

She shivers, but says, "It's the truth."

"So before I get into the details," I announce, "this is where I ask: Do you want to do this? Any of you, *any* of you, can say no, and I will understand. Anybody makes fun of you for it, tries to blame you for anything that comes next, even gives you a funny look in the Rootbeerium, they can come to me to get the hard time of a lifetime."

Smiles and frowns and confusion bounce back and forth across the table, hitting everyone except Miss Mighty. She just rolls her eyes at the rest.

"When my person made me," she says, "I was there to fight bullies, jerks, and villains. This guy is all three. If I said I wasn't going to help you with this, you'd know Dr Atrocity replaced me with a clone."

Breaker looks gratefully at Miss Mighty, and a little more fearfully at me. "I can't let people get hurt. I can't let memories go bad. That's not... Sasha wouldn't..." She wads her arms up in an approximation of fists. "I'm going to help."

Spiderhand drums on the table, an insistent beat that doesn't need any gestures to bring across its meaning. Percival slaps a flipper on the table with the same emphasis.

Freedom Frieda is the first one who hesitates, her beak quivering, her eyes a deep, sorrowful navy blue. "I can't..."

"That's okay," I say. "You don't have to."

"Me either," says Golem Jones, fat stone fingers fidgeting with his teacup. "I don't fight anymore. Not since..." His words slide down into a guttural growl.

"That's okay too," I say, as bright in tone as I am bleak in spirit. "Can you two make sure that anyone else the Teatime Man sends here gets the help they need?"

"Absolutely," Freedom Frieda says, eyes white and resolute.

"I'd never do anything else," Golem Jones croaks. "I never *do* do anything else." Even in the middle of this, he takes time to act comically put upon.

"Thank you," I say, as the lump forms in my throat. "Then – okay, then..."

I look out over my companions. These are the Friends who took me in from the cold when I got kicked into the Stillreal. These are the Friends who have always stood by me, who have trusted me even when I indulged my witticism addiction at their expense. They signed up for this, and they are ready to help with this.

I let myself take a second to breathe. The next part's harder.

"So then, about that help we're getting Breaker..."

"No."

Yeah, this is how I figured it would go. Miss Mighty is pacing up and down my living room, the rest of the council of tea-and-war watching from the sidelines like we have dynamite strapped to us. At least I can still accurately predict some things.

"But Mighty," I say, "Dr Atrocity is the only one who can–"

"No," Miss Mighty says again. Her face drifts into a snarl, a sneer, a frustrated pucker. "There's someone else. There has to be someone else." If you look in her eyes, you can see I've won this argument already; it's just about getting to where everyone is comfortable admitting that.

"Mighty," I say.

"Don't 'Mighty' me! We can't trust her."

"No, but we can trust that we'll all defend ourselves."

She flares her nostrils, shakes her head again.

"Look," I say, "the Teatime Man has us all messed up, he has everything messed up. But bottom line, even if we're evil, or selfish, or whatever, we all like existing. He's something, maybe the one thing, that we can count on Dr Atrocity for."

Miss Mighty laughs. It's not a nice laugh. "You been to visit her recently?"

My back stiffens. Time to pull the pin out of the grenade. "Yeah, actually."

Miss Mighty stops pacing. Everyone in the room tenses, but the award for most worried goes to either Breaker or Spiderhand.

"Big Business attacked her a couple days ago. Had her strapped in to her own death ray."

"How did you find her?" Miss Mighty snaps.

"Alibi Lounge," I say.

She rolls her eyes, frustrated with herself. "The minions always know."

"Mighty – Miss – okay, look, I want to explain, okay? I was there because I knew I needed to talk to Big Business, and then it turns out I needed to rescue someone *from* Big Business. Emergency situation, not a casual visit. I would have told you. Okay?"

She twitches, but she nods. We both know I also kind of liked doing it on my own. We are what we were made. "Okay."

"Great. Thank you. The Doc has been monitoring all the changes to the Stillreal. She knows where all the new Ideas are, she knows where the teacup bits are showing up. She's how we're going to get this done."

Miss Mighty shakes her head. "She'll turn on us. She'll twist this to her advantage."

"I have no doubt."

Mighty takes a deep breath, cracks her knuckles. She looks disgusted, but more importantly, she looks me in the eye. "I'm going along with this because I trust you," she says. "But she's going to turn on us."

"Won't it be nice to only be dealing with her, though?"

She stops, and cocks her head, annoyed in that way that says I got it right in one. She scoffs at herself, and smirks, and I remind myself to breathe.

"Great," I say. "Great. Thank you. Let's go, then? Before either of us has second, third, maybe fourth thoughts?"

She nods, and leans down to peer out our window, looking for a touchstone to get us over to Avatar City.

"Oh," I say.

Everyone turns and looks at me. I look at Miss Mighty.

"This part? This part is also going to be dangerous."

Mighty's smile almost makes the past few days worth it.

We think to Avatar City through the bell-tower on top of Playtime Town Hall, floating through some medieval city Idea Mighty knows before we hit the big gothic church in the South End. I don't have time to make a quip before she scoops me up and launches into the sky.

"Where is she?" Mighty asks, already at zero patience.

"The observatory. I'd point to it, but I'm afraid to look down."

Her brow furrows. "Observatory?"

"The one that looks like a skull from the far side."

She nods like that makes sense to her, and speeds off over the patchworks of green and brown that make up the Avatar City countryside. We're over the observatory in seconds, on the ground in half that. We spend more time hesitating outside than we do traveling there.

"Afraid of robots coming out to greet us?" I ask.

Mighty narrows her eyes at the observatory door. "I'm more afraid of the part where they aren't."

A lot of reassuring thoughts occur to me, and get thrown away as not actually reassuring. I settle on, "Remember: self-preservation is the trump card."

"And it'll trump *us* too," Miss Mighty mutters. But hey, she starts toward the door.

The outer door opens without fanfare. The inside of the place is quiet. I pick up humming machinery, the rattle of pistons and gears, but no signs of life. Miss Mighty seems to be having the same problem. She floats ahead of me, looking around like she can't quite believe what she's seeing, and it only gets worse when we get into the main room and she sees the death ray. I wonder how many times she's been hooked up to that thing.

Miss Mighty turns toward me, scowling. "You getting anything?"

"I–"

The noises from the machinery change; I hold up a paw while I focus on it. The new sound is the soft whoosh of something big traveling at great speed, starting below us and getting closer. I point in the direction I think it's coming from, and Miss Mighty turns with banked rage to the door now irising open in the wall, revealing a bemused Dr Atrocity.

She stays in the elevator, hands tucked into her lab coat, posture stiff and unrelenting. "Detective Tippy," she says, with a nod my way. She turns toward Miss Mighty, and her demeanor ices over. "You."

"Doc," Miss Mighty says back, way, way too sweet.

One tiny fraction of Dr Atrocity's mouth tilts upward. "You need my help."

Miss Mighty's gloves squeak. Yeah, this is on me now.

"It's the Teatime Man," I say, stepping forward. "The Man in the Coat."

"He's been getting more active," Dr Atrocity replies. Her smile grows at my unnerved reaction.

"No kidding," Miss Mighty says.

Dr Atrocity swivels toward her. I step forward again.

"Your monitoring machine," I say. "You can trace the teacups he leaves behind?"

"That's a... simplified, but accurate, view," she says.

"You can talk to us like civilized people," Miss Mighty snaps.

Dr Atrocity's human eye bulges. She looks Miss Mighty up and down, sighs, and lets her shoulders slack.

"You are correct, this once," she says with resignation. "This is not the occasion for verbal salvos." She flares her nostrils, tension balling up her face. "Miss Mighty... I do not suppose that under the circumstances you would consider... a truce?"

And like that, all my concern and attention is on my friend.

Miss Mighty grinds her teeth, sighs the same sigh Dr Atrocity just let out, and runs an aggravated hand over her face.

"Yes," she grunts.

Dr Atrocity smiles. "Good, then–"

"But," Miss Mighty raises a hand. "But. Truce doesn't mean forgiveness." She stares whole murder mysteries' worth of daggers at the Doctor. "I remember what you've done, what you think, better than anyone else in the Stillreal. This fight never really ends. Not until all of that changes."

Dr. Atrocity gives Miss Mighty a sour, uncertain look, and shrugs like she's shucking a backpack off her back. "Very well. For now, the war can move to a different front." She steps backward, opening up space in the elevator. "Come with me."

I waver on whether or not to come when called. Miss Mighty doesn't. She zips in and stands right next to Dr Atrocity, the two of them looking the most uncomfortable I have ever seen them.

"Are you coming?" they ask in unison, and turn to each other, baffled.

Did their person do this on purpose? Not a question I can answer today...

Once I'm in the compartment, Dr Atrocity flips a few switches, and we head downward at speed. I feel the world shifting around us, bubbling here, buckling there. It's making me dizzy in places I didn't know could get dizzy.

"Been upgrading your elevator?" I ask. "Or did you think I wasn't properly scared last time?"

Dr Atrocity smirks. The door opens. She marches through without even pausing to let it open all the way. "Follow me."

Miss Mighty looks down at me. "Now are you getting anything?"

"All I hear is machines. So, maybe?"

Mighty snorts, and follows her nemesis. I'm grateful she's made the decision for me.

Dr Atrocity leads us down the same cavernous hallway she took me down a lifetime of beatings ago, but with less rock and more steel and rubber. She's strung cable back and forth overhead, enough to hang an army's worth of laundry, and connected to an equivalent amount of new machines. The hallway is the source of the humming, a motorboat sound like someone's drumming on its back. Detective stuff says whatever it's all powering is huge. Miss Mighty drifts along behind me, judging everything with a negative eye. I just trust and follow. It's all I have left.

We head down that same dead-end hallway, and Miss Mighty all but hisses when she sees the monitoring station unfold. "How long have you had this?" she demands. She's trying for outraged, but she's hitting awed.

"As long as your Teatime Man has been around," Dr Atrocity replies with relish. She tickles a few keys on the control console, and the screens blink over to nine apparently random Ideas. There's the crayon-drawn forest I saw last time, there's the Memory Reefs, there's an empty apartment in Smile House. That's what I was afraid of.

"The oneiric infection has spread to Playtime Town," Dr Atrocity says. "It hasn't reached Avatar City yet, however. If you're looking for a place to dig in…"

"I didn't want them traced so we could hide," I say, boxing up my terror for later.

Dr Atrocity straightens her posture. "Are you implying what I think you're implying?"

"We're taking the fight to him," says Miss Mighty.

Dr Atrocity leans against the control panel, a hand to her head. You don't need special senses to hear the sigh of relief.

"You were expecting this?" Miss Mighty asks, a foot sliding forward, ready to fight.

The Doctor shakes her head. "Hoping." She sweeps an arm out to indicate the monitors. "The infection is spreading, without regard to whether or not the original Friend entered the Idea in question."

"He actually entered Playtime Town," I say.

"But how?" Dr Atrocity asks.

"He seems to be able to track any Friends he or his creator have touched," I say. "Or maybe that should be creators. Look, I'm less worried about exactly *how* he works and more worried about making him *stop* working."

"A lofty goal. But don't you think the how might matter in this regard?"

"It's rarely mattered with you," Miss Mighty responds, proving bad timing isn't exclusive to me.

"I don't break the rules," Dr Atrocity responds.

"Excuse – no," Miss Mighty says, hands up. "No, you're taunting me."

Genuine concern flicks into the Doctor's eyes. "I apologize. Habit." She presses a few more keys. "This Friend does not operate like other Friends do. He is not governed by all the same rules we are. We need to understand how he works if we are to be sure our countermeasures will affect him in the expected manner."

I know she has a point. I really do. But I've also got a brain full of dead friends. "Do you have a way to figure that out? Like... fast?"

Dr Atrocity sighs. "No."

"Then that pretty much settles that," I say.

"You make a valid point," she says without praise. "What is it you wanted me to do, then, if my advice is not to your liking?"

Right. I think about Spindleman instead of what I'm about to say. "Two things. First of all: You can track the teacups."

"Easily."

"Can you tell which ones are the oldest?"

Of all the reactions, I am not expecting excitement. "Yes. Yes, I can."

Miss Mighty snorts. "That was what you were working on before we showed up, wasn't it?"

"Not for the reasons you think."

"You were spying on us and hoped we would ask this question?" Miss Mighty says.

"That, too," Dr Atrocity says with a smirk.

"I need you to find those oldest teacups," I say, throwing myself between the implied fists. "And I need you to find me some touchstones I could use to get there."

"Child's play," Dr Atrocity says. "But, you said 'first of all.' I assume that means you have a second of all?" She curls an eyebrow, making sure we know how clever she is.

And the second Hail Mary… "You have cameras and stuff in other Ideas. That means you can make stuff that lasts."

"It stands to reason."

I nod. It's the only movement I can make aside from panicking at what I've got myself involved in. "Can you help a friend of mine build a trap?"

CHAPTER TWENTY-SIX

Miss Mighty and I think back to Playtime Town in silence, both trying very hard not to let the other know they're terrified.

Dr Atrocity said yes. She's agreed to meet us in Playtime Town as soon as the materials are ready, and I've agreed to let her into my apartment. Frankly, that's the least of my worries.

My apartment door has repaired itself, but the noise level inside is higher than ever. I'm pretty sure I know what's up, but Miss Mighty and I still share an uncertain, hopeful look before we go inside.

Spiderhand's still there. So are Breaker and Percival. With them, crowded into our living room, are the rest of the Sadness Penguins, Chip Dixon, Officer Cold, Lieutenant Burrows, Azure Armadillo, Farmer Nick Nefarious, and Big Business. Miss Mighty straight-out gasps. I deal with it the way I deal with all new and weird information.

"Golem Jones recruiting drive?" I ask Spiderhand.

Hand-nod.

"Thank you for coming," I say to the penguins.

They nod in a cascading row, right to left and left to right. I respond with a smile, and move on. I'd be lying if I said I wasn't worried about them, and I'd be underplaying it if I said that worry wasn't all-consuming. I stomp it down into the depths of my thoughts, and turn to the unpleasant heap of denim we call Farmer Nick.

"Corn wouldn't stop screaming?"

Nick gives me a dry, unstable look. "This is my fight, too."

"I'm surprised Fran didn't come along."

Nick gives me a look like a funeral procession. "Someone has to tend the crops if I die."

I could taunt him, suggest ways their conversation came around to who should go and risk their neck. But every addict needs to go into recovery some time, right? "I'm glad you're here."

Nick's face just about turns inside-out.

Next up is Azure Armadillo. He fades back a second as I come near, and I settle for a wave and a welcoming smile. I give him time to settle into a meek smile of his own, and move along to Big Business. He's been here long enough the floor next to him has sprouted a drab potted plant.

"People dying is unprofitable," he says, heading off any longer conversation.

"I figured it was something like that." I make sure I've got eye contact. "Listen, this whole thing… it's going to involve Dr Atrocity."

Big Business' smile flickers.

"She's going to be here in a little while. It's alright if you have to go—"

"People. Dying. Is unprofitable," he says, as unyielding as petrified wood.

"Glad to have you on the team. I have an idea, actually…" I raise a paw. "I'll get back to you later."

"Looking forward to our meeting, sport," Big Business says, and claps me on the shoulder as I walk away. I try not to twitch in pain.

Officer Cold and Lieutenant Burrows are already talking, so that's one small note of convenience, at least. They turn to me as I approach, the lanky look of disdain and the affable, mustachioed smile both aimed at me. It's a little intimidating.

"You good to talk tactics?" I ask.

Officer Cold looks to Lieutenant Burrows, gives a 'you can have this' shrug. Burrows adjusts his monocle and asks, "What about tactics?"

"The fact that I'm terrible at them."

Burrows chuckles. "But you're good at information, yes?"

"That's sort of where I was driving this conversation, yeah."

Burrows gives me a grim smile, and nods down the hallway to the bedrooms. "Let's do this part in private, yes? Officer, do you want to come?"

"Playtime Town doesn't really do SWAT training," Cold says, with an uncertain look at his tea. "Or training at all."

"But you're a police officer," Burrows says, not so much doubtful as telling Cold he's wrong about himself. "Come along. I would appreciate your insight."

Cold looks at the rest of the party, and follows with a dismissive shrug. "Better than this."

I lead them into my room, hop up into my office chair, and get myself into a listening kind of mood. Lieutenant Burrows gestures for Officer Cold to close the door. He complies with an annoyed twitch of his lip.

"I don't like to discuss tactics in front of the troops," Burrows says.

"Are you saying they're disposable?" Cold asks, teeth already grinding.

Burrows looks at him in horror. "No. Never. But no army benefits from frank discussions about chances."

Cold raises his eyebrows, and once again I'm the guy who has to prevent the fight.

"Cold and I obviously disagree with that," I say, "but you've got a lot more experience than we do, and we don't have much time. Are you good to listen and trust for now, Officer?"

Cold narrows his eyes at me, but gives another icy shrug. "It's that or do nothing."

Burrows nods in both acknowledgment and dismissal. "How long do we have to plan?"

"We should operate assuming we have hours."

"And assuming we don't?" Cold asks.

"Then the Teatime Man shows up in the middle of my apartment and we all fight until one side is dead," I say.

Lieutenant Burrows gawks, monocle clicking in and out of different focuses. He shakes his head, and resumes his old airship-captain demeanor. "I am the tactics. You are the information. What do we know?"

I clear my throat, and consider briefly the flask of root beer in my desk drawer. Later. "The Teatime Man is a Friend, but he breaks a lot of the rules that govern us. He can travel freely just like us, or at least close enough we should assume it works the same way. He can permanently kill Friends, like, the Idea never brings them back when it resets. He leaves behind broken teacups everywhere he hunts, and if he's there long enough, he leaves a duplicate of himself that's almost as powerful. He's fast, he's dangerous, and the only weakness we've found so far is that he for some reason stayed inside a cage even though he could have walked right out of it."

"So, very much like a ripper in this regard," Burrows muses, not talking to either of us.

"Sure," I say.

Burrows considers, expression bleak and body slack while he conserves momentum for his brain. Officer Cold fidgets, the kind of rotten-lemon expression that says he feels proven right and hates it. I think again about the root beer and the dryer, and try not to count just how many people in my front room are depending on me.

Burrows nods, and gives me a smile. "Very well. Then we have to attempt some fancy flying."

"Are you good at fancy flying?" Cold asks him.

"No," he says, with that rakish smile on his face I suspect won him many a clockwork lover. "But with a crew behind me, I can work miracles."

He unscrews the tip of one of his clockwork fingers to reveal a pen nib, and gives the wind-up key on the back of his hand a couple of cranks.

"Let's draw up a plan."

Lieutenant Burrows is right about one thing: nobody benefits from hearing about the planning.

Over the course of the hour we spend theorizing, the sounds of the gathered group outside flow from hushed whispers to worried murmurs and back again. No one disturbs us, but that's because Big Business and Miss Mighty convince them not to. (That's not a team-up I ever expected.)

I take point coming back into the living room. Not everyone knows Burrows or Cold, and a familiar face is the least I can do. Dr Atrocity is here now, with an armful of wood, metal, and fishing line, along with a backpack that clanks when she moves. Miss Mighty is only the third-most uncomfortable person in the room; Big Business and Dr Atrocity herself are tied for the prize, with Business studying the Employee of the Month plaque he's sprouted in his corner and the bad doctor nervously chuckling at something Breaker and Spiderhand are discussing. I step into the living room, and everyone's attention is on me.

Why me? I'm just a detective. I found the guy. The evidence he did it is right in front of us. This should be up to someone else. But I'm the best-traveled and the best-known of our chosen leaders, and more important than any logic, they've decided to hang their hopes on me. I need to give them what they want. Let's see if Sandra taught me how to do it.

"Most of you are expecting a speech," I say. "And I don't want to disappoint you."

There are some smiles, Burrows and Miss Mighty and of all people Dr Atrocity. Everyone else is busy being afraid.

"I want to say three things before I get all Big Hero on you." I plant my paws firmly, look everyone in the eye. "First of all, I want to thank you all for being here at all.

"Second, I want you to know that we do have a plan, and that we are going to tell you the whole plan. We're not going to lie to you as part of a trick, or use you as a sacrifice, or some nonsense like that. I know some people think that's good tactics, but that's not what the Stillreal should be about."

Big Business looks at his feet, dismayed and embarrassed.

"Third, I want to say, again: if at any point you decide you can't handle this, you can leave, and I will still admire you for having stayed

233

as long as you did. What we're doing today is unbelievable and scary and maybe deadly, in a way Friends have never had to deal with. There's no shame in deciding it's too much."

Breaker almost cries. Dr Atrocity's smile just gets bigger.

"What we're doing today... except for maybe Burrows, this isn't what we're built for. We find things and we fix things and we fight the bad guys, but we don't go to war. That's for the soldiers, the Friends who played war or robbed stagecoaches or... or whatever."

"The killers," says Big Business. "The merciless ones."

I nod to him. "And that makes this even scarier. We're up against a killer, and we're not killers. Not like him. And that sounds like we're at a disadvantage, but there's something we are that matters here. Something that we are and he isn't. We're fighters."

Miss Mighty cocks her head.

"Every one of us came into being because someone needed to believe in us. Because with us around they knew they were never alone," – I gesture to Spiderhand – "or that it was possible to stand up to the bad people," – I gesture to Miss Mighty – "or that there was some purpose and reason behind this all." That one's to Big Business, the living conspiracy theory. "And every one of us wound up here because something happened that meant our people couldn't believe in us anymore."

Breaker squirms. Spiderhand nudges against her side.

"But we're still Real, just like the name says. We're still Real, and we're here, and if we could go back to our people?" I let that hang in the air for a second. "If we could help them again, even if it's just one more time, is there any pain, any punishment, any awful thing we wouldn't endure to make that happen?"

I pause. Nobody is moving. None of the ones who breathe are breathing. But then Miss Mighty, with great determination, starts to shake her head.

"Exactly," I say, pointing to her. I see courage spark in the others, backs getting stiffer, loads getting lighter. "We've survived awful things already. And that's what we have that the Teatime Man doesn't have. We all know we're here for the same reason, and we all know that the last thing we want is for anyone to be lost again the way we were the first time. And because of that, I believe we can win. Because us? We're fighters.

"So if you're staying – if you're fighting – I'm going to tell you the plan, and we're going to take the Teatime Man out of the Stillreal. Once. And. For. All."

Half the Friends are staring at me, and the other half are staring at each other. There's some shock, and some uncertainty, and gallons and gallons of fear. But there's also fire, and confidence, that wasn't on their faces before.

And then, there's applause.

Thank you, Sandra. Thank you for helping me do this. Thank you for making me who I need to be to fix this problem.

I just wish I knew for sure it helped.

CHAPTER TWENTY-SEVEN

When the plan has been explained, and then re-explained for the youngest among us, Dr Atrocity distributes photographs of the Space Kingdom. The assembled Friends are either baffled or excited by the ability of the photographs to stand up to time in another Idea; Big Business manages both reactions at the same time. Dr Atrocity gives everyone time to look over the photos, and treats us all to a cold, condescending smile when we're done.

"The photographs are perfect reproductions of the Stillreal Idea that the Teatime Man first appeared in," she says. "Using these, you should be able to think your way to the designated clearing. If you cannot, team up with someone who can. If you can, make sure no one needs to team up with you before you leave. Any questions?"

Miss Mighty is itching to ask a few, but to my eternal gratitude, she stays quiet. Dr Atrocity sniffs, and nods to me, once again handing me the burden of everyone's attention.

"Right," I say, hopefully loud enough to drown out my heartbeat. "The advance party will go scout things out now. Everyone else, meet at the clearing in half an hour. No more, no less. You show up and no one's there, you wait three seconds and you think back here for a little bit before you try to return. Nobody waits there alone. Period."

Spiderhand raises himself, standing tall until he gets my attention. "Yes?"

He signs out, in worried little motions, a query about whether or not he should put the kettle on, just in case. Big Business is the only one who doesn't smile.

"Fill it up, but don't leave the burner on," I say. "Half an hour, everybody?"

There are nods and murmurs of agreement, and the other Friends think out of the apartment, some gathering materials, some just taking a second for themselves. The advance team of Lieutenant Burrows and Miss Mighty head out, followed by a grim Dr Atrocity and a reluctant Breaker, our engineering team. That leaves me and Spiderhand. Spidey signs to me, a frenzy of curls and snaps and crosses that takes a few seconds to complete. He says, "This is a wonderful experience. Thank you."

Everything's gotten a little dusty and foggy all of a sudden – I mean, there's no way I'm crying.

"Here," I say. "Take my paw."

Spidey obliges, nervous energy coursing through him. I look around at the apartment, trying to memorize it. It's a good apartment. If I could thank the creator of Playtime Town for how well he furnished the Welcoming Arms, I would.

"We can't go home," I say, "but we can't stay here." And before I have time to doubt, I think the advance party out of our home and straight into the photograph. No sense delaying the inevitable.

The leaves on the floor of the clearing are gorgeous, gold and bronze and every non-metallic color in between. The river at the edge of the clearing sounds like a rushing rapid, but looks like a friendly creek, a branch large enough to serve as a bridge fallen across it. The surrounding forest is thick, dark, and endless in all directions. It smells like fresh, unsullied pine. The only thing messing up my calm is how everything looks like a crayon drawing. The leaves are little half-star shapes, the river a curving blue line, the branch a rectangle with a single twig sticking out of it. The forest around us is just row upon row of scribbled-in brown cylinders topped with cloud-like blobs of green, all of it with patches of white peeking through the color. I see the castle from the photograph poking out of the trees in the distance, a solid rectangle of eggshell white that you might mistake for just another uncolored spot if it weren't for the blue outline marking where the walls end.

"You made it," Dr Atrocity says from behind me, dragging me back to the present.

Dr Atrocity is standing on the other side of the fallen branch, next to one of the thickest trees. Her hands are busy tinkering with the screws on some huge, film-reel-looking gizmo that Miss Mighty is holding in midair. Neither of them looks pleased with this arrangement. Behind them, Breaker is hard at work with the bad doctor's heap of materials, arms blurring as she attaches wires and rope and hinges to metal poles. For the first time, she looks calm.

"Your photograph was darn good," I say to Dr Atrocity. "Thank you."

Dr Atrocity smirks. "The device will be done shortly. Your octopod companion is very efficient."

Next in is Lieutenant Burrows. He's alone, as planned, looking at the pocket watch bolted to his hip.

"Lieutenant," I say.

Burrows' monocle hums as it adjusts itself. His expression is stiff and unemotional, just how he likes it. "Your pronunciation is still barbaric."

"I love your positive attitude," I say. "Everything ready?"

He looks at the watch again, closes it up. "Everything I can control."

Next in are the Sadness Penguins, all done up in capes and makeshift helmets, carrying a variety of household implements that may or may not serve them well as impromptu cudgels. What they lack in armament they at least make up for in determined expressions. After them is Big Business; he smiles that hungry predator smile, and gives me a big thumbs-up. I feel the fact-finders around us more than I see them.

Officer Cold thinks in, dressed in what I think is supposed to be riot gear, but honestly looks like he's strapped a bunch of blue balloons to himself. (That may not be wrong, actually.) Then comes Farmer Nick holding, of all things, a scythe, then Azure Armadillo, Scrapyard and K'kota (but no Dame Rouge, which doesn't surprise but does disappoint). The last in is Chip, looking nervous and sporting a shoulder holster that contains, if I'm not mistaken, a child-sized revolver.

Chip adjusts his hat, turns his baby-fat-rounded face toward me, and gives me a determined nod that does not belong on a fifth-grader. Armadillo and his crew go over to Dr Atrocity, distracting Breaker from her work and raising Miss Mighty's hackles even further. Everyone else looks to me and Lieutenant Burrows, expectant, twitchy, and fearful.

We've done the speech thing. We've done the planning thing. Now it's time to do the really scary part.

"Phase One," Lieutenant Burrows barks, his voice resonating as it projects over the crowd. "Take your positions, confirm placement when ready. Signal at the first sign of the enemy."

The Friends scatter off to the fringes of my vision, with the exception of Big Business and the Alibi crew, who hang back with Dr Atrocity and Miss Mighty. Spiderhand gives me the most backward glances.

"It's ready," Dr Atrocity says.

I turn at the pronouncement. Dr Atrocity is crouched over the assembly Breaker made, attaching it to the film reel gizmo. The contraption slides all the way into the reel and out of sight, no bulges or protrusions to indicate something as thick as one of my paws is now filled with around a hundred linear feet of metal. She hands the reel off to Mighty, who answers with a nod and flies up out of sight, rummaging around in the forest canopy. My detective stuff thinks it has her located, but honestly, I don't pay much attention. The less I know for sure, the better this will go.

And we wait. Big Business pulls a phone out of his coat long enough to silence it. Lieutenant Burrows nervously toys with the wind-up key for his clockwork arm. Azure Armadillo, Scrapyard, and K'kota trade six-packs of uneasy glances. There's no noise in the crayon forest except the rushing of the river and the sounds we make ourselves. I smell the woods, but nothing underneath it, no tea or fish or anything else that might stick out. I don't hear anything, but that doesn't necessarily mean the Teatime Man isn't right behind me. I'd stop scanning the clearing for any evidence of an intruder, but that might give me room to think about what I'm actually doing.

And we wait, and we wait, and we wait. I'm about to make a joke at the expense of Azure Armadillo's fidgeting when the pop of fireworks takes a cheese grater to my nerves. Sparks fly up above the canopy, formed into a birthday cake for a few shimmering seconds before dissolving into individual flecks of color. That's the signal for movement sighted in the forest. (Thanks, Mr Float.)

The scouts come sprinting back out of the trees. Spiderhand pelts up and hides behind me, spinning in place as he tries to guess where danger is going to come from.

Crudely drawn branches snap somewhere out in the forest. Leaves crunch under someone's feet. And slowly, but unmistakably, there comes the footfall of heavy boots.

This is the tallest version of the Teatime Man we've seen, and the skinniest, too. His coat is made of rough green fabric. His hat is a broad-brimmed felt thing, with a black feather that looks like it was just plucked from a chicken. He's holding less of a bat and more of an unpolished tree limb, dangling at his side like it weighs more than the heaviest thing I can imagine. Here and there, when the sunlight catches him, I see rough textures, the waxy flash of crayon, but that bare nod to the Space Kingdom doesn't make him any less terrifying.

He pauses at the edge of the clearing, looks at the knot of cowering Friends, and cocks his head.

"Drink," he announces to the world at large.

His eyes, a sickly, toxic green, crinkle like he's smiling… and he charges. He gets halfway to us before Miss Mighty sonic-booms out of the canopy and punches him in the face.

He's a foot shorter when he stands up, his coat draping on the ground; he gets both hands on his club, before Miss Mighty gives him a kick that launches him so high he grazes the tops of the trees. He craters into the ground, and he's about the size of Spiderhand. I'd cheer, but we're not ready for that quite yet.

The Teatime Man stands up, swings the club, but he's too weak to face Miss Mighty now; she catches it and throws it away from him. He disappears into his clothes, starts to slither away, but Mighty gets his lapels in her hands and slams him into the ground, and again, and again, and again. Breaker's arms death-grip onto my tail.

Miss Mighty roars, and slams him one last time. There's a sound of shattering glass, and Mighty is standing in the clearing alone, holding a couple tatters of green cloth. She drops them, spits, and retreats back to our position at the center of the clearing.

"I hope we're right about this," she grumbles.

"You and everyone else," I say.

Lieutenant Burrows twists one of his many wind-up keys and shouts an order, magnified like he's got a loudspeaker in his mouth. "Formation Baker, on the double!" he shouts, gesturing to any Friends who hesitate for even a second. "Be ready for the next wave!"

The Friends fan out again. Breaker and Spiderhand get close to me, watching the underbrush. Officer Cold takes up in a hole (well, a black oval) in the side of a scrawled-together tree. Chip Dixon and Azure Armadillo slide down the riverbank and lurk under the branch-bridge. The others all form a line near the center of the clearing, armed, coiled, and alert.

Lieutenant Burrows clicks his monocle back and forth a few times, and gives a bleak but approving nod before flipping a switch on his belt and careening up into the sky with a burst of steam. Dr Atrocity gives me a salute that I'm painfully sure is sincere, and does the same, humming with electricity and antigravity.

My detective stuff keeps me posted on my allies' moods. Fear is the overall theme, along with anger and, to my heart's great heaviness, more than a little regret.

"Thank you all for coming," I call out to the clearing.

Everyone tenses up at the loud noise, but what comes after that looks a lot like relaxation. Breaker turns and gives me a long look. Spiderhand signs to her that it's going to be okay, because Tippy's here. I have no idea what to do with that.

Next to me, Big Business sniffs. "Complete failure of personal reality is a poor investment decision anyway."

The villain refusing to admit he's got emotions. That brings me back to the Stillreal I'm used to.

241

The bushes rustle, but whatever's doing it is pretty light, a bird or something, whatever the little kid who drew this thought passed for normal. I feel the ground starting to transform under us, warping to match the outside Friends standing it; I see a knot in Officer Cold's chosen tree warp into the beginnings of a smiley face. Too much longer, and this plan might be a bust.

More rustling sounds out in the forest. The ground under my feet is starting to look like it's paved with felt. Come on, come on…

And then footsteps, huge, heavy, and slow, even more so than the last ones, thunder through the forest to my left. Everyone in the clearing clenches up.

"Is this the action item we're looking for?" Big Business asks, looking the same direction I am.

"Yeah," I say, as the footsteps pick up speed. "There's no mistaking that sound."

"I hadn't heard him before," Big Business says, eyes wide.

Underbrush thrashes at the far edges of the clearing, a green mist rising up from between the trees. I squint, and I see scribbled twigs and leaves being hurled up into the air, like something is impatiently swatting trees out of the way.

"I don't want to die," Breaker says, barely a squeak.

"That's a rational response," I say.

I look around the clearing, checking on Officer Cold, Chip, the Sadness Penguins, everybody who agreed to be here with me. I just barely finish before the light in the clearing dims.

It's him. The original, the biggest one in the blackest coat, with the bat like a staff made of shadow and the hat wide enough for an army to hide under. He pauses as he comes into the open, and he looks right at me. I can tell he recognizes me by the way he hesitates.

"We're here to stop you," I shout at him. I come out from the group a little, hunker down for a charge. "We're not letting you hurt any more Friends."

He cocks his head, still looking at me.

"It ends here," I say. "It ends now."

The Teatime Man straightens, glances for just a second at Big Business. I feel the entire clearing hold its breath.

"Drink," he says into the silence.

He raises his bat over his head, and charges at me with a speed I've never seen – until Officer Cold nails him with the freeze ray, anyway. The ice only holds him for a second, just a few crystals down around his ankles, but the effect on his demeanor is the important part: for one beautiful second, he's startled.

"You killed my partner!" Cold snarls, and blasts the Teatime Man straight in the face.

The Teatime Man stumbles back, clawing the ice out of his eyes. Farmer Nick lunges in, swinging the scythe in a serpentine pattern that doesn't hurt the Man, but does delay and confuse him. Nick dodges away as the Teatime Man gets his bearings, one hand up in mock surrender. The Man comes for Nick until another blast from the freeze ray catches him in the back, then he whirls and charges toward Cold's tree, bat swinging in an endless black streak, gouging cavernous holes in the trunk.

That's Chip's cue. He pops out from his hiding place and starts shooting, again aiming at the Teatime Man's exposed back. The Teatime Man wheels toward Chip and bull-rushes without a thought, bat cocked back for a swing, the bullets rippling his coat without slowing him down.

Anyone who attacks him becomes the primary target. Just the reaction we were hoping for.

Chip dives back under the branch-bridge, and Azure Armadillo pops up, letting rip with blasts of lightning from his gloves. The Teatime Man breaks off his pursuit of Chip and heads for Armadillo, who curls up and rolls downriver behind Chip.

Breaker gets his attention next, hurling a fishing net out of her tool belt. The Teatime Man catches it in one hand and barrels toward her. Spiderhand steps in front, fingers up in a 'halt' gesture, but the Teatime Man doesn't slow. He brings the bat down with both hands, headed straight for my favorite Friend – and then Miss Mighty grabs onto the bat.

I hear the crack as her hand stops the swing, the awful crunch of breaking bones. Mighty doesn't even flinch; she's too busy putting her unbroken fist straight into the Teatime Man's face.

Didn't see that coming, did he?

She hits him again, and he stumbles, even lets go of the bat. Miss Mighty discards it, and before he can recover, she follows through with a shoulder tackle, smashing him to the ground. He doesn't shrink, doesn't even wince, but detective stuff confirms he's moving a little slower. Miss Mighty throws a left cross that spins the Teatime Man around, puts a knee into his back, and brings her broken hand back for another punch. And there's where she makes her mistake.

It's just one wince, one second of pain – but at the speeds they're moving, that's more than enough opening. The Teatime Man snatches the bat off the ground and swings it straight into her temple. Miss Mighty cries out in agony as she collapses. The Man steps over her, as triumphant as he's ever looked.

"Drink!"

And that's where he makes *his* mistake.

Lightning comes crashing out of the forest canopy, one thick, sizzling blue bolt turning everything black and white. It hits the Teatime Man with pinpoint accuracy, hurling him to the ground. He stands, coat smoldering, and looks up as the brown-wax branches snap and crack under the bulk of the descending airship.

Burrows' crew lets the Teatime Man have it with the lightning gun again, throwing him across the clearing. The sky-pirates cut loose with their blunderbusses, peppering the open ground with bullets and broken bottles and whatever else they could stuff into the breeches. Burrows barks orders, sending his crew to recharge the lightning gun's capacitors while the pirates launch pot-shot after pot-shot. They're not actually hitting the Teatime Man – even slowed down, he's too fast for that – but they are keeping his attention, enough that he doesn't seem to realize they're herding him toward the riverbank, over to the tree where Dr Atrocity and Breaker did their work.

The airborne assault continues for another few seconds before the Teatime Man gives up on dodging and leaps right for them, lunging into the air to an incredible height. Without flinching, Burrows raises his hand, and the Teatime Man's forward momentum halts. Next to me, Big Business grins.

Big Business makes a small gesture, and the Teatime Man is slammed back to the ground by the half-hidden things surrounding him. One second, the fact-finders are smears of black and awful, forms just barely suggesting arms and stingers and beaks, and the next they're businessmen, shouting like someone just canceled their company credit cards. Whatever they look like, they're relentless, punching and stomping at the Teatime Man, who I am pretty sure has no idea how to process what's going on. Up above, the sky-pirates whoop and cheer; the soldiers keep their guns trained on the melee, frowning just like Burrows as they wait for the inevitable.

Two fact-finders go flying as the Teatime Man stands up and swings. One bounces across the clearing, rolling to a halt on the riverbank. The other dissolves in midair, reduced to scraps of fabric fluttering in the breeze. Big Business grits his teeth, and gestures for them to keep attacking.

Another swing; another fact-finder reduced to tatters. Another, and another, and another. The fact-finders start to retreat on instinct, and the Teatime Man strides after them, swinging like he's Farmer Fran harvesting wheat. We've lost the element of surprise, and we're not likely to overpower him. But, I force myself to think, we've got him going the right way.

Miss Mighty goes for another tackle, catching the Teatime Man around the midsection. He brings his bat down on her head, and she splays out flat in front of him. He prepares for the killing blow, but Chip fires on him again, diverting his attention back toward the river.

We need to get Mighty out of there. Officer Cold is on it, but he's the last person who should be. The freeze ray blast snaps the Teatime Man's attention back to Cold, back away from the tree. Cold yells, fires again, and the Teatime Man swats the shot out of the air, shattering the ice on contact.

He's three trees away from Cold, spitting distance from the tree we want him under. My turn to save the day, then. I put my head down, and come charging right at him.

A pair of fact-finders wrap their arms around his neck, sink long probosci into his collar. The Teatime Man chucks them off him, destroying one with an off-handed swing. I'm thirty feet away...

Cold fires again. Again the Teatime Man clubs it away. Twenty feet...

His boots thunder against the ground as he heads for Officer Cold's tree. The blunderbuss fire from above isn't even getting a sideways glance. Ten feet...

He crosses in front of me, and I throw my horns into his legs as hard as I can.

His knees come out from under him, and the bat tumbles out of his hands. His weight on my horns is enormous, the heaviest thing I've ever moved. But I am moving him.

A fist clubs me in the back. My stitches rip. I think about Cable and Plug exploding into nothingness, and Spindleman's claws gouging at the top of the staircase, and I put the pain away and keep moving.

The sound when we hit the tree is unbelievable, like dynamite just went off in my ears. I follow through, shouting against the noise and the pain and the fear, until my neck insists I can't go forward anymore. The weight of the Teatime Man sags against me, stunned.

I can't move. I can't see. But I can hear. And what I hear is Miss Mighty, in pain but still with us, saying, "Now!"

Dr Atrocity pulls a click-button out of her labcoat, and gives it an intense smack with the palm of her hand. There's a click, and a whirr, and I throw myself backwards as the bad doctor's device lets out a bang like a whole birthday party's worth of firecrackers. The Teatime Man looks up at the same time I do, and steps back a half-second too late to avoid Breaker's contraption falling from the trees above. The heap of metal unfurls like a skinned umbrella, hinges swinging wide and ropes snapping taut to form a cylindrical cage whose bars slam into the ground around the Teatime Man, separating him from the rest of us. He stands up stock-straight, swamp-green eyes bulging.

"Got you," I say.

The Teatime Man lets out a yell like nothing I've ever heard, like he's been lit on fire, like he's dying and he's angry about it. The silence when he finishes is filled in with a cheer.

The pirates are whooping, Burrows' soldiers are chanting "Huzzah," Breaker and Spiderhand are flailing at the air. I hear someone say "Yes!" and someone else say "Victory!" I just stare at the Teatime Man, and wait for the noise to subside again before I give him my speech.

"We figured it out," I say. "We figured it out from the darn copies you kept leaving everywhere."

The Teatime Man glares with dinner-plate eyes. Everyone is silent, the readers watching the detective accuse the criminal. This part feels right.

"You don't like cells. Or cages. Even if they shouldn't be able to hold you. Even though you should be able to break anything imaginary you can get your hands on."

The Teatime Man snarls. It sounds like we've got a tiger caged in there.

"It's over," I say. "You're done. You stop killing. Today."

I think I see a tiny smile in the shadows of his face. He's daring me to say what I want to say next. It comes out a little hoarser than expected.

"We're never letting you out," I say. This part doesn't feel right. "We're never letting you hurt anyone again!"

He hunkers down, shoulders up around his ears, but it's less 'ashamed' and more 'ready to pounce.'

"Do you hear me?" I shout. This definitely doesn't feel right. "It's over!"

The Teatime Man stands back up, looking down at me with those huge, dangerous eyes. And he reaches out, and with that same terrifying, man-on-fire scream, he grabs two of the bars, and he pulls… and the bars start to bend.

Now he's not the only one screaming.

He's in pain – you can tell that without even looking at him – but he keeps on bending the bars. I start backing up; the other Friends are doing the same. He's in pain… but he's not stopping.

The copies of him are weaker than the original…

Big Business thinks out of the clearing. His fact-finders go with him. The sky-pirates panic, their ship sending down cascades of leaves as they wrestle it back into the sky. Farmer Nick drops his scythe and follows suit, mouth dropped open in horror. Everyone else is stuck in place, until we all hear the long, high moan of the bars buckling in the middle, leaving a gap more than wide enough for a looming figure in a trenchcoat to step through.

"Drink."

The Teatime Man steps out of his prison, and almost everyone who's left flees into the woods.

Officer Cold points the freeze ray at him, fires, and for a hanging second the Teatime Man looks down at the ice coating his arm. He shrugs, and the next blast misses completely. For an eye-blink, the forest sun is blocked out as the Teatime Man steps over me and thunders across the clearing, reaching into the shadows of his coat.

Miss Mighty flies past me at speed, but he's armed with a new bat before she can get to him. He takes a double-handed swing that makes my stomach clench. Mighty yowls as she sails across the clearing, grunts when she goes hip-first into a scribbled-in tree trunk. Dr Atrocity runs over to her, swinging one of the fishing poles like a sword, and the Teatime Man turns away from them, focused on Officer Cold.

"Go!" I shout to Cold, as he tries to aim again.

He looks at me, face blank with fear. The Teatime Man puts his head down and rushes.

"Go!" I shout again.

The bat connects with bare tree trunk where Officer Cold had been. The tree crashes to the ground, jagged blocks of crayon falling amid the scattering herd of Sadness Penguins.

"Go!" I yell. "Go! Go! Go!"

The Teatime Man turns toward me, eyes blazing. The Sadness Penguins wink out around him. Chip disappears from the corner of my eye. Behind me, I hear Dr Atrocity say, "I'm sorry." A second later, my detective stuff tells me her and Miss Mighty are gone.

It's just me, and him. Good. Let's slow his hunt down as much as possible.

"This ends here," I say. But even I know I don't mean it.

That smile appears under his eyes, the tiny hint of teeth. He knows he's won.

"Come on," I say. "If we can't put you in jail, let's at least have a fight scene."

He stays still, stays smiling, drawing out and relishing this horrible moment. I won't yell. I won't break.

"Come on!"

I lied.

The Teatime Man readies the bat, hurtles toward me, and stumbles as something brown and dog-sized hits him right in the chest.

Spiderhand.

No.

The Teatime Man pauses, unfazed by the blow, but confused by the interruption to our little story. Spiderhand responds by again balling himself into a fist and leaping up to punch the Teatime Man in the chest. It's not anywhere near the force I can get going, but it makes him back up a step.

"No!" I say.

The Teatime Man sucks in a breath.

Spiderhand turns toward me, and in a quick, worried gesture, he conveys three simple things.

Go.

You can stop him.

Take care of our home.

The Teatime Man brings his bat down, and with a horrible crunch, Spiderhand splays out on the ground.

"No!" I bellow, charging straight at the monster in the black coat.

Spiderhand hops up, shaking, and does another jump-punch. He connects with the Teatime Man's knee. He turns to me, and gestures one more time: You can stop him.

The Teatime Man cocks back his bat. "Fine."

Like heck, Spidey.

I charge in, head down, aiming not at the Teatime Man, but at the wobbling bundle of kindness in front of him. Spiderhand struggles, but in his state that isn't saying much. I get my nasal horn under him, and toss him across my back just in time for the bat to come down hard across both of us.

I feel a stitch split, and fluff wafting free; but I also see, through the welling tears, a shard of teacup peeking out of the dirt. I bite my lip, and I concentrate as hard as I can. The wind of a deadly blow bellows down at me, right as I think us back to a dining room table covered in glued-together teacups.

I blink. I look around. It's our living room. It's our apartment. It's our hallway, and our smell of tea and root beer, and our view of Playtime Town out the window and our wondering if our friends are okay.

We're okay.

We're okay?

"Spidey?" I ask the weight on my back.

No response.

"Spidey?!"

He's there, says my detective stuff. It knows the weight of him, the feel, the scent.

"Spidey!"

I kneel to one side, realize what I've done too late to prevent him banging limp into the carpet. He's still a hand, still brown and soft and curvaceous, still Spiderhand. The Teatime Man didn't take that from us.

"Spidey?" I ask.

I lift a finger, let it go. It falls right back down to the floor.

"...Spiderhand?"

He just lies there, even when I start to cry.

CHAPTER TWENTY-EIGHT

The dryer barks as it hits the end of its cycle. I slump out, press the Extra Dry button, and climb back in. It's the only thing I know for sure I can do right.

Saint Sunbeam's was waiting for us – Golem Jones called ahead the minute we left. Nurse Pawsome and the teddy bear doctors were at the ready, prepped with as much needle and thread and Panacea Potion as they could set aside. Miss Mighty was up and moving already when we got there; I didn't take much longer. But Spiderhand…

Panacea Potion can cure everything. Panacea Potion can even raise the dead if you use enough of it. Panacea Potion is magic. But so are a lot of other things in the Stillreal…

His knuckles healed. His fingernails unchipped. His skin sloughed off its cuts and scrapes and went back to its healthy tan color. He was, by every measure they could take, alive. But alive and awake are two different things.

He's in a bed. Under observation, they say. We're working on it, they say. We don't know, is really what they said, and kept saying as I stumbled out of the hospital, trying to understand why, and how, and what to do next.

Maybe defeating the Teatime Man will break the spell? Maybe a kiss from a prince will undo the curse? Maybe he just needs time?

Maybe my best friend will never wake up.

Miss Mighty stayed at Saint Sunbeam's after I left – just for observation, according to the after-action report Lieutenant Burrows slipped under my door. It's not the only letter I've gotten since the clearing; Big Business sent a formal letter on high-grade paper, explaining that while he enjoyed our partnership and we would discuss my debts in the future something something something – I didn't finish reading before I tore it in half.

I remember seeing Chip and Farmer Nick on my walk home, both leaning out of the doorway of the Rootbeerium with fear in their eyes, wanting to know if I was alright. I remember the Sadness Penguins waddling slowly alongside me, signing a similar question. I didn't answer any of them.

Golem Jones knocked on the door once. Officer Cold knocked, too, claiming he was 'doing the rounds.' Freedom Frieda apologized through it in the highest, most piercing voice I've ever heard. I didn't answer for any of them, either. I'll answer when I'm ready.

I'm never going to be ready.

I haven't heard from Breaker, or Dr Atrocity, or any of the henchmen from the Alibi. I'm hoping it's because they've gone to ground, because the Teatime Man is almost certainly on the hunt for all of them. The good news is, the one Friend I am absolutely sure he's going to come after is me.

I've messed up his plans. I may have gotten the closest to beating him anyone ever has, and even if not, I know something that hurts him. He's going to kill me, and he's going to kill anyone who tries to stop him.

I wish I understood how getting drunk worked.

The dryer stops. I sit in its cylinder, watching the plain white wall with the big bright sign reminding us not to steal each others' clothes because stealing is wrong.

The Stillreal needs me.

Or does it? Dr Atrocity is smart. Lieutenant Burrows figured out the tactics. There are better fighters. All I am is a detective. A sense-maker for a world that doesn't make sense.

I slide out of the dryer, into the cool air. I climb the stairs to our – to my –apartment, and head inside, kicking aside a snowdrift of letters I never want to answer just so I can lock the door.

I wake up at my desk. I'm not sure how long I've been in the chair, but by the number of empty root beer bottles on the floor, I'm guessing either a couple days, or one really bad one. I think about Spiderhand, and I groan my head back down onto my desk, relaxing at the feel of my stuffing pressing against the hard wood surface.

I wake up at my desk again. People are knocking on the door. I can't help them, so I put my head back down.

I wake up at my desk once more, to the sound of my front door shattering. Footsteps come booming down the hallway. I watch my bedroom door, waiting, ready. The door bursts open, and Miss Mighty stands before me, arms crossed. I wish I could say I was relieved.

"Tippy." She's angry, but not as angry as she's acting.

I study the wood grain on my desktop. It has a pattern, knots in the wood that form little maps of the state of Hawaii. Sandra liked Hawaii.

"Tippy, it's time to get up," she says, closer to me this time.

My stitches ache. Sleeping might help. Did I used to sleep before the accident?

Miss Mighty grabs my chair, dumps me onto the floor hard enough I bounce. I probably deserve it.

"I said, get up." She looms over me, fists at her sides, teeth locked together. I've got her good and mad.

"Why?"

"Damn it – dangit – no, damn it. Damn it, Tippy, we need you!"

The world blurs out. I must be crying. "I'm not what the world needs."

"How do you know?"

"I didn't catch the bad guy, Mighty." My voice is like glue. "I'm supposed to catch the bad guy, but he got away. He got away and Spiderhand's never going to wake up, and... and I can't do what I used to do anymore. I can't. It's gone." I sniff, paw at the ground. "I can solve all the little stuff, but when the big problems come around, all I do is fail."

Miss Mighty stays stock still. Detective stuff is registering anger, shock, and frustration. And sadness. Big, memory-whale-filled oceans of sadness.

The carpet rustles as she turns and walks out of the room, without even a glance back my way. I hear her walk down the hall and shut the door, very, very gently.

She couldn't prove me wrong.

I nudge at my chair, but setting it back up is too much effort. I climb into bed, and without bothering to get under the covers, I fall asleep.

I wake up to a tapping on the window over my bed. If it weren't for the curiosity Sandra gave me, I probably wouldn't even look up. But I do, and… why is a tiny black bird pecking at my window?

My detective stuff wakes up right after me, and tells me it's a nightingale. A nightingale with glowing gems for eyes.

The bird taps once more, a rhythmic little three-beat chord, and flutters off into the sky. My eyes follow it as it flies off toward the stars… and the moon.

I can see the moon's face now. I mean, I can't really help it with it staring right at me. It's got three enormous eyes, with big golden eyelashes and stars for pupils, bright against its green-cheese skin. It has one mouth, an oval crater lined with soft, kind lips. There's a lunar lander sitting on top of it like a hat.

"Hello, Tippy," says the moon, in a voice like my favorite song being hummed to me while I sleep.

"… Hi…"

"You seem sad," says the moon. "I thought you might need to talk."

If you're having trouble, the moon will talk to you. That's the legend of Playtime Town. Of course the legend is true. This is the Stillreal.

"Do you talk to every Friend who seems sad?" I ask.

The moon smiles. It's not a smile I'm ever hoping to comprehend. "Only the ones who really need it."

"That seems judgmental."

The moon laughs. It seems to be enjoying itself, but if that's the laugh of enjoyment I hope it's sad forever.

"You're a good person, Tippy. No," it says, with enough authority to silence me, "no quips back. You're a good person, because your person made you that way. I know, because seeing to the heart of people is how my person made me."

"Right." I nod. It's the most motion I can handle without feeling things. "Sort of useful in your line of work."

The moon smirks again, a little chiding, a little kind. (That describes nearly everything it does, really.) "Right now, the whole Stillreal needs that goodness."

That exact burden is why I'm stuck in bed.

"I know," it says, and honestly the creepiest part is how blasé it is about responding to what I'm thinking. "It's a lot to handle. But I know you can handle it."

"How do you know?" I ask, with an aggravated thrashing of my head. "How do you know I can handle it? I'm dealing with something one of a kind."

"He's just one more monster of a very old kind," the moon says.

I arch my eyebrows. The moon looks down at me like I'm a baby bird struggling to fly.

"He's a bad guy," the moon insists. "He's a criminal."

My detective stuff is ringing off the hook. The moon's exact wording matters, but my main brain isn't working quite right.

"I need more…" I say.

"Your companions will help you figure that out."

"My 'companions' all hate me."

"That is not strictly true. And all anger passes in time."

My toes curl in annoyance. "I really hate it when people talk in riddles."

The moon just smiles. "Nothing I say will get you out of bed. But don't worry. You'll hear it soon."

"Hear what?"

"Remember that people love you, Detective Tippy," the moon says. "Remember that Friends love you, and that people loved you, and that there's a reason for both. Remember that reason, and you will win."

"This is garbage."

And again, the moon smiles that too-meaningful smile. "For now."

And it turns its face away from me, and I'm just looking up at cheese and craters.

I could go get another root beer float. I could go take a spin in the dryer. Or I could sit here, and try to figure out what the moon means.

I try that for a while. Then I sleep again.

I wish I could say it felt good.

I wake up again in the middle of the night. Someone in the living room is insisting on playing 'Chopsticks' on the piano. Badly.

I roll out of bed, and the piano player switches without warning from 'Chopsticks' to Spiderhand's favorite Beethoven piece. My back turns into a steel cable of fear, but I still step out into the hallway. If death is going to kick down my door, I'm going to face it standing up.

I stride along to the opening strains of the 'Ode to Joy,' and stop at the edge of my living room. Miss Mighty leans back from the piano, regarding me with a melancholy smile.

"Are you back to yell at me?" I ask.

Miss Mighty shakes her head. "Yelling at you isn't going to help."

"Yeah. I'm allergic. So, then, why *are* you back?"

"Because you need help," Miss Mighty gives me an exaggerated shrug. "Duh." And a smile on the end of it, just to take the edge off.

I give her my own harm-reducing smile before I let it lapse back to a frown. "Listen, I–"

Miss Mighty holds up a gloved hand. "Don't worry, tough guy. I know nothing I say is going to convince you to square up for another round." She gives me that crooked smile that means she knows she's got me. "So I brought someone who can."

My detective stuff switches on before I can look confused. There's someone in the kitchen. Right as I register that, Officer Cold comes out into the living room, hands in his pockets.

"Hi, Detective," he says. He's not smiling, but he wants to be.

"What are you doing here?" I ask.

Officer Cold drops his arms to his sides. He looks so, so uncomfortable. "I…" He clears his throat. "Well. I understand you're not coping well."

I snort. "You could say that."

Officer Cold looks at Miss Mighty. She urges him on, looking as uncomfortable as he does. He tetches, looks at me again, and blurts out, "Do you need a hug?"

"Um," I know the answer, but I feel weird saying it. "Yes?"

Officer Cold clears his throat again. He looks at both me and Mighty with uncertainty. And then he hugs me. He's not very good at it, but still, that's where I melt.

I think it's just going to be sniffles, but it doubles down at that special speed reserved for strong emotions. There's a choke, and a wail, and I end up sobbing into Officer Cold's shoulder so hard it feels like I've pulled my back.

I bawl. I scream. I pound my hindlegs into the carpet. I don't care that my tears are freezing me to him. All I care about is crying, and sagging, and not being the only one carrying this anymore.

"I know," Cold whispers, in a softer, gentler voice than he has ever used on me before. "I know how you feel."

I stiffen, get ready to push free – and I make myself stay where I am, and I melt again. It feels right. Cold, but right. I let that go another second, and peel myself away with a crackle of shattering tear-ice.

"Thank you," I say. "I want to say thank you and say I mean it before you and I inevitably start bantering again."

Cold gives me an ironic half-smile. "You're welcome."

"Great, moment duly noted," I say. "Now, why are you here, risking the possibility we might decide you have a heart after all?"

"Because I need your help."

"What? *My* help?" My mouth runs out ahead of my panicking brain. "What, did you run out of Friends who don't reek of failure?"

Miss Mighty looks at me like I just said the sky is a horse. "Because you're the smartest Friend we know who isn't evil?"

Now I look at her like she said the sky is, in fact, a donkey. "But... I failed."

"Okay," Miss Mighty says, biting down frustration, "'failed' implies we're done. I count three of us alive in here," – she encompasses us with a twirl of her finger – "plus plenty more out there. We're not done."

I shake my head. I have the ominous feeling Miss Mighty is about to say something that makes sense.

"And also," she continues, "you didn't fail. You came up with the plan, but this butthole doesn't work the way we're used to things working. There are gonna be mistakes. And yeah, it sucks, and yeah, Spiderhand got hurt, and yeah, you get to be sad and angry and whatever you have to do to process all that. But Tippy, that doesn't mean you stop trying."

Officer Cold smirks darkly. "If it did, wouldn't I have stopped arresting you by now?"

Miss Mighty points at him for emphasis. "So this is more complicated than we expected? Okay. Don't we still have a duty to help people?"

The moon's voice is echoing in my skull. *You'll hear it soon.* I try to chase it out through sheer verbiage. "'We'?" I say. "You're a superhero. I'm just a detective. What am I supposed to do, evidence him to death?"

"You're not just a detective, Detective," Officer Cold says. "You—" He stops, looking the most uncomfortable I've ever seen him. "You hugged me when Officer Hot died."

"I..." I have no defense for that. I've got nothing except a bag of hot gravel shaking around in my guts.

"Tippy," Miss Mighty says. "You know I suck at feelings. But seriously, you are one of the most helpful, kindest Friends I know. Why the heck do you think Friends come to you with so many of their problems? It isn't because you like to act smarter than them, trust me."

My mind is carbonated, thoughts bobbing up and diving down and capsizing all over the place. What Miss Mighty just said sprints headlong into my memories, and I think I get what the moon meant. It feels like someone just rolled a boulder off my heart.

"Oh," I say, and that pulls the cork free of my tear ducts again.

"Uh?" says Officer Cold, both disarmed and disgusted.

Miss Mighty shakes her head. "Pretty sure those are happy tears. Let him feel his feels."

"No," I say, swallowing the saltwater. "No, no. I can... I can..."

I come out of the tailspin with two things staring me in the face. Cold and Mighty meant to give me a pep talk, but they just gave me a whole lot more than that.

"I think I'm ready to help." I sniff, choke, sniff again. "Yeah. Yeah. Distract me, please. What do you need?"

Officer Cold says, like it's obvious, "I need to catch him, before he does this to someone else."

Someone besides me. I nod. "I can help with that. I think. But – I don't know how to star–"

And then the rest of what the moon said makes sense. I feel the idea inching along my brain, back to front, dredging clues up as it crawls, slow and steady and overwhelming, into my conscious thoughts.

"He's thinking," Miss Mighty says.

"I know what deducting looks like," Officer Cold says with a familiar, welcome disgust.

I go back over the events in the clearing, in Memory Reefs, the Freedom Motel, Spindleman's house. I add up all the little moments in our encounters with the Teatime Man, seeing them with much clearer eyes. My theory is just a theory, but it's more than I had when I woke up.

I think I've got a plan for the Teatime Man. But for the first time… literally ever, actually… I think I've got a plan for me.

"I need a little more info before I say for sure," I say. "But I think I might know what we need to do."

"What's that?" Miss Mighty says.

"Well, I…" I stop, and I sigh. "I need to talk to Chip. I know how mysterious that sounds, but, I want to wait to discuss plans until I'm absolutely sure. We…" I shiver. "We obviously can't afford to go in half-cocked on this."

Miss Mighty smiles. "Congratulations. That's the most straightforward you have ever been."

Officer Cold sniffs. "More proof the Stillreal is coming to an end."

I give Officer Cold a smile and a pat on the shoulder.

"Come on, Officer," I say. "Let's go catch a bad guy."

CHAPTER TWENTY-NINE

I hate coffee. It's bitter, and it looks like mud, and it turns your teeth a funny color. Also, Sandra told me coffee is something I should hate. But it also made her Dad feel better, and Miss Mighty and Mr Float say it'll make me feel better. So I sit here in the Rootbeerium, and I drink it. And you know what? I do feel better. Of course, I also feel more awake, which is not necessarily what I want right now, but I can have a breakdown about that later.

The Rootbeerium is almost empty again, just Mr Float and my little band of coffee-sippers: Miss Mighty, Chip Dixon, and Officer Cold. According to Chip, pretty much everyone else has abandoned Playtime Town. Lucky them.

"Okay," I say, now that 'ready' is as close as it's getting. "Chip: Give me the news. What's going on with the Teatime Man in the real world?"

Chip shakes his head, a frown nailed to his face, but the words tumble out of him anyway. "The hunt for the Teatime Man has reached a fever pitch! The Portland Police Department, aided by agents from the Federal Bureau of Investigation, continue to tighten the net around the man who is already being called one of the most heinous criminals of this young century. Three days of searching have turned up nothing, but the police assure the people of Portland that it is only a matter of time–"

I hold up a paw. "Thank you. That's what I needed to know."

Miss Mighty scowls into her root beer. "So his person is being hunted, too."

"Exactly," I say. "The Teatime Man isn't just after us because he's mad. He's after us because his person is getting desperate. Okay, so the next thing I need is… a little more unusual."

Chip raises his eyebrows, baby face waiting in fear and confusion.

"At the fight. What did you see happen?"

Chip blinks. "What?"

"You're the ace reporter. If you had to write an article about that battle, what would you say happened? Assume you can use as many words as you need. Editor's being nice today. Or drunk, if that fits better."

"Gosh," Chip sighs, like I've described a dream. "I mean, we measure articles in column inches…"

"Unlimited column inches, then."

Chip coughs. "Gosh. Okay…" He pulls his glasses off, gives them a polish. "Okay." He sits there, chin in hand, while he mulls over his memories. After a few seconds, he clears his throat, and lets the story take him away.

Chip is a journalist, the best one in the Stillreal, and that means everything is recounted with total neutral objectivity – and total awareness. I hang on every word, and I listen to my detective stuff as it turns each one over and rubs the dirt off to make sure there's nothing underneath.

He describes the forest clone of the Teatime Man showing up, and the quick, brutal beating Miss Mighty gave him, and I learn that in those brief seconds of combat, the monster showed fear.

He describes the approach of the Teatime Man, the way it recognized me, and the startled way it reacted when Officer Cold shot at it, and I start to see what the moon was talking about.

Chip finishes up by describing the Teatime Man imprisoned in the cage, the way it looked at me as I yelled at it, the way it reached out and put itself in incredible pain to escape – and there we go.

He's a bad guy, the moon said. *He's a criminal.* I let Chip finish, even though Miss Mighty loses patience the second I start smiling.

"What?" she says. "What?"

"I know how to beat him," I squeak.

Miss Mighty's eyes go almost as wide as Chip's. "You got that from that?"

"I think my reporting was top-notch, but honestly I'm pretty shocked too," Chip says, adjusting his glasses.

"You gave me clues," I say. I'm about to start laughing. Maybe crying. Maybe both. "And Miss Mighty helped me realize how I'm supposed to use them."

"So how do we stop him, then?" Miss Mighty asks.

I look at her, and my heart breaks. I don't want to tell her this part. But I know it'll just be worse if I play games. "We don't," I say, with a shake of my head. "This fight's for me and Officer Cold."

Officer Cold chokes on his root beer. I wait for him to stop coughing before I continue. Miss Mighty's teeth grind halfway to stubs in the meantime.

"You want to prevent what happened to your partner from happening to anyone else?" I ask.

Cold's eyes flicker with that shattered rage he aimed at me back in the jail. "It's what I do."

"It's what I do, too. But it needs to just be us. If Miss Mighty's there, she could die, and if we fail, we need someone with her kind of power protecting the rest of the Stillreal. It needs to be just me, and Cold, and…" My stomach tries to run away.

I don't want to say this. I don't want to do this. I want the dryer. I want Sandra. I want Spiderhand…

"We need to talk to Freedom Frieda," I say. "And we need to talk to her friend Wrrbrr."

Getting back to the apartment in Santa Erzulie is a cinch; it's kind of hard to forget walls halfway made out of crayon, and once you have that all you need is a wall. I take us back to our – to my – apartment, and I think from there straight into Wrrbrr's secret home, Miss Mighty, Officer Cold, and Chip Dixon all trailing along with me.

I know bringing these three is going to make Frieda more annoyed, but I also know that I am not leaving a single Friend alone right now. Still, I wish I had a way to call ahead.

There's no one in the living room when we arrive. All three of the Friends with me are uncertain about their surroundings, but the Abject Horror award goes to Officer Cold, who looks revolted when he sees the crayoned-in parts of the scenery. Enjoy those deductive skills, Officer. Kind of sting sometimes, don't they?

"Where are we?" Chip whispers.

"It's better for everyone if I don't tell you exactly where," I mutter back. "This is supposed to be a safe place."

Detective stuff picks up movement from the depths of the apartment, someone shuffling around in one of the bedrooms. It's slow, careful, trying to be stealthy. As tempting as it is to do some kind of dramatic flourish, today of all days is the day to be straightforward.

"Wrrbrr?" I call. "Frieda? It's me, Tippy. I have a couple Friends with me."

The gasps that sound out from the back room make me flinch. Could that have gone smoother? The sound of Frieda's talons stomping on the floor says yes.

"Tippy?" she growls as she stalks around the corner, her eyes fireworks-red. She sees me, and drops the crayon-drawn golf club she was brandishing in one wing. "Tippy, what the heck are you—"

"Sorry," I say. "I'm so sorry. If there was any other way—"

"Any other way to what?" she demands. "What the heck do you think you're doin' here? What the heck are *they* doin' here?"

Without a good comeback, I go for disarmament. "Thanks for not swearing."

Frieda's eyes flash white, but that half-second is all the respite I'm getting. "He's huntin' you," she snarls, "and you thought it was a good idea to come here?"

"It's the only idea that's going to work."

"That's goin' to—" Her irises turn the color of fresh-drawn blood. "What are you up to, Detective?"

I inhale. Might as well ask at this point. "I need to talk to Wrrbrr."

Frieda's eyebrows arch. "Why?"

"Because I have a plan."

"And your last plan went so well?!" she shoots back.

Ow. "I deserved that."

"Not so sure," Mighty growls.

"Mighty–" I start to say.

"No," Chip says. He's balled his hands into uppercut-ready fists. "No, Miss Mighty's right."

Frieda recoils like she's just smelled something terrible. "Excuse me?"

"Speaking as the journalist in the room," Chip says, making up for confidence with volume, "Tippy did everything he could. The enemy had an advantage no one could have planned for."

Frieda's eyes narrow, crimson light pouring out between the lids. "If his tactics were so sound, why are we still hidin' in this apartment?"

"Because we're dealing with an enemy outside of anything any of us understand," Chip says.

Frieda scoffs. "That's an understatement."

"Aren't you supposed to be a great unifier?" Miss Mighty asks.

Frieda's eyes flash white again, and come back even deeper red than before.

"Mighty–" I say.

"No," Frieda slashes a wing at me. "Miss Mighty, I have sacrificed for the Stillreal. I have dedicated my existence to makin' it a safe place for Friends of all stars and stripes. You, of all people," – she jabs a feathered finger Mighty's way – "do not get to make claims about a lack of commitment to unity."

Miss Mighty's voice sounds out from the bottom of a furious pit. "What?"

"Your kind of solutions are how we wound up in this mess."

Miss Mighty's glove squeaks. "Say what you mean, Frieda."

"I mean–"

A car zooms by on the street below, and Frieda jumps backwards, gawping in the direction of the window. The rest of us hunker down, ready for the fight she seems to think is coming. When all we get is an engine growl fading into the distance, Frieda looks more embarrassed than anyone.

"He could be comin' any time," she says. Her eyes are blue now, pupils bouncing as she examines the patchy crayon shadows.

"That fear you're feeling?" I say. "That's why I need Wrrbrr's help."

That brings her out of the fugue. "No," she says. "Out of the question."

"And why is it your call?" Miss Mighty demands.

On the list of things that were not going to make this easier…

"Because I'm her protector," Frieda says, matter-of-fact, but with red eyes backing it up. "I'm *the* protector. So I'm goin' to do that. It's the only thing I can do."

Officer Cold glowers at her. "And what are you going to do when there are no safe places left?"

"I'll die!" Frieda squawks.

As ways to kill a conversation go, that's certainly efficient. Miss Mighty is too angry to speak again, Cold and Chip are too shocked, and I'm too busy trying not to drown in sympathy.

"I'll protect her…" Frieda says, hunching in on herself, withdrawing back into the hall. "And then I can die knowin' I did what I could."

All my stitches ache, and I'm cold, and instead of big speeches, all I think when I look at Frieda is how much her eyes look like headlights…

"She was the first Friend he tried to kill," I insist from under the weight of myself. "He'll be attracted to that. He'll… if we can keep his attention on her, we can stop him…"

Frieda's eyes flicker between fear and anger, a house-fire raging in her sharp-beaked head. "Get out," she snarls, advancing on me. "Get out!"

"Frieda," I stammer. "I'm sorry, I didn't–"

"Get out!" she shrieks. "Get out, get out, get ou–"

"Miss Frieda?"

That tiny, lispy, uncertain voice drops into the conversation like a depth charge. Frieda and I exchange horrified looks.

Wrrbrr has come out from her room, her blobby body rolled up into a perfect round ball. She's looking around at the visitors to her home, not scared, but sort of curious, like she's trying to tell which of us is full of snakes.

"Hello?" she says.

"Go back to your–" Frieda starts.

"Hi, Wrrbrr," I say. Oh, no you don't, birdie. "I need your help."

"My… help?" Wrrbrr sounds both surprised and hopeful. Was she actually engineered for heartbreak?

Frieda steps back, standing next to her little buddy. "He wants your help dealin' with the Man in the Coat."

Wrrbrr looks at Frieda with her eyes terror-wide. "Dealing with? How? What does that mean, please?"

I'm not playing anymore. I'm not hesitating. "I have a plan to stop him. Me and Officer Cold here."

Cold salutes. "Afternoon, ma'am," he says, as formal as ever.

"A plan?" Wrrbrr asks.

"Yes," I say. "But for it to work, I need you to…" I breathe deep. "I need you to help bring him to us."

She slides backwards like I just jumped out of the shadows. "What?"

I don't sugar-coat it. I'm not dying a liar. "The Man in the Coat always tracks down the Friends that escaped from him. You were the first one to do that, and we're betting you're the one he's angriest about losing."

"Me?" If you'd ask me before today if scared and flattered could appear in the same sentence…

"Yeah. We know how to bring him to us, but we think if he sees you, he'll be too focused on you to notice us doing anything weird."

Wrrbrr flattens against the ground. Her face rises up just the tiniest bit as she asks, "But why do you want him to come to you?"

That look on her face, that quivering around her mouth… can I ask for this? Maybe waiting for death is better, or at least easier–

A frigid hand rests on my back. Officer Cold steps up next to me, and relieves my burden.

"Our plan requires you not to know our plan. We think the Teatime Man might be able to tell when he's being faked out. So when you see him, as horrible as it might sound, you have to be scared for real."

Wrrbr's face sinks back to the floor. All that's left is those huge, unblinking black-dot eyes.

"If you don't want to help," I say, "we will not make you help."

"And we will do everything in our power to protect you," Cold says. "That doesn't mean we'll succeed, though."

That was unnecessary, but then, that's Officer Cold. Wrrbrr looks at him, at me, at Miss Mighty.

"You could get very badly hurt," Freedom Frieda says. "You could die." Her eyes are electric blue.

Wrrbrr's mouth twists in on itself, and her eyes screw shut. She's shaking like a little kid staring at their closet door.

"This is ridiculous," Frieda says, swiping a wing through the air so fast it sheds feathers. "All you're doin' is scarin' her."

"Let her say that," Miss Mighty says.

"I'm protectin' her," Frieda snaps back. "You don't know how to deal with newcomers to the Stillreal. It's my job to know. Let me do my job, and we'll all be happier."

"We'll all be dead!" Miss Mighty responds.

"We can't change that now!" Frieda caws.

"And yet everyone else in the room is saying we can?" Miss Mighty crosses her arms, daring Frieda to respond.

"I've been around longer than any of you," Frieda says. "I've seen how things work here. This is worse than anything. This is the end."

"Because no one in my stories ever claimed all hope was lost," Miss Mighty responds dryly.

"We're not in your stories anymore!"

Wrrbrr's eyes are filling with tears. I'm starting to hear the rain.

"This plan is ridiculous," Frieda insists again, more feathers dropping from her flailing wings. "This is just goin' to get more of us hurt."

"And your amazing plan gets us hurt a little bit slower and is therefore better?" Mighty stomps her foot, shooting a crack through the floorboard beneath it.

Wrrbrr's mouth is a vibrating line of stress.

"My plan will at least—"

"Frieda."

Everyone stops talking and looks at me. I must have been the one who spoke, then.

"You keep talking about how we should let you protect Wrrbrr," I say. "I take that to mean you think we should let you do what you're good at?"

Frieda flails again, one eye red, one eye blue. "Exactly!"

I nod. "Okay. Well… stopping bad guys is what we're good at."

Miss Mighty gasps almost as loud as Frieda.

Frieda's beak quivers. "But – it killed people who trusted me–"

"I lost someone who trusted me, too," Cold says, voice quaking. "So did Detective Tippy, actually.

"We're all incomplete," Cold continues. "That's why we live here. But Tippy wants to give us a chance to make that right."

"But what if he…" Frieda gasps for air. "What if it kills–"

"You said it already," replies Cold. "We're all going to die anyway. Why not die trying to do something meaningful?"

Exactly, Officer Cold. Exactly.

Frieda's eyes are fading from blue to white, but still not quite all the way there. "But why his plan?" she asks, gesturing at me. "Why is his plan what you believe in?"

Officer Cold gives me a judging look before he replies. "When my partner was killed, I arrested Tippy. I suspected him of being involved with the – the monster. And when he convinced me that it wasn't him, the first thing he did when he got out of that cell…" There's a crackling from somewhere near Officer Cold's eyes. My detective stuff says it's ice crystals forming. "The first thing he did was hug me. The first thing he did was make sure the person who arrested him was alright.

"If Detective Tippy has a plan, I will guarantee that it's the best plan he could think of. That it's a plan that's meant to help all of us. He wants what's best."

I want to hug this jerk all over again. How did I ignore what people were telling me?

Frieda looks at me. Her eyes are all the way white. I need to be honest with her. She deserves that. I deserve that.

"It might not work," I admit. "I will not absolutely guarantee any plan. But I will guarantee we'll try as hard as we can, to stop the Teatime Man and to keep Wrrbrr safe. That's all I can do." That sense of revelation courses through me again.

Frieda's eyes blink blue, white, blue. She ruffles her feathers as she sighs. "Wrrbrr has to agree to help you. I won't let you take her anywhere without her say-so."

"Of course," I say.

"I wouldn't do it otherwise," says Officer Cold.

Behind us, Miss Mighty chuckles.

"So…" I turn to the Friend in question. "What do you say, Wrrbrr?"

Wrrbrr frowns at Frieda. She looks at me, and the frown deepens. "Is everyone telling the truth?"

"Yes," I say. "Including Frieda. You're safer if you stay here. But the Man in the Coat *is* looking for you."

"I know," Wrrbrr says, sinking again.

"If you come with us, we will put you right in his path. If we mess up, we could all three be killed. But we might stop any more killing from happening. We might actually end this, the way I was hoping we would before…" I'm getting misty again, better wrap up. "So, what do you say? You want to help?"

Wrrbrr looks up at me, tension lines stretching at her half-drawn face. Frieda watches her, lit up pale blue, a wing frozen halfway to reaching for her charge.

"You think this will work?" Wrrbrr asks.

"Yes."

Wrrbrr looks at me, and I see ruins in her eyes. "I am a space knight," she says. "I will not fail again."

Again. That one word makes my heart ache.

"You don't have to…" I say.

"Yes," Wrrbrr responds. "I do." She extends an arm, forms it into a hand ready for a shake. "Let's beat the bad guy." She swallows. "Please?"

"Yes," I say. "Let's end this."

And we shake, and Freedom Frieda sighs. She sounds defeated, but that's only the second most heartbreaking sound I've heard in the last few minutes.

"Well," Miss Mighty says, cutting short any other tearful babbling, "that's my cue."

Wrrbrr blinks. "What?"

Miss Mighty shrugs. "Tippy didn't want my help for this next part. He wanted yours."

"If you thought I meant we were all going, Wrrbrr, I'm sorry I misled you," I say. "If that changes anything–"

"No," Wrrbrr says, shaking back and forth. "No. A space knight doesn't back down."

I like this kid.

"Hey, Mighty," I say, before she actually says her goodbyes.

Miss Mighty watches me, telling me with her eyes to go on.

"Do me a favor, will you?"

She hints at a smirk, like she can't believe I'm asking. We both know she can.

"Dr Atrocity," I say. "Will you check in on her? And K'kota and his amazing friends, too?"

Her expression darkens, but at least there's a smile in there. "It'd be my pleasure to tweak their noses."

I nod. "Thank you. And, um – and Breaker? I don't know where she went after, if you can–"

"Done," she says. She rolls her shoulders, starts to turn away. "Now, before you dorks get any more touchy-feely, I'm just going to–"

"I'm sorry, Miss Mighty," I say.

She stops, and looks me right in the eye. Her face wants to be angry, but it's too busy being sad. "Apologize by getting rid of him."

"I'll do my best."

She nods. "Good. Good." She looks around the room, trying to find a touchstone for her grand exit. "Just tell me we'll fight bad guys again?"

"I'll come and tell you that myself. Tomorrow morning. The Rootbeerium. If I don't come…"

"I'll get on my butt-kicking boots," she says. "And take as many butts down with me as I can."

I smile. I always smile when people are being perfectly themselves.

She turns her head, focuses on a traffic light outside the window, takes a deep breath… and she's gone.

That might be the last conversation I have with her.

No. I'm not thinking like that.

I turn, and look at an expectant Wrrbrr. "Ready to end this?"

"I…" She closes her eyes, panting, a little kid's idea of deep breathing. "Yes. Dame Wrrbrr is ready."

"Alright, dame knight," I say. "Let's go be good guys."

Wrrbrr puts a tendril in my hand without hesitation. On the other side, Officer Cold does the same.

"Bring her back," Frieda says.

I nod to her. It's about all the emoting I can safely do right now.

CHAPTER THIRTY

I think around as rapidly as I can. Wrrbrr is shaken by every new Idea, but also awed, her mind forming connections her person never planned. Officer Cold, on the other hand, is getting agitated, his sneer doing backflips with every new city we go to. When we stop in Chrometown I explain myself in my most apologetic voice. "I need to find an Idea where the moon is full."

Officer Cold nods, understanding but not pleased about it. "A big black building, and the moon."

Of course he gets it. He went there before I did.

I zip us into Avatar City, in the shadow of the Cape and Cowl Club, and look past the buildings to the moon rising high above them. It's full, of course – Avatar City likes its moon full, crescent, or conveniently eclipsed. A shape streaks across it – maybe Captain Candela, maybe Thunderbolt, but very likely Miss Mighty. I really, really hope I don't have to miss her.

I focus on the moon, and I imagine it bigger, and colder, and orange.

Autumn wind brushes along my horn-tips. I turn from the moon to Spindleman's house, looming coal-black on the dark lawn, illuminated only by the nightlight glow from the top-story windows. The chill I'm feeling has nothing to do with the wind.

This is what a detective does, I think, as I lead my little trio into the house. A detective puts together the clues, and traces them back to the beginning of things. The vital clue. The origin of the case. Of course, later on, Sandra figured out that detectives also sometimes get shot at…

Spindleman's house is fully reset, a cavernous living room decorated in early broken tea service. I see the couch the cloned Teatime Man shattered, the shadow-filled hallway where the monster appeared. I hear the floorboards settling in distant rooms, the scary sounds that Spindleman's home demanded. The wood under my feet is cold, the cold as imagined by a little boy terrified to get out of bed. I see every detail. I've always seen every detail. But I don't always stop to appreciate them. This little Idea is scary, and cold, and lonely… but it's perfect at being all of those things.

I act before I have time to reconsider.

"We're here!" I shout.

Wrrbrr jumps. Officer Cold goes rigid. I stay between them, hunkered down for a charge.

The house goes silent, its creaks and crackles fading to the far edge of hearing. Its shadows grow deeper and thicker, suggesting even more horrible shapes inside. The cold wind blows by, rattling the windows, and Wrrbrr presses up against me, a quivering but resolute little ball.

And then, for what I hope is the last time, the heavy tread of big black boots. They're coming from the hallway, and they're getting closer at a very familiar speed.

"Drink," announces that voice as it approaches.

I turn to Officer Cold. "Time to repeat ourselves."

Cold's hand shakes as he pulls out the freeze ray.

The footfalls come closer, grow louder, shaking the house like an angry kid with a snow-globe. The shards of teacup juke and judder, skipping back and forth under the onslaught. And without shift or fanfare, the big, shadowy clone of the Teatime Man steps out of the hallway, already taking practice swings with his bat.

"Here we go," I say.

"Drink!"

Cold has the gun out, so the clone comes for Cold first. The beam catches him right in the face, just like in the forest. My mind's eye watches Spiderhand crumple again, until I realize Cold is shouting at me. The clone has almost clawed the ice off its face, the bat swinging blindly at the air. I charge in, and plant my horns right in its stomach.

The clone isn't as heavy as the real thing. He sprawls out on the floor on contact, much smaller already. Cold gives him another blast of the freeze ray, and he's anchored in place, twitching and struggling to get free. I back up to get distance for another charge, when I hear a twang and a spangly woosh, like wind chimes in a hurricane, and a column of golden dust streaks over my head straight into the killer's belly, detonating him in a blast of black and glittery gold.

Wrrbrr?

There's a cannon hovering in front of her – huge and golden, its muzzle shaped like a star, its shaft decorated with swirling galaxies, drawn in crayon but as detailed as a Renaissance painting. Sparkling dust wafts from the opening. The clone is gone, and Wrrbrr's face is a shivering, struggling red.

"Star Power," she says. The cannon disappears in a ringing of bells.

She warned me.

"Just don't do that when he actually shows up," Cold says.

"No," I say. "If that's what you would do, do that. But once we start fighting him, give us room."

Wrrbrr nods, eyes darting around at light-speed as she watches for anything else that might jump out. Officer Cold stands beside her, both hands on his freeze ray. I cross the room, duck down behind the couch, and I listen, ready to move the second I hear someone coming, ready to put the couch between me and any new set of eyes. We wait, as the house once again begins to creak.

"Where is he?" Wrrbrr asks. She's got a shield shaped like a star now, a sword with a blade made of light, drawn just like the cannon.

"He comes around after his clones get beat up," I call from my hiding place. "It's totally reliable. He's done it every single time."

"You've fought him more than once?"

"I've run from him more than once," I say.

Wrrbrr bites her lip, and returns to her slow study of the room. "Where does he usually appear, please?"

"From somewhere you can't see," says Officer Cold, our emotional blunt instrument.

Wrrbrr gasps. Officer Cold emits a self-conscious huff.

The floorboards settle in a predictable rhythm, starting in the back of the house and moving forward, creaking through the walls on their way into the hallway. I can just imagine Spindleman creeping alongside the creaks, timing it perfectly so its person would know that their approach meant its own. I can also imagine the way they both felt the night that the monster that came into the boy's room wasn't Spindleman.

Wrrbrr shivers, tries to stand up taller. It's not very effective. "I'm scared. I'm not supposed to be scared."

My stitches ache. "Lots of heroes are scared, Wrrbrr. Trust me."

Wrrbrr lets out that worried hum again. "Mmm, really?"

"We're living proof," says Officer Cold.

"Listen to the icicle man," I say.

Wrrbrr hums again. She's still a bundle of tangled nerves, but the tangles are a little bit looser. "That... makes me feel better?"

"Yeah," I say. "It confused me the first time, too."

"I hope you have a chance to get used to it," says Cold.

The footsteps come again, this time from outside. Officer Cold moves slowly, tactically away from Wrrbrr, joining me behind the couch. Wrrbrr lets out a determined version of her little hum, shivering, but defiant. So are we, Wrrbrr. So are we.

"I'm a space knight," she insists. "I'm Wrrbrr!"

The glass in a front window shatters. Wrrbrr screams; Officer Cold shudders. I peek around the corner of the couch again, and lock up.

The Teatime Man is here – the real one, for sure. No other Friend has that much raw hate in its eyes. Actual oblivion is clambering through a window on the other side of this couch, and I'm wounded, and tired, and not in any shape to have an actual fight. If this doesn't go exactly how I need it to, everything falls apart.

The Teatime Man stands up to his full height, his slick black coat smoothing out as he rises. Wrrbrr slithers away from him, her eyes so bright they're casting flashlight beams on the Teatime Man's face. He looks down at her, not even glancing in the direction of the couch, and he raises his bat. Wrrbrr raises her sword in answer, face a rough-draft sketch of determination.

"Drink," the Teatime Man demands.

"No," squeaks Wrrbrr. "No more drink. Not ever. This – mmm – this ends tonight, monster!"

The Teatime Man lets out his swamp-mud chuckle and strides toward Wrrbrr, every footstep rolling thunder. Wrrbrr cedes ground, baiting him closer to the wall, closer – and then I step out from behind the couch, Officer Cold following behind. My little cloth heart pounds like a set of bongo drums as Officer Cold yells, "Freeze!"

And he does. Thank Sandra, he does. The Teatime Man literally stops where he is, the bat raised over his head.

My idea might be working.

"Teatime Man," Officer Cold says. "You're under–"

The Teatime Man throws his bat at Cold. It hits with a horrifying crunch, and Cold stumbles backward, his face crumpled and wrinkled, but not bleeding.

My idea might be working, but I knew it wouldn't be easy.

"You're under–" Officer Cold begins again, and barely dodges as the Teatime Man lunges for him, avoiding the attack but leaving the Teatime Man free to recover his bat.

"Fine," the Teatime Man proclaims. He pivots to confront Cold, and over the ice-man's shoulder, I see Wrrbrr's sword and shield transform back into a cannon.

"Don't!" I shout.

Wrrbrr lets her shot off. It doesn't hurt the Teatime Man, but it does make him stumble – and then turn back toward Wrrbrr.

"I am a space knight!" shrieks Wrrbrr, in the stratospheric register of the truly terrified. "I am a hero of the Space Kingdom, and I will bring you to justice!"

Of the things I thought I'd feel right now, awe was not on my list.

The Teatime Man shifts his feet, hunkers down for a sprint. Wrrbrr flinches, but fires again, backing away from him as he swats the dust aside. The Teatime Man barrels at her with that awful speed, but Officer

Cold shouts "Freeze!" again and the Teatime Man comes up short, his raised foot not even touching down on the floor.

"You're—" Officer Cold says.

The Teatime Man wheels on him, eyes searing pools of acid, and Officer Cold stumbles over his words.

"You're – you're—"

"Fine," the Man responds.

Darn it. I was trying to avoid this. But sometimes, when violence is already happening, violence back is unavoidable.

I charge right into the Teatime Man's path. He doesn't even break his stride; he clubs me hard enough to send me sailing back over the couch. The world turns into stars and lightning as I impact against the coffee table.

My vision is uncoupled. My legs are each interpreting my instructions differently. Everything sounds like I've got a pillow strapped to my head. Another direct hit like that, and I'm joining Spindleman. Or Spidey...

"Coward!" shouts Wrrbrr.

I hear the angry chorus of another cannon shot. I hear the Teatime Man's footsteps grind back toward Wrrbrr. I hear Officer Cold stammering. Okay. Time to improvise.

I struggle to my feet, and I shout, "We have all the evidence we need, Teatime Man! It's all over!"

The footsteps stop, and there's a whoosh of air and a horrible hiss as the Teatime Man vaults over the couch. He shatters the coffee table when he lands on it, gouges up a floorboard with a menacing swat of his bat. I think he's taller than he was a second ago. I duck a swing that once again vaporizes the couch, another that busts a me-sized hole into the wall. The Teatime Man readies an overhead chop, but before he can swing, he's knocked aside by another blast of golden dust from Wrrbrr's cannon.

"You will be brought to justice, Teatime Man!" she shouts. No humming, no 'please.' She's in her element. Let's hope we all are.

The Teatime Man stands so fast it's like he never even fell, and readies his bat with just as much speed. "Fine," he says, and steps through the ruin of the couch to get at her. I let him get a few steps toward her before I lob another pitch.

"The jig is up, Teatime Man!" I shout.

He looks at me, his eyes going berserk. I'm inches from the wall on my right, blinded by falling stuffing on my left, and I'm sure the original is fast enough to make a game of keep-away pointless. The Teatime Man's green eyes blaze as he cocks the bat for a homerun swing. But behind him, I finally hear the click of Officer Cold's freeze ray coming online.

"You're under arrest!"

The Teatime Man goes stiff. He doesn't look triumphant anymore.

When that car accident took Daddy from Sandra, I failed for the first time ever. I failed because something broke the rules I knew the world operated on.

The Teatime Man broke the rules, too. So I worked the case the best I could in all my inchoate panic, and the minute I saw a rule he had to live by, I jumped all over it. Here's the solution. Overwhelming force of darkness, meet the overwhelming force of teamwork.

But this is the Stillreal. There are no simple endings. And I was so prepared to believe that he didn't make sense – so ready for him to be another car accident – that I didn't stop to think about what else the clue might mean.

The cell in the Memory Reefs didn't stop that Teatime Man clone because cages stop the Teatime Man. It stopped the clone because of something much more fundamental than that.

I back away from the Teatime Man, out of range of the bat. "You can't help it, can you?" I say.

He watches me, frustration boiling over in his eyes. I know that look very well. It's Freedom Frieda when she insisted on protecting Wrrbrr. It's Officer Cold when he arrested me for Officer Hot's murder. It's me when I made every mistake I've made on this case. It's the look of a Friend, a being who is Real because someone needed them to be, running up against the limits of what they are, even though they know it's not what they want.

He's just another monster of a very old kind, the moon said. That was the key.

"The evidence was right in front of me the whole time," I say. The Teatime Man twitches, and I have to admit, I like it. "You're the Friend of a serial killer. An abuser. A monster. Maybe that's part of why he needed you. One person who actually saw eye to eye with him."

The Teatime Man knocks on the floor with the bat. It doesn't sound as menacing as it used to.

"You went after Wrrbrr first. You butchered everyone in the Space Kingdom. Or, almost everyone. One got away, and that never really sat right with you. But you couldn't focus on that. Your person had needs."

While I'm revealing all the evidence, I barely even notice how much pain I'm in. (It's a lot.) Because a detective catches the bad guy in a web of deductions, and reveals their conclusion to the murderer, face to face. "So you kept claiming victims. Victims like the whales in the Memory Reefs. Victims like the Friends in this house when your person abducted Matthew. But that was when the real problem started, wasn't it?

"Spindleman escaped you. Just like Wrrbrr. Just like one of the kids escaped your person. You could maybe stomach missing one, especially if they just disappeared like Wrrbrr seemed to. But another one? One that dared to go live where other Friends lived? That might mean people would see your failure. You had to find them, and thanks to your creator poisoning an entire city's dreams, you had the power to find them. So out you went into the rest of the Stillreal."

The Teatime Man is shaking, the epicenter of his own personalized earthquake.

"You had to get the ones you missed, no matter what. Not even witnesses mattered. Of course, witnesses meant the police came looking for you, but in your mind, that was simple: you'd take them down, too. Or… one of them, anyway. But that wasn't the plan, right?"

Officer Cold grunts behind me. He sounds almost pleased, but I know better.

"Unfortunately, you had rules you had to play by," I grin. "The rules of killers."

The earthquake inside the Teatime Man climbs up the Richter scale.

"Oh, yeah. Your person knew what he was trying to be, what he really was, so you knew the whole time exactly what you were too, and you knew that other Friends were bound to figure it out."

The Teatime Man snarls like a dog with a strange hand near it.

"It was the cell in the Reefs that really tipped me off, actually. Your double should have been able to walk out through those rotted old bars. But he couldn't. And you hesitated when you saw me the first time because you knew what I was. The same way you hesitated when you saw Officer Hot, right? You know detectives and cops when you see them."

The Teatime Man goes very, very still.

"So when I showed up, you did your best to either stay away from me, or to kill me so I couldn't do the one thing that could stop you."

I pause, because this is where I'm supposed to pause. The Teatime Man doesn't look angry anymore. He doesn't look *anything* anymore. His hands are at his sides. The bat is gone. His face is two glowing eyes and a flat, expressionless mouth.

"You were what your maker couldn't be – the relentless killer. The unstoppable monster." I walk closer, and I look right up into that shadowy face. "But if a detective – a real detective – managed to put together the clues, and figure out what you were and why you did it… and if a cop managed to put you under arrest… then the hunt was over.

"That was why you left evidence everywhere you went, even though you hated it. That was why you tried to silence the witnesses, even though you knew it would mean our paths crossed again. That was why you couldn't leave the cell until somebody let you out." My guilt doesn't quite catch up to me, but I know it's coming later. "And that's why you can't move now that Officer Cold has you under arrest.

"Because killers get caught.

"And when killers get caught, they stop.

"It's over, Teatime Man. It's time to face your punishment."

The Teatime Man's features shift; he's sad. He shrinks to half his height when Officer Cold puts on the cuffs.

"You have the right to remain silent," Officer Cold says, sniffing away frozen tears. "Anything you say can and will be repeated from memory in the Playtime Town Courthouse…"

The Teatime Man hangs his head and takes it all in, not even trying to fight.

"Hey, Cold?" I ask, when the litany has been recited.

Cold breaks off from looking for a way back to Playtime Town to look at me.

"When you're done, bring Frieda back her master key, yeah?"

Cold furrows his brow, lights up in understanding, and nods. "Thank you for reminding me, Detective." For once, the title doesn't sound like an insult.

"That's what I do, Officer," I reply. That statement carries more weight for me than I'd expect.

I let them think away without me, leaving me and Wrrbrr to look around at the shadows.

"You did good," I say to the little blob. "You did amazing."

Wrrbrr's face reddens on either side of her mouth. "I did what a space knight would do."

"We couldn't have done it without you," I say. "I mean it."

She smiles. "Is it over?"

By the light in her voice, she knows the answer. But she still needs to hear it. I gesture to the floor, and I say, "Just watch."

It takes a few minutes, long enough for Wrrbrr to start fidgeting, but eventually, the Idea returns to normal, and the teacups recede in favor of a few more patches of bare hardwood floor.

"What the Teatime Man did?" I say. "That takes time to heal. And for some of us it might never go away all the way." I think of Spiderhand in his hospital bed, and I swallow a new raft of tears.

Wrrbrr nods. "But he won't be able to hurt anyone else."

I smile, and for the first time in days it's not for anyone but myself.

"Do I go back to the forest now?" Wrrbrr asks.

"If you want to."

She frowns. "Can I go back to the big rooms in the big city?"

"Depends on if you can pay the big rents."

"What?"

"Never mind." I know I don't have to snark, but it's so easy. "You can travel the Stillreal all you want now," I say. "Live in any Idea you want."

Wrrbrr looks around the house, tall and dark and scary. "I think I want to go back to the big rooms."

"They're called an apartment," I say.

"A-part-ment," Wrrbrr says, sounding out the word.

Is it dusty in here? "Do you need me to take you back?" I ask, voice cracking.

"Yes please," Wrrbrr says, and takes my paw in her tendril.

"Okay," I say. "We're going to make a couple stops on the way. I figure it might be good to teach you the basics of thinking around."

She squeezes my paw. "Thank you."

I take one last look at the house where Spindleman lived. I'm not sure if this will stick around in the Stillreal without its core Friend or not. After all, it's not like Friends have died permanently before, so I don't really have case files to work off...

"Goodbye," I say, and think us to Avatar City.

Goodbye. That's what I need to do next.

CHAPTER THIRTY-ONE

One moon to another. That moon to yet more. And then we're in Santa Erzulie, at the midnight hour on a humid summer night that you just know is full of zombies and critters. Freedom Frieda shoots up out of the cheap armchair she's collapsed into, looking at Wrrbrr with an offensive amount of shock.

"She's... you..." Her words keep sticking, eyes flickering with a whole sea of emotions.

"Safe," I say.

Wrrbrr bounds over to Frieda, and swings long, stretchy arms around the bird's mid-section. The hug crushes Frieda about half as hard as it crushes my soul.

"Safe," Frieda repeats, looking at me over the shaking blob.

"We're safe," I say. "We're all safe. Officer Cold should be bringing your key back soon, too."

"Is he..."

"No," I say. "He's going to jail."

"Where bad men go," Wrrbrr announces from below.

Frieda strokes Wrrbrr with a quivering wing, looks at me, and nods. "Thank you," she says.

The pure, calm white of her irises is all the thanks I need. Except...

"We all need a few days," I say. "A few weeks, maybe. But... I was thinking..." I scratch at a stitch with a back paw. "I was thinking of

283

having a, a dinner. Just something small, a few of the people who were stuck in this with me. A few. Um. Friends."

Frieda stops mid-back pat, and between you and me, this is scarier than every second I spent in Spindleman's house.

"Friends?" she asks. "Or Friends?"

"That first one."

Frieda smiles. "May I bring Wrrbrr?"

The blob's eyes peek out from the hug.

"Wrrbrr is my friend, too, if she'll have me," I say. "I'll send the invite to this apartment."

"Send mine to the motel," Frieda says.

I sigh to myself. "Okay," I say. "Okay."

I think out before this gets any harder.

Detectives are cynics. Sandra knew that, and she made me as cynical as she knew how. It's not enough to keep me from smiling as I walk down the street from the History Building to the police station and see nothing but wan smiles and relieved faces. I think it's Boss Raccoon and the Worst Cat lurking in the alley, divvying up coins on a trashcan lid, that really convinces me we're getting back to normal. But I won't pretend I don't see their eyes dart toward me when I walk past, or the fear in their eyes when they see me turn toward the police station. Of course it isn't that easy. Nothing's that easy. That's kind of what I had to figure out.

I'm in the Stillreal because I exist to make sense of things, and it turns out not everything will always make sense. There isn't always a villain, a conspiracy, a motive that will put a deserving jerk behind bars. Sometimes, the road is just wet, and Daddy is just struggling with the car, and bad things happen to good people. Sandra couldn't cope with that, and I was supposed to help her cope. So away I went.

When I arrived, I took detective work because it was what I knew how to do. I solve a mystery, and for a little while, I can keep the feeling at bay. The feeling that I'm lost. That I'm bad at life. That I'm a failure. But 'at bay' isn't the same thing as 'gone.' When the clues didn't add up, when a witness didn't cooperate, or when a media-fueled nightmare monster came rampaging through my backyard, the feeling came back, and no amount of time in the dryer would drag me out of it. Just more solving. Just the end of the case. And then, when that was over…

Miss Mighty and Officer Cold said that mistakes were okay – or at least, that we have to own up to them and move forward from them. That in itself was a bucket of cold water on my soul. But it was the next thing they said that got me: that being a detective is just the way I help people.

When Sandra and I were hunting the Co-Spirity, and Daddy came home in the middle of it, we abandoned the case. Nowadays, that would be a stick blender straight to my calm, but back then, I was fine with it. Because I knew in my heart of plush hearts that, and I quote myself, mysteries were all well and good, but Sandra's happiness came first.

Happiness comes first.

I thought I was treading water doing my detective work, stroking my ego and helping people while I did it. I thought I hid under being smarter so they didn't see my stitches coming loose. I thought I was nothing pretending to be something. Then Miss Mighty said that. That I don't have to be perfect. And I gave myself permission to try, and to focus on helping people…

I could go on, but getting to the police station disrupts my thought process. Time to do the next difficult thing.

The jail is much as I left it, stony and ominous and possibly impregnable. The Snitching Snipe is in his usual spot, watching from the shadows and failing to blink. Officer Cold is waiting for me in front of the furthest-back cell. Miss Mighty is next to him, leaning against the bars, watching nothing in particular.

"Hi," I say to her.

She looks at me, and smiles.

"Dr Atrocity tell you?" I ask.

She nods. "She was monitoring the whole thing, I guess." She gives me a crooked smile. "You did good."

"Coming from you, that means a lot. And… um," I look at Cold. "How's the…"

Cold just turns and points through the bars. I give my body a chance to remember what 'normal' feels like before I follow the gesture and look in on the Teatime Man.

If it weren't for the thick glasses, I might not believe it's him. He's taken off his coat, doffed his hat and boots, and it's left him even smaller than you'd expect, Officer Hot's height and Officer Cold's weight. He's wearing a white t-shirt and beige pants that are the plainest clothes I've ever seen, both blended into a uniform dirty-sock gray. His skin is a pasty white I only see on Friends who live underground, with teeth almost as yellow as Farmer Nick's, and there's just enough dishwater-colored hair left on his head to tell you most of it's fallen out. The only thing that isn't less menacing are his eyes – forest green, furious, eyes that want to hurt you the way they've been hurt and know they can never manage it. I don't smile at the sight. I can't smile at someone in so much pain.

"Did he resist at all?" I ask Cold.

The skinny ice-man shakes his skinny ice-head. "Kept his head down the whole way here. Didn't so much as give me a nasty look."

"Because that's what killers do when they're caught," I say.

I turn back to the Teatime Man. He's staring at the ceiling of his cell, his fragile little fingers rubbing together like they need something to fidget with.

"Hi," I say.

The Teatime Man retreats like he's been slapped, huddles against the back wall.

I'm a helper. But that doesn't mean I just help good guys. I mean, if that were true, I'd never have taken Farmer Nick's job. I'd never have found Spindleman…

"There's another thing killers do sometimes," I say, projecting for his benefit.

He glares at me, daring me to keep speaking.

"Sometimes, killers reform."

Miss Mighty tenses. Officer Cold sniffs. The Teatime Man's eyes glow with their old, murderous heat, and he tears his attention away from me. But for just a second, I think he might smile. For today, that'll have to be enough.

"The cell going to hold him?" I ask Cold.

Cold's eye twitches. "Is that a jab?"

"More like paranoia."

He sniffs. "It'll hold."

"Good." I take a deep breath. That means it's time to do the really hard thing. "Do you want to come with me, then?"

"Come with you where?" Cold drawls.

Oh. Mouth got out ahead of my brain, I guess. "The Rootbeerium. I'm going to… I think folks need closure. And I'm not going to get more ready to people."

Cold's jaw works as he parses out what I'm saying. His eyes widen just slightly.

"I should stay here," he says, a little too fast. "I don't – we can't risk him escaping. Just in case the, the bars don't…"

I smile, and I nod. "Whatever makes you happy, Cold." I turn to Miss Mighty. "How about you?"

Mighty detaches from the bars with the ghost of a smile. "Celebrating the defeat of a villain? Seems like my kind of party."

That warms most of me. "I'll be back later," I say to Cold. "Just… one thing at a time."

"Sure," Cold says. He's not looking at me.

I turn back toward the stairs, take a deep breath, and get ready to do the harder thing.

The Rootbeerium is starting to edge back toward normal when Miss Mighty and I enter. It's not exactly packed to the rafters; the population is small enough they're just barely crowding the bar, with the exception of one lone fact-finder I catch skulking in a corner. I see Mr Float, of course, serving a couple Brass Legionnaires. I see Golem Jones sitting next to the Kingdom of Living Marbles. I see Focred, and the Sadness Penguins, and Prince Hekau and Rocky and Lloyd. They're all talking more than they're drinking, running over with concerns and questions. Golem Jones is doing his best to palliate, but results appear to be mixed. The throng shifts a little, and I'm relieved to see Chip in their midst.

"Tippy," he says, and grinds the conversation to a halt.

Everyone turns and looks at us, the detective and the superhero, standing frozen in the doorway. Everyone's doing their own version of holding their breath. Only Chip and Golem Jones remain placid.

"The rumors true?" Jones asks. By the relief in the crowd, he's giving voice to everyone's question.

A part of me wants to drag this moment out. That part of me is not the part I want to be. "The Teatime Man has been captured," I say. "He won't hurt anyone anymore."

The Brass Legionnaires let out a throaty cheer, toasting each other with their sodas. Rocky buries his pallid face in his pallid hands, sobbing with relief. Everyone else just sort of deflates, like the nerves were the only thing keeping their posture correct. Golem Jones smiles, and nods, approving like the uncle I never had. That feels warm and fuzzy.

"There room at the bar for us?" I ask.

"Always," says Jones, waving people to make a hole for us to stand that conveniently puts us right next to Chip.

"Nice job, Tipster," Chip says. "Nice job."

I smile at him. Then I don't.

"What'll it be, Tippy?" sing-songs Mr Float, once again cleaning out his glass. "On the house."

I smile again, and again, I don't. "Can you line up six shot glasses of root beer? And the same for anyone else who wants it."

Mr Float raises a spectral eyebrow. "Wants what?"

"To help me toast the fallen."

Miss Mighty looks at me in surprise, but a smirk manages to edge it out. "Expositioning." She looks to Mr Float. "Six for me, too."

"And me," says Chip.

"And me," says Golem Jones.

"And me."

"And me."

"And me."

Everyone echoes the call. Mr Float gets briefly overwhelmed by the flurry of identical orders, but after a quick headcount he starts lining them up like an assembly line, the soda gun working overtime in his translucent hand. While he does that, I take a deep breath, try not to shake, and turn to Chip.

"Chip?" I say.

"Hm?"

"Tell me the news."

I hear Chip's smile in the way he inhales. "Citizens of Portland today are as exultant as they are mystified, for the nightmare of the Teatime Man is finally over – by his own hand. The Teatime Man, one Frederick Harbor of Sandpoint, Idaho, has turned himself over to the authorities, saying that he knows it's time for him to be punished for, quote 'what a bad father he's been…'"

There's more, stuff about how long Fred Harbor's reign of terror was, how many children he kidnapped, how many of those are going to the hospital. I think Chip mentions a trial date. I log it all, setting it aside to comb through later for evidence of how the heck this all came to pass. For today, I let myself focus on the part where it's over.

Eventually, Chip finishes reciting the article, sounding the most pleased I've heard him since the door to Smile House broke. Mr Float starts doling out the shots of root beer, handing them off on trays to make it easier on everyone. I notice he's poured six more than he needs, then I realize he's counting himself. I take one of the shot glasses in my paw, the smell of vanilla and sassafras tickling my sinuses, and I let myself take a couple seconds to be sure I'm ready for the feels train before it leaves the station.

"To the fact-finders who fell facing the Teatime Man," I say, holding the shot glass high.

That jangles a few nerves. I guess they didn't think villains would figure into the toasts. Welcome to my world.

"To the fact-finders," says Golem Jones, his hand soaring overhead compared to the rest of us.

"To the fact-finders," agrees Chip.

The others repeat it, though not without some shades of reluctance.

I slam the shot back, and raise the next one. "To the soldiers of the Mousehole Wars." I hate lumping them together like this. If this ever happens again, I'm learning all their names. I'm making sure the fact-finders don't have them, too.

"To the soldiers," everyone says, with a little less confusion.

The third shot is to Victor Crane. Miss Mighty belts out his name, and the others speak it with reverence, too. The fourth is to Plug, repair-octopus of the Memory Reefs, and by then people aren't reluctant anymore, though Mighty and Jones are still the loudest. The fifth is to Cable. The sixth… the sixth I have to hesitate on. Mighty next to me has figured it out, judging by the way she lets her hand hover near my paw on the bar. But I swallow the latest fusillade of nerves, and I lift the shot-glass.

"To Spindleman," I say, my eyes misting up.

Everyone hesitates. Focred and the Sadness Penguins trade anguished looks among themselves.

"To Spindleman," agrees Golem Jones, with sadness in his voice.

"To Spindleman," echoes the group.

To Spindleman. To a life far too short. To a Friend I'm certain was wonderful. I won't pretend its death was worth it. I won't pretend the Teatime Man's arrest makes it all right. But I will say that at least we can honor it with some amount of justice.

The crowd falls silent, looking at each other, hanging on their closer friends among the group. There's still sadness hanging over us, but there's a lot less tension; I even see relief on a few faces. We needed that. I needed that.

"Thank you, Tippy," says Golem Jones, a warm, rocky presence next to me.

"Yeah," says Miss Mighty, as she gestures for another drink. "Thanks."

"Of course," I say. "I mean, what am I for if not helping people?"

Miss Mighty tilts her head back and laughs, and the brightness goes up on my world. Usually, Miss Mighty only laughs about how foolish a villain is being. This laugh is her happy laugh. It's loud, and it's high, and it's just a little bit musical. I like it.

"Hey," I say, riding the wave. "Do you… do you want to come to a party later? In a couple days? Give us all time to recover and then–"

"Of course," Miss Mighty says. "Any party you invite me to I'll be at. 'Less Dr Atrocity is stealing the moon again or something," she finishes with a smile.

"Great," I say. "Great." Usually I'm okay at small talk, but her mentioning Dr Atrocity has thrown me for a loop. I'm more fragile than I was admitting, and that's saying something. "Do you mind if…" I swallow. "Is it okay if I go?"

Miss Mighty furrows her brow. "You askin' if you can be excused?"

Yeah, okay, I'll smile. "I guess I am."

"I mean, of course," Mighty says with a shrug. "But, you sure you want to be alone?"

"Yes."

Mighty shrugs again. "Okay." She gives me a smile that I know is genuine, if worried. "See you around, then, Tippy."

"I'll make a point of it."

"You'd better."

I wave goodbye, turn around, and stop, feeling nailed to the spot. The fact-finder is looking directly at me – not near, not past, at and in and deeply. I'm not sure if it's trying to intimidate me, or if that's just the way it looks at people. I maintain eye contact, feet planted, and say, "Thank you."

The fact-finder flickers into their much less welcoming form, a throbbing mass of what looks like roadkill and burnt crayons. They shift back to their businessman form, and they mouth without sound the words, "You owe us." And then they're gone.

I shudder, for sure, but I don't let it bother me too much. Owing Big Business a favor isn't as scary as what I have to do next.

I head for the door, stopping and talking to just a few Friends – Mr Float, Chip, Golem Jones, – to make sure they'll come to my party.

The smiles they give me keep me warm all the way up until the door closes, and I'm alone outside. I'm not sure if Playtime Town has actually gotten darker since I was inside, or if it's just my mood. Either way, I know what I have to do.

I start walking, and head down the street to Saint Sunbeam's.

I stay for an hour. Spiderhand doesn't wake up.

CHAPTER THIRTY-TWO

I walk up the Welcoming Arms stairs, walk into my little apartment. I swim through the treasure-trove of letters I've been neglecting, and I let my mask of confidence drop as I look around and see what's changed.

Spiderhand's room is still exactly the way he left it, organized chaos with a tea-party theme. The spices he loved to rub between his fingers are still in the kitchen cabinets. The big round table is still there, right next to the tea service he served us from at that last big meeting. And in the corner, big and black and well-cared-for, is the piano. The kettle he filled up before we went out to the Space Kingdom is even still there, still full of cool, clean water.

Take care of our home, that's what he told me. Playtime Town is our home. And the Teatime Man is now a part of our home. He'd want me to take care of that, too. He'd want me to believe the best of others. I will. Eventually.

I pick up some of the mound of letters, head back to my room, sit down at my desk. I take a long, nose-tickling pull from my flask of root beer, and I start sifting through the letters.

One of the Sadness Penguins is missing – they never came back after we scattered in the Space Kingdom. Golem Jones says a Friend visited him recently, saying their home Idea's volcano just erupted for the first time. And a smeared note from Wrrbrr says the Santa Erzulie Cinema is being haunted by something she calls a 'popcorn ghost.' There's a lot for me to do.

Good.

There's a knock at my door. I twitch, and when the knock comes again, I realize the twitch is because I'm expecting them to kick the door down. I smile, relieved, and swing the door wide.

Standing at the door is Breaker. She's wearing a new tool belt, some new tools and some old, a screwdriver and a drill and a hammer and some things I couldn't explain if you handed me an instruction manual. But, more importantly, she's wearing a worried expression. Did Miss Mighty check on her? Should I have checked on her?

I should have checked on her.

"Are you alright?" I ask.

"Y-yes," she says, massaging her arms with each other. "I w-was – Miss M-Mighty told me what you were d-d-doing. S-she found me…" She smiles up at me. "Dr Atrocity took me in after the… after e-everything."

I guess I can still get surprised.

"I'm glad you're safe," I say, guilt and snappy phrases traffic-jamming my brain. "Is there something I can help you with?"

"Can… I come in?"

I step back, and gesture for her to follow. She glides into the living room and stops, studying the piano.

"What is that for, anyway?" she asks, enthralled.

"It's a piano," I say. I shake my head. No sarcasm. Not today. "Sorry. It's a musical instrument. You make music with it."

Breaker twists her arms into her version of a nod. "Sasha experienced music a few times," she says. "She really liked, um, rock and roll?"

I chuckle. "Yeah. Sandra did, too."

Breaker's worry has tripled in the last couple seconds. "Your m-maker's name was Sandra?"

"Yep," I say. "I… that's all I want to say right now, but…"

Another arm-nod. "I understand. But I would like to hear more someday."

Um… "What did you need to see me about?"

Breaker's arms twist up under her, a noodle bowl of uncertainty. They come undone with a shiver, and she blurts out, "I need a place to stay and I was wondering if you wanted a partner."

I stare. I stare for a long time, while my thoughts pinball around each other. Breaker decides to fill the void by looking hurt and ashamed at my carpet.

"I'm sorry, I'm sorry, I just… liked helping you and planning with you and I want to learn, and, and your j-job is all about learning and thinking and, and, and f-fixing and… I wanted to help people the way you helped me and…"

She doesn't stop. She probably can't stop. I would say I feel awful, except I now know a new definition for that word.

She's smart. She had to be to help Sasha with what she did. She's got a great memory. She's quick-thinking. She's inventive. And she's good, deep-down good, the octopus who stayed kind when the Teatime Man forced them to figure out a new way to survive. From the moment she came to Playtime Town, behind the fear, all she wanted to do was help. Help, just like I help. I should have checked on her. But also, underneath the rest of the crisis, a part of me wanted to check on her. To be a Friend who checks on Friends like Breaker… and to be someone Breaker would want to check in on her.

Teaching her could be difficult. She might not take to it. But I have to let her try.

"Yes," I say.

Breaker stops.

"Yes," I say again, before she can start back up. "I'd love to have you be my partner."

"I…" Her eyes are saucers. "I… I…"

"You're welcome," I say with a smile. "Listen, though: I've never really had a partner." Not that I acknowledged, anyway… "I've never really worked with anyone but hired muscle. And I have some bad habits when it comes to clues that I'm still trying to get past. So this is going to take some learning for both of us. And if we're going to work together, it's important you get along with Miss Mighty, and with Chip, and I think these days with Big Business and Dr Atrocit–"

"Of course!" she says, arms flailing. "If they want to help, I'll figure out a way to help them help. J-just as long as I can help, too…"

"You'll always be able to help. I'll make sure of it."

"Thank you," she says. "Thank you, thank you, thank you."

"You're welcome," I say again. "And now… the but."

Her arms twist up again. "Yes?"

"You can't stay here."

Breaker's mood plummets. "What?"

"That room? That's Spiderhand's room. He's hurt. He's hurt bad. But he's not dead. If I give his room to someone else… if you overwrite his things accidentally, maybe he…"

"Oh. Oh gosh. I wouldn't want to – I don't – I d-didn't mean–"

"You're fine," I say, with less truth than I'd prefer. "You didn't do anything wrong. There's never anything wrong with asking for a favor."

"I h-hope I didn't hurt y-you–"

"Not at all. Partner." The good news? I don't have to dig too deep to find a smile.

"I… thank you," she says, with a faint sigh.

I shake my head; it's way too full of feels. "Look, I need a few minutes to gather my thoughts, but then, why don't we go visit Golem Jones? He should be able to hook you up with a place to stay."

"I – yes! Yes! Let's do that!"

"Great," I say. "Just a few minutes. I'll meet you downstairs."

"Thank you!" Breaker says. "Thank you, thank you, thank you!"

She rushes out of the apartment, leaving me alone with the worst possible company: my thoughts.

I take as deep a breath as my remaining stitches will allow, and inhale deeply the smell of detergent, root beer, tea, and just a tiny hint of sea air. My smells. Spiderhand's smells. Those aren't going away soon. Those aren't going away at all.

An idea crosses my mind. I walk out to the kitchen, and I pull down two of Spiderhand's teacups from one of the cabinets. When we're done finding her a place to live, Breaker might want some tea. It's what Spiderhand would do.

This case doesn't end the way I want it to. But it ends the way I need it to. And besides, the story doesn't end here.

I return to my desk, go back over the letters. There aren't a lot of clues here, really, and I wouldn't expect there to be. The writers aren't detectives, or they wouldn't have to come to me. They have other jobs to do. They were made for other reasons. I keep shuffling through, seeing if anything clicks for me and my detective stuff, and set them aside to be sorted through later.

I need to help these people. I need to see what I can do with the Teatime Man. I need to help Breaker, my new partner. And I need to help Spiderhand, my original partner, the one I never gave the satisfaction of a chance to actually partner up.

No, not never. Never means we aren't going to fix it, and we *are* going to fix it. We're going to fix a lot of things.

The next case could be harder than this one. The next case could redefine how I think about the Stillreal and the Imagination and everything else that humanity cooks up between their ears. Again. Or, it could be totally routine. Both are okay; because no matter what, we're going to take it. That's what we do. We're the Stuffed Animal Detective Agency, Detective Breaker and Detective Tippy, and their third partner, Detective Spiderhand, out on injured reserve, and all their friends and allies and contacts. We make sense of a world that sometimes refuses to make sense. We remind everyone that the world is basically a good place, even – especially – when it seems to be anything but. We help people.

I like solving mysteries. I like gathering clues. I like feeling a puzzle come together in my mind. But those are tools, a means to an end. What I really do is help people, both with their problems and with believing the best of the world. That's what Sandra needed me for. That's what... that's really what got me stuck here in the first place. But as long as I do that – as long as I help – I know everything will, eventually, work out alright. Even if getting there hurts. Feeling smart and like I made something make more sense will just be a bonus on top.

Losing Daddy ruined Sandra. But that doesn't have to mean it ruined me.

Have I mentioned I love the Stillreal? Because honestly, no cynicism meant, I do.

ACKNOWLEDGMENTS

This job can feel so incredibly lonely at times, but the truth is that no writer really writes alone. *The Imaginary Corpse* is the product of my imagination and labor, yes; but also a whole mess of feedback, comfort, empathy, understanding, and other peoples' hard work. I couldn't have done this without their help.

To that end: Thank you to my family, the first people to read something I wrote and see it as something besides a hobby, and the people who brought the original Tippy home to me all those years ago. Thank you to my agent, Lisa Abellera, who helped me navigate these first huge steps into a big wide world and made me feel like I belong here. Love and emoji to the Isle of Write, who helped me feel like a Real Writer doing Real Writing and were with me through the lowest lows and the highest highs. You're the best cadre of writers I could ever hope to be a part of, and the best people I could hope to know.

Endless thanks to my wife, Sonya, who was the first to tell me this story was amazing, who took on so many extra chores so that I could sit just a little longer at the writing desk, and who saw every convention and pitch party and feedback session as an investment in someone and something she believed in. You're amazing, sweetheart.

And thank you, always, to Yossarian, one of the best cats I have ever known, who snuggled me through the hardest parts of this novel and so many other aspects of my life. He passed on during edits, but I am grateful the Worst Cat will live on forever through this story.

I'm sure I've forgotten someone, so let me end with: to everyone who gave me a kind word and told me I had something here, this is for you. You helped me keep writing, and I am overjoyed to get to repay that with a novel. I hope you like it.

ABOUT THE AUTHOR

TYLER HAYES is a science fiction and fantasy writer from Northern California. He writes stories he hopes will show people that not only are we not alone in this terrifying world, but we might just make things better. His fiction has appeared online and in print in anthologies from Alliteration Ink, Graveside Tales, and Aetherwatch. *The Imaginary Corpse* is Tyler's debut novel.

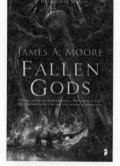
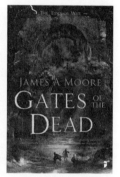

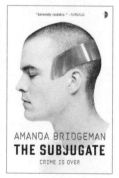

Science Fiction, Fantasy and WTF?!

@angryrobotbooks

UNDER THE PENDULUM SUN BY

JEANETTE NG

PAPERBACK & EBOOK
from all good stationers and book emporia

Two Victorian missionaries travel into darkest fairyland, to deliver
their uplifting message to the godless magical beings who dwell
there… at the risk of losing their own mortal souls.

*Winner of the Sydney J Bounds Award, the British Fantasy Award for
Best Newcomer*

Shortlisted for the John W Campbell Award 2018 & 2019